Eileen Stafford was born in Bristol. She lived there for some years and frequently returns to research her novels. She moved to Devon twenty-five years ago and now lives on the edge of Dartmoor. A former teacher, her first novel was published soon after her sixtieth birthday. A BOUQUET OF BRIARS is her first saga and she is currently at work on her second.

A Bouquet
of Briars

Eileen Stafford

KNIGHT

First published in 1992
by HEADLINE BOOK PUBLISHING PLC

First published in paperback in 1992
by HEADLINE BOOK PUBLISHING PLC

This edition published 1998 by Knight
an imprint of Brockhampton Press

10 9 8 7 6 5 4 3

ISBN 1 86019 6535

Phototypeset by Intype, London

Printed and bound in Great Britain by
Mackays of Chatham PLC, Chatham, Kent

Brockhampton Press
20 Bloomsbury Street
London WC1B 3QA

For my mother and for Carol
and in memory of my grandmother
who lived for most of her life in St Paul's

THANKS

I should like to thank the staff of my small local library for their unfailing interest and for their help in finding many obscure books and facts.

O, how full of briars is this working-day world.
      (*As You Like It* – William Shakespeare)

CHAPTER ONE
1910

Dorothy peered enviously through the iron railings of the playground at the shining new motor car parked across the street. It stood there opulent and luxurious next to the coalman's grimy horse and cart.

'Look at her sitting there just like a queen or something,' Dorothy said to her friend and they both stared at the girl, who was studiously ignoring them. Amy Harding sat proud and tall, staring straight ahead.

'Ma made that coat she's wearing,' Dorothy said. 'She was always taking it up to their house for fittings. She tried it on me two or three times too. I'm just the same size as Amy Harding. It made me that jealous.'

Vera looked at her friend with a trace of pity. 'Fancy putting on clothes like that and then not being able to keep them. I'm glad my ma don't make things for them rich folks.' She turned back to stare at the girl in the motor. 'And the hat, that's scrumptious.'

Dorothy particularly remembered the hat. She had been sent to the draper's with a bit of the coat material and instructions to buy velvet ribbon to match – for the bow that now adorned the hat's lovely, soft floppy brim. 'I tried that on too.' A dreamy look flashed across her face for a second. 'It was beautiful.'

Suddenly Vera gripped the railings of the playground fiercely and turned towards her friend, her eyes wide and serious. 'I can tell you a secret about that Amy Harding,' she said. Then, with a hungry look at the paper bag Dorothy was holding, 'What'll you give me for telling?'

Dorothy considered the proposition. It couldn't be anything important. Vera was only trying to get some of her sandwich and she'd intended to give her a bit of it anyway. She didn't reply at first but watched Dr Harding, Amy's father, come out of the house opposite the school and smile at his daughter. He went to the front of the car and swung the handle to start the engine. Eventually the amazing contraption sprang into life.

'He'd be better off with his old horse and carriage if you ask me,' she commented, deliberately ignoring Vera's anxious words. 'That thing do look good but it seems terrible hard work to make 'em go.'

'I got a secret that you won't believe, Dorothy Miller,' Vera repeated insistently. 'Do you want to hear it or no?'

Dorothy relented. 'Course I do. You can have half my dripping sandwich if you like.' She carefully opened the bag and took out two enormously thick slices of bread stuck together with rich creamy-coloured beef dripping. Her mother had wrapped the bread in grease-proof paper and given it to her to take to school because Dorothy's dinner hour had been spent going to the draper's shop for yet more ribbon and thread. It was for Amy again of course: another dress that had to be finished by tomorrow.

She tore the sandwich into two and held one out temptingly to her friend. 'Well then,' she asked as Vera took the proffered morsel and bit into it with appreciation. 'What do you know about that Amy Harding?'

'Wait till I've finished,' Vera said annoyingly.

Dorothy ate her own share and wiped her greasy hands on her large home-made handkerchief. She was still hungry and, as she watched her friend eating

2

slowly, obviously enjoying the unexpected treat, she regretted her generosity. The secret had better be worth it, and be something bad. She had always had an uncomfortable feeling about Amy Harding, a kind of antipathy for the rich doctor's daughter whose life was much more comfortable than her own.

'Hurry up,' she said impatiently. 'The bell will go soon. What about her then? What have you found out?'

'Don't know that I ought!'

'You've got to now. You've promised and had half my dinner.'

'All right then.' Vera paused as if savouring the importance of what she was about to say as much as she was enjoying the last remnants of the sandwich. Then in a solemn, slightly frightened voice she announced, 'She's your twin sister. Your true twin sister. That stuck-up, la-di-da Amy is your real blood sister. Your ma sold her to them when she was born! Sold her for a purse full of sovereigns. I heard my gran telling Ma the other night. Just before Gran died it was.' Vera shivered. 'Horrible, like a sort of secret that she wanted to tell. Her voice was all gurgly and faint.'

The two girls stared at each other, the enormity of the pronouncement making a sudden hostility between them. Both were silent, as if the will to move or speak had been taken away. Dorothy felt giddy with shock and she stood looking at Vera without comprehension. Then feeling returned, and thrusting out her hands she gripped the other girl's thin shoulders and shook her violently. How could Vera joke about something like that! 'Don't you dare say such wicked things ever again, Vera Price,' she shouted. 'It's a wicked, wicked lie. My ma would never have sold her baby. Just you forget everything you've said. It's all lies, do you hear me?'

When Dorothy released her, her anger finally spent,

3

Vera crumpled against the railings. Dorothy looked at her with cold pain-filled eyes. Then the strident clashing of the school bell interrupted her stunned horror and, instinctively obedient, she walked almost without seeing to her place in the silent lines of children ready to march into the classroom.

She found herself in the familiar and large dismal room that was cheered here and there by some flowers and by a flamboyant picture of the late King in all his coronation robes. Pulling herself together, Dorothy tried to brush the angry tears away and turned her face to the window so that Miss Davis should not see. At thirteen it was important not to be vulnerable, always to be in command of yourself. It was especially important if you were a girl and poor.

'Dorothy Miller!' She jumped as she heard her name called and tried to summon some shreds of composure.

'I should like you to read the story to the little ones please, during dictation.'

She was often excused the hated spelling tests, mainly she supposed because she did them easily with never a mistake. She rose unsteadily and took the book that her teacher was holding out and walked over to the part of the room where the infants sat. Her reading was clear and fluent, and those moments when every small face was turned towards her in pleasure and excitement were precious. It was then that the yearning to become a teacher was strongest and the thought of Buxtons Chocolate factory where she was expected to work next year was most abhorrent. But her mother, struggling to feed and clothe herself and the two children with the money she earned from her constant sewing, needed the extra wages that Dorothy's job would bring. There was no hope of any more education for Dorothy after her fourteenth birthday. She was already fortunate to have been allowed this extra year and she was grateful for that.

She knew the stories in the book almost by heart and her voice gave each character life and meaning even while her mind was occupied elsewhere. She tried to reject Vera's improbable story but the seed of doubt had been sewn. It was true, Vera's gran *had* died recently and she had been the local midwife for years and years. If such a thing were true that was how she would know. But could Ma truly have done such an awful thing? The thoughts went round and round in Dorothy's head and when the bell rang at last for prayers and home-time she jumped nervously before collecting herself and shepherding the little ones to their orderly lines in front of the rest of the school.

She listened to Miss Davey's mellow cultured voice reading the afternoon prayers and by the time they were finished and the long monotonous hymn had come to an end, her sturdy common sense had reasserted itself a little. She helped the small children into their shabby coats, buttoned her own against the chill wind outside and looked round for her brother.

'Coming?' she asked, anxious for his reassuring presence.

He glanced at her in surprise.

'What would I want to go with you for?' he said. 'Girls can't run. I'm going to race with Bill.'

The two boys were off in a rush of dust and shouting and she stared at their backs with a sigh. Of course she could run if she wanted to, but they wouldn't let her race with them. If she'd been a boy, she'd have been able to beat Franky at everything. Well, she thought crossly, she could anyway. He was a year her junior and she knew that he had always been resentful of her. He was constantly telling her that girls shouldn't be clever, and that with that brain of hers she'd never find a husband. She usually laughed at him but behind the amusement there was frustration, for she knew that there was some truth in his words. And there were so many things she wanted to do with her life, most of them impossible for a girl!

She walked out of the school gates and stared across at the spot where the doctor's new motor had been standing, and her heart started to pound furiously in her body as she thought again about Amy Harding. Could it be true? Could it possibly be true? She walked slowly along the grey dusty street and gradually some of the feelings of which she had been dimly aware ever since she could remember began to come into sharper focus. She recalled the look in her mother's eyes whenever she spoke of Amy, a far-away look that had frequently given Dorothy an unpleasant shut-out sensation.

Dr Harding and his wife and daughter lived in one of the big houses in City Road. It stood back from the street with a drive and big trees in the garden. There were servants, and just recently the motor car had appeared. Dorothy had been there once to the surgery at the side of the house to fetch some medicine when Franky was ill. She remembered the peace of that garden, the smooth lawn and lovely flowers. She knew that Amy's mother came from a wealthy family, landed gentry, whatever that meant. There was always gossip about their way of life. All the money they spent on the house, the elegant clothes, the carriage and the motor, came from the beautiful Lady Patricia – as she had been known before she married the impoverished young doctor. At least that was what everyone said. What he earned would never be enough for all that luxury they said. He was popular in the poor streets of St Paul's, never demanding payment for his services when he knew there was nothing to pay with; always ready to help whenever he was needed. He had a special smile for Dorothy too when their paths occasionally crossed. She had often wondered about it and sometimes thought wistfully what it would be like to have a father like that. Perhaps now she was beginning to understand his interest in her!

She thought about her own father. Was he then Amy's too? Frank Miller was a shadowy figure in her own life and Ma seldom spoke of him. But there was a framed photograph on the mantelpiece and his letters arrived regularly from Canada, each one enclosing a few dollars, each one asking if they wanted to join him. And he had been home once. It was when Dorothy was small and she could remember little but the smell of cigarette smoke and the surprising noise he made. The episode had been a grave disturbance in the well-ordered life Ma made for her and for Franky, and as soon as he left they had returned with relief to their quietness and their peace.

Her thoughts kept coming back to that stuck-up Amy, the pampered only child, secure in the love of her wealthy parents. Well, if Vera's statement were true Amy had a shock coming to her! Dorothy felt jealousy welling up in her mind, filling her head almost as if it had a power of its own. And then there was the horror of her mother's betrayal. She fought to try and disentangle the two emotions and felt herself failing. But was Vera right? Suddenly it became desperately important to know the truth but she knew it was impossible to ask her mother. Dorothy could never do that. Yet if she didn't know, if it always remained a mystery, could she ever love and trust Ma again? To sell a baby! Tears blurred her eyes once more as she turned the corner into the road where she lived.

She pushed impatiently at the small iron gate in front of the house. Ma was very proud of that gate. 'I hope I'll never have to live in a house with the front door on the pavement,' Rose Miller would frequently say. The tiny path was lovingly swept each day, the brass step cleaned to a shining perfection every morning, and in summer the painted wooden door was protected from the sun with a bright blind of striped canvas.

She let herself in and walked slowly through to the back kitchen where her mother was sitting, as always, by the old treadle sewing machine. In spite of her jangled nerves and confused thoughts Dorothy smiled, a small tight smile.

'Hello, Ma. Shall I make a cup of tea?' she said quietly.

'That would be lovely, Dorry. I haven't stopped all day from this sewing. Mrs Harding wants it by tomorrow. There's a party that Amy's going to.'

Numb anger flashed through Dorothy's mind as she heard the words. Was there a special feeling in them, a kind of love? She turned and stared at her mother. She had been sewing for the doctor's wife for years, sewing for Amy: lovely clothes, dainty muslins and glittering things; uniform, too, for that posh school up at Clifton. Her mother was a skilled tailoress as well, and she made coats and suits, smart outfits in the latest fashions. Suddenly Dorothy felt her anger explode inside her. The room, the table with the sparkling dress spread upon it, and her mother's kind, concerned face all seemed to spin in a confused mass of colour and sharp jagged lights that criss-crossed down one side of her vision. 'A migraine,' she stuttered. 'I'm having a migraine, Ma,' and stumbled out of the room and up the stairs to the comfort of the large feather bed that received her with its lumpy warmth. Then, as she closed her eyes against the light and against the turmoil of her mind, and slept, the shocks of the day receded into dreams of wealth where she was a princess and Amy Harding, dressed in a maid's cap and apron was bringing her a cup of tea . . .

When she awoke the next morning the headache was still there and she stumbled downstairs glad that it was the weekend. There was always a lot to be done on

Saturdays though. Franky must black the kitchen range, clean the silver and polish all the boots while she had to shop, brush the carpet in the front room and polish the few bits of furniture of which her mother was so proud. Then there was the washing! Dorothy thought of it with a sigh of resignation. The usual ritual of Monday washday had been changed to Saturday as soon as she was old enough to help. That left her mother free to sew on the five school days.

Wearily she went out to the wash house in the back yard, filled the boiler with water and started the difficult job of lighting the fire beneath it. There was newspaper to fold into long paper sticks to set alight first, then small pieces of wood to go on next, and only one bundle to be used because they cost precious pennies. Finally coal must be set carefully on the top.

She had to scrub much of the underwear, shirts and tablecloths and even towels before they were boiled; then they must be rinsed, mangled, starched and blued to a pristine state of whiteness. Her dress and that of her mother were washed separately, and with great care. They possessed two each and there was no money to buy material for new ones.

As she worked Dorothy was surprised to find that the hard physical toil helped to calm her thoughts, and her anger began to seep away with the swirling water as she tipped it into the drain. The mangling of the clothes took a long time. It was something that she and her mother often did together, and when the washing was almost finished Rose Miller bustled into the yard, pushed her sleeves well above her elbows and pulled the cumbersome mangle out of its corner, placing it near the tub.

'How's that headache of yours, love?' she asked her daughter with concern. 'I can do the rest of it if you'm still bad.'

'No, Ma. I'm lots better now. Hard work seems to

do me good.' It was an attempt at a joke, an attempt to stop any further probing.

She folded the thick twill sheets and fed them between the wooden rollers while her mother turned the heavy handle. Each sheet must be put through several times, being folded and refolded to take out as much water as possible.

'You'm a good girl,' Rose said. 'I thank the Good Lord every day for my Dorry.'

Dorothy blushed at the familiar words, embarrassed and slightly guilt-stricken at her hard thoughts about her mother. The two of them were usually so close. It was seldom that they had any serious disagreements and there were few secrets or problems that they did not share. Dorothy knew she didn't want to lose that closeness and, as they worked steadily together, she began to feel a kind of protective love for her mother replacing yesterday's fury. Yet she constantly found herself looking at her ma's round rosy face and kind eyes with speculation. Was it true? Did she do it? Had she really sold her baby? Her mind flitted from one idea to another trying to find a reason for such an outrageous act. Perhaps it was her father who had insisted? Maybe it was his fault? Or could it have been out of love? For certainly any child brought up in the Harding household would have every luxury, and the doctor and his wife were good people. Good as well as rich, Dorothy speculated. Was Amy lucky then? She suddenly realized that the chosen twin could just as easily have been herself and not Amy. Her mind reeled at the thought, envisaging herself sitting in that motor, wearing those clothes, and more important, going to a good school, perhaps to university. A few women were getting places now. Her mind wandered almost luxuriously through all the wonderful possibilities but at the end of it all she was filled with guilt once more. Ma! She wouldn't have had Ma, she realized. Tears filled her eyes. How could she have even imagined life without her mother? What mattered was not daydreaming but finding out what had really happened. But how? The only one who could help was Vera Price. She thought of her with unexpected anger. Then suddenly like a shaft of light she had another idea. Dr Harding was the one she would ask. She remembered his smile the last time she had seen him. Would she dare? She hadn't got any choice, she told herself firmly. She wouldn't be able to rest until she had discovered the truth.

It was late on the Saturday afternoon when she finally managed to make some excuse to leave the house.

'Don't be long, deary,' Rose called after her. 'And mind the horses. It'll be dark soon.'

Dorothy pulled her shabby coat around her and ran most of the way along Grosvenor Road, not stopping to look in the shops or to read the newspaper boys' notice boards. At last she reached the wider City Road where she slowed her pace, tried to arrange her hat a little more decorously, and pulled on the gloves which she had stuffed into her pocket. At the front gate of the doctor's house she paused and looked up at the twinkling lights in the windows and at the motor car standing on the drive. The front door seemed to be a great distance away. As she reached it her nerves almost overcame her, but she summoned all her strength and taking the great brass knocker, banged it three times. Encouraged by its confident noise she rang the bell for good measure but, immediately startled by her own boldness, found herself stepping back from the porch, overcome by fright at what she had done.

It was Amy who opened the door. 'The surgery door is at the side. This is our private entrance,' she said. She stared with distaste at the girl who was standing nervously on the gravel beyond the porch and wished

11

she had not rushed to answer the impatient knocking and the ringing of the bell. It was Myrtle's job but the maid had the afternoon off, Cook was busy with the evening meal, and none of the other staff seemed to be around.

Amy's gaze fell on the shabby patched clothes of the visitor and she tried not to notice them. She didn't want to know about the poverty and the suffering in the poor streets around her home. Her father's patients were usually kept well away from her safe and protected little world. The surgery and waiting room were separated from the house. There was only one connecting door and this was through her father's study, and it was usually kept locked. There must be no fear of that harsh outside world entering her mother's well-ordered domain, the spacious and comfortable rooms in which Amy had been brought up.

Immediately she had acknowledged her thoughts about the girl she felt ashamed of them. To live in this place and yet to have no part in the lives of the people who came each day for help was a constant source of trouble to her. Because of the grinding poverty and the misery that she saw all around, she sometimes felt like the oyster with grit in its shell, grit chafing the delicate flesh and calling out for a covering, a surrounding pearl to protect from the irritation. There were so many girls about her own age, and older women too, all with the same defeated look on their faces. She couldn't help noticing them. Some had great swollen stomachs or babies wrapped in dirty shawls, and the ones who were unencumbered filled the streets in their hundreds in the early mornings on their way to the dismal buildings of the chocolate and cigarette factories. She usually turned away in disgust, sometimes in pity, and always with guilt.

The girl was still standing there. She didn't move obediently to the side door. She just stood and stared

12

back. She seemed familiar too. Amy pushed her long shining hair nervously from her face and recognized her as the daughter of the sewing woman, the dresssmaker who made her lovely clothes so skilfully. Perhaps she had come about the new outfit, although she had never done so before. It was always Mrs Miller who came, and never to the front door!

When she saw Amy try a polite smile of recognition, Dorothy found she couldn't return the gesture. With the knowledge of Vera's statement hammering inside her brain she stood and stared, and for a terrifying moment she felt as if she was looking at herself, looking in a mirror and wondering who she was, why she existed! There was the same fair wavy hair, the same round full face, but there was more, some indefinable quality that she could not name but immediately recognized.

'I want to see your father.' Dorothy made the statement briefly and without apology or explanation.

Amy stiffened at her rudeness. Her brief desire to be pleasant vanished as quickly as it had come. 'You're Mrs Miller's daughter aren't you? So you haven't come about my new things?'

Dorothy made no more efforts to be careful about her speech. 'No, I aint,' she said brusquely. 'It's your pa I wants to see.'

'He's busy. You can't see him now unless it's an emergency. You must come at the proper time, during surgery. It's finished for tonight. The next one is on Monday.' Amy's words were definite and final.

'I'm not ill. It's something else, something important.'

'I'm sorry. If you are not ill you'll have to wait. It's not convenient now.'

Dorothy heard the antagonism in the girl's voice and realized she'd probably provoked it by her flare of temper. Shocked at her own forthrightness, she took

13

another step backwards and watched helplessly as Amy, obviously taking the move as a signal that she was going, pushed the door shut between them leaving her standing alone in the garden. Dorothy stood staring bitterly at the dark brown paint and heavy brass letter box and felt her brave resolution crumbling around her. But then she suddenly realized that she had achieved what she had come for. That moment when she had been face to face with Amy had confirmed her fears. It was true. There was no need to ask anyone else. She had not noticed the startling likeness before, but now that it had been pointed out to her she could see that it was certainly there. That girl was her twin sister and she would have to live with the knowledge for the rest of her life and not tell, not let anyone else know. She couldn't sort out her reasons at that moment, but it suddenly became the most important thing in the world to hug the knowledge reluctantly to herself and not share it with anyone. That way she could control it.

Then, with a jolt, she remembered Vera. How could she persuade her friend not to tell? She turned and her feet crunched noisily on the gravel path as she walked down the long drive and out into the street. There were all those brothers and sisters too. She wondered whether any of them had also heard the whispered confession of their grandmother. Dorothy thought of Arthur, Vera's older brother. Arthur with his clever sensitive face, the one she liked the most. Did he know too, and if he did would he despise her mother for what she had done? She walked home slowly through the grey streets, one idea after another filling her mind and then being rejected. Tomorrow was Sunday, a day of Chapel and a certain amount of freedom from all the chores that filled every other day. Tomorrow she would go and see Vera.

But even Vera's promise of secrecy, if she could be

14

persuaded to give it, wouldn't answer the one question that still tormented her. 'Why, Ma? Why, why, why did you do it?' The unspoken words went round in her head like a refrain that would not be quietened and she knew that her trip to Amy's home had only deepened her unrest.

As she closed the door, Amy felt a sudden shiver of fear that she couldn't understand. She went to the hall window and watched the slight figure disappear round the corner of the drive. Why had the girl's simple request disturbed her so? She was still cross with herself for having answered the door.

Tobin, her small dog was waiting for her at the foot of the stairs and she picked him up and fondled him gently. He was always a comfort, the recipient of all her secret worries and joys. She buried her head in his silky coat and setting him down, watched him run before her up the wide staircase past the great portraits of her mother's parents. She glanced at them as she frequently did. Her grandmother had been so pretty when she was young. She paused for a moment and stared more closely. Then she went into her room and looked for a long time at her own reflection in the large mirror above her dressing table. She would like to look like Grandmama, but however hard she tried she could never achieve the calm cool beauty that she saw in the portrait. Mama had it too, the high-cheekboned aristocratic features that seemed to have passed her by. Perhaps she was more like Papa.

She took her hair brush, the silver-backed one that had been one of her thirteenth-birthday presents. It had her initials engraved beautifully upon it. She traced the letters 'A H', with her finger and then impatiently brushed her long hair. The waves sprang back each time she dragged them down and little golden tendrils curled round her face. She recalled that the girl at the door had hair that looked just the same, but hers was tied back in a single neat plait, hanging down over her collar. And she'd had a big bow on the end, the ribbon broad and shining. It was the only nice thing about her otherwise shabby appearance. Amy had surprised herself by noticing it from the window when the girl was walking away. She had noticed a droop to her shoulders, too. It made her feel guilty, privileged and guilty together. They were not pleasant emotions.

Suddenly there was a welcome tap on her door and thankfully she replaced the brush and pushed back her hair. It would be Myrtle probably. Tobin could always tell and he hadn't barked.

'I've brought your clothes for tonight, Miss,' the maid said. 'Madam asked me to remind you that Mr and Mrs Buxton, and Miss Laura and Mr Clifford are coming to dinner. Your Mama would like you to go down early.'

She carefully put the new frock on the bed and Amy looked at it with pleasure. It was longer than the ones she wore for school, only a few inches above her ankles, and the bodice was shaped with countless tiny tucks. The neckline was high, finished with layers of delicate lace and a small bow of blue shining satin matching the wide sash which set off the gathered silk skirt. There were long white gloves and new undergarments too, a frilled petticoat and a pliable corset bodice. Amy picked the bodice up and held it against her slim body. She saw the maid looking at her and blushed.

Accountably she thought of Clifford. He was fifteen, tall and handsome, with laughing brown eyes and long-fingered artistic hands that could coax the most wonderful music from the cumbersome old grand piano. He played the violin too and she liked listening to that most of all, but his father frowned when he did so. It was an unmanly thing to do, Geoffrey Buxton irritably told everyone.

16

Amy's depression vanished as she thought about Clifford and began to look forward with pleasure to the evening ahead. Laura was good fun too. They had been friends ever since she could remember. She turned to the maid and said anxiously, 'Can you help me to get ready please, Myrtle? I want to look my very best tonight.'

Ralph Harding sat at his desk in the surgery as the last patient of the evening shuffled out. He had seen the girl, Dorothy, standing at the front door and the customary dismay filled him. He was haunted by her and her mother. Every time he saw either of them he felt threatened. The fragile façade of his happy family life was too vulnerable to be held in the hands of people who lived so close, and he cursed his stupidity, his stubborn refusal to move out of this district, this place where the natural mother and the twin sister of his much loved adopted daughter lived. He thought of Rose Miller, the dressmaker, and of her frequent appearances in his home. How had he ever been persuaded to allow Patricia to engage her to make Amy's clothes? He supposed that Dorothy's purpose in calling this evening had been something to do with some garment or other that Rose was making, If so it was strange. He had never seen her here before. The two girls were so alike that it was deemed unwise for them to be together.

Eventually he stood up, the problem unresolved as always. He cleared the papers spread out before him and went through into the house. He must concentrate on being the perfect host this evening. He liked the Buxtons and wanted nothing to mar Patricia's dinner party. Geoffrey Buxton was the only friend who shared the knowledge of Amy's birth. Perhaps he could unburden some of his fears tonight if they had any time alone together. He went across the landing and tapped gently

17

on his wife's door. Patricia was resting and he went in quietly. She turned to him and smiled.

'You seem worried, Ralph,' she said. 'Is anything troubling you or have you just had a hard day?'

He bent to kiss her and his heart thudded as it always did when he saw her like this. He loved her more now than when he first married her, yet she seemed so fragile, so breakable that he never forced himself upon her. She would frequently turn away from him when she sensed his need and he had learned to be gentle and to subdue his desires. He had never been unfaithful and sometimes, in his most honest moments, he wondered why. There were women in plenty who would be happy enough to oblige him without demanding more than he could offer.

'A busy day,' he lied in answer to her question. 'Only that. I'll go and bath. We have an hour before they arrive I believe.' He glanced at the incredibly shaped corset on the chair and at the gown hanging on a rail ready for Patricia to put on. It was an elaborate affair of lace and some shining fabric and he sighed knowing that it was her own money that bought such luxuries, and paid for the staff too. She would certainly need a maid to help her into those garments he thought wryly, wondering for a moment why it was necessary for women to force their bodies into such an unnatural shape. Some of his rich patients had various ailments and fainting fits which he repeatedly told them were caused by their tight waists. But they refused to take his advice, preferring to suffer. The poor ones suffered anyway, but not from overtight clothes! For a moment he mused on the irony of it and then paused with his hand on the door knob. 'A beautiful gown, my dear. I long to see you wearing it.'

He grinned at the inconsistency of his remark as he left the room. But it was true. He did enjoy seeing his lovely wife doing justice to her glorious clothes.

Perhaps it was the contrast with his daytime life that made the pleasure more intense. Patricia was to him a creature of magic, free of any connection with the everyday toil and poverty of the people with whom he mainly worked.

In his study he stripped off and dropped his clothes in a heap on the floor. They smelt of the surgery and, he had to admit it, smelt too of the poverty and unwashed bodies of his patients. He stepped into the enamel bath which had been placed before the fire. He preferred it to the splendid bathroom with its great cast iron bath that Patricia had installed. That was left to his wife and daughter.

Even in summer there was always a fire when he finished surgery, a fire and hot water ready – with vast towels laid on the wooden airer. He was glad to wash the smell of doctoring from his skin and he glanced down at himself as he rubbed the soap violently over his body. At thirty-nine he was still slim and fit, his belly flat and his chest broad. There was no superfluous fat anywhere and he was moderately proud of his good health. He sat in the shallow and rapidly cooling water and smiled to himself as he contemplated, with pleasure, the evening ahead. His worries about his daughter, about Rose and Dorothy Miller, were momentarily forgotten as he thought of his friends.

How did a man like Geoffrey Buxton with his rigid mind and unbending principles come to be married to Felicity he wondered? Felicity the ardent campaigner for women's rights, the militant suffragette. It was a question he often asked himself. She was so full of life and enthusiasm while her husband was solemn and dour, but he was a good friend nevertheless. It was bound to be an entertaining evening.

And then there were the children. Patricia had decided that it was time that Amy learnt more about formal dinner parties and therefore Laura and Clifford

Buxton had been invited too. He liked Clifford he reflected, wished he had a son like that. Geoffrey should appreciate the lad more, give him credit for his music. At fifteen he was quite brilliant on the piano and with his violin. But Felicity's son would of course be both clever and sensitive, as well as full of life. Laura too was a bright star, at thirteen, the same age as Amy, already beginning to challenge some of the repressive ideas and rules of her father's strict regime. Ralph stood up suddenly and laughed aloud at the thought. Then he stepped out of the bath scattering droplets of water around him on the thick mat that had been especially placed close to the fire. He reached for the largest of the towels and briskly rubbed himself dry and the warmth from the glowing coals was pleasant, almost sensuous on his skin. His clothes were lying ready on the bed and he dressed carefully – enjoying, in spite of himself, some of the luxuries that Patricia's money brought.

The dinner was good for they had an excellent cook. There was asparagus soup followed by duck and then apple tart spiced with cinnamon. As Ralph felt the food and the wine helping to dispel the tensions of the day, he looked at his family and his guests with satisfaction. He glanced frequently from his wife to Felicity and wondered how two women brought up in similar privileged homes could be so different. Patricia was calm and beautiful like a precious jewel that glittered in the light, reflecting all the colours of the rainbow, while Felicity glowed too, but differently. Her attraction lay in her voice, her words, her enthusiasm for life.

'I should like to take Amy with us to the next meeting of the Women's Social and Political Union,' she said. 'Laura was very impressed with the last one.'

'Don't let her go,' Geoffrey advised. 'Bad for women

to get filled with all these stupid notions. They should be content to be good wives and mothers, nothing else.'

Felicity laughed at her husband and turned to Patricia. 'Don't listen to him,' she said. 'We'll go together, all four of us!'

Ralph knew that his wife would never do anything without his approval and he looked at her and smiled.

'Take Amy if you want to,' he said. 'I think I agree that women should have a vote. Go and see what they're up to anyway.'

It was meant to goad Geoffrey into further remonstrations. Ralph enjoyed the frequent to and fro of argument with his friend and he wanted to hear Clifford's views too. He guessed that when the ladies left them to their brandy in a few moments the conversation would be fast and furious.

'Yes. Amy and I will come,' Patricia said. 'I have no wish to join, but I should like to hear what they have to say. I am quite sure that we should have the vote, but I must say I'm not too happy about breaking the law to get it.'

Felicity laughed again but Ralph detected an iron determination in her voice. 'I think we'll have to go on breaking the law if we are ever to have equal rights with men. The government won't listen to us unless we force them to,' she said.

Ralph looked at her. It was a daring statement and went much further than he himself was prepared to go. Equal rights indeed! An interesting concept but not practical. It could never happen. Although he wasn't prepared to admit it he secretly felt that there was a vague but uncomfortable threat in the words.

His wife stood up decisively. 'We'll leave the men for a while,' she said. 'They can argue our futures without us to inhibit them!'

It was a typical Patricia sort of comment Ralph

thought. She would seldom say anything that caused controversy and always backed quickly away from argument. But it was one of the things about her that he loved, he mused to himself as he stood while the ladies left the room. Her serenity, and his pleasure in her company had even helped him to forget the troublesome presence of Dorothy Miller at his front door earlier that day.

CHAPTER TWO
1910

'Yes, I'll keep your secret,' Vera said and Dorothy breathed a sigh of relief. 'Not just because you're asking me,' Vera continued. 'Ma don't know that I overheard, and if she did, and if she found out I'd gossiped to you she'd half kill me. She won't want no trouble with Dr Harding. I been real worried since I told you. You got to keep it secret too. Don't go and say nothing to that Amy or to your ma or anyone will you? You'll get me into proper trouble if you do!'

It was a consideration that had not occurred to Dorothy but it seemed to make the burden all the greater. Since yesterday she had thought about little other than this terrible new knowledge and she had found her feelings had shifted a little. At first she had felt that it was a secret that she must respect for ever, a burden that she must always keep locked away inside her. But gradually self-interest had taken over and although she was anxious that no one should find out through Vera, she realized that she rather valued the information in a perverse sort of way. It was a kind of secret weapon to her and, if she promised Vera never, under any circumstances to reveal it, then the knowledge was clearly useless.

'Can't I even talk to my ma about it? It ain't a secret to her. She knows!'

Vera looked doubtful. 'Well of course she knows, but I'd rather she didn't find out that you know, cause then she'd say something to my ma and the fat would really be in the fire!'

'Well I probably won't anyway. It'll be a secret between us, but not for ever, Vera. For ever is a long time.'

'Well keep it till we'm grown up then,' Vera said. 'Then Ma can't do anything to me!'

'All right. Till we'm grown up.' Dorothy's words were slightly grudging but 'grown up' could mean anything and she realized that if she wanted her friend's co-operation then she must give something too. 'Does anyone else know? Does Arthur?' she asked anxiously.

Vera looked at her and grinned, the worried lines vanishing from her face. 'No. I'm sure he don't and Fred and Molly was out. All the little ones was in bed and you could hardly hear what Gran was saying anyhow. I was just taking some hot water in so it was only me what heard, and I pretended that I hadn't.'

'So you think it'll stay a secret then.'

'Of course it will. My ma'll see to that. She promised Gran just before she died. She promised her faithfully. I stayed outside the bedroom door and listened to all of it. I heard Ma promise on the Bible so you can stop worrying about us. It's only you what's likely to spill the beans one day I suppose.'

'Why do you say that?' Dorothy said sharply.

Vera turned away. 'Well it might be some use, mightn't it. I been thinking what I'd do if it were me.'

She wouldn't say any more and although her assurance of secrecy made Dorothy less anxious, yet her words were worrying. Sometimes she felt her friend understood her just a little too well. But she wanted to talk and it seemed now that Vera was the only person with whom she could share her concern.

'I saw Amy Harding really close up when I went round,' she said. 'And she really do look like me but she's all bossy and stuck-up like I said. I'm sure that

24

you was right. She'm my twin. It's hard to believe though.' A note of despair crept into her voice. 'Don't know why I didn't notice it before. That we'm alike I mean.'

'Well you wouldn't would you, not till I told you.'

'No I suppose I wouldn't. She looked at me as if I smelt bad or something and then she said I was to go round to the surgery and that I shouldn't be at the front door. Don't know how I managed not to shout out at her what I knew, I was that cross.'

'I'm glad you didn't. But she'm bound to hear about it one day and what a shock it'll be!' Vera's voice held some satisfaction, and it made Dorothy feel better that her friend felt the same urge to see Amy hurt as she did.

'Wonder how she'd find out?' she commented. It was an interesting thought and she smiled to herself with sudden perverse pleasure. Perhaps it would all come out right in the end. The situation might work to her own advantage even if she wasn't the only one to tell the secret. How could she be expected to feel any loyalty to Amy who, though tied to her by blood, was otherwise almost a total stranger? What's more she was a stranger who was the heir to wealth and privilege to which she had no true right, no right of birth anyway. And they were privileges that Dorothy passionately envied.

She and Vera were strolling slowly through the green oasis of St Andrew's Park. Sunday afternoon was a time of precious freedom, two hours in the week that they could truly call their own. Dorothy stared at the sloping lawns and well-kept flowerbeds. This park was not too far from her own depressing street but it could have been another world. She breathed the cleaner air deeply and tried to imagine life in one of the large houses that she could see across the wide tree-lined road on the other side of the iron railings. She pictured herself in one of those front rooms. 'It could have been me that Ma gave away.' She still couldn't get out of her head how differently her life might have turned out. It made her feel a strange sense of loss, as if part of her was misplaced. Yet even that failed to dispel completely her previous sudden optimism, her sense of the possibilities the future could hold. She scuffed her boots in the autumn leaves that still lay in abundance on the path, until Vera broke into her jumbled thoughts with a fresh and welcome train of thought.

'Arthur said he might come up the park to meet us,' she said. 'He've got the day off. Hasn't to be back until ten o'clock tonight.'

Dorothy blushed and turned to her friend.

'Do he know you'm with me then?'

'Course he do. I told en we were coming up here for the afternoon, just you and me. He seemed pleased.'

The two girls sat down on a seat at the edge of the path and were silent for a time. Dorothy was glad that she was going to see Arthur. Since he had left school and gone to work as a gardener and handyman at one of the posh houses in Clifton he only came back now and then to the uncomfortably overcrowded house where his large family lived. There were so many of them crammed into the four rooms, and Dorothy felt sorry for Vera and all the others, nine children altogether. She was grateful that there was only her and Franky in her own family. She knew it was because her father had gone off to Canada just after Franky was born. She often heard her mother telling friends that it was a blessing, and there was always an odd note of thankfulness in her voice. Dorothy wondered what had happened to make her father leave.

'There he is. I seed'n just coming through the gate,' Vera said and Dorothy felt the colour rushing to her face again. Arthur was tall and fair with sensitive blue eyes and a shy smile that he always seemed to keep in reserve especially for her. She watched him quicken his pace when he saw them and she put an anxious hand to her hair ribbons hoping that they were still in place. Her hair was tied in bunches today. The plait was for the other six days. On Sunday the fair curls were allowed more freedom.

'Hello both of you,' he said. 'Can I sit down?'

They made room for him and he sat between them self-consciously. He groped in the capacious pocket of his shabby tweed jacket and brought out a bar of chocolate.

'Got some spare money now,' he said proudly. 'Thought we'd have a bit of a treat.'

He broke the bar into small squares and divided it between the three of them.

They ate in silence enjoying the smoothness of the dark covering and the white peppermint cream inside.

'Lovely,' Dorothy said and then her voice changed perceptibly. 'But I don't suppose I'll like it much when I'm working there, at Buxtons I mean. I think you'm allowed to have some of the rubbed stuff now and then.'

'Rubbed?'

'The stuff what isn't quite perfect enough to sell. It goes into a box and you can have it cheap or free, I don't know which. But them what works there says that they don't like it no more. It's being in the smell of chocolate all day I suppose.'

Arthur laughed.

'Then you can bring it home and give it to me, Dorothy,' he said. 'I'll never get tired of chocolate.'

They licked the last delicious morsels from their sticky fingers and Vera suddenly jumped up.

'I've just seen a friend over there,' she announced grinning and, turning her back on them, rushed away along the path until she was out of sight behind the bandstand.

'What did she want to go and run off like that for?' Dorothy said, embarrassed.

Arthur laughed. 'That's just like our Vera. Always up to something or other.' Then he moved closer along the seat and Dorothy could feel the warmth and sturdy comfort of him beside her. It was a new sensation and she felt suddenly safe and content. He looked at her with concern in his eyes.

'You don't want to work at the factory do you?' he said.

'How do you know that?'

'I just know. It's in your voice, and with you being so clever at school and all that. You've really got to go have you?'

'Ma needs the money. She works so hard at the sewing. If I can earn a bit it'll make things easier for her.'

'But you could earn a lot more if you stayed at school. In the end I mean. You could be a pupil teacher.'

'That's just not possible Arthur Price and you ought to know it. I'd get almost nothing for a long time.'

There was a sadness in her voice, a sadness for both of them. She knew that, like her, he was clever. He had always been top in arithmetic at school and used to say that he wanted to learn accounting and work in an office, or else do something with the new motor engines. But there was ready money, and board and lodging offered in the big house where he worked now. His mother needed every penny she could get to feed all those hungry mouths, and for him there had been no choice either. It had been more than a year ago that he'd left school and since that day he had just been a labourer. His hands, calloused and rough, showed it clearly and she stared down at them angrily.

'It's not fair is it?' she said. 'Some can have as much schooling as they want, even if they'm real dunces, while you and me have to leave as soon as we'm old enough to bring in a bit of money.'

Arthur suddenly took her hand in his.

'Never mind,' he whispered. 'We'll get there some time, Dorry. We'll have a big house and lots of money and a motor, you just see if we don't.'

He was staring at her and the depth of feeling in his sensitive blue eyes frightened her. She moved away from him, pulling her hand gently from his grasp. 'Some hopes of that,' she said, jumping up. 'Come on. Race you over to the bandstand. Let's find Vera.'

Amy, too, was out walking with a friend on that Sunday afternoon. She felt perfectly happy, but there was a frown of dissatisfaction on her companion's face.

'I don't know why I work so hard at school,' Laura Buxton said. 'Papa praises Clifford every time he does well, but me, oh no, he just tells me to speak properly, stand up straight, learn to embroider and play the piano. I hate the piano and I hate embroidery!'

Amy laughed. 'You should have been a boy,' she said. 'Clifford plays brilliantly.' She glanced away at the thought of Clifford. She had known him for a long time and he had looked at her with pleasure and in a new way when the family came to dinner recently. Odd sensations had flooded through her body, feelings that she vaguely knew were not to be mentioned under any circumstances. There must have been a special tone to her voice and Laura turned and grinned.

'You two were very friendly last week,' she said. 'You had better not let Papa see you together. He'll soon put a stop to that. Mind you,' she reflected, 'I sometimes think he has plans. . . .'

'What plans?'

'Just plans!' Laura was annoyingly vague. 'He likes everyone to dance to his tune you know. I mean, any friendships have to be in his time and his way!'

29

'I don't know what you're talking about!' The blush deepened on Amy's face and she looked down at the River Avon far below and hoped the cold November breeze would cool her flustered thoughts. She loved walking along the path over the Clifton Downs, especially the part where she could look at the graceful span of the great Suspension Bridge that linked the high cliffs of the deep gorge which separated Clifton from the countryside of Somerset beyond. There was a road far below, winding along beside the muddy banks of the river, and she could see an occasional motor car and a carriage now and then. They looked so tiny, like toys in a magic landscape. It was so beautiful but today she could think only of Clifford.

'I wish Papa would leave St Paul's and come and live up here,' she said. 'I hate it down there. The streets are dirty and noisy and the people are so poor and rough.'

'But he can't, can he. It's his work,' Laura said. 'I think your papa is wonderful. I should like mine to be a bit more philanthropic. All he thinks of is that awful factory and the Chapel!'

For a fleeting moment Amy felt ashamed of her thoughts. She disliked the lower orders, the people of the slums amongst whom she was forced to live. She looked at her friend. Laura had such high ideals. She was always talking about Elizabeth Fry who had gone into prisons and helped poor women. She shuddered. 'It's all right for you,' she said resentfully. 'You don't have to live there. A girl came to our front door the other day instead of to the surgery and she made me feel quite awful. She looked very poor and there was something about her that frightened me. Her mother is our dressmaker actually, and I suppose I should have been friendly. You'd think Mrs Miller could have made her daughter a decent coat wouldn't you?'

'No money for the material, I suppose,' Laura said.

'But what do you mean, she frightened you?'

'I don't know really. She was about our age I should think and it was like looking at myself!'

'You're an odd one, Amy. You are always telling me you can't stand those sort of people and then you say something like that!'

Amy wanted to forget the girl who had come to the door and who had stared at her with those penetrating blue eyes. She changed the subject again. 'What about this Women's Social and Political Union, then?' she asked. 'Do you want to go to their next meeting? Do you really think that women ought to have the vote?'

Laura stopped walking and stared at her without comprehension. 'How on earth can you even ask such a thing?' she demanded. 'Of course we have to have the vote. We are totally equal to men. Mama has been telling me that ever since I could understand. We have to fight and fight until we get it, and I mean to be there fighting as hard as I possibly can. I just wish I was five years older.'

Amy shivered. She had mixed feelings about the militant antics of the suffragettes but she certainly didn't want to appear stupid and frightened in front of Laura. Unlike her friend she was glad that she was still only thirteen. At least she wouldn't be expected to take an active part.

'I can't think why your papa allows you to go,' she said.

Laura laughed. 'Oh he gets furious but he's no match for Mama when it comes to an argument. She just says and does what she wants.'

Amy was constantly amazed at what she heard of the Buxtons' family life. She herself was terrified of Geoffrey Buxton. He seemed so stern and strict yet his wife and daughter had no fear of him. 'How can your mama be like that?' she said. 'Standing up for herself I mean. I don't know anyone like her.'

31

'Well she came from a rich family and she has her own money so she isn't dependent. My grandmama is the same, always fighting for women's rights. She's been in the suffragist movement for years and years.'

'Why did she let your mama marry your papa then?'

Laura laughed. 'I'm always wondering about that myself,' she said. 'I think Mama must have loved him. She's determined enough to get her own way. In fact I know she loved him, she still does.'

'But my mama is rich too and she isn't at all. . . .' Amy groped for the right word. 'She isn't sort of free like yours.'

'I suppose it's how they were brought up. Yours was trained to be a good wife, but mine was told that she must aim to stand for Parliament.'

Amy gasped in shock. 'She couldn't do that. Women haven't even got the vote. They'll never be in Parliament.'

'You don't know what'll happen one day though.' Laura skipped a step or two. 'Perhaps we'll be the first women members!'

'Not me,' Amy said decidedly. 'I want to get married. I haven't any other ambition!' She brushed a speck of dust from her skirt. 'And I always want to be able to have nice clothes.' The suit she was wearing was warm and comfortable, made for her by Rose Miller a few weeks ago. It was one of her favourites, fashioned in fine light grey tweed and it came almost to her ankles. The jacket had large revers trimmed with red braid, and her hat, made to match, was finished with a great red velvet bow at the back. For a moment she thought uncomfortably of Dorothy Miller and the ancient coat.

'I can't think how I put up with you for a friend, Amy Harding,' Laura said in mock disgust. 'Clothes aren't at all important. But anyway Clifford will be pleased.'

32

Amy blushed again. 'What do you mean, Clifford will be pleased?'

'Well, men are supposed to like nice, quiet decorative little wives aren't they?'

Amy swung her bag at her friend in reproof. 'Shut up,' she said. 'I don't know what you're talking about.'

They walked along in silence for a while and pleasurable thoughts of Clifford filled Amy's mind banishing other uncomfortable ones. She was glad he was not at all like his father.

She sighed suddenly. 'Isn't life complicated,' she said. 'There's you wanting a career, wanting to go up to Oxford or Cambridge or somewhere one day, and your father absolutely adamant that girls shouldn't be educated.'

'And you don't want to go at all do you,' Laura said. 'Yet you could?'

'If I was clever enough, yes. My parents would both be pleased.'

'And Clifford is desperate to study music while Papa is quite firm about him going into the factory to learn to take over in the future,' Laura added.

'Chocolate for ever,' Amy said trying to lighten the conversation, and both girls laughed. We're too gloomy for such a nice day. Let's wait for our mothers. Perhaps they're feeling more cheerful.'

Felicity Buxton and Patricia Harding were walking behind and the two girls stopped and waited until they caught up. Felicity wore one of the latest walking costumes and Amy looked at it with admiration. The long straight skirt was bordered at the ankles with serviceable leather, and the handsome jacket was bound with the same material. Her own mother was more conventionally dressed. Her lovely afternoon gown was covered with a long blue coat, its severe shape emphasizing her tiny waist, and her hands were warmly encased in a huge sable muff.

33

The women smiled at their daughters. 'Why so solemn?' Felicity asked.

'Just life, Mama,' Laura told her. 'Women's rights and all that.'

Felicity laughed. 'And what have you decided between you?'

'Laura wants to enter Parliament, as a member if you please,' Amy said. 'She's not even content to get a vote!'

'And Amy merely intends to get married.' Laura laughed good-naturedly. 'Fancy that, Mama, just to get married. What can we do about her?'

'Find her a good husband then I suppose.' Felicity's tone was bantering but Amy was embarrassed. She looked to her mother for support, but Patricia joined in the laughter.

'I suppose I am to blame for my daughter's lack of ambition,' she said. 'I shall have to try and remedy it.'

'But you haven't any ambitions either have you, Mama?' Amy asked bravely.

Patricia considered the question. 'To make your father happy I think,' she said. 'And now I suppose that with that remark I've earned Laura's scorn.'

It was Laura's turn to blush. 'Of course not, Aunt Patricia,' she said. 'Perhaps to make someone else happy is the best thing of all.'

The afternoon sun was dipping quickly, leaving the sky grey and cold. 'I think we'd better return to the house now,' Felicity interrupted. 'Papa will be worried and cross if we are not back before dark. He'll want to have tea and then get ready for the meeting tonight.'

'There you are,' Amy said triumphantly to her friend. 'You aren't so liberated are you? You go to that Chapel every Sunday and I know you don't really enjoy it.'

'It keeps Papa happy,' Laura replied with a grin. 'You surely approve of that.' She addressed her

34

mother. 'We want to keep him in a good mood, don't we Mama!'

'Of course, dear,' her mother said. 'We must rule with devious means sometimes.'

They turned to go back to the large and comfortable Buxton house. It overlooked the Gorge, and the house and its setting always filled Amy with a sense of security and happiness. She was as much at home here as in her own house. This was the world she knew and loved, a world of order and privilege. Tea would be set in the drawing room and Clifford would be waiting for them. She shivered a little with pleasure. She hoped she looked good and that he would approve.

When Dorothy reached home later that same afternoon her mother was waiting anxiously for her. She had spread the best cloth on the table over the usual green baize one and there had been enough margarine and a couple of eggs to make some cakes for tea. She looked at her daughter critically. She'd been too long up in that park, she thought. Damp air was no good to anyone. But she said nothing. No cross words must be allowed to spoil this day.

Sunday was always special for Rose Miller since she had started going to the Chapel. It was a day different from all others and she would have liked her children to share all of it with her, but she realized they needed a little time of their own, Dorothy especially. She was a good girl and helped with the work every day when she came from school. They all went to Chapel together every Sunday evening though. Rose insisted upon that.

She glanced at herself in the big mirror above the fireplace before moving the kettle closer to the heat of the coals, and she was pleased with what she saw. Her blonde wavy hair was tied neatly in a large bun at the nape of her neck, but tendrils of curls always escaped and framed her face. She smiled at her reflection. 'Not bad for thirty-three,' she thought, and then laughed a little, shamed at her own vanity. She was wearing the better of her two dresses. It was a soft dark violet with tiny tucks all down the bodice and a high neck set off with her one piece of jewellery, a large cameo brooch. She ran her finger lovingly round the gold frame for it reminded her of her other child; the one she must not think about but constantly did; the child she touched sometimes when she measured her for a new dress, but for whom she must never show a glimmer of affection. She brushed unwelcome tears quickly from her eyes and hoped they hadn't been noticed. The brooch often took her like this. It had been a present from Mrs Harding, a present given anonymously, but she knew of course where it had come from. It was so beautiful, like Amy, and it had never been to the pawn shop. However little money there was in her purse she would never take this.

She turned away, guiltily directing her thoughts back to Franky and Dorothy. She could feel their rebellion as if it were a tangible thing, but she knew that neither would dare to complain. Both would accompany her to the Chapel wearing their best clothes and they would smile and be polite.

Franky was standing by the window dressed in a thick suit and white shirt with a huge starched collar that had taken her a long time to prepare. The effect was completed by a splendid bow-tie and shining black boots. Apart from his scowling face his mother was proud of him. She turned her attention to her daughter.

'Come on, Dorry,' she said. 'The kettle's boiling and everything's ready. I'll tie your hair neater for you when we've had tea.'

She saw her daughter's unhappy face and was saddened. The little Chapel on the corner of the street had made such a difference to her life that she desperately wanted it to influence them too. She could remember when the drink had ruled her, when there was never a spare penny for a ribbon or a bit of decent food. She had been a slave to the gin and she shuddered at the remembrance. But when Frank went off to Canada she'd given it all up and signed the pledge. She wasn't sure quite why, now, after all these years, but she'd kept her promise. Not a drop had passed her lips. It was something to be proud of.

For a moment she allowed her thoughts to wander back to those early days of her marriage. She and Frank had been happy enough in the first couple of years and there had been many pleasant times. A small secret smile crossed her face as she remembered her husband's rough embraces when he returned from the pub on Friday nights. He had never been violent like some she knew of, and she had loved him in a way, almost enjoying his love-making now and then. She frequently used to tell her friends that he was always considerate and kind. There hadn't been any babies immediately either, and they'd had more than a year to enjoy each other. She looked back on that time with pleasure.

But his dismay, almost anger when she produced twin girls, had surprised her, and his instant readiness to part with one of them had further distressed her. He'd said they had enough to cope with with one extra mouth to feed, and two might break them. Secretly, she'd known he was disappointed that she'd not had a son. But she had agreed to Frank's proposition mainly for the child's sake. Dr Buxton was such a good man, and that dear lovely wife of his; well, how could she deny a home like that to one of the pathetic little scraps she had just produced so painfully and only briefly seen? The midwife had chosen one of the babies. They were so alike that it didn't matter which, and she had thought then that there would be plenty more, a constant stream of infants to pull her down, pull them all down into the terrible poverty she saw all around.

So the little unnamed thing had been taken away and when Rose saw her again months later, out with her nanny in a posh pram and swathed in laces and satins, her heart had thumped and raced and she'd wept lots of tears, but she was glad. Glad for Amy, for that was what they'd called her, and sorry that little Dorry couldn't have all those frills and furbelows too. The doctor had given her money, not payment he told her, but a gift in gratitude for his precious daughter.

Then little Franky came along and, although she was happy to have a boy, and relieved at her husband's pleasure in his son, she'd hoped there wouldn't be another too soon. Birthing didn't come easy to her. She remembered the hours of pain and the months of weakness afterwards. Big Frank and little Franky she called her two menfolk, and although in many ways she was happy, she wanted to love her Big Frank without fearing that she'd become like all the other women. There was her mother for example, with thirteen babies arriving one after the other until the poor dear soul just died of work. She remembered seeing her dressed for once in a beautiful spotless white dress, her lying-out dress which she'd saved for, a penny a week in the club for years. 'I shall go beautiful to my coffin,' she'd said, and the young Rose had looked in scorn at her father weeping on his knees beside the bed. She knew that most of it was his fault. If it wasn't for this great clumsy passionate man her lovely mother would have been alive and laughing and well. Only by dying could she put an end to his constant demands on her. It had made a great impression on Rose and she had determined that somehow the same fate wouldn't be hers. But after Franky's birth there seemed to be no way in which she could escape.

But then her husband himself had provided the

solution. 'The Ford Motor Company,' he had announced one gloomy winter day. 'They're advertising for workers in their factory in Canada. It's a chance, Rose. A chance in a million. There's nothing for me here. Would you come?'

He had been out of regular work for the previous year and she had kept the family from starvation by her sewing. But she found the effort of being sole provider almost too much even with only two children. Frank did nothing to help. It didn't occur to him. Even when she asked, he would only carry in the coal and occasionally sweep the back yard. Rose had supposed she must be grateful for that, but as she heaved vast loads of washing to the mangle while Franky yelled in his pram and the small Dorry ran about getting herself wet through in the water that slopped from the enamel pail, resentment began to fester in her heart. Frequently she would sit up late into the night, straining her eyes over the old treadle sewing-machine in order to finish an important order while the children were asleep. She could usually hear Frank's loud snores from the room upstairs and she could clearly remember the bitterness that constantly boiled up inside her at his easy uncaring life. The thought of yet another pregnancy had constantly filled her with horror too, preventing her natural affection from bubbling over. She tried to keep herself rigid and unloving when she would have preferred to throw her arms round her man and give him a hearty kiss now and then, for in spite of his laziness he had been handsome and masterful. She blushed at the memory. But kisses usually led to other things so she had decided that they must be avoided at all costs!

And then he had made his surprising suggestion. He was proposing to take his share of the burdens at last. She had been jolted out of her dilemma by his novel proposal. He was offering her a new country, a new life, some comforts at last.

But Rose's natural caution had quickly come to the fore. She pondered her marriage and her life for a short time and she came to her decision fairly easily. St Paul's was her home, always had been and she liked it in a way; she had friends and brothers and sisters all around. And there was the other thing as well, her constant dread of endless babies. Living in Canada wouldn't solve that. In a foreign land too! The idea frightened her out of her wits. No, she wasn't brave enough to leave her comfortable little house, for in spite of the hand-to-mouth existence they led she was proud of her home. She struggled, with moderate success and in spite of the gin, to keep it clean and pleasant.

At last her mind was made up. 'You go on first,' she had said. 'If it all works out, then I might follow later. Get us a place to live, Frank. Write to me regular, and I'll write back to you.'

He had fallen in with her decision with surprising speed and for a few days she had misgivings, wondering if she were doing the right thing. Her friends thought she was a little mad too. 'You'm a fool not to go along to Canada, Rose Miller. Just give I the chance!' It was a comment she was well used to hearing when her husband's proposal of going to find wealth and prosperity across the sea first became known.

But eventually it was all arranged and Frank had sailed from Avonmouth, his fare paid for by the Motor Company, and Rose had waved him off with mixed feelings. Now, many years after, she remembered mainly the overwhelming relief she felt because there was no new baby on the way and no fear of one for a long time to come! He had promised to return in a year or two and had told her that he hoped she would then go back with him. Well that was as maybe, she had thought. Meanwhile she would enjoy her new freedom, or as much freedom as she could manage with a couple of small children. Without Frank around all day drinking her money away, she felt fairly confident of being able to earn enough for the three of them. And there would be no more men and no more drinking in *her* life she decided.

She started going to the Chapel on the corner and signed the pledge. Life slowly began to improve. A few comforts appeared in the little house; there was always food and to spare. Then that lovely Mrs Harding asked her to make clothes for Amy, for her own Amy, and Rose felt that her happiness was complete!

On the whole it had been a good life. Frank had returned once and she had managed to get away with his month's visit without conceiving another child. That had been a small triumph. She hadn't promised to go to Canada either and she suspected that he wasn't too eager about the idea anyway. The invitation was probably out of duty. She'd been glad to be asked though and she boasted of the fact to her friends. But he seemed happy enough without her and she made no enquiries about his life out there, not wanting to know, preferring to keep him always in her mind as a good faithful husband. It gave her a kind of inner security, a shield against various fortune-hunters who came her way. Not that she had much of a fortune, but there were those who were attracted by the small degree of security and comfort she and her home had to offer. And sometimes she thought she'd like a man around, like one in her bed too, but men meant babies and Rose was quite determined that she didn't want those!

Frank continued to write, and as long as the letters kept arriving at regular intervals she was perfectly happy. Sometimes he sent money and on the whole the arrangements suited her admirably.

All these thoughts went round and round in her head

as she lifted the heavy black kettle from the fire and poured water on to the tea leaves that she had carefully measured into the best teapot that afternoon. Only on Sundays did this fine piece of china appear. She liked to keep some special things for a special day. The pot had been standing warming in the grate for a full half an hour.

'Come and sit at the table, both of you,' she ordered. 'There's bread and jam first and then you can have a cake, or even two for a treat. And be careful of that suit, Franky. I don't want no jam down the front of it mind!'

An hour later they sat at the back of the small bare Chapel on hard chairs and stared up at the man on the raised platform in front of them. Dorothy knew that the preacher tonight was the factory owner, the high and mighty Mr Geoffrey Buxton.

He lived in Clifton and had a son and a daughter about her age. People talked about them, usually with envy. The daughter was a friend of Amy Harding. She had seen her a couple of times in a big motor car arriving at the house in City Road. As she stared at him her mind was off in another bout of daydreaming, and it wasn't until her mother nudged her and tapped the red Sankey hymn book on her lap that she returned to the present and stood up to sing with everyone else. As she sang the familiar words she stared at the old piano with its ancient pianist. The woman was thumping out the tune and hitting many wrong notes and Dorothy couldn't help noticing the look of pain on Mr Buxton's face each time there was too terrible a discord. Suddenly she wanted to giggle. Chapel often affected her like that. She wasn't sure why, but she sternly bit her lip until it hurt, to prevent the disgrace. Her mother would be very upset if there was even the tiniest hint of amusement on her face.

As Geoffrey Buxton led the singing with his fine tenor voice, and tried in vain to keep everyone in tune, he looked down on his small congregation with a mixture of compassion and boredom. As an elder of this parish he had to take his turn at preaching each month, although he would much have preferred to be at the more fashionable meeting-place in Clifton. He thought of his wife and two children there at this moment and his face lit up momentarily as the image of Felicity flashed into his mind. He loved his wayward brilliant wife more than he cared to admit, more than he even wished. She had him totally entranced in spite of her modern ideas and refusal to submit in any way to his will. A good wife should submit in everything, he thought grimly, just like the Bible said. But it was no use, Felicity just laughed at him.

He stared around at the small motley crowd singing with various degrees of enthusiasm and his attention was caught by Rose Miller and her two brats towards the back. He looked at Dorothy and shuddered a little. How like Amy that twin sister of hers was! How long would it be before the Hardings' secret was out? Well it would never be from his lips. He sometimes felt quite burdened with the enormity of the confidence that Ralph had shared with him. But every time he saw Amy he thought of her real background.

The mother was staring up at him as if he were God and he smiled a little. Rose Miller was a good-looking woman: a pity she had no man to share her bed! He couldn't imagine why her husband had gone off to Canada. She wouldn't be an uppity character. He felt sure of that. Nice and round and soft and submissive that one! The sensual nature of the pictures that suddenly filled his head took him by surprise and suffused him with disgust at his own frailty. He mentally shook himself and firmly looked down at his shining black shoes with their fashionable grey spats and then at the hymn book in his hand, and formed a silent prayer for forgiveness. But then women shouldn't come to Chapel looking like that, all those fair wisps of curling hair that he could see beneath her large saucy hat. They framed her contented face, and then there was the swell of her bosom beneath that tight dress to torment him further! He'd seen pictures of Arab women swathed from head to foot. Perhaps that would be a good idea for Christians too!

They were singing Amen and with the long hymn finished it was time for him to lead the prayers. He waited until everyone had shuffled into their seats, and he stood tall and resolute in front of them all, ready to beseech the Deity for a blessing. He prayed for sanctification and for peace, and most of all for release from the desires of the flesh, and then he opened his great black Bible at the text he had selected for tonight. It seemed wonderfully appropriate.

'First Epistle of Peter, Chapter Three,' he boomed. 'Ye wives be in subjection to your own husbands; that if any obey not the word, they also may without the word be won by the conversation of the wives while they behold your chaste conversation coupled with fear. Whose adorning let it not be that outward adorning of plaiting the hair, and of wearing of gold, or of putting on of apparel. But let it be the hidden man of the heart, in that which is not corruptible, even the ornament of a meek and quiet spirit, which is in the sight of God of great price.'

Dorothy, listening to his long sermon and yet not really attending to a word of it, had her Bible open on her lap at the place he had chosen. Shouldn't she plait her hair then, she wondered as his words boomed over her. It seemed to her a stupid text to take. As if any of them had any gold, or much in the way of apparel to choose from. And what was the hidden man of her heart? Her thoughts ran to Arthur Price. Perhaps that was what it meant. Perhaps he was the hidden man of her heart!

Rose, trying to listen attentively nevertheless glanced further down the page of her Bible and read, 'Ye husbands, dwell with them according to knowledge giving honour unto the wife, as unto the weaker vessel.' Well, she thought, maybe St Peter's wife was the weaker vessel, but she knew who was the strong one in her marriage. Hadn't she kept things going, fed them all, while Frank lazed his time away? And he wasn't dwelling with her either like the good book said he should. She looked up at Mr Buxton and thought what a handsome figure of a man he was. Her heart beat a little faster. Now if she had a husband like that, maybe . . .

CHAPTER THREE
1911

Dorothy greeted the morning of her fourteenth birthday with mixed feelings. Her mother was already up. She could hear her bustling about downstairs and she knew that the fire would be burning, and the kettle set on the coals and probably boiling by now. It was the last day of freedom. Tomorrow an interview had been arranged at Buxtons. She had been worrying about it for weeks. Friends had told her of the fearsome looks of the women who sat behind the large desk, of the dismal room, and of the mental arithmetic which would be fired at her – figures to be added up, multiplied, subtracted until she would almost faint with dizziness. But everyone agreed that Buxtons was a good place to work and that if she were offered a job there she'd be lucky. Privately Dorothy was not so sure, but she kept her thoughts to herself. Vera was always telling her that she had ideas too big for her boots and Franky, too, had used the same words only yesterday when she'd started to moan.

She shivered as she slipped out of the warmth of the big bed. Her mother's thick shawl was lying on the chair and she pulled it round her shoulders for comfort and went over to the window and stared down at the street below. It was unusually quiet, the first day of a new year. She wondered what 1911 would bring. It was strange having your birthday on New Year's Day she thought, making it twice as special somehow, a new beginning on two counts. Well this one was even more important than all the others. She was grown up. There would be no more school. She would be earning some money to help Ma. She determined to enjoy this last day of freedom and to make great efforts not to think of tomorrow. But in spite of her brave resolutions she sighed. Fourteen was too young to be grown up. She wanted to go on learning, go on reading and studying, to become really clever and to have a good job one day. A stab of jealousy for Amy Harding shot through her but she quickly tried to banish it.

'You up, Dorry? I've wet the tea,' she heard her mother call. Regretfully she took off the shawl, folded it neatly and pulled on her clothes.

'Coming Ma,' she replied and she ran down the narrow stairs to the little back kitchen.

'Many happy returns of the day, dearie, and here's a present for you.'

Rose held out a large package and Dorothy gasped at its size. Surely it couldn't be . . . yes it must be a new frock. She wanted nice things to wear more than anything and Ma knew of course. With trembling fingers she took it from her mother, felt its softness with excited anticipation and untied the string impatiently. She put the brown paper aside and looked at the folded material with reverence. Then she held up each lovely garment separately, breathlessly, and her eyes sparkled with delight. She had never, in all her life, owned such beautiful things.

She laid them down again on the table and ran to her mother and threw her arms around her. 'Oh, Ma. They're so perfect. Where did you . . . ?'

'Don't ask questions. I made them for you special for your birthday.'

There was a dark blue velvet skirt and a white silk crepe blouse with lace at its collar and cuffs. Beneath lay a small bolero of the same blue velvet. Dorothy stroked the soft material of the skirt and then the many

48

narrow tucks that adorned the front of the blouse. Tears began to streak down her face. There was a hat too and even a pair of white gloves.

'Now don't cry all over it,' Rose said. 'Take it upstairs and try it on so's I can see if it's right for you. I wanted it to be a surprise, so I couldn't measure you. I've made it big though with plenty to let out so it'll last you a fair time.'

Dorothy kissed her mother and leapt up the stairs. She threw her old skirt and blouse on the bed and carefully stepped into the new things. She took the hat and put it on her head. It was large and its brim was decorated with veiling rucked and gathered into delicate folds.

Then she stood before the glass and suddenly her heart beat faster. It was Amy Harding who was looking back at her from the old chipped mirror. She stood staring and speechless. She had tried so hard during the past weeks to put her secret knowledge about Amy to the back of her mind. Her promise to Vera and her loyalty to her mother forced her to try to forget the whole affair for the time being anyway. But she had not been very successful. Amy's clothes were often in the back kitchen, her mother frequently busy with them, and Dorothy had even been called upon now and then to model for a new frock to save a visit to the big house. 'You'm just the same size as Miss Amy,' Rose had said only a week ago and Dorothy had wanted to tear the half-made dress from her body and run screaming from the room. But she had forced herself to be calm, gritted her teeth and said nothing. One day she knew that she would triumph, one day all the wrongs would be righted. She didn't know how, but it was important to keep her head. Losing her temper wouldn't achieve anything.

And now she couldn't take her eyes away from her reflection in the mirror. There was no looking-glass downstairs and she had never seen herself in anything but her own familiar shabby things. Her hair was loose, not yet restrained in its usual plait and the long waves fell about her shoulders. 'Amy Harding, Amy Harding, my twin sister,' she whispered to her likeness. The blue eyes looking back at her seemed to be pleading for friendship and whether it was her own features or Amy's that she saw there she couldn't be sure. In these new clothes there was little difference. It felt as if part of herself were missing and she stood transfixed, her pleasure in the birthday present destroyed.

'What's the matter?' Rose called. 'Can I come up and see?'

Before she could think of any words to reply, her mother was in the room and as Dorothy turned and saw her white face, she knew that she had seen it too. The old shabby clothes kept the likeness hidden, but these lovely ones stressed it.

'You've made me look like a lady, Ma,' Dorothy whispered. 'When am I to wear clothes like these?' She knew the words sounded ungrateful and for a moment she regretted them.

It was a moment before Rose gathered herself together. 'There'll be a chance. You'll see. Everyone should have something pretty in the cupboard.'

Then suddenly Dorothy knew where the material had come from. Her mother had been doing a lot of sewing for the Hardings lately. It was either something left over from one of Amy's outfits or a gift from the doctor's wife. There could have been no money for anything so expensive out of their own meagre funds. And the hat. It was probably one of Amy's, refurbished and altered.

'It's like what that Amy Harding wears isn't it?' She couldn't stop the cruel probing words and she searched her mother's face anxiously as she spoke. She knew that today was Amy's birthday as well as hers, and of course her mother would be thinking of that too. For a second she wanted to hurt, to wound, and then just as suddenly she felt sorry, filled with love for the kind little woman who was looking at her with such concern and affection.

For fourteen years Rose had lived with the grief and the joy of seeing Amy grow up, and of concealing the knowledge of what she had done. The likeness between the two girls shouldn't have too much power to disturb her now. But it did. As they grew it became more obvious, and now she had caused it to be more so. She stared at Dorothy with a great rush of love and pity in her eyes. This child had so little compared with the other one.

'Yes, I suppose them are the kind of things the gentry wear,' she said steadily in answer to Dorothy's comment. 'But there's no reason why my girl shouldn't have them too!' She smiled and went over to her daughter. There was a stony look on the young face and Rose kissed her briefly on the cheek. 'You look lovely dearie,' she said. 'But put on your old things now and come on down for breakfast. I think Franky has something for you too.'

She turned briskly and walked down the stairs.

Dorothy heard each creak of the old staircase as she went, and then she looked at herself again in the mirror.

'I'm just as pretty as she is,' she addressed her reflection. 'And I'll make myself speak like she does and I'll learn things too. I'll get equal to Amy Harding one day, just see if I don't!'

How she was to do it she had no idea at that moment, but the battle was on. She would win eventually. Yet in her heart was an element of doubt. Her need to excel, and perhaps even to hurt Amy Harding was combined with a feeling of wanting to be close to her, to know her. Not as a friend though. What was a sister? She had no such knowledge. Perhaps Amy was a missing half of herself, a half that wouldn't be comfortable to be with, yet in some way necessary. Slowly Dorothy took off the clothes, found hangers for them, stowed them away in the big built-in wardrobes, and dragged on her more familiar shabby things, trying as she did so to shake off all her strange uncomfortable feelings. Then she brushed her hair and tied it back with an old ribbon at the nape of her neck. She couldn't be bothered with the effort to plait it this morning, yet she wouldn't put it in bunches. That was how Amy wore her hair, in two fat bunches each side of her head. When she went downstairs, Franky was holding out his present to her with obvious pride. 'I searched a long time for these,' he told her proudly. Ma gave me a bit of the stuff of your new frock to match up.' Carefully she unwrapped the small piece of brown paper and found a string of blue glass beads.

'Them's lovely, Franky,' she said, and was once more moved to tears. They must have cost him considerable self-sacrifice. 'Fasten them for me will you?'

Embarrassed he lifted her hair and clipped the ends together. 'You like them then?'

'Oh yes. I shall wear them all day.'

'And you can put on your new clothes tonight for Chapel,' Rose said as she put bread and margarine on the table for breakfast. 'And I thought you might wear your hair up. I'll do it for you. Now you'm fourteen you can have it up round your head instead of hanging down like that.'

Strangely Dorothy felt a little sad at the suggestion. Wearing your hair up was a sign of being a woman. It told everyone that childhood was over, and it made her think of tomorrow too. Tomorrow and the interview at Buxtons. The frightening prospect cast a shadow over her birthday morning.

Vera came to see her in the afternoon bearing a bar

of chocolate as her offering and carrying a further small parcel. 'From our Arthur,' she said with a grin as she handed it over. 'He can't get no time off but told me to give you this. Said that it might help you get on, whatever that do mean. He wouldn't let me see what 'twas. Hurry up and unwrap it. I wants to know what he been spending his money on.'

Dorothy could feel her friend's eyes upon her as with trembling fingers she untied the string and laid aside the layers of old magazines that had been used as wrapping paper. Inside was a shabby old leather-bound book, its spine coming away from the yellowing pages, but Dorothy looked at it with almost breathless delight. Then she unfolded the piece of paper inside and read the letter that Arthur had written to her.

Dear Dorothy,

'I hope you have a nice birthday. I'm sorry this present is so shabby. I couldn't afford a better one, but I thought you'd like it. I don't know what it's all about, but you used to read fairy stories to the little ones so nice in school that I thought a book was a good present. I listened to you sometimes instead of doing lessons. Got caned for it once.

I tried to read the book a bit by the way and liked it where the girl says something about briars. (Page 24) Hope your interview isn't full of them tomorrow. Good luck!

Love from Arthur Price

Dorothy read the letter over twice and wondered what he meant, then she turned the pages reverently. She'd heard of Shakespeare. Miss Davey had told them about him, and had read some bits to all the children now and then. She couldn't believe that she had a real copy of her own, and from Arthur too. That made it even more precious.

She turned to Vera. 'It's lovely,' she said. 'When'll you be seeing him again?'

'Don't know. He don't get much time off. You'll 'ave to write and thank 'im.'

'Yes, I will.' She ran her fingers lovingly over the leather. 'Look what it do say on the front, Comedies, them's things to make you laugh. I could do with something to make me laugh, couldn't I, Vera, what with having to go to Buxtons tomorrow.'

'You'll be all right. I can't wait to get there. Ma won't let me leave till I turns fourteen though or I'd be going along with you.'

Dorothy was so engrossed with her present that she hardly heard her friend's words. 'Look,' she said, 'there are pictures in the book, too, old brown photographs of actors and actresses.'

'I don't agree with acting,' Rose interrupted. 'Mr Buxton says 'tis Devil's goings on.'

'Oh Ma, you don't really think he'm right do you?'

'Well, I ain't clever enough to know so I be content to leave them things to those wot do.' There was a definite twinkle in her eye and she winked at Vera as she poured three cups of tea.

Vera laughed. 'Well we ain't got enough money to go, have we, Mrs Miller? My ma likes the music hall though. She saves up for it.'

Dorothy was still engrossed. 'Look,' she said suddenly, 'I found the briars bit wot Arthur wrote about.' She pointed to the lines and read, 'O, how full of briars is this working-day world!' She laughed. Trust Arthur to pick that out. Probably because he's a gardener. 'Ma,' she asked. 'What are briars exactly?'

'They got prickles but they got roses too. Pretty things when all the blossoms are on 'em,' her mother answered. She carried the big teapot out to the scullery and started to clear away the last of the dishes on the table. 'Hurry up you two and get on out of my way if you'm going out,' she said. 'I wants a nice quiet Sunday afternoon.'

'Right, Ma. I'll just take my presents upstairs.' Dorothy ran up to her room and looked at her other books. There were just four of them, all prizes for being top at school. They were simple little stories that she read at night sometimes to her mother, all of them telling of the good things that happened to those boys and girls who were good, and the bad things that befell everyone who didn't go to Church or Chapel on Sundays and who went to the pub or drank gin on a Friday night! She had already decided that real life wasn't quite like that, but Ma liked the stories and they both hoped that hearing them might have some good effect on Franky. Get them young, Ma said.

This book looked quite different and if Arthur Price thought that she might enjoy it, then she'd do her best to prove him right. Amy would certainly be reading things like this, she thought and that made her quite determined to read every word!

'What's it all about then, that book?' Vera wanted to know later when they were walking arm in arm up the Ashley Hill.

'I told you, Shakespeare,' Dorothy said. 'Plays. Hard to read, but I'll manage. I'm that pleased with it.'

'Funny thing for our Arthur to choose,' Vera commented. 'But he always had his head stuck up in the clouds. Not that he'm much for books and stories though, more for arithmetic and engines. He do keep going on about motors and things. Last summer he couldn't talk about nothing but flying, would you believe. He got a picture of someone who flew over the sea. Stuck it up in our kitchen. It's still there and it do give me the shivers every time I looks at it.'

Dorothy laughed at the horror on Vera's face. 'He told me he'd like to be an aviator. That's what they call them who fly. Some hopes though for folks like us. You got to have money to do them things.'

'Well we'll never have that,' Vera said impatiently. 'Unless we finds a rich husband.'

'I'm going to get rich myself first,' Dorothy said with a grin. 'Then I'll find a rich husband!'

At least the interview was not until nine o'clock. Dorothy thankfully turned over in bed and pulled the blankets over her head and wished the day would go away. But it was here, Monday the second of January 1911, the day when she must go to Buxtons and face her future.

An hour later she left home and walked with faltering steps along the cold grey streets towards the entrance gates.

The interview room was bare of furniture except for a large desk at the front with some chairs set behind it. Dorothy stood nervously with two other girls. Her hair was plaited and wound round her head and no fair curls were allowed to stray. She was wearing a grey skirt of sturdy wool and a white blouse free of all ornament. She had polished her tall black boots until they shone brilliantly and she stood and stared down at them, unwilling to lift her head to the two severe-looking women who were sitting stiffly on the other side of the table.

'Dorothy Miller, stand forward,' one of them ordered.

Trembling she looked up and took a step in front of the others. She allowed herself a brief glance at the spokeswoman before lowering her eyes again. In that second she took in the plain angular figure, the hair screwed tightly into an enormous bun and the severe and dismal black dress. She was aware of the other woman as well. They were both staring at her, obviously summing her up, 'As though I were for sale in the animal market,' she confided later to Vera.

'We have read your school report and your letter of testimonial and we have looked at your needlework sample,' the taller of the two said. 'All are satisfactory and your careful stitches show a diligent attitude to your work. As you know, we look for cleanliness, honesty, strict punctuality and a neat appearance.'

There was a pause and Dorothy wondered if she was supposed to say anything. She continued to stare at the table and at the ink stand set upon its shiny top.

'You may start work for a trial period of one month beginning tomorrow,' the voice continued. 'Be here at seven sharp. Your wages will be three shillings a week. Have you anything to ask?

'No Madam,' Dorothy whispered.

'Your reports and your testimonial were excellent,' the woman added. The words were a little grudging, but very welcome. 'We have therefore decided that an arithmetic test is not necessary. You may go now.'

Dorothy was overcome with relief but she felt humiliated too. They would never have treated Amy like that! She turned to go but before she reached the door it swung open and Geoffrey Buxton entered. He stared at her and she could see sudden recognition in his eyes. She remembered that he had spoken to her mother that Sunday evening a few weeks before at the evening meeting in the Chapel.

'Just a moment, young woman,' he said. 'Dorothy isn't it? Dorothy Miller?'

'Yes, Sir.'

She was surprised that he remembered her name. There was a pause as they gazed at each other and Dorothy felt immediately nervous under his staring gaze. He seemed to be slightly disconcerted. Was there something wrong with her appearance?

Then he smiled, a strange half-smile. 'We've met haven't we. At the Chapel. I'm glad that you attend regularly with your mother. So you're coming to work in my factory?'

It was a statement rather than a question and she nodded dumbly.

'Yes, Sir.'

'Then work hard and do well. I heard what Miss Jenkins said about your school reports. We are sometimes looking for girls who can do slightly more responsible jobs.'

Dorothy heard a displeased snort from one of the women behind the desk but she dared not look round.

'Yes, Sir,' she murmured again and she glanced longingly at the open door.

'All right. That'll do, Miller.' The female voice behind her was dismissive and impatient and she fled thankfully into the corridor.

As she walked home through the cold grey streets she pondered the slightly strange behaviour of Geoffrey Buxton. The more she thought about it the more she felt it odd that he should single her out for attention, remember her name so easily and suggest that there might be promotion for her one day. What could he possibly mean? In charge of a section? She didn't want to look like those old frights who had interviewed her. She'd heard that a few girls were employed to write in the great ledgers in the office. You had to be able to do copperplate writing for that, beautiful looped sloping letters and never a blot or smudge. Well, she'd always been neat and had prizes from school to prove it. She could write as well as the best. Perhaps that might be her way to better things.

Her thoughts returned to Mr Buxton and suddenly she remembered that his family were friendly with the Hardings. She stopped and stood still for a moment with shock, realizing that he might know the secret. Did he see Amy instead of herself standing there when he entered that room? Could that be the reason for his strange friendliness? It was just possible, and if so it made an extra complication. She walked on slowly, her mind full of this new insight. Then she smiled a little grimly to herself. Perhaps it wasn't a complication though after all. Maybe it could become another way of turning events to her own advantage. 'More responsible jobs,' he had said. Well whatever he might mean she knew she was clever enough. Just wait and see. She would do it! She clenched her fists tightly inside the old fur muff and strode purposefully on towards her home.

'How did it go then?' her mother wanted to know as soon as she entered the front door.

'It went well, Ma. Very well. I start tomorrow,' she replied, and there was a glint of triumph in her eyes now. 'Three shillings a week at first, but I reckon I'll soon get better'n that.' The boredom and humiliation with which she had previously viewed her proposed job had disappeared. There was hope now, hope and a challenge. Perhaps that stuck-up Geoffrey Buxton was the key. Perhaps through him her chance would come!

It was just a week later that the new school term started for Amy. Although she didn't board like some other girls she knew, she had always disliked returning after the holidays. But one of the things that pleased her about the school in Clifton was that Laura Buxton went there too. At least she would be seeing her every day now. Nevertheless she longed to be grown up, to finish with education and to learn all the accomplishments that her mother could teach her instead.

'I wish I could leave school,' she told her friend at the end of that first school day of the new year. 'I'm fourteen now, quite old enough, but Papa won't hear of it.'

'What on earth would you do with yourself all day

if you did leave?' Laura wanted to know. 'I should be terribly bored.'

'Visit with Mama, go to tea parties, read a bit, have sessions with my nice dressmaker, play the piano, that sort of thing.'

She could feel Laura's amused scorn. It was almost tangible but Amy laughed. She was used to her friend's modern ideas and outrageous ways.

'We must be educated and take our place alongside men as equal partners,' Laura lectured her severely. 'I'm truly ashamed of you, Amy Harding.'

'You sound as though you're quoting Mrs Pankhurst,' Amy replied, laughing at Laura's stiff seriousness. 'Well I agree with her of course, but I don't want to be forced to have a career just because someone else thinks I should.'

The two girls were waiting in the school hall for Ralph Harding to take them home. Sometimes it was the Buxton chauffeur who met them but today it was to be Amy's father. It was one of his few days away from the surgery. Amy glanced at herself in the mirror over the huge fireplace and rearranged her hat, pulling her gloves more smoothly between her fingers. It was quiet in the elegant and spacious hall. All the other girls had been collected. Ralph was late. Then the sound of a motor engine broke the silence and Amy ran to the front door.

'There he is,' she said. 'Come on, Laura. We don't want to keep him waiting.'

'Did you work hard on your first day?' he wanted to know as he greeted both girls. He came round to the back passenger door of the Ford and held it open for them to climb in.

'Of course, Papa,' Amy said. 'We had hockey this afternoon though. I can't really run fast enough but Laura's very good. She always manages to score goals!' Amy knew that her father was very much in favour of sports for girls. She had heard him arguing with Laura's father about it.

Ralph laughed. 'Then you'll have to practise running,' he said, 'However much your Mama says that it is unladylike.'

He tucked a rug round their knees and arranged his long legs into the driving seat. They drove through the wide Clifton streets, carefully overtaking the carriages and tradesmen's carts and avoiding the hordes of children just coming out of the Board School, many of them with large iron hoops which they bowled merrily along oblivious of other road users. The car jolted uncomfortably now and then on the uneven cobbles of some of the roads and Ralph drove with extra care when he encountered them.

They passed the Church and then drove through the shopping Mall, where Amy stared at the various stores on either side. There was a fruit shop, a hairdresser's, a large grocer's, and many more. She wrinkled her nose as they passed the fishmonger, and then the delightful smell of coffee from Carwardines masked the other unpleasant odours. She began to feel hungry.

When they arrived at the elegant Buxton home Ralph pulled the car into the drive and prepared to help the girls down. He saw Felicity standing at the window watching for them and she came to open the door herself.

'Have you time for tea?' she asked, smiling. 'It's ready in the drawing room.'

'Of course,' Ralph said. 'The girls will have a lot to tell us I expect.'

The beautiful room overlooked Clifton Down with its green acres and many trees. The steep sides of the Avon Gorge could just be seen and he stood admiringly at the window as he always did when he came to this house. He experienced yet again the usual guilty conscience about keeping his own family in St Paul's when he knew that both Felicity and Amy longed to move up here.

Amy came and stood beside him and he put an affectionate arm around her shoulders.

'I should love to live here, Papa,' she said.

'Perhaps one day you will.'

He saw the hopeful glance she bestowed on him and he smiled at her. 'But not for a while yet. The folks down there need me. You know that.'

When Clifford Buxton came into the room a little later all eyes turned towards him. Ralph looked with approval at the upright way he stood, at the ready smile and the clear brown eyes that looked back directly into his. He held out his hand to the young man.

'Hello, Clifford. All prepared for the new term then?'

'Not quite, Sir. I still have some vacation work to finish.'

'Been spending too much time on that violin of yours instead of your other studies, I suppose?' Ralph's voice held amusement and a measure of approval.

'I suppose I have,' he said. 'But once term starts there isn't so much opportunity.'

'But you must keep at it,' Ralph said. 'You have a gift. Don't neglect it.'

'I wish my father would tell me that!'

'He will one day.'

Clifford laughed a little grimly. 'I should like to believe you. He shows no sign of it at the moment.'

A maid set the tea on a small table as they spoke and Felicity rose and poured from the elegant silver teapot. She handed a cup to Ralph.

'I agree with you,' she said to him. Then she turned to her son and smiled. 'Your father is not so hard as you sometimes think, Clifford, I am sure that he is secretly quite proud of your musical ability.'

Amy sat on the sofa drinking her tea and looking

from one to the other as they spoke. Although she and her parents had been close friends with this family for as long as she could remember, she sometimes felt inadequate in their company. She knew that she hadn't the brains of Laura or the bright spirit of Felicity, yet the more she glanced at Clifford the more she hoped for his approval. As if answering her thoughts he smiled in her direction and came and seated himself on the sofa next to her.

She had already thanked him for his birthday present to her but now wished to say more about it.

'I love the book you gave me,' she said. 'I've read a lot of it already.'

Clifford had spent a long time choosing, and at last had decided on a leather-bound copy of Tennyson's poems.

'Do you really? I wasn't sure if poetry was your sort of thing.'

Amy hadn't been sure either at first, but just to hold the beautiful volume in her hands was pleasure enough and to turn the pages and read a few lines here and there, imagining Clifford's voice speaking them, made her glow with happiness.

'Yes,' she said. 'I hadn't got a copy of Tennyson. Thank you so much.'

There was a pause, neither quite knowing how to continue the conversation. Clifford broke the silence.

'How did school go today then, Amy?' he asked.

She blushed violently, feeling his nearness although there was a respectable gap between them. 'Quite well I think. But I should like to leave soon. I'm not very clever really.'

'I'm sure you are. Laura tells me that you are very good at needlework and cookery.'

Amy could feel the blush deepening. To her dismay it seemed to be spreading right down into her neck. 'But those things are so ordinary,' she said quietly. 'So unadventurous and boring to talk about.'

He leaned forward to take the plate of cakes from the table. He offered them to her and in so doing moved another few inches nearer. 'Not boring at all,' he told her. 'You could say they're the most important accomplishments really. We couldn't do without them could we? And you play the piano too. Could you play for me some time, to accompany my violin I mean? Laura has been doing it, but she's hopeless.'

He turned his most dazzling smile upon her and her body seemed to turn to jelly. She had never felt more terrified or more deliciously excited in her life!

'Of course, Clifford,' she whispered. 'I'll do my best.'

'Good. Then I'll lend you the music of the piece I'm studying at the moment. I have two copies I think. Perhaps you could practise it and we'll have a session together.'

He sprang up and went to the grand piano that stood beneath the window and took a sheet of music from the stand. 'Dvořák's Ballade,' he said handing it to her. 'Could you try it?'

Amy glanced at the pages and tried to conceal her dismay. She knew that she could never reach the necessary standard without hours of painful practice. Yet she would do it. For him she would do anything, anything on earth.

'I'll do my best, Clifford,' she said summoning all her resources. 'I'll have it as perfect as I can by next weekend.'

Buxtons Chocolate Factory dominated a whole area of the town and the two great chimneys towering above the rows of warehouses seemed to dwarf everything else in sight. Dorothy felt completely intimidated as she made her way along Union Street in the cold darkness of her first morning of work. She shivered with apprehension. Now that the moment was actually here her jaunty optimism of the previous day had vanished. What would it be like? Could she possibly survive the boredom? Some of her friends went into service but she had always firmly rejected that idea, and since discovering the truth about Amy it had seemed even more impossible. Amy had servants! Dorothy shuddered at the very thought of being like one of them. Yet factory workers were almost as despised, more so by some. With a heavy heart she wrapped her long scarf more tightly around her neck and plodded along the road, completely inconspicuous in a crowd of others all going in the same direction, to the same place. As she looked at the expressionless faces and bent shoulders she felt that she had lost all her individuality and much of her hope.

She was the only new girl that morning. The other two must have been refused a job, so she supposed she ought to be grateful for her own good fortune. She stood just inside the factory entrance waiting to be told what to do and where to go. Eventually one of the grim-faced women who had interviewed her bore down upon her.

'Ah, Miller,' she said. 'This way. I'll show you where to leave your things.'

Dorothy noticed that the dark frock she had been wearing was completely hidden now with a long alpaca overall. She knew that she herself would be issued with a white one and she would soon look just like all the others, completely anonymous in the all-concealing garment that she had been told about. 'They'm good,' one of her friends who worked here had said. 'You don't have to think what to wear. Any old thing does under them overalls.' Dorothy supposed, grimly, that it was one way of looking at it. At least she wouldn't wear out her clothes.

After trailing along endless corridors they came

eventually to a room with rows of hooks and a great cupboard. 'Hang your things here, Miller,' the woman directed, indicating one empty space. Then she took a folded starched overall and handed it to her. 'Put this on, and keep it clean. Our girls are always clean.' Her voice reminded Dorothy of the parrot who lived in the pawn shop in Grosvenor Road. This ancient crotchety bird was always screeching at his owner's customers in some unknown language and the noise was fearsome to hear. 'Cleanliness and punctuality,' the voice went on relentlessly. 'Those are two of the things Mr Buxton's known for. Twopence will be taken from your wages each time you're late. We pride ourselves on the honesty of all our workers too, Miller. That of course goes without saying. I'm your supervisor by the way and you will address me as Madam. Name's Miss Jenkins. You're on a month's trial. I stand no non-sense. So work hard and behave yourself if you want to stay here. Now follow me and I'll allocate you a place and a number. You go to the same place every day and stay there until the bell goes for your dinner hour. Half an hour for dinner and then you'll stay until half past five. Is that clear?'

'Yes Madam,' Dorothy said, and her heart sank. She was filled with overwhelming deadness as though all hope had disappeared for ever.

An hour later she was still seated in the place that had been allocated to her at the end of a long row of girls. There was a table with a moving belt in front of them with an endless stream of chocolates upon it. Her job was to put a little whirl on top of any succulent mound that had been missed by the other girls further along the table. Not one chocolate must get through without its little decorative curl. She sat with the special rod in her hand and her eyes fixed on the endless procession as if hypnotized like a rabbit before a stoat. The chocolate was soft, and had to be kept so until the process was finished and to achieve this the room had to be kept reasonably warm. At the end of that first hour Dorothy began to feel that she might be able to survive after all. On a cold January day at least it was not an uncomfortable place to be.

Every now and then the moving belt stopped to allow the girls to look up, to speak for a few moments, and to check on the chocolates in front of them.

'This your first day then?' the girl next to her said in one of those precious seconds.

Dorothy turned to her in relief. 'Yes it is. How long you been here?'

'About a year now. You can eat the chocolate you know, as much as you want.'

For a second Dorothy looked down again at the creamy confections suddenly immobile before her. 'Yes, they told me. I had two, but that's enough. No good to feel bad if you got to stay here all day.'

'Can't stand the things meself. I ate a lot at first. Got proper ill I can tell you. That's why they lets you take 'em. They knows that you'll soon get so's you can't stand the sight of the things.'

Dorothy laughed. 'Not much good if you can't bear to look at them,' she said.

'You knows what I mean,' her companion replied. 'I buy some of the rubbed for me ma and me brothers and sisters now and then. It's that cheap it seems a pity not to get some, but not for me. My name's Win by the way, Winifred Gale. What's yours?'

Dorothy told her and smiled. She seemed nice enough and it would be good to have a new friend. 'We'll be pals then,' she said. 'What's it like here? You'd better tell me as much as you can.'

What d'you want to know?'

'Well, the bosses? Are they good to you?'

The girl shrugged her shoulders. 'Depends what you

do. As long as you don't give no trouble they're all right. Some of the men make passes now and then.'

Dorothy was surprised that there weren't more women in charge. A lot of the supervisors seemed to be men. Some of them were young too, much younger than many of the women under their control.

'Aren't there many women bosses?' she enquired. 'It was women what interviewed me.'

'They're the only ones. It's only Miss Jenkins here. Miss Enderby's in the packing section. Makes me mad,' the girl said.

'Why's that then?'

'Well Mr Buxton don't hold with women in top jobs. He thinks we'm only fit for doing this.'

'But he . . .' Dorothy was about to mention his strange comment to her but she decided that it might not be very prudent at this moment.

'He what?'

'Nothing, just that I heard he got a wife who believes in women getting the vote and things.'

'He don't approve though. We gets a bit of laugh about it to tell you the truth.'

Dorothy had heard murmurs of gossip about Felicity Buxton from time to time. She was a prominent member of the Women's Social and Political Union, and people said that this was a cause of great annoyance to her rather pompous husband. 'You know anything about this WSPU?' she enquired of her new friend.

'A bit. I can't go to the meetings though cause my pa don't approve. Wait till I get away from him. I'll go then all right, see if I don't. How about you? Your pa let you go will he?'

'He'm in Canada. Me and Ma can do what we like!'

'Lucky you,' Winifred said and Dorothy was deeply impressed by the envy in her voice. Yes, she supposed she was lucky, very lucky. She considered her own words. It was quite true. The thought hadn't really occurred to her before. They could do more or less what they liked. Freedom was important and, as she gazed at the assembled chocolates, she decided in that moment that it was something worth having, worth keeping and struggling for. But to be truly free you had to have money and power and those were things that were more difficult to come by.

'I want to get rich,' she said, half to herself.

Her companion laughed. 'Better marry a rich bloke then,' she said. 'There ain't many other ways that I know of to get rich.'

'I want to do it on my own,' Dorothy replied firmly.

'Better learn to use one of they newfangled type-writers then,' was the next suggestion. 'I heard tell that you can get good jobs if you knows about they.'

With a melancholy grinding noise the belt started to move again and Dorothy put an extra-sized squiggle on the chocolate in front of her in her sudden excitement. Maybe that was it. Learn to type. It wasn't much but it might take her out of this factory, give her a chance. Perhaps her lovely copperplate writing wasn't the answer after all. And she'd have to make sure she could talk properly too. Being here on the chocolate-line wasn't going to help in that direction very much, she thought. Reading in every spare minute might do it. Books were written in good grammar. Where could she get an endless supply of them? For the rest of the morning she had little to say. Ideas of self-improve-ment were going round in her head as fast as the chocolates were passing beneath her nimble fingers. At last the bell rang and she trooped out with the others to eat her sandwiches in the big yard beneath the belching chimneys and she shivered with new excitement in the bright January sun.

'Can I have a candle to take to bed?' she asked her

mother at the end of that first day. 'I want to read before I go to sleep.'

Rose was doubtful. Fire was a constant hazard. 'Can't you read down here, lovey?' she asked. 'It's all quiet with Franky doing his homework and that. You can sit right up under the lamp.'

The back kitchen was lighted by a flickering gas lamp that hung in the centre of the room. The rest of the house had oil lamps or candles.

'All right then,' she said, capitulating easily. 'I want to read the book Arthur gave me.'

'Did you see them magazines what he wrapped it in?' Rose asked. 'I been reading them a bit today. Some real nice stories in them.'

Dorothy looked at her mother in surprise. She seldom read anything but her Bible.

'No Ma. Show me.'

Rose produced a battered copy of *The Girls' Own Paper* and Dorothy looked at it a trifle scornfully. 'But it's old, Ma. Look at the date, May 1906. That's five years ago.' She flicked through the pages. 'Wonder where he got it. I suppose the book shop wrapped it up for him.'

'There was a lot of wrapping,' Rose continued. 'Look at this.' She held out another paper even more tattered. '*Chums*, monster edition,' she read. 'This one's all blood and thunder. Not the kind of thing for you and me, Dorry.'

Dorothy glanced down at the cover illustration of three men apparently in the process of killing each other. 'Captain Bill's great new Russian Story,' she read aloud. 'It's horrible, Ma. I'm surprised at you.'

They both laughed and Rose opened the paper up and pointed to a notice at the bottom of the page. 'Look, Dorry,' she said. 'There's a competition for a story and this one's modern, just last week's. They'll give a whole guinea to the winner.' She suddenly became wistful. 'That was what I always wanted to do when I was your age. Write stories like that Charlotte Brontë I heard tell of. Never could of course. I hadn't the education. But it would have been nice. I still got ideas all the time in my head, but I never learnt to spell proper or do grammar.'

Dorothy looked at her mother in astonishment. 'But Ma, that's wonderful. I didn't know.'

All at once Rose was ashamed of what she had said. 'Just you forget I ever said them silly things, my girl,' she commanded. 'The sewing suits me. I can do that and I shan't never do anything else.'

'But *I* might, Ma. *I* might.' Dorothy looked again at the competition. A school story, it said. For boys of course and only the first part. It was to be a serial. 'I was always top in Composition and Grammar at school,' she stated. 'Ma, do you hear me?' Could I do it d'you think?'

'Have a try, love,' Rose replied. ' "Nothing attempted, nothing won", as they says.'

With all thoughts of Shakespeare put temporarily aside, Dorothy sat for the rest of the evening beneath the yellow flickering light reading every word of the scrappy little magazines. Excitement was rising within her with every sentence she read. And when she had finished *Chums* she turned to *The Girls' Own Paper* and studied that too.

'I shall be a writer, Ma,' she declared when she had finished them both. 'Then I'll show them folks at that factory that I can do something better'n decorate their silly little chocolates all day long.'

'You'd best learn to talk proper first, lovey,' Rose said with down to earth practicality. 'I never heard tell of a writer who didn't speak the King's English as it be called. You and me be proper Bristol. That won't be no good. You got to learn how to talk like the nobs first.'

71

The remark was discouraging, but Dorothy rose above it. 'I'll do it, Ma,' she said. 'I'll learn to talk like the nobs somehow if it kills me.'

'Then it won't be no good will it!' Rose said, and her remark set them both laughing again. 'Come and have a nice cup 'o tea anyway and then you can read me a bit of that Shakespeare of yours before we goes to bed. I bet he spoke the King's English.'

'Yes, but it was another King,' said Dorothy, grinning at her mother in amusement.

'Well, just fancy that,' Rose said as she poured three cups of tea and turned to Franky who was sitting at the far side of the table, bending unwillingly over a page of sums in his exercise book.

'Come and listen to your sister,' Rose said to him. 'She's going to educate us with that ole Shakespeare.'

Franky closed his book thankfully and picked up the copy of *Chums* that Dorothy had temporarily discarded. 'Gosh, Ma. Where did this come from?' he asked, ignoring her remark about Shakespeare and peering at the gruesome picture on the front. 'This is more like it!'

His mother grabbed it away from him. 'Never you mind,' she said.

'Our Dorry's going to be a writer.' She pushed his cup of tea towards him and put a home-made cake on a plate. 'Eat your supper,' she commanded. 'Do you hear me, a writer my boy, so you'd better listen to her.'

Franky looked at his sister for a moment in awe and then he too laughed. 'You'm joking,' he remarked his mouth full of cake. 'Our Dorry couldn't be a writer. Them's clever educated folks.'

In bed that night Dorothy wondered if she could indeed ever achieve such a wonderful aim. The magazines were safely stowed away in her box, the one that held

72

her few treasures. The key was on a string round her neck and she held it in her hand as she drifted into sleep. Perhaps dear Arthur, with his lovely present had given her, in the wrapping paper, an even greater gift?

CHAPTER FOUR

With the flush of new ideas to fill her head while her hands were busy, Dorothy found that the days in the factory passed reasonably quickly. She was careful not to say a word about her longing to become a writer to the other girls. Winifred had become quite a good friend but not one to be completely trusted. She'd laugh and call her ambitions just silly highfalutin ideas, but to Dorothy her dreams were precious and not to be trodden on or ridiculed. It was only to her oldest friend Vera Price that she felt she could really open her heart, and Vera hoped to join her at Buxtons when she left school. Dorothy longed for that.

Her first story was well on its way, written for *Chums* and suitably full of action. She wrote one page each night and then read it to her mother and to a bemused Franky who looked at her with a new respect.

'Where do you get all them ideas, our Dorry?' he asked after a particularly dramatic episode.

'Out of my head,' she replied brightly. 'Pity you can't help me being a boy and boys being reckoned to be cleverer than us girls.'

Rose's comments were usually predictable and tonight was no exception. 'Couldn't you put in a nice moral somewhere,' she said. 'Something to turn them lads what are going to read it into good upright young men, make 'em go to Chapel on Sundays.'

'Then it wouldn't win the prize, would it, Ma. The editor don't – doesn't,' Dorothy corrected herself, 'doesn't want things like that. I've read the magazine over and over and there aren't any preachy bits anywhere!'

Rose sighed. 'Pity you can't use your pen for the Good Lord,' she said. 'I been reading *Our Own Magazine*. That's full of morals.'

'If I win this competition maybe I'll do a little story for that as well,' Dorothy said. 'When I'm famous and rich I shall have plenty of time to write for them all! Try to find some other old magazines, Ma, children's ones. I'd like to write kid's stuff. I used to enjoy reading stories to the little ones at school and the tales were easy. I know I could do it.'

'If you did a nice Christian story Mr Buxton would be pleased,' Rose cajoled.

'And who would tell him?'

'Well you would wouldn't you? I'd be that proud of you, Dorry.'

Dorothy laughed. 'Oh, Ma,' she said, 'You're incorrigible.'

Rose looked shocked. 'In-what? It don't sound nice to me. And I don't like you using them long words.'

Dorothy laughed again. She had come across the word in some of her reading and had looked it up in the old battered dictionary that she had managed to buy for twopence from the bookstall on the market. Now she was trying to use the word and make it her own as she did with every new one she met. 'It means that you can't be changed I think,' she explained. 'Something like that anyway.' She wasn't sure whether she should use it of her mother. The dictionary said that it meant hopeless or hardened and Ma certainly wasn't either of those things, but it sounded right somehow and very impressive.

'In-corr-ig-ible,' Rose said. 'Well you learns something every day don't you!'

Dorothy grinned at her affectionately. She had

finished reading the evening's instalment of her story and she put the sheets of paper aside and went to put the kettle to boil for a cup of tea. 'By the way, Ma,' she said as she placed cups and saucers on the table. 'You remember that I told you about the Women's Social and Political Union Meeting on Friday? Are we going? I do want to, but I couldn't go without you.'

'Yes,' Rose said decidedly. 'We'm certainly going. Not that I can do much to help, but I definitely think women ought to have a bit more say about things.'

Geoffrey Buxton frequently walked round the factory and as Dorothy watched him on the following morning she thought about those determined words of her mother and laughed bitterly to herself. The great Mr Buxton wouldn't agree in any way with Rose's sentiments. In spite of his liberated wife, or perhaps because of her, women certainly had very little power in his factory. There was really only one and that was the angular, stony-faced Miss Jenkins. She was following at his heels again as usual. Dorothy frequently wondered about her. Whenever she came into the factory she would glare at everyone with condescension, but it was always on Dorothy that most of her venom seemed to fall.

'Don't know what I've done to make her hate me,' she said once to Winifred.

'It ain't any one thing what you've done,' her friend had commented. 'It's just that you gives yourself airs sometimes. She don't want nobody to get into the boss's good books. She's jealous. Better be careful.'

As Geoffrey Buxton walked slowly into the room Winifred glanced up at him. 'Handsome ain't he,' she whispered. 'Not my type, but handsome for someone that old.'

'How old do you think?'

'Forty-ish I suppose.'

'He wouldn't approve of the meeting that Ma and I are going to on Friday,' Dorothy said with a small grin. 'The WSPU. He's that against women's rights.'

'His wife do go regular.'

'Yes, so you said. It's funny.'

'You must tell me about it.' Winifred's voice was envious. 'I told you, my pa won't let us go.'

Geoffrey Buxton walked down the row of workers and the room became silent. He looked sternly at each girl and the nervousness that his presence evoked was almost tangible. Dorothy shivered a little. Nothing missed those shrewd eyes and she hoped that she had no smears of chocolate on her overall or strands of hair escaping from her white cap. Eventually he drew level with the end of the table and stopped in front of her. She looked down not wishing to meet his gaze and feeling the antagonism of the ever-attentive Miss Jenkins who hovered just behind him. 'Dorothy Miller again, isn't it,' he said. 'Are you still liking it here?'

'Yes thank you, Sir. Very much, Sir,' Dorothy lied.

'Good. I am gratified.' He inclined his head ever so slightly in her direction and then walked on.

'Blimey,' Winifred said. 'What's so special about you then? And what do gratified mean?'

'I don't know, but I'll find out,' said Dorothy with grim determination. 'I'll look it up.'

Her dictionary once again, that evening, yielded up its treasures and the next day on the way to work she told Winifred. 'That word he said, *gratified*. It means pleased or delighted. Now why on earth should he be delighted that I like it here? Which I don't.' She added the last words in a whisper hiding her mouth with her hand, and the girls giggled.

'Perhaps he'm sweet on you, Dorothy Miller,' her friend said in a similar furtive manner.

'Go on, don't be so stupid. He'm more my Ma's age. Now she likes him. She'm quite dotty about him as a matter of fact.' Dorothy saw the surprise that swept over Winifred's features at this admission. 'No you ninny, I don't mean like that!' she protested. 'She thinks he'm splendid and good, something like God. Especially when he'm preaching in our Chapel.'

'Well, would you believe it. Our Mr Buxton like God.' Winifred tucked her arm through Dorothy's and still laughing they went cheerily through the factory gates for another day of chocolate and boredom.

'Can I wear my new things, Ma?' Dorothy asked two days later when they were getting ready to go to the meeting. 'I want to look as good as possible. I feel better when I look nice.'

'I suppose you can, love,' Rose said. 'It'll be crowded though. I don't suppose anyone'll notice either of us.'

Dorothy was feeling pleased with herself. She had been paid her wages that day and she had proudly given all the money to Ma as usual as soon as she got in the house, but her mother had insisted that she take a whole shilling back to buy a book or anything else she fancied. Dorothy put the money safely away, locked up in her private box until she could go to the second-hand book shop down on the Haymarket.

She was excited, too, about tonight's meeting. 'I want to join the junior section of the WSPU,' she said. 'I can, Ma can't I?'

'We'll see.' In spite of her enthusiasm for women's rights, Rose sounded doubtful. 'I don't want you or me mixed up in any of them rough goings-on, mind. They'm all right for the gentry. They've got friends to get 'em out of trouble when they get arrested. No stone-throwing or anything like that for us, Dorry.'

Rose's voice was severe and Dorothy knew the sound sense of her words. Suffragettes had frequently been imprisoned and even had food pushed down their throats through tubes when they refused to eat. She

79

shivered. It was a terrifying idea.

'There was that Lady Constance who got herself put in jail,' Rose went on to voice her daughter's thoughts as she stood in front of the small hall mirror and skewered her hat firmly in place with long fierce-looking hatpins. 'She were force-fed, remember, and that's terrible from what I hears.'

Dorothy was at the top of the stairs and she looked down at her mother. 'You mean that one who dressed up poor at first and they didn't know?'

'Yes. I don't think that made much difference though. I've heard they'll do it to anyone who won't eat. But p'raps if they'd knowed she was a lady they might've treated her a bit better. But we've got to mind it don't happen to us. We don't want no trouble. She had a rich brother to get her out and look after her when she was poorly, after. An Earl I think he were. That's the important thing, having no need to earn a living and being able to give up lots of time. No good for us, so you be careful. Hurry up now anyway. I'm all ready to go.'

Dorothy rushed into the bedroom and carefully lifted her blue skirt out of the big cupboard that filled the space between the tiny blocked-up fireplace and the wall. She ran her hand over the soft material and laid it reverently on the bed along with the blouse and bolero, glad that there was some place at last where its glowing colour and fashionable lines would be suitable. She took off her working things and put them just as carefully on a sturdy wooden hanger inside the cupboard. She knew that each garment must be looked after, brushed and ironed and regularly washed. She would never allow herself to deteriorate into the slovenly ways of some of the people she saw every day. She had long ago determined that she would always be clean and neat, whatever she was doing.

She poured water from the big jug into the bowl that

stood on the washstand and soaped her hands and face and then she brushed her hair carefully and tied it with two big bows one each side of her head instead of the usual plait or bun. Finally she put on the blouse, pulled the skirt over her head, and added the bolero. Then she stood and surveyed herself in the long cracked mirror, pleased with what she saw, except for the reminder that the thick bunches of fair hair made her look like Amy. That was just how Amy Harding wore hers. But it was too late to change it now.

'Put on your coat,' Rose was calling up the stairs. 'It's cold and beginning to rain.'

The meeting hall was only two streets away and Dorothy would have braved the cold rather than cover all her finery with the shabby old tweed coat, but rain would spoil the velvet. Unwillingly she pulled her coat on and rushed down to join her mother.

'Votes for women!' Franky shouted after them as they closed the front door and Rose laughed.

'We'll 'ave to take Frank along one day and educate 'im a bit, won't we?' she said, huddling against the drizzle. 'Want to get the lads on our side too!'

'Franky won't be any good,' Dorothy said scornfully. 'He don't – doesn't – want to do anything with his life except go round with that old horse and cart. I can't understand him at all. Him being a boy and all and could do lots of things.'

He'll have a good job when he'm fourteen,' Rose said defensively. She tucked her arm into Dorothy's. 'Jennings Hardware Stores is a good place. Lots of chances to get on. Folks will always want paraffin and candles and the like, and he'm getting sixpence a week for the bit he do evenings and Saturdays.'

Dorothy laughed. 'Sixpence for that and him not fourteen yet. And what do I get? A measly three shillings for all the hours I slave away with them – those – chocolates!'

'Never mind,' Rose said. 'When we get the vote we'll have the same money as the men, you'll see.'

Dorothy looked at her mother in surprise. Equal pay was a dream sometimes talked about in hushed voices by one or two of the most militant girls at work, but she couldn't imagine it ever coming. After all a man had a family to keep hadn't he?

They walked along the dimly lit street and turned into Grosvenor Road. The shops were shut and the gas lamps spluttered here and there with the wind. Dorothy pulled her coat more tightly around her and was glad that she had worn it. It would have been stupid to leave it at home however proud she was of the blue velvet!

The meeting was in a small room above one of the shops and they turned in thankfully out of the rain. Rows of hard rickety chairs were set out close to each other and an old wooden table stood below the small uncurtained window with two glasses of water and some writing paper ready upon it. Rose prepared to sit herself at the back but Dorothy stopped her.

'No, Ma,' she said. 'The front. Let's sit at the front.'

They were early and Dorothy stared with interest at the assortment of women and the sprinkling of men who were gathering there, some of them talking with gusto, others silent, and some obviously nervous. When most of the rows were filled and it was almost time to begin a sudden hush fell on the room. The organizer, a young woman in a fashionable coat and hat, went to the door and greeted the couple who stood there. Dorothy noticed the new slim line of her hobble skirt and the fashionable small hat perched on her shining well-groomed head, and for a moment her pleasure in her own clothes was dimmed. The blue skirt seemed too full now that some of the gentry were wearing the hobble. She had left her old tweed coat at the back of the hall and she suddenly felt slightly self-conscious sitting right on the front row. Why ever had she done that, she wondered?

The meeting was about to start. The young woman had brought her two guests to the table on the raised platform and she was looking around at the assembled company.

'Ladies and gentlemen,' she announced in a ringing tone. 'Our advertised speaker has not been able to come owing to a sudden indisposition but I am pleased to tell you that Mrs Felicity Buxton has agreed to fill her place at the last moment. May I introduce her to you, and also her son Mr Clifford Buxton who kindly consented to accompany his mother and who is favourably disposed towards our movement.'

Everyone stood up and there was loud applause. At first Dorothy had no eyes for anyone but the woman she had heard so much about: Felicity Buxton who took no notice of her husband's bossy ways, the wife who always had her own way, or so everyone said. For someone married to the great Geoffrey Buxton that was quite an accomplishment. But her gaze was soon riveted on the young man standing beside his mother. He was tall and handsome, with an immaculately tailored suit and an assured and confident manner. She was aware that he was staring at her too and that he was as gripped by her as she was by him. Suddenly she knew with an intense and blinding certainty that Clifford Buxton's destiny somehow lay entwined with hers. It was frightening to be so sure, and she looked away. She was being silly she told herself and she tried to think of Arthur whom she liked, Arthur with his big work-roughened hands and his good-natured face. But the picture of him failed to materialize. She was too much aware of the presence of this other man.

She sat trying to concentrate on Felicity's talk for more than an hour, but her thoughts and frequently her eyes were focused on the young man behind the table and she knew that he was constantly looking at her too. Geoffrey Buxton's son! He's my boss's son, she kept telling herself and so far above me that I shouldn't even presume to speak to him! But still she felt the link between them, felt sure that he sensed it too.

She managed to grasp something of what his mother said however and she found that she was in total agreement with all that she understood. In fact she was so carried away by the general excitement of the evening that during question-time at the end she found the courage to ask about equal pay and whether this was an aim of the Union. She blushed as she saw the interest in Clifford Buxton's eyes deepen as he listened to her words, and her embarrassment was more intense as she saw him smile at her. She was so overcome that she scarcely heard Felicity's reply.

When it was time to go she was still moving in a kind of dream.

'Come on, Dorry. What's the matter with you?' Rose wanted to know. 'You'm behaving very strange tonight. That was a good question though. I don't know how you had the pluck to ask it.'

She was jerked back to the present, back to the stuffy room and the need to find her coat. She pushed through the crowd and pulled the garment roughly down from the hook on the wall and put it over her arm as she followed her mother towards the door. Felicity and Clifford were standing there talking to a group of enthusiastic volunteers.

Suddenly as she passed close to him he turned and smiled at her again. 'Have we met somewhere?' he enquired. 'Your face seems familiar.'

'No. No we can't have. You'm making a mistake,' she said and was immediately suffused with shame for her grammar. The words had come out all in a rush. She turned away from him, her heart thumping and

84

she pushed anxiously through the door into the dark rainy street. Only then did she pull her old coat angrily over her beautiful clothes, only then did she stand still and calm herself, breathing the cold damp air in great gulps as she waited for her mother.

Clifford Buxton's thoughts kept returning to the fair-haired girl in blue sitting in the front row of the dingy meeting room. She reminded him vividly of Amy. In fact the likeness was almost uncanny. Yet there was a difference. He tried to determine exactly what it was that stood out so strongly in the young face. He had caught her staring at him frequently during the long meeting and each time their eyes met he had felt oddly disturbed. There was a frankness in her gaze that disconcerted him, and also a sense of purpose and determination that was more typical of his own sister than of Amy. He sensed a polish, too, that one seldom found in the working classes. He had been impressed at the perceptive question she had asked and surprised by the words she used, the thoughts not matching the strong Bristol accent. She intrigued him.

'Who was the girl in the front, Mama?' he enquired of Felicity on the way home. 'Do you know her?'

'Who dear?' His mother was, for once, vague and tired. Her mind was still on her talk.

'The one in the ill-fitting blue outfit who looked like Amy.'

'Oh yes, I remember. Yes, there was a likeness to Amy. I noticed it too. I don't know her name. Is there a reason why I should?'

'No. I don't think so. Her question was well thought-out.'

'Yes it was. She might be a good worker when she's older. Very young I should think. About the same age as Laura.'

Clifford suddenly felt uncomfortable. He wanted to

push the memory of the girl away from him. He could still see her startling blue eyes in his imagination and she vaguely troubled him. He fell silent and let his mind wander to other things. He had accompanied his mother to this meeting because his father insisted that she should not go alone. He knew that his school friends would laugh at him if they guessed that he was even mildly interested in women's rights. Most of them, if they thought about it at all, were strongly against giving the vote to women. He sighed. He was perfectly happy at his expensive school in Clifton, but sometimes he would have liked to board, to get away from home each term.

Then as the sleek and handsome Rover purred its way through the quiet streets, his thoughts turned to Amy. The girl tonight had brought her back vividly to his mind. He felt a little guilty and troubled when he thought of his sister's friend. She was so anxious to please him, so sweet and adoring. He wondered doubtfully if he could live up to her obvious hero-worship. And he sighed, remembering that he had given her a difficult piece of music to practise so that she could accompany him on the piano. He must be careful not to use her just because she was so amenable and willing.

Then he realized that his mother was speaking to him.

'Thank you, Clifford,' she said as the chauffeur pulled the motor to a stop in the drive-way of their house. 'I was so glad to have you with me tonight. I always feel a little nervous when I have to speak to a group of people I don't know.'

He jumped down and went round to the other side of the vehicle to help her out. Not that she needed helping, he thought with sudden amusement, but she took his hand gracefully.

'I mustn't impose on you any more though. You

have your school work to attend to. Papa will just have
to accept that I must go out alone sometimes.'

Clifford knew that whenever she found it acceptable,
his mother deliberately bowed to his father's will, but
her fierce independence would assert itself at any time
if she so wished. He laughed a little grimly to himself
at the thought. Even his sister knew how to deal with
their father, however rigid a disciplinarian he appeared
to be. He longed to be able to stand up to him as the
two women of the family did and he wondered why he
found it so difficult. He was not afraid of anyone or
anything else. It was only his father who could humil-
iate him and make him feel useless and incompetent.
He was standing in the hall ready to greet them when
they arrived.

'Good meeting?' he enquired without interest. 'I'm
glad you're home safe and sound. To bed with you
now, Clifford. Otherwise you'll be tired for your work
tomorrow.'

'Yes, Sir,' he said bleakly. He watched his mother
take the pins carefully from her large hat and hand it
to the waiting maid. She removed her coat with its
beautiful fur collar, every movement graceful and
elegant. Her hair gleamed in the light from the great
chandelier above them and she turned to her husband
and kissed him gently on the cheek. Clifford saw the
adoration in his father's face as he looked at her and
he felt shut out and alone as he went up the wide
staircase to his room.

'You look very tired, my dear,' Geoffrey said
as he guided his wife into the drawing room. 'I shall
ring for a cup of hot chocolate for you, and some
sandwiches.'

She smiled at his solicitude. 'Thank you. That would
be nice. Yes I do believe that I am tired.'

'I wish you wouldn't do these things,' he said.
'You know how much I dislike you going out alone,

and to St Paul's too. Not a pleasant place to be after dark.'

Felicity sighed. 'I had the chauffeur to take me right to the door. And you knew Clifford accompanied me too.'

Geoffrey grunted. 'Stupid place for a lad to go,' he grumbled. 'The whole thing's ridiculously misplaced. If women were meant to have votes and rule they would have . . .' He groped for an end to his sentence but could find none and Felicity put her hand to his cheek and traced her finger round his mouth and determined chin.

'They would have what?' she asked. 'Beards perhaps?' She smiled at him. 'You're just old fashioned, dearest,' she whispered. 'We're just as capable and clever as men, more so than most, I think. We're merely suppressed.'

'If that's so then I wish you would keep your ideas to yourself and not infect my workers. You'll have my factory girls demanding things soon. Damned uncomfortable that would be.' He spoke in an affectionate, almost amused tone, which took the sting out of his words.

Felicity put her fingers on his lips in mock reproof. 'Swearing, my dear! The good preacher! Better not let them hear that at your Chapel.'

They laughed together and finished the sandwiches and chocolate.

'Shall we go to bed?' Felicity said to him taking his hand and half pulling him from the deep sofa.

He jumped up and took her in his arms. 'Perhaps there are some advantages in having a liberated wife,' he murmured. 'As long as no one else knows!'

That was just it, Felicity thought as she preceded him up the stairs. He was so very ashamed of her political activities that he would like to keep her hidden away like some Arab wife. It made her very sad. It was the great flaw in their relationship and a great burden to both of them. 'I love you. I love you so, you stupid man,' she said to herself. 'When will you grow up and be a true husband to me?'

'How did the meeting go then?' Winifred wanted to know on the following Monday morning.

Dorothy wasn't sure how to reply. She was strangely reluctant to tell anyone of her odd feelings about Clifford Buxton. One of the things she hated was to be laughed at and she knew that she would be teased unmercifully if she dropped even the slightest hint of the effect he had had on her. She decided to concentrate on his mother, but there was danger in that too. Everyone would be interested in the boss's wife and she'd be pestered to tell all about it.

'It was good,' she said. 'And the speaker was Mrs Buxton, but you've not to let on!'

'Blimey,' Winifred replied. 'All right. Just tell me later in secret.'

'Some time I will,' Dorothy said. 'When there's no fear of her husband being in earshot. She's nice though. I don't know how she got married to him.'

'His looks I suppose,' Winifred commented. 'Them's important. A fellow got to look good.'

Dorothy grinned at her. 'Looks aren't the only thing,' she said, but as she spoke she was unwillingly thinking of the handsome sensitive face and the flashing brown eyes of the boss's son.

Winter gave way to spring and then to summer but the seasons meant little to Dorothy. Shut away in the factory the days were long and tedious, and all her plans to better herself had had little success so far. Now with the lengthening summer days she was beginning to feel more restless than ever.

'I want to learn to type,' she confided to Winifred one day when they were eating their sandwiches during the dinner hour. 'You told me it was the way to get on. Well I've decided to try.'

Her companion looked at her with a doubtful expression on her face. 'Them what can afford it go to a special typing school. My ma was telling me about the daughter of the woman she works for.'

'There's no hope for me if it needs money,' Dorothy said. 'I got to find a way that don't – doesn't – cost anything.'

'This girl goes to some college with a fancy name.' Winifred pondered for a time while she enjoyed a mouthful of moist and delicious bread-pudding. 'Let me see,' she said as she swallowed the last bit, 'Lavender Hill I think it was. I don't know where that be but it ain't round here anyway. She stays away.'

Dorothy sighed. Money seemed to be the key to everything. If you had plenty of it there was nothing you couldn't do. Even if you were a girl there were still plenty of possibilities, but without it life was pretty bleak. Her story for *Chums* magazine had been sent off to the editor with great hopes and much approval from her mother and Franky, but the carefully written sheets of paper had been returned to her with a short polite note. Her competition entry was reasonably good the letter said, but needed more plot, more excitement, and if she could get the use of one of the new typewriters for her work it would look more professional. She had been depressed for days after that and for a long time hadn't written anything else. But eventually she had taken out the letter again and read it over and over, coming to the conclusion at last that it wasn't as discouraging as she had first supposed.

The word 'professional' interested her. The old dictionary told her that it meant 'businesslike, making a trade', and she was very intrigued. That was what she wanted, a trade of her very own and the thought of learning to type began to dominate her mind again – for even if she never became a writer she'd have a skill. Girls who could type could get jobs as private secretaries.

'Miss Jenkins types,' Winifred said breaking into her thoughts. 'I seen her machine when she called me into her office the other day. It looks pretty hard to use I can tell you and it makes a great clatter when she'm writing on it, but she goes fast and she don't seem to look at the letters. Pretty clever if you ask me. I had to stand and wait while she finished something.'

'She'd never let me learn to use it. No hope of that.'

'They got a typewriter in Benjamins. I expect it be pretty dear. I saw it in the window when I went past yesterday.'

For a second Dorothy's heart thumped in excitement. Benjamins was the pawn shop in the Haymarket and she often stared at the various items that had been left there by owners who couldn't afford to claim them back. She had never liked the sad lost look about the shop, and as she walked on past its dirty brown windows she would sometimes weave stories in her mind about the men and women who had to trade precious possessions for money to pay for food or rent. At least she and Ma had only had to do that twice. It was her dad's old watch that Ma had taken both times and they had always found enough money at the end of the week to get it back.

The factory bell rang stridently at that moment and Winifred jumped up. 'Come on,' she said. 'Stop your daydreaming. We got another four hours on them blessed chocolates.'

During the winter the warmth of the factory had been a comfort, but now its heat was proving to be a trial that Dorothy could sometimes hardly bear. On that bright June day she dragged herself back to her place on the production line hating each sickly

91

chocolate cream that seemed to swim before her glazed eyes. The factory often felt like a prison from which her mind frequently escaped as surely as her hands expertly performed the dreary automatic actions required of her.

It was towards the end of the afternoon when she was feeling at her worst that Geoffrey Buxton paid another of his frequent visits to her section. As she watched his progress down the production line, she wanted to scream out to him that she was capable of better than this, that she wanted to learn to type, to work in the office, to use her brain, but she controlled herself as always. He stopped in front of her as usual and looked at her with a vague sort of concern, almost annoyance. Some of the other girls, as well as Winifred, were beginning to notice the attention he gave her and teased her now and then. She could only assume that it had something to do with Amy Harding. He must know about the connection between them. The thought always disturbed her.

And there was another thing of course that plagued her, although he could have no knowledge of it! Sometimes she couldn't avoid seeing the likeness between the boss and his son. It was now some months since she had seen Clifford, but he still featured in her dreams. The sight of Mr Buxton striding regally around seemed to stress the difference between Clifford and herself, the great chasm of wealth and social class which it was almost impossible to cross.

These thoughts filled her mind now as she looked up at the man standing autocratically in front of her. His hair was similar to his son's, dark and glossy. They shared that determined set of the mouth too, and the way they talked, the easy fluent use of words that she admired so much. But there the likeness ended and for an unwilling moment she saw, vividly in her imagination, Clifford, as he had been back at the meeting in the early spring. Clifford of the smiling eyes, the strong hands with long artistic fingers and clean well-shaped nails. She had noticed so much on that memorable night when he'd sat beside his mother at the WSPU meeting for almost two hours. Their eyes had met so many times. She wondered if he remembered her as vividly as she could recall him. Every line of him was etched on her memory.

Dorothy tried to pull herself together for here was his father staring at her, her boss, the all-powerful Mr Buxton. The colour rushed to her face in response to the pounding of her heart. She desperately hoped that he was not aware of her thoughts. Of course he couldn't be, she told herself fiercely. He didn't know she'd even spoken to his son. Once again she reminded herself of how stupid she was being.

The moving belt stopped at that inopportune moment and her fingers were stilled, the room suddenly quiet. It seemed that all eyes were turned in their direction.

'Dorothy,' he said. 'Is everything still satisfactory?'

'Yes, thank you, Sir,' she stammered. And then, suddenly and with the thought of Clifford vividly in her mind, she burst out, 'But I should very much like to learn to type, Sir. Is it possible?'

There was a deep gasp from the girls who heard her. No factory worker dared to speak to him apart from a quick 'yes' or 'no' if he should deign to ask them anything. Certainly no one ever made suggestions like that!

He stood transfixed, the enormity of the idea for a moment causing him to remain speechless.

'An interesting idea,' he said at last. 'You have something in common with Laura I think. Quite out of the question of course.' Then he turned without the usual nod and was gone. The moving belt resumed its relentless course and the buzz of critical comment that

93

Dorothy knew would inevitably follow was postponed until the next break.

It was some time before Dorothy lived down her daring suggestion. She was teased, looked at with concern as if she should be in the town's lunatic asylum, and often ignored by the other girls as being different, not one of them. Her efforts to improve the way she spoke also brought much unfriendly comment.

'Trying to be a swell, that Dorothy Miller!' The words were unkind, frequently repeated and some-times much more cruel than that.

Even Winifred told her that she had ideas above herself. 'I didn't mean you to go and blurt it out like that when I said about typing,' she complained. 'You got no sense, Dorothy Miller!'

But however much her friends laughed at her, Dorothy persevered with her efforts, and if no one wanted to eat their sandwiches with her in the dinner hour, well then, she would try not to mind. She always kept something in her bag to read!

And every night she scribbled. The pile of exercise books under her bed grew bigger. Each one was filled with stories and there was a special one to which she confided all her secret longings and fears. This little book, unlike the others, was lovingly locked away. She felt fairly confident that her mother wouldn't pry into her things, but it was better to be sure, especially as she'd written about her feelings for Clifford as well as for Arthur Price.

Eventually her isolation ended, for Vera, Arthur's sister and still her greatest friend, joined her on the production line at Buxtons. The two girls had kept faith with each other during the past year, neither mentioning the secret about Amy Harding to anyone. It had created a bond between them and now Dorothy felt a sense of relief that there was someone at work who understood some of her worries, who knew about her burden. On Vera's first day she persuaded the supervisor to allow them to have permanent places side by side.

With the onset of the colder weather, life became a little more bearable in the factory, and with Vera's cheerful presence the long hours seemed less tedious.

'Our Arthur's got himself a new job,' she announced one day. 'He starts in January.'

'Doing what?' It had been some time since Dorothy had seen Arthur. He worked long hours and their time off seldom matched.

'Driving. He's that thrilled. He've always been keen on motors as you know. He learnt to drive at his last place and they taught him how to look after them too, the mechanics and all that.'

'Our Franky's more interested in horses. He loves them. I don't know what he'll do if they get motors instead.'

Vera laughed. 'They won't use motors for pulling carts, you ninny. Motors is only for posh folks. But our Arthur reckons that all them what have got enough money will have 'em soon instead of carriages.'

'Where's this new job then?'

'Up at the boss's place in Clifton just in the next road to where he is now.'

'You mean he's going to work for Mr Buxton?'

'Yes. A chauffeur, he said he was to be called. It's the new name for the man what drives and sees to a motor. What's wrong? You don't sound very pleased.'

'Yes. I'm pleased for Arthur if it's what he wants.' Dorothy paused for a moment and considered her reaction to Vera's news. 'It's just that I wonder what he'll be like for a boss, our Mr Buxton. In his home I mean, and then there's the son.' She paused for a moment, thinking about the implications. The two young men she liked the most, together: master and servant. It was an uncomfortable thought. 'There's a daughter too,' she added.

'I've never seen neither of 'em. What are they like?'

Dorothy's hands worked efficiently on the chocolates in front of her as she considered her friend's question. The moving belt had been improved a little, made quieter, and it was possible now to talk sometimes without waiting for it to stop. Her thoughts went winging back yet again to that evening last spring when she and Clifford had spoken together. It seemed a long time ago now and although she was always hoping that they would meet again it hadn't happened.

'I don't know the girl. The son's nice. Not a bit like his dad. I rather took to him when I saw him at a WSPU meeting I went to with Ma.'

Vera laughed, and the bell rang out at that moment to tell them the long morning was over. It sounded stridently throughout the building. 'Not our sort,' she said, over the noise. 'You'd better forget all about him. I thought you was sweet on Arthur anyway.'

Dorothy blushed. 'Arthur's nice,' she replied. 'I hope he likes it, the new job I mean. He'll do well. He works hard.'

'He've grand ideas like you. Wants to improve himself he do say. Tries to speak like them, the gentry I mean. He's a clever one, our Arthur, not like me. I shan't never be anything but a skivvy.'

The girls crowded through the wide doors into the street outside and Dorothy took Vera's arm in hers. 'Don't say that, Vera,' she said angrily. 'You'm – you are – as clever as you want to be and you can do anything you make up your mind to do.'

Vera laughed again. 'Not me,' she said. 'Your grand ways aren't for the likes of me. You'm always reading books and I can't be bothered. Just give me a nice lad and I'll be happy.'

They usually ate their lunch together in the small

park a couple of streets away and if it rained they sheltered in the bandstand or stayed in the factory's bicycle shed. Dorothy thought about Vera's words as she ate and wondered why her friend was so content and happy with the little she had. She herself was still driven and harassed by dissatisfaction. Apart from her scribbling she had found no way yet to overcome it. She had sent two more stories away to editors, but both had been returned, and with each rejection had come a gigantic hopelessness. Ever since her stupid remark to Mr Buxton about learning to type he had carefully ignored her and she felt that she had made a stupid mistake. She would have to be more subtle.

She started to think about Arthur Price. He was ambitious. Perhaps he was a kindred spirit and she remembered he'd once talked about money and power, the two things they both wanted. She recalled the time they'd spent together in St Andrew's Park some months ago and the present he had sent her. She'd written to him but she'd never mentioned the effect on her of the magazines he'd used as wrapping paper.

She turned to Vera. 'When'll you see Arthur again, then?' she asked.

'He'm coming home round Christmas some time. He've got a day off.'

'I hope I'll see 'en then,' Dorothy said firmly. She decided, in that moment, that she must banish all her silly thoughts about Clifford Buxton. He was, as Vera said, not her sort, as far above her as . . . her mind groped for a comparison and she could find none. He was far above her. That was enough. She sighed, folded her sandwich paper neatly, put it into her pocket for tomorrow and stood up. It was almost time for the soul-destroying afternoon to begin.

CHAPTER FIVE

'Sorry to have to leave you for a moment, my dear,' Ralph Harding said to his daughter. 'I have to give Mrs Benjamin a bottle of medicine. Will you be all right?'

'Of course, Papa,' Amy replied bravely. She hoped he wouldn't be long. She hated it when he left her sitting in the motor in these dismal streets. It didn't often happen and today it wasn't too bad. The worst place to be abandoned was outside St Barnabas' School. One of his patients lived opposite the playground and he sometimes needed to stop there. If it was playtime the children always crowded around the railings and stared at her. Sometimes they shouted rude remarks too. She shivered at the thought.

It was old Mrs Benjamin whom he had to visit now though. She and her husband kept the pawn shop and Amy could see the little bow window from her place in the passenger seat of the motor. Although the glass was dirty and stained she noticed the black typewriter that took pride of place in the centre. She stared at it with interest. There were two machines in her school now, and a few of the girls had asked if they could take a typing course. She vaguely wondered if it might be an interesting thing to learn. She doubted that there was very much you could do with a typewriter that couldn't be accomplished by nice neat handwriting but some of her friends were enthusiastic.

'Look at that, Papa,' she said when he came out of

the building. 'A typewriter. Do you think it might be a good thing for me to learn how to use one?'

Ralph laughed. He had heard that women were beginning to find jobs in offices. Their small nimble fingers seemed more suited to pounding the keys of these newfangled machines then were those of men apparently. 'You ladies will be taking all the jobs away from the lads if we don't watch out,' he teased. 'Now why would you want to learn to type?'

'I don't know. It was just an idea. I saw it there and wondered if . . .'

'I'll buy it for you if you like,' Ralph said. He was about to swing the starting handle of the motor car but he turned back to have another look in the window. 'Though I would prefer to get you a new one.'

'Oh no, Papa. You said that the Benjamins are poor and don't do much trade now. Wouldn't it be better to get it from them? Actually I'm not even sure if I want it. It was only a thought.'

'Like to come in and meet Mr Benjamin?' Ralph asked. 'He's a nice old soul and very worried about his wife. She'll get better but it means good food and a lot of nursing. Perhaps we should give them some trade.'

Amy accepted her father's hand to help her down from the vehicle and together they pushed open the shabby old door, and to the accompanying peel of a chime of swinging bells entered the dim interior of the shop. Amy looked around her in fascination. There were dolls with lolling wax heads and long dingy white gowns, piles of lace covered in cobwebs, endless books, a box of old jewellery, clocks in abundance, a small writing desk, and several paintings hanging on the walls. A pall of dust covered everything and the dirty musty smell almost choked her.

The old man who came in answer to the tinkling of the bell looked in surprise and some concern at the reappearance of the doctor. 'Dr Harding,' he stammered. 'Is there something you forgot to tell me? About my wife is it?'

'No, no of course not. She's going to be well again in a few weeks' time I assure you. This is my daughter.' Ralph's tone was kind and reassuring. 'Amy would like to see the typewriter you have in your window.'

The shopkeeper seemed to be transformed before their eyes. He straightened his back and his face was suddenly full of hope. 'Yes, yes of course. It's a good one, almost new. I'll get it out for you.' He pulled a vast array of items from the window and at last appeared triumphant, staggering under the weight of the ungainly black machine. He swept a pile of tableclothes and old newspapers from the great oak counter that dominated the front of the shop and placed the typewriter reverently upon it dusting its keys with his handkerchief. 'There you are,' he said. 'And it has the book of instructions too. Nothing's lost. The young man who left it needed the money. He came back and told me he couldn't afford to redeem it. Sad, but . . .' He shrugged his shoulders, 'Life's hard, Dr Harding, and we all have to try to make a living somehow.'

'Of course, Mr Benjamin.' Ralph looked from him to the ugly cumbersome machine. 'I know nothing about such things.' He turned to Amy. 'Do you, my dear?'

'Not really, Papa.' She was beginning to feel a little guilty. Her parents were so generous with her. She only had to show an interest in something for it to be hers, however flippant or unnecessary the item.

'We'll take it.' Ralph made up his mind quickly. Even if it was a complete waste of money he couldn't disappoint the anxious little man in front of him. 'How much?'

When the deal was done and the typewriter stowed

carefully away behind the driving seat, Amy climbed back into the motor. Mr Benjamin was standing at the door of his shop looking as if the wealth of all the world had suddenly come his way. She wondered what it must feel like to be so poor and she was glad that she had unwittingly been the cause of his happiness. She didn't know many poor people. For a moment she thought of her dressmaker and that daughter who was about her own age. She knew that Mama had ordered some new dresses for Christmas and for her fifteenth birthday on the first day of January, so she was giving some employment and money to them too. A small glow of satisfaction filled her.

Her father's thoughts must have been running along the same lines. 'We paid far too much for it, of course,' he said on the way home, 'but I don't mind. He needed the money more than we do. Do you think you'll bother to learn to type?'

Amy laughed. 'I might, Papa. It depends how easy it is. What do you think Mama will say?'

'She'll be appalled. She'll say that no daughter of hers will ever work in an office.'

'Well of course I shan't.' Then another idea came to Amy. 'It might be useful for me though if I ever get involved with Aunt Felicity's political ideas. I could type pamphlets about the Women's Social and Political Union couldn't I?'

Ralph was relieved to see that she was joking. Patricia wouldn't approve of her doing that either he thought. 'Just amuse yourself with it,' he said. 'I might get you to do some letters for me one day, so you'd better watch out!'

He parked the motor car on the gravel in front of the house. The old gardener had learned to drive now and he could be trusted to put the vehicle away in the old stable. He would carry the new purchase in, too.

Father and daughter entered the front door together

102

in a glow of shared well-being, and by the time Amy had done her homework and changed for dinner, she had forgotten all about the typewriter. It had been placed on a corner table in the breakfast room.

'Fancy the master buying one of them things,' one of the maids commented the following morning. 'I reckon we ought to cover it up. Not very pretty is it!' She took an embroidered chair-back and placed it decoratively over the offending black keys. 'There,' she said to herself. 'That's better. No one'll see 'en now.'

On her way past Benjamins the next afternoon Dorothy looked at the vacant place in the window. The typewriter had been there for a long time, and there was now a clean dust-free space where it had been. She would never have enough money to buy it of course, but while it was there it had been like a sort of beacon of hope. She knew the old couple who kept the shop and she pushed open the door and went in.

'How's Mrs Benjamin?' she forced herself to ask first out of politeness.

'Dr Harding says she's going to get better,' the old man replied. 'And he bought that typewriter what I been trying to sell for so long, so I got some money now to buy her the things she needs.'

'Dr Harding did you say? Dr Harding? What did he want it for?'

'His daughter took it into her head to have it. I don't suppose she'll bother to learn how to use it, but she wanted it and I was glad she did, I can tell you.'

Dorothy turned to the door but remembered her manners sufficiently to say a mumbled goodbye before the tears began to streak down her face. She stumbled out and walked unseeing almost all the way home. She had tried for so long to cope with her feelings about her twin sister. Now there was this to make her efforts even more difficult. Just a word and Amy had the thing that she, Dorothy, wanted more than anything else in the world at that moment. It was monstrously unfair. She pushed open the door of her house and the rage within her threatened to boil over, to erupt in a great wave of tears and anger.

It had long ago been agreed between Rose Miller and Patricia Harding that the fact of their daughters' birthdays being on the same day should, as far as possible, be kept from the girls. Neither believed that they would immediately ask awkward questions if they found out, but it was better all round if they didn't know. The girls never met of course. That had been another of the agreements. Rose had always gone to the Hardings' home to measure Amy for clothes and so far their paths had never crossed, or so their mothers believed.

Every year as the first of January came around, Rose found herself thinking back to that day – almost fifteen years ago now – when she had given birth to her twins. Her feelings were so mixed about it that she scarcely knew whether it had been a bad thing to do or a good thing. She was quite sure at least that for Amy it had been all for the best. The child had so many advantages and so much love, two parents as well, both mother and father. She sighed now as she cut out yet another new frock for her and wondered what she would get Dorothy for her fifteenth birthday. Last year's clothes were still serviceable, still big enough, since she had made them with room and to spare.

She was always on about learning to type and although Rose couldn't see any advantage in it she would have liked to help her somehow. She remembered that Dorothy had longingly pointed out a great ugly black machine to her one day when they were passing Benjamins. It had been in the window for weeks, and for a time Rose had wondered if perhaps there might be some way to buy it, something that she could ask the old man to take in part exchange. She had frequently and lovingly fingered her cameo brooch but couldn't quite make up her mind to the sacrifice, and then the typewriter had disappeared. She was half relieved and half disappointed.

And now the birthday was nearly here. There was Christmas too. It was a pity, she thought, to have them so close. Two presents in a week were far too much of a problem. She'd made Dorothy a serviceable blouse and she'd managed to buy a big packet of nice quarto paper all ready for those stories of hers. The presents weren't much Rose reflected sadly, but they were all she could afford.

There were two letters pushed through the box on the Saturday before Christmas. The postman came early and Dorothy, hearing him, stumbled out of bed. In the winter darkness she peered at them eagerly and just made out the writing. One was addressed to 'Mrs Rose Miller'. She recognized her father's scrawl and the Canadian stamp, but the other had her name upon it, written with a typewriter. Trembling, she carried both of them through into the back kitchen, put her mother's down on the table and found a knife to slit open the other. She pulled out the piece of paper inside and her whole future seemed to be enveloped suddenly in a great golden glow of achievement.

She bounded up the stairs. 'Ma, Ma. They liked my story. The one about the two boys who got lost on the moors. Do you remember it? Do you? They're going to print it and pay me a guinea, a whole guinea.' She jumped on to the bed right on top of her mother and waved the letter under her nose. 'It's happened, Ma. I'm going to be a writer. I'm going to be famous.'

'Get off, you great lump,' Rose said. 'You're proper squashing me. But it's wonderful, lovey. Let me see.'

105

She took the paper from her excited daughter and read it over twice. 'So you've got to sign your name and send it back and then you get your money.'

'Yes, yes!' Dorothy scrambled off the bed and was shaking too much to be able to hold the jug, to pour any water, to wash. She just pulled on her clothes and brushed her hair and then danced round the room holding her letter above her head. 'Oh, Ma. I've never been so happy in all my life. We're going to be rich.'

'Well I hope you're right, but mind it isn't just a flash in a pan. You'll have to work hard now and keep it up.'

'Of course I will, Ma. I'll work every hour I possibly can. I've got loads more ideas.'

'Was there a letter for me? We haven't heard from your father for a bit, and he usually sends us some extra of them dollars before Christmas.'

'Oh yes, Ma. I'm sorry. I was so excited that I forgot.'

'It don't matter. You go on down and get the fire going while I get dressed. And I shall wash, not like some I know. The letter 'ull keep till I gets me clothes on.'

'I can't wait to tell Franky,' Dorothy said as she pranced down the stairs. 'I heard 'en go out ages ago. He do have to start jolly early at that hardware place.' She went into the back kitchen and looked around at all the jobs waiting to be done, but this morning she was not daunted. As she cleaned out yesterday's ashes and relit the fire she dreamt happily of the day when she'd be able to liberate them all from such drudgery. By the time her mother appeared the kettle was boiling merrily.

'You been a long time,' Dorothy said as she handed the other letter to her. 'What do – does – he say, Ma.'

Rose sat for a long time at the table reading and rereading the letter before she spoke. 'He'm asking me to go out there to Canada,' she said at last. 'Says we could all go. There's work for you and Franky and he've got a new job with more money. I shouldn't have to do any sewing.'

Dorothy put the breadboard down on the table and thumped the loaf upon it. 'What did you say? Did I really hear right, Ma? Go to Canada, all of us?' Oh please, God, she thought, not that, not Canada. Not now, when life just seemed to be opening up in all sorts of exciting ways. 'Oh Ma. You're not thinking of going are you?'

Rose saw her distress and laughed comfortingly. 'No, of course I'm not. I don't hold with foreign countries. He went away and left us all when you and Franky was small and if he wants us again he can come home to Bristol.'

'But he went to get work didn't he!' Now that she knew they were safe, Dorothy refused to hear bad things said of her father. She had a vision of him that wouldn't tolerate any faults although in her more honest moments she acknowledged that having a parent in far-off Canada who wrote fairly regularly, often with some welcome dollars, was probably the best possible arrangement. She had seen family strife in the homes of some of her friends. There was poor Winifred for example with a bossy and often violent father who was regularly drunk, and who made life a misery for both her and her mother.

Although she was vague about the more intimate details of the things that went on between men and women, Dorothy also realized that if her father lived here in the normal way, then there would be an endless stream of babies for Ma. Much better to leave things as they were. But she often wondered what her father thought about his other daughter, about Amy. Did he in fact know about her at all? Perhaps the baby had been smuggled out when she was first born? There were so many things that she would like to ask Ma, so many answers she wanted. She sighed, knowing that there was no way in which she was going to find out, not yet anyway, not for a long long time.

Rose cut herself a slice of bread, stuck it on the toasting fork and joined Dorothy beside the fire where she held it out to the hottest part. Neither of them spoke for a time, each busy with her own thoughts. Rose kept looking at her bread and when one side was done she deftly took it off, turned it round and put the white side to the flames. 'Fire's not really red enough for good toast yet,' she remarked. 'I wonder if they have proper fires in Canada?'

'Well, it don't – doesn't – matter does it, Ma, seeing we're not going?'

Rose laughed and got up from the fireplace. She put her blackened piece of bread on her plate, picked up Frank's letter, folded it, slid it determinedly back into its envelope and placed it behind the clock on the wide wooden mantelpiece.

'Well that's that,' she said. 'He've sent us some dollars though and when I've changed them for proper money we'll have a nice bit of meat for Christmas. That's another thing I couldn't abide,' she added as she stuffed the notes into her apron pocket, 'using them funny bits of paper instead of pounds shillings and pence. I likes a nice bit of silver and even better, a gold sovereign in my purse.'

Dorothy was amused by her mother's reasoning. 'But he couldn't send sovereigns, could he, Ma?' she said.

'Suppose not.' Rose replied. 'Come on, then, let's finish our breakfast and then you can make some paper chains to put up. It's Christmas, Dorry. Nearly anyway. And we're going to have a nice time!'

Dorothy knew that they certainly were. She would soon be fifteen, her first story had been accepted for a guinea, a whole pound and a shilling of her very own. And she was going to spend Sunday with Arthur and Vera, well mostly with Arthur. The future looked decidedly promising!

On the first Saturday of March 1912 the postman once more delivered a letter to the little house in St Paul's rather than a returned manuscript. Rose was beside herself with joy when Dorothy opened the envelope and told her what it contained. 'It's from *Our Own Magazine*, Ma,' she said. 'They've taken my children's story and they want more.'

'So you've done it, our Dorry,' she said. 'You've gone and used your pen for the Lord like I wanted you to.'

'I got more money from *Chums*,' Dorothy said with feeling. The little story had caused her a lot of trouble and two rewrites. 'I'm only getting three shillings for it. That's not much for all the time I spent writing it.'

'Three shillings and a mansion in heaven,' Rose said jubilantly. 'That's good value, deary. I wonder if I'll get a mansion too on account of your being my daughter!'

Dorothy glanced at her mother and realized that there was a glimmer of amusement in her eyes.

'I'm sure you will, Ma. If you don't you can share mine, and Mr Buxton might be next door.'

'Now you'm teasing me,' Rose complained.

'Don't tell him mind, about the story I mean.' Dorothy didn't want any more special attention from her boss. Since her outburst about the typing he had ignored her and she had been very relieved.

'Now when would I have a chance to talk about a thing like that?'

'If he comes to preach at Chapel you might. I just know you, Ma. I'm sure you would in fact.'

'Well he ain't coming for a bit as far as I knows, so

you're safe, though why you aren't proud of it I just don't know.'

Dorothy shrugged her shoulders. 'I've sent off two more stories, one to *Girls' Own Paper*, and another to *Boys' Own*, so keep your fingers crossed for me, Ma.'

'I shall do no such thing,' Rose told her. 'You know that I don't believe in all that wicked superstition. I'll ask the Good Lord to help you though. That'll have more effect.'

'Thanks, Ma,' Dorothy said doubtfully. 'Can I go round to see Vera now? I've got a bit of spare time and I want to tell her. I don't mind Vera knowing. I won't be long.'

'All right. Mind the horses,' Rose called after her. 'Look where you'm going.'

Vera hardly listened to Dorothy's news, she had something of far greater import to tell. 'It's Mrs Buxton,' she said. 'Old Bossy Buxton's wife, she'm in prison!' She was standing at the old sink in the tiny scullery, her hands buried in soap suds.

'You must be going mad. She can't be.'

'It's the truth I tell you. She've thrown a stone through a window in the prime minister's house. She was with them suffragettes. She's brave, aint she? It's exciting. I wish I was as brave. They been smashing windows in the Parliament and throwing stones in lots of big shop windows. I don't know how they dare!'

Dorothy thought for a moment of Felicity Buxton and she felt that she certainly knew how she dared. She remembered the ringing tones of her speech at that meeting a year ago. 'How did you find out?'

'Arthur came down for a quick visit last night. He said that old Buxton's in a terrible state.'

'How awful.' Dorothy was filled with horror at the thought of that lovely Mrs Buxton in prison. It just didn't bear thinking about. And there was Clifford. Her heart thumped dangerously. 'How long are they keeping her in for? Did Arthur know?'

'Nobody do, but one thing for sure is that Mr Buxton will be vexed out of his wits. He don't hold with such things, with women having the vote and all.'

Geoffrey Buxton was indeed vexed. He paced up and down in his study and glared at anyone who dared to disturb him. How could his wife have made such a fool of him? How could he ever preach in the Chapel again or even for that matter open his Bible and read those verses about a man keeping his house in order? He had failed dismally. Failed with his wife and even with his daughter. Neither of them obeyed him. He was not master of his own home. Felicity, his own precious Felicity whom he loved more than his life had thrown a stone through the window of Number 10 Downing Street. His blood pressure rose furiously and his pulse seemed to hammer a tattoo in his brain as he thought of it. Her name was in *The Times* for all to see. He would be the laughing stock of Bristol!

He wrenched open the door and strode down the hall and outside into the cold March air. 'Price!' he called. 'Price, where are you?'

Arthur Price appeared quickly from the coach house that was now dedicated to the gleaming Rover – to be greeted by, 'Is the thing ready? I want to go over and see Dr Harding, now at once.'

As he was driven grandly through the streets Geoffrey Buxton's splendid motor car for once gave him no comfort. He could only think of Felicity in prison. He recalled some of the terrible things he had read about in the papers lately. There was the awful force-feeding and the unspeakable things they did to the women who suffered it. Surely she wouldn't be stupid enough to refuse food? The more he thought about it the more he knew that she would. Her bright determined spirit would never capitulate. He clenched his fists angrily. Why had he the misfortune to have fallen under the spell of such a woman? Why was Felicity not more like Patricia Harding, quiet and gentle Patricia who never gave her husband a moment's worry.

It was Patricia who stood to greet him in the drawing room when he was shown into his friend's home.

She smiled graciously. 'Ralph has had to go out to visit a patient. He shouldn't be long,' she said. 'Would you like some tea, or something stronger?'

He ignored her offer. 'Have you heard the news?' His angry words fell strangely on the peaceful room, and he noticed the effect they had. Patricia's lovely aristocratic face paled and she took a step backwards away from the fury in his eyes.

'No, Geoffrey. No I haven't. Tell me.'

'It's Felicity. She was in the suffragette rally in London. She threw a stone and broke a window in Number 10 Downing Street. They've arrested her and put her in prison.' He almost spat the words out and was immediately ashamed of himself for his venom. He had no right to inflict his anger on this lovely woman. She was standing in front of him gripping the back of the tall chair that stood between them. He glanced, embarrassed, at her, and could hardly believe what he saw in her face. It was only a fleeting thing, a glimmer of amusement quickly corrected, but it stabbed him to the heart. This was what he must expect then!

She came to him and put her hand on his arm. 'I'm sorry, Geoffrey,' she said. 'But they won't keep her long I'm sure. And I don't think you need to worry too much. Felicity is well able to look after herself.'

It was not the right thing to say. Geoffrey almost choked with frustration, and for the first time in his life wanted suddenly to hit a woman. He controlled the impulse and moved away from Patricia impatiently. He most definitely did not want a wife who could look after herself. He wanted one who was frail, who would cling to him, obey him in everything, and always be there when he needed her.

'I'll not wait to see Ralph,' he said. 'Tell him when he comes in.' He strode to the door and then regained his manners. 'Thank you for the offer of tea, and I am truly sorry to have disturbed you.' He bowed slightly. 'I'll see myself out.'

He picked up his hat and stick from the hall table and dismissed the nervous little maid who rushed to open the door for him. Price had better be waiting by the motor car, he thought. He needed to get away, needed to think. Patricia's quickly concealed amusement would be typical of everyone he met. He was right when he had decided earlier that this news would make him the laughing stock of the whole city.

Arthur Price was not waiting obediently beside the shining Rover. Geoffrey looked round with considerable irritation, but he did not give way, did not call out furiously in case Patricia should hear and laugh again. Instead he adjusted his hat carefully and strode down the drive and out into the street, his silver-topped stick tapping angrily on the pavement. Perhaps a walk would calm him a little. He walked quickly through the wide tree-lined City Road, his mind pondering the impossible situation that he felt engulfed him. Then suddenly he found himself in poorer side streets. He looked with distaste at the little houses with their front doors right on the pavement and at the net curtains moving curiously as he passed. He realized that he was quite well known around here. The Chapel was nearby. It had been stupid to come here in his present mood. He hurried along looking neither to the right nor the left.

He walked for an hour, up the Ashley Hill to cleaner fresher air that was more like his own Clifton, round the pleasant St Andrew's Park and then down again until he reached the narrow cobbled streets and the noise and smell of St Paul's. He stared at the small shops in Grosvenor Road and watched the women with their weary eyes and work-roughened hands, and for one fleeting unwelcome moment he remembered Felicity's high ideals and wondered if she were fighting for something worthwhile. He pushed the thought away swiftly and turned up one of the side streets that would take him back to Ralph Harding's house, back to his own beautiful car and his privileged world.

He had not bargained on meeting someone he knew. She stood outside her house, her hand on the little brightly painted iron gate of her minuscule garden.

For a moment he couldn't place her. Then he remembered. Of course, Mrs Miller! She was a member of the Chapel too. He recalled her face shining up at him from amongst the congregation. He recalled, with embarrassment, how he had basked in her adoration, and a slight flush suffused his features as he remembered his guilty thoughts.

'Mr Buxton,' she said, smiling shyly at him. 'A nice surprise to see you down here, Sir. And I want to thank you for giving my Dorothy a job. She likes it.'

He nodded. 'A bright girl I hear. I'm thinking of putting her in the office. We need someone to help with the insurance stamps and that sort of thing. She has no idea of course, so please don't mention it to her.' The words came to him almost unbidden.

'She'll like that, Sir. She'm always reading and trying to better herself is my Dorothy.' She paused for a moment and then continued, looking up at him with a mixture of uncertainty and concern. 'I don't suppose you'd like to come in and have a cup of tea, would you, Sir? You look proper tired and the kettle's on the fire all ready. We've talked at the Chapel now and then,' she added as though an excuse was needed for her forward behaviour.

Geoffrey was taken aback at her words and even more surprised at his own reaction. He wanted to see the inside of her small house, wanted to sit down and take a cup of tea from this nice uncomplicated woman, and most of all he suddenly needed comfort.

'Thank you, Mrs . . . Mrs Miller isn't it? Yes I do believe that I am tired and a cup of tea would be very welcome.'

She led the way inside and he noticed the cleanliness of everything, the gleaming brass step, the spotless white-painted treads each side of the narrow thread-bare stair-carpet, and the cracked but shining linoleum beneath his feet. The smell of carbolic soap hung in the air.

'The parlour is cold and damp. We only use it on special days. Would you mind coming in the back kitchen where the fire is?' she asked.

'The back kitchen would be very nice,' he replied, wondering just what such a room comprised.

She took his hat and cane and put them carefully on the otherwise empty hall-stand and opened the door at the end of the passage. As he passed into the tiny room he had an immediate impression of cosy warmth. There was a table in the bay window covered with a green baize cloth and adorned with a huge aspidistra, and three sturdy oak chairs were pushed up to it. A small glass-fronted cupboard stood in the corner and a trea-dle sewing-machine in the other. There were two red plush armchairs before the fire, one large and full of cushions, the other smaller. Geoffrey Buxton watched his hostess nervously brush the seat of the bigger one with her hand and plump up the cushions.

'You'll be comfortable here, Mr Buxton,' she said. 'It won't take a minute for me to wet the tea.'

He settled himself into the chair and felt some of his tension falling away. She had to lean over close to him to take the big black kettle from the fire and he noticed the clean washed smell of her, not the scent of expensive perfume of which he was always aware when in the company of Felicity or Patricia, but a simple wholesomeness that he liked.

She went to the cupboard and took two china cups and saucers from it and dusted them with a clean cloth. They were obviously not for every-day use. She went out of another door which he presumed led into the scullery, and returned with a jug of milk, some of which she poured into each cup. He watched every movement. When she handed him his tea he stood up and she blushed. She was probably unused to such gallantries he thought, almost tenderly. They looked at each other awkwardly. She seemed to be unwilling to sit down.

'Won't you sit,' he said and she did so but without the embarrassment he expected.

Rose studied his features, scrutinizing the troubled look on his handsome face. She felt a sense of pity, an emotion she was sure few people experienced when looking at Geoffrey Buxton. Here was a man who needed a bit of comforting and cosseting and she suddenly realized that those were things that she had to give. Like most men, Frank had needed it, and when he went to Canada there were the children. But they were growing up and didn't need her so much now. She had no one to fuss over.

'I'm so sorry about Mrs Buxton,' she said quietly without, he noticed, any trace of amusement. The words brought him back to the unwelcome reality that he had momentarily almost forgotten. He drank the scalding tea quickly and his previous rage returned, and with it a tremendous grief that threatened to overwhelm him.

'I am more angry than sorry,' he exploded. 'Angry that she could do such a thing.' He stared at Rose and suddenly he saw in her an attractive woman whom he could master and use, who could answer his needs as Felicity never could. She was staring at him with understanding and compassion, but there was more. In her face he saw a gentle kindness. It was the one thing he wanted just now. His pulse quickened and he put the cup down on the grate inside the brass fender, his eyes riveted on the swell of her bosom inside the constraining dress.

He jumped to his feet, took her cup from her and put it down beside his own. Then he took her hands in both of his and pulled her up beside him and in a moment she was in his arms and he was kissing her full on the mouth. He felt the shape of her against his body and he was filled with desire and desperate need. All his high standards and ideals vanished as though they had never been and he pulled her through the door and up the narrow stairs.

Rose felt that she was in a dream, that all this was happening to someone else and she was helpless to resist. It was a long time since she had had any man, and she wanted this one, not only to comfort and succour, but for herself. Perhaps she had always had a secret dream of having him. When she sat listening to him in Chapel, was she wanting him then? Was this the fulfilment of all her deepest hidden desires? She felt his body strong and hard close to her and when they reached the top of the stairs she guided him into her room, towards the bed with its clean lavender-scented sheets.

Geoffrey realized, when they reached the landing that she was leading the way. He saw nothing of the room and as he dropped his clothes on the cold lino he watched her, saw that she was wholesome and attractive, noticed again the roundness of her, and the infinite gentleness.

She held out her dimpled arms to him and he went to her and felt the welcoming warmth of the big feather bed beneath him and smelt the lavender. Then her soft body was close, moulded perfectly to his, and as he took her, swiftly and without care, all his anger and frustration, his unacknowledged fear of women seemed to go into the act. His sense of power and conquest was complete and he knew a moment of total triumph. Then when it was all over, her hands were still upon him and he could feel that she was, even then, ready to give comfort and a kind of selfless love. He raised himself on one elbow and looked down at her in amazement, and she smiled at him without any shame. He quickly slid from the bed and put on his clothes and he was conscious of her eyes watching every movement he made.

'Thank you, my dear,' he said. 'Thank you!'

Geoffrey failed to experience any guilt as he walked swiftly back to the Hardings' house. As he thought about what he had done he was amazed at his composure and his feeling of complete satisfaction. He had betrayed his wife and his God and he was happy! Perhaps the questioning and the self-disgust would come later but for the moment he was immersed in the total glory of those moments with Rose Miller. Power was the all-important emotion for a man he reflected. Only power over others, particularly women, could give him the self-confidence that was essential for his well-being.

His motor car was standing where he had left it on the gravel drive and there was no sign of Ralph or of Patricia, for which he was very grateful. Arthur Price was standing beside the vehicle polishing the wide blue mudguards.

'Ready, Price?' he called. 'Get the thing going. I want to get away.'

Arthur straightened himself and saluted. 'Right, Sir,' he said. He gave a final polish to the already shining brass and opened the rear door for Geoffrey. Then he swung the starting handle until the engine turned over with a satisfying purr. He leapt into the driving seat and they were off. Geoffrey noticed a surprised Patricia waving at him from her front door. He waved back cheerfully. He had wanted to talk to Ralph who had always been a good friend, but he had found another source of comfort now, altogether more satisfactory, and he smiled to himself as the car carried him effortlessly through the streets to his home. Let Felicity do her worst. He was not dependent on her any more. He still loved her very much, but not with the complete devotion that had dominated him for so many years. For the first time since their marriage he felt free.

It was not until his daughter mentioned something about Amy later that evening that the full import of his encounter swept over him. Suppose there were to be unwelcome consequences from what he had done today? He felt his whole body drain of strength while his mind grappled with the horrific possibilities, his earlier triumph swiftly dissipated. Rose Miller was not just any anonymous woman whom he could pay well and forget. She was Amy Harding's natural mother. That knowledge had hung heavily about him ever since Ralph had entrusted him with the secret of Amy's birth fifteen years ago, but he had never thought to be personally involved. He went to bed that night pondering all the implications of the situation he had brought about and his shame was like a knife stabbing and twisting in his gut. He wondered if it was only God and Felicity whom he had failed!

When Geoffrey left her Rose didn't move for a time. She just lay in the rumpled bed cradling her body in her arms and staring at the afternoon light between the half-pulled curtains. He had slipped from between the warm flannel sheets, put his clothes on with care, not looking at her, and then he had moved quietly to the door and turned and smiled. She lay and pondered that smile. There was triumph in it, she was sure of that. But there was more, a kind of amazement too. She could hear him going down the stairs, fumbling with the front door, letting himself out. But she did not throw the bedclothes back until long after she heard the click of the front gate. Then she gathered up her scattered garments, heaped them on the chair, and poured water into the big china bowl. It felt cold and pure and she was glad that habit always forced her to keep the jug filled and covered with a clean towel. It was a small rule of housekeeping for which she had never before been so grateful. She soaped herself vigorously and shivered as she washed all trace of him from her body.

When it was done to her satisfaction and she was dressed again, the bed made, and all evidence of the last hour removed, she smiled a little grimly to herself. There had been no pleasure in it for her except that of giving. He had taken her quickly and without any gentleness. She stared at herself in the small mirror as she put the final hairpins into the bun at the nape of her neck and wondered why she had been so willing. It was getting on for ten years since Frank went back to Canada that last time and there had been no one else until today. She had not wanted anyone, not wanted any more babies.

The thought chilled her suddenly and she pulled her shawl closely round her shoulders and went downstairs. She poked up the fire, washed the two cups, put them carefully away in the cabinet and made herself another cup of tea. Then she went to the sewing machine, took the half-made frock that was lying there and began to stitch the seam at the side of the bodice. Each action she made was cool and calm but her mind was in a state of shock. The whole of the last hour seemed to belong to a dream world and she had no understanding of why she had allowed it to happen, encouraged it even.

She sat there for an hour, her hands busy with the garment while her thoughts searched for some explanation, something she could grasp that would make sense and reduce her steadily increasing pangs of guilt and confusion. The thought of Felicity Buxton in prison for her ideals, ideals they both shared, troubled her greatly and made Rose feel a deep unworthiness. She was still working at the frock when Dorothy came home.

'Hello, Ma. Shall I make a cup of tea?'

Rose looked up at her daughter and smiled. This girl was a great joy to her, a strength and a prop now that she was no longer a child. It wasn't so necessary to be the strong one continuously. Dorothy was beginning to share the burdens.

'That would be nice, Dorry. I just want to finish this hem and then I'll pack it away and we'll see about supper. I've got a bit of fat pork and some potatoes.' She bent over the material beneath her hands and for a few uncomfortable seconds prayed fervently once more that she was not about to bring any additional burdens into their lives, or create another barrier between herself and the daughter she loved so much. There was still the secret of Amy that would have to be told one day. She constantly dreaded the thought of doing so. That alone was enough. Geoffrey Buxton's baby would be an added and unthinkable disaster!

She came to the end of the hem, pulled the thread through and cut it carefully so that she would not have to rethread the next day. Then she folded the frock, a lovely one in a soft silk with a lower neckline than of late. She wrapped it in a piece of muslin and placed it in her large work box. Mrs Harding had ordered three new dresses for Amy and there was a new coat too on

121

which Rose had laboured lovingly for many long hours. They were almost ready to be delivered. She sighed a little, remembering Dorothy's envious glance when she'd seen the coat on its hanger in their bedroom.

She swung the heavy sewing machine over and fastened it beneath its wooden surface with a loud and satisfying click. The welcome sound always heralded the end of her day's labours and she stood up thankfully and stretched, rubbing her eyes which felt sore and tired.

Dorothy looked at her. 'I'll make the supper, Ma,' she said. 'You just sit there and put your feet up.'

'Thanks, Dorry. I think I will. I do feel a bit tired. Mind you does plenty of potatoes. Franky'll be in soon and he'm always hungry lately since he started working for Jennings full time.'

'You all right?' Dorothy asked as she handed her a steaming cup of tea. 'You look worried. Anything happened today then?'

Rose took the cup and settled herself luxuriously in the chair and she smiled up at her daughter. 'Nothing, deary,' she lied. 'Nothing at all.'

CHAPTER SIX

Much to Geoffrey Buxton's annoyance the subject of his wife's imprisonment was on everyone's lips. And from most people there was great praise and admiration for her daring escapade. He was well aware that the girls in his factory were all buzzing with the latest news and he tried to take no notice, knowing that to forbid such talk would merely increase their amusement at his expense, and their sympathy for Felicity.

Whenever there was any opportunity the conversation between Dorothy and her friends turned to their favourite subject.

'Them suffragettes hid hammers in their muffs, would you believe,' Winifred said one day in their dinner hour. 'That was how they smashed the windows in all them posh shops in London. I just read about it. Ever so brave, weren't they?'

She had recently drifted back into an easy friendship with Dorothy partly because of their shared fascination with women's rights, and, together with Vera, the two girls usually spent their small amount of free time together.

'Better not let the boss hear you say that,' Vera said anxiously. 'He'm that mad about what Mrs Buxton did that he can't bear anything said in praise of her.'

'Well she'm jolly brave and he ought to be proud to be married to her,' Winifred stated firmly.

'Ever such a lot are in prison as well as Mrs Buxton. I wish I'd been there.' Dorothy bit into one of her substantial cheese sandwiches. 'I don't know how they can refuse to eat. Going on hunger strike it's called. I'd never be able to do that.'

Vera shuddered at the thought. 'Nor me. Food be one of the pleasures I looks forward to most.' She threw a few crumbs to the pigeons who were strutting hopefully around the old iron seat.

In this park at the Haymarket there was no grass, just dirty cobbles stained with the droppings of the birds, and littered with dead leaves from the trees in the churchyard nearby. There were cigarette ends, too, and other debris left by the old men who sat there for hours on end each day.

Dorothy looked around her with distaste. 'I reckon that if women had the vote and got some say about things, places like this would be cleaned up a bit.'

'I wonder why men have always been in charge of everything?' Winifred said thoughtfully.

'Just because we got to have the babies,' said the worldly-wise Vera. 'You get married and then you ain't got no more strength to do anything else 'cept 'ave kids, and that's the men's fault.'

'Mrs Buxton only had two,' Dorothy commented.

'There are ways if you'm rich,' Vera added darkly. 'Not for the likes of us, but for the nobs . . . well.'

The other two girls looked at her questioningly. 'Go on then, tell us.' There was a trace of desperation in Winifred's voice.

'No, I won't. My Ma says it's wrong. I don't reckon 'tis, but I'm not saying, and anyway we ought to get back.' She stood up and brushed the crumbs from her coat for the excited pigeons. 'Come on, else we'll be late, and that old Jumpy Jenkins'll have words to say.'

'She's been worse since she was promoted to top lady supervisor.' Dorothy's last words were mocking. 'Lady! Her a lady. Well if she's one then I'm glad I'm not.'

'Jumpy Jenkins be a good nickname for her,' Vera said. 'You was clever to think of it, Dorry. She'm always jumping out of nowhere when you don't think she'm around.'

'She's not in favour of suffragettes or women's rights. She thinks men are wonderful.'

'That's because she ain't got one,' Winifred added sarcastically. 'Just give her my pa and she'd soon change her tune.'

To Dorothy's surprise her mother failed to show any enthusiasm for Felicity Buxton's exploits. She put her lips firmly together when the matter was raised and refused to comment.

The following Sunday as they were getting ready for Chapel, Dorothy was thinking about it again. 'But Ma,' she said, 'aren't you a bit thrilled? She actually threw a stone into the prime minister's house. It broke a window. I wish I could have seen her. I wish I could have done it.'

'No, you don't, our Dorry. I've told you before, them antics aren't for the likes of us. That husband of hers'll have her out in two shakes, you just see!'

Dorothy was taken aback by the sudden bitterness in her mother's voice. 'What ever is the matter?' she asked. 'I thought you'd be pleased about her being brave enough to do that. It gets us a bit nearer having the vote don't it – doesn't it?'

'That's as may be. I know I went to the meeting and she was very likeable and spoke up well, but I've decided to have nothing more to do with it. Finding enough money to feed and clothe the three of us is all I can think of.' Rose carefully put her wide-brimmed hat over the blonde waves that would not lie flat however much she pulled them tightly into the bun at the nape of her neck. 'Come on now, Dorry. We'll be late for Chapel else.'

Dorothy sighed. Her mother had behaved very oddly during the last few days and she wondered what could have happened to change her so much. She was usually quite cheerful and bubbly. Nothing bothered her for long. But she obediently put on her coat and waited on the pavement while Rose locked the door carefully behind her. Then they walked down the road together.

'Is it Franky, Ma. You worrying about Franky?'

'No,' Rose said sharply. 'If he don't want to come with us no more that's up to him. He'm fourteen now and I shan't force him. I'm not worrying about anything so stop your bothering.'

Dorothy knew better than to probe further. Her thoughts turned to Arthur Price.

'Arthur drove Mr Buxton to London,' she said. 'Vera told me. Just think, Ma, all that way in a motor car. I wonder why he didn't go on the train.'

'What he likes or doesn't like isn't for you or me to know about,' Rose said sharply. 'Now, can you talk about something else a bit different from that family please? I be tired of hearing about them.'

Her mother's words worried Dorothy even more and she could think of nothing further to say. She thought about Arthur again. The last time they had met he had been thrilled with his job as chauffeur to the Buxtons. All he wanted to talk about was engines and motor bikes and even aeroplanes. He had bored her. Well, the long ride to London would have pleased him. She presumed he was still there.

'What's it like in London, Ma?' she asked. 'I'd love to go there one day.'

'What's the good of asking me, my girl. I've never been and never likely to go neither.'

Dorothy sighed as they reached the small and rather dismal entrance of the Chapel. Amy would go to London one day, she was sure of that. The usual envy overcame her as it did more and more lately, and she shuffled into her seat full of resentment. Well at least it wasn't Mr Buxton preaching tonight she thought thankfully. She couldn't do to listen to him for the next hour, and by the sound of her mother's remarks she wouldn't welcome the sight of him up on the platform either. She idly leafed through the hymn book in her hand and hoped that some of their favourites would be chosen tonight. Singing always cheered her mother and she certainly needed something to lift her out of her doleful mood.

With two stories now in print Dorothy began to feel more confident and more determined than ever to learn to type. She knew that handwritten manuscripts wouldn't always do if she really wanted to succeed in her chosen career.

'You'll just have to get round old woman Jenkins,' Vera told her sternly when they were walking home together one day. 'I don't know why you don't want to shout out from the roof top that you'm a successful author. I know I should.'

'Two stories don't make a successful author,' Dorothy said. 'Now if I'd written a whole book or lots of stories I might think about letting on. Until then it's a secret, so just you remember that Vera Price.'

'Can I tell our Arthur? He'd be so thrilled about it. He'm a reader too, well a bit of a reader, not as such as you though.

'Yes. I don't mind Arthur knowing now. It was because of him I got started really. I told you didn't I? It was the old magazines that his birthday present to me was wrapped up in that gave me the idea.' Dorothy paused for a moment thinking of the long months that she had laboured, the countless pencils she had worn down and the sheets and sheets of paper that had filled the dustbin. 'I been working for more'n a year now and I only got two published stories to

127

show for it so far, so I've a long way to go yet.'

'Well I think you'm really clever, and you only fifteen and all. You can't expect to write like that old Dickens or them Brontës you'm always telling me about. They was old.'

Dorothy laughed. 'Not so old as all that,' she said. 'Anyway, come on, let's run. I'm cold and if we were properly grown up we couldn't could we? Run I mean.'

The two girls abandoned all attempts at looking ladylike and sprinted along the street, each trying to outdo the other until they arrived restless and laughing at Dorothy's home.

'Coming in?' she enquired. 'I expect Ma has done some baking.'

'Not now,' Vera said. 'I got to get along and help with the little ones.' She stood for a moment and looked enviously at the tiny garden and the brass frontdoor step that gleamed brightly with the evidence of its daily vigorous treatment with Brasso and much rubbing. 'You really got to pluck up your courage, Dorry,' she said. 'I want to see you get on. You just got to ask to use that typewriter. I want to tell all my pals that I knows a real live author!'

Dorothy laughed, but she was moved by her friend's confidence in her. 'I'll think about it,' she promised. 'See you tomorrow.'

'Will you do it if you get two more stories bought then,' Vera persisted. 'That'll prove that you're really clever and impress all of em.'

'All right. When I've sold four altogether I'll pluck up my courage and ask, but I think it had better be Mr Buxton. Best to go right to the top!' Dorothy felt it was a promise without much hope. She had been writing so much for so long that she had given up thoughts of quick success.

But her expectations received a pleasant and very unexpected lift much sooner than she thought. The following day a letter from *Chums* confirmed another story sold, and an envelope addressed to 'Mr D. Miller' enclosed a money order for a guinea and a half, and a request for more similar stories.

'Who's Mr D. Miller then?' asked Rose suspiciously.

'Well I couldn't let on I'm a girl when I was sending in a story about lads could I?' Dorothy held the letter in her hand and was surprised to feel tears threatening behind her eyes as she stared at it. At last perhaps she could believe that her first successes were not merely luck. Now she might be taken seriously by everyone.

'That's dishonest,' Rose persisted. 'Calling yourself by a lad's name.'

'But I didn't, Ma. I merely put my initials, just "D. Miller". If they like to think I'm a chap, well that's their lookout!'

'But you might be getting more money as a man than you would as a woman.'

Dorothy stared at her mother in disbelief. 'I thought you were keen on women's rights,' she said. 'I thought you believed in equal pay. It took me just as long to write those stories as it would if our Franky had written them, and do you really think that he should have got more than me?'

'Franky?' said Rose, completely missing the point. 'He can hardly write more'n a few words. He couldn't write no stories.'

'I know he couldn't, Ma. I'm just saying that . . .' She looked at her mother's disgruntled expression and gave up trying to make her point. 'Never mind. I shall just go on being "D. Miller" for *Chums* and for *Boys' Own Paper*. Plenty of other women have done it. Charlotte Brontë did. She called herself Curer Bell I think, when she published her book.

'You'm getting too clever for me altogether,' Rose declared. 'I just don't know where you got them brains from. I wish our Franky had 'em, him being a boy.'

'Oh, Ma, I give up. I just give up! It doesn't matter whether you're a lad or a girl, both need brains, and a girl more probably, because we have to struggle more. Mrs Buxton is in prison for these things, Ma. *In prison*.' Dorothy stressed the last words as she threw on her coat and dashed out of the door. The excitement of her two letters had made her late for work or would if she didn't rush. And that would mean twopence off her wages. She would have to run nearly all the way now.

As the door slammed, Rose stood for a moment before she gathered up the letters and put them safely behind the clock. Dorothy's words brought further distress to her. Any mention of the woman whom she had wronged made her heart sink and a heavy leaden feeling would fill her body and her mind. Wearily she turned to the table and cleared the breakfast things away. She had more to worry about now than votes for women!

Miss Jenkins was furious. 'My typewriter!' She glanced at her precious machine. 'What terrible cheek. You really mean to say that that girl,' she paused and repeated the last two words as though she were speaking of some poisonous reptile, '*That girl* wants to learn to type and on my machine!'

Geoffrey looked at her and vowed that never again would he appoint a woman to any position of authority. 'She has asked if she may stay for half an hour each evening and use the typewriter. Of course I told her that it was probably not possible, but after giving the matter some thought I wondered if you had any . . . any ideas.'

Geoffrey desperately hoped that Miss Jenkins would never have the remotest clue about the reasons that lay behind his staggering benevolence. As he looked at her he thought of the unfortunate incident with

Rose Miller. Suddenly, unbidden, there came the tiniest glimmer of amusement in his mind, carefully hidden, as he contemplated for a second, the shock such a revelation would give the woman now confronting him.

'Ideas? Ideas for what may I ask? Perhaps you wish me to teach her to type?' Miss Jenkins had never looked so outraged and shocked in all her time at Buxtons.

Geoffrey realized that his behaviour had indeed been completely out of character, ridiculous to a degree. He had put himself in an unbelievably absurd situation with a woman for the third time that week. First there had been his fall from grace with Rose, then his feeling of obligation to listen to her daughter's preposterous ideas, and now finally, he was reduced to asking favours of Miss Jenkins. He was inclined to blame Felicity for it all. Had she been here to look after his needs instead of allowing herself to . . . he could not bear to think about the behaviour of his wife!

The girl, Dorothy had ideas above her station, and above her sex as well, but for once he was at a loss what to do about it. When she had timidly approached him two days ago he had asked himself whether she could possibly know about what had passed between him and her mother and whether that had given her the courage, but her attitude had partly assured him that she could not.

She was extremely apologetic and very frightened, yet he sensed a trace of pride in her voice when she made her request. Her accomplishment in becoming a budding author was obviously the cause of this and he had to admit her success had surprised him considerably. He had no idea that anyone so young and with so little education could even string intelligent sentences together let alone write something that was worth publishing. How many stories did she say? Four he thought, and one of them a religious one. For that alone he knew that he ought to help her.

Yet he was, in spite of this curious accomplishment, staggered at her audacity – especially as she had mentioned the crazy idea of learning to type once before and he had carefully ignored her for a long time after that.

However, he confessed to himself, had it not been for his unfortunate lapse with her mother he most decidedly would have refused to have anything more to do with the matter. Factory girls always remained factory girls until they married and became mothers. It was the natural order of things. Their sex and their background saw to that. For them there was never any promotion. Of course there was another element to this whole unfortunate affair, he reflected. She was twin sister to the Hardings' Amy. He was quite fond of Amy Harding, saw her frequently in fact since she was his daughter's best friend. A nice sensible girl too with no ambitions. But that shouldn't really make any difference to his treatment of Dorothy Miller, and until now it had not. He had long ago decided that he had to bury away out of sight and thought the disturbing confidence that his friend, Ralph Harding, had imparted to him more than fifteen years ago. Yet the two girls were so alike. He found it disconcerting in the extreme.

Miss Jenkins was standing looking at him as if he had completely taken leave of his senses and he was inclined to agree with her assessment. 'You have no ideas of any way we might help this girl then?' he asked. Once he'd taken up this line of enquiry it seemed difficult to relinquish it.

'No. I certainly have not. If she wishes to learn to type then she must save up and buy herself a machine. I refuse to let her touch mine, unless you command me to do so.'

'I would not, of course, dream of doing anything of

the kind, Miss Jenkins,' Geoffrey said through clenched teeth. It angered him to think that here was another woman whom, like Felicity, he could not rule. This one was in his employ too. The trouble was, she'd been in it far too long. He longed to give her the sack, hand her her cards and bid her leave. If there was ever any way of doing so then he would do it. For now he turned on his heel and strode out.

When Mr Buxton first called her in and told her that he could not help her, Dorothy was extremely downcast, and even further depressed when she was moved away from the production line and into the packing section. The job was even more tedious than doing those awful endless chocolate whirls on each sickly cream and there was no Vera or Winifred next to her, ready with a bit of friendly chat and a joke now and then. But she couldn't remain miserable for long. Her successes with her writing brought her a satisfying inner glow that helped her through the long frustrating days.

One afternoon a week later she was full of an idea for a further story and she bounced into the house after work ready to tell the plot to her mother, and to receive the usual uncritical praise and the comforting ever-ready cup of tea.

She put her coat on the hall-stand and pushed open the door to the back kitchen. It was the coldness of the room that first struck her as odd. Then she saw her mother sitting at the table with no ready smile, no greeting. Suddenly all her bright positive feelings collapsed. She stood for a moment and stared unbelieving. 'What's the matter?' she asked. 'Oh, Ma, whatever is the matter? You've been crying.' She was completely unprepared for the pain in her mother's face and the blank look in her eyes and she ran over to her and threw her arms round her shivering body. 'Whatever is it?'

For a few moments there was a silence broken only by sobs. They were the most frightening sounds Dorothy had ever heard.

At last her mother spoke and her voice was barely audible.

'There's going to be a baby, Dorry. God please help me, I'm going to have a baby!'

To Dorothy the words had a hollow sound as if they came from a long way away and as their import gradually registered in her mind she felt herself swaying on her feet, the room seeming to spin and rotate alarmingly until it ceased and became still again. She looked at the dying embers of the fire and for a few seconds she could think of nothing except how cold she was, and how she trembled, her whole body out of control. She felt helpless, unable to think of anything to say, just totally numb all over.

Her mother got up from the table, crossed to the fireside and slumped into the red plush armchair and refused to look up. 'Get some wood, Dorry,' she whispered at last. 'Stir up the fire and put the kettle to boil.'

Glad of something to do Dorothy rushed out, took two precious bundles of sticks and impatiently pulled the string from them. She stacked them carefully on the ashes, placed small pieces of coal over the top and watched as the tiny glowing particles of warmth beneath gradually caught the fresh wood and the flames began to leap up cheerfully between the black coal lumps. She held her hands out to the welcome brightness and then took her mother's cold lifeless fingers and rubbed them gently, first one hand and then the other.

'Are you sure, Ma?' was all she found to say.

'Yes, Dorry I'm sure. And I can't talk about it. Not yet. Don't ask me any questions.'

Dorothy made a pot of tea when the kettle eventually boiled, then she put vegetables into a pot, washed up all the dishes that had gathered during the day and laid the table for the three of them for supper. There was no material or needles and thread anywhere and the sewing machine had obviously not been used all day. Rose did not stir while Dorothy was working. She did not speak either and Franky was due home in another hour. If she and her mother were to talk it would have to be before he came in.

'Will you talk to me now, Ma?' Dorothy said. Her tasks done she went and knelt on the floor beside her mother again. 'You'll feel better if you can.'

'You're too young to understand, Dorry,' she said at last. 'But I done wrong and I'm being punished. That's all. I'm just sad that the punishment is going to be on you as well, and Franky a bit I suppose.'

Dorothy closed her eyes for a second as she thought of all her friends at Buxtons, of the laughs and callously crude jokes that she had frequently heard made at the expense of any woman who got herself wrong like this. And then there was the Chapel, oh dear, dear God! It was more prayer than blasphemy that went through her mind. What would they say there?

Then, swiftly following these thoughts, she experienced a sudden defiance. She loved her mother and whatever she had done she would stand by her, defend her to the end. But how could it have happened? Dorothy's face was already a vivid red with her closeness to the now cheerful fire but she felt the blood rush to her features, hot with intense embarrassment. She knew that shameful things went on in bedrooms, things that women had to put up with for the sake of men. Had Ma been forced? There was a word for it, a word breathed now and then with horror and shame, rape. Had Ma been raped? She must have been for she would never have willingly agreed to anything so awful. Dorothy began to feel anger rise inside her like a

135

mighty rushing wind, and with it a great protective surge of love for her mother.

'Oh, Ma,' she murmured. 'Don't think about us. I'll help you all I can, I promise. And it don't matter what folks think. I've got my writing now, and no one can take that away from us. Everything will be all right, you'll see.'

'You're not ashamed of me then, Dorry?'

'No, Ma. Of course I'm not. In fact it'll be nice to have a . . . a baby in the house.' Dorothy hardly knew how she spoke the words but she felt she had to say them. It was the only way she knew to comfort her mother.

She knelt there for a long time holding her mother's hands, beseeching her to look up, trying to give her some of her own strength and determination, and although she knew quite well that somewhere there was a man who was responsible for all this trouble, yet to her he was without form, a faceless creature whom she refused to acknowledge. The baby would be theirs, theirs alone, and no man would have any part in her thoughts or her considerations.

Geoffrey returned from London a couple of days later, exhausted and furious at his inability to do anything to procure his wife's release.

'She refuses to eat and refuses to agree to any terms that might cause them to let her out,' he fumed to Ralph who had called to offer any comfort he could. 'The governor won't allow them to go without food for too long, a few days I think and so she'll be force-fed from tomorrow.'

'She's a very brave woman.'

Geoffrey sensed the admiration in his friend's voice and it further inflamed his anger.

'Brave! Totally stupid, self-willed and thoughtless are more suitable words to describe her behaviour I think!' He flopped into a chair beside the fire and took the brandy Ralph held out to him. Brandy was one of the evils of the flesh, but an extremely necessary evil at times like this he thought. He sighed, suddenly deflated, and as the rich burning fluid coursed through his body he carefully placed the glass on the small table at his side and covered his face with his hands.

There was a long uncomfortable silence in the room and he was ashamed of the feelings that swept over him. His love for Felicity was as powerful as ever and the thought of her being manhandled by prison warders was too repulsive for him to contemplate. Yet in her absence he had experienced a more compliant and gentle satisfaction of his baser needs, and thoughts of that hour in Rose Miller's house returned to haunt him yet again. Against his will he often remembered the feel of her hands on his skin and the clean smell of her, even now when he should be concerned only with Felicity, his own annoying Felicity. He tried to pull himself together, took another sip of brandy and looked at Ralph.

'Yes. I suppose I am proud of her in a strange way,' he admitted. 'Angry but proud, too. And I want her back, Ralph. God how I want her back.' Suddenly it was true. His need of her was desperate if he were to fend off the temptations that constantly assailed him since his foray into adultery. The word circled round in his mind, the word he had avoided. It sounded too crude to describe the perfection of that hour. But he forced himself to admit the truth of it. In the moment of Felicity's need he knew that he had not only failed her, but also had committed one of the sins that he had always most despised.

Suddenly the sound of a knock on the door intruded into the turmoil of his thoughts. His daughter entered quickly and Geoffrey saw at once the reddened eyes and the pain in her face.

The two men stood. Laura was an attractive girl now, almost a young woman, demanding the courtesies due to her sex. She crossed the room and kissed her father gently on the cheek, and shook hands with Ralph before speaking.

'Sorry to disturb you, Papa,' she said. 'But I've been reading a terrible description of force-feeding, and Mama is refusing to eat, isn't she? Can't you do anything, Papa? Surely there is something we can do to save her from that?'

Geoffrey almost recoiled from the grief in Laura's face. 'I've read the newspaper report too,' he said quietly, 'And I too am appalled, but there is nothing more I can do. If that is your mother's choice then we cannot interfere however much it hurts us to stand by and know it's happening. I have spent five days in London. I have pleaded with her, all to no avail. We must just be ready to receive her back to us when the time comes and to give her all the love and care we can.'

'You could go to London again couldn't you, Papa? Keep worrying the authorities?'

'I shall of course, Laura, but I have no great hopes of achieving very much.' He turned away from her, away from them both and stared blankly through the window. In his imagination it was his wife's face he could see, rather than the graceful trees and the daffodils that were just showing in all their golden beauty around the edges of the well-kept lawns. He could almost feel the accusing eyes of his daughter boring into his back as though she somehow blamed him for Felicity's plight. Then the image changed and it was Rose he could see and she too was accusing him.

Felicity sat on the bare wooden bench and felt sick with apprehension. Not eating had been hard at first. The food had been left with regular precision and recently it had been more carefully prepared. The prison governor was unhappy about force-feeding apparently, and did everything in his power to tempt his charges to eat. But she had refused all the dainty offerings that were brought to her, accepting only water. It had been difficult but she had won, and now the sound of the feeding trolley being pushed along the stone floor outside came ominously nearer. Then suddenly the door of her cell was open and she was surrounded by people, their white coats and hard faces making a blurred picture before her frightened eyes. There were women there, wardresses, and she wanted to scream at them that she was doing this for them. Why were they fighting against themselves? Men she could contend with, but women. . . .

She was grabbed roughly and thrust upon the wheeled chair that they had pushed into the centre of the cell. She felt pillows beneath her head and her face was forced violently back and a towel wrapped round her neck. One of the white-coated men grabbed her nose in a tight grip and she opened her mouth to breathe, to scream. The wardresses were holding her arms and legs and as her mouth was prised fully open by the man in front of her, she felt a long tube being pushed into her throat and down into the depths of her body. It felt like rape. She couldn't breathe, she was about to choke to death and the panic that overcame her was the most terrifying she had ever experienced in her life. Her lungs were bursting and her brain wanted to scream at them to go away, to stop, but she was totally helpless and their words came to her from a long distance.

'If you just stopped struggling it wouldn't hurt!'

Dear God, how could she stop struggling? She felt warm liquid seeping down the tube. She knew she was going to die any minute. She couldn't breathe and their faces above her swam in a loathsome blackness. Then they were pulling the tube out and the pain was worse than anything that went before. It was searing her insides and she could do nothing. Her arms were still held in that vice-like grip, her head forced back until her neck felt as if it were about to break. She retched and yet could not retch, and then the tube was out and her throat and mouth were burning centres of pain. She heaved into the towel that was held now in front of her and gradually her tormentors lessened their grip, pulled her up and roughly wiped her face. Her every movement was accompanied by tearing pain and she was lifted and placed on the bed. Dirty blankets were thrown over her and she shivered helplessly. The all-encompassing smell was vile, and one that she knew she would never forget. There was no escape from it. But as the heavy prison door clanked shut and Felicity was left mercifully alone at last, she thought for a second of Geoffrey. She longed to feel his comforting arms around her and for a fleeting moment she seemed to see his face. She smiled weakly in spite of her pain and whispered to the dank silence, 'Sorry my dear, so sorry to shame you but I had to do it. I do love you.' Then she sank into blessed sleep.

As the days slowly passed, Geoffrey became more frustrated with each news bulletin from London. There had been more force-feeding episodes and still Felicity would not give in. He paced the floor of his bedroom angrily at night, wrote letters to *The Times*, visited every influential character he knew, and went to the prison each weekend. The more he did for Felicity, the more guilty he felt about his lapse with Rose Miller. All his frantic activities on behalf of his wife failed to assuage his self-reproach. His first surge of triumph and satisfaction that had accompanied that one lapse into adultery, as he firmly called it, had long passed away.

Yet sometimes and much against his will he longed for the comfort he had received in Rose's simple home. Not now the comfort of her arms, for his conscience would never allow him a repeat of his shameless misconduct. But there was a wholesome and uncritical friendliness about her that he knew he needed. He now bitterly regretted his behaviour. Had he restrained himself, he reasoned, then perhaps, in the guise of a pastoral visit he could have gone to her home more often. In his capacity as a Chapel elder it would have been perfectly acceptable and he could have basked innocently in her adoration. He felt desperately in need of someone to believe in him, to look up to him for leadership and advice. Rose Miller would do all of those things. He thought of his beautiful self-willed Felicity for a moment. Oh God, how he loved her and how he wanted her back, yet he acknowledged unwillingly that since her arrest it was sometimes an unreal woman he saw when he thought of her, a sort of cross between Rose and Patricia Harding: an elegant and sophisticated Rose Miller.

Eventually his need for comfort overcame all other considerations and, carefully leaving the motor car in some inconspicuous place, and making a plausible excuse to Arthur Price, he went to see Rose again.

But as he stood in the small room and looked at her all the feeling of superiority and power, which he had enjoyed so much on his last visit, disappeared. She was not offering a cup of tea this time either or even smiling, and her round homely face was pale and frightened. He was so concerned with his own problems that her words at first failed to make sense to him.

'Yes it's true, Mr Buxton. The Good Lord has seen fit to punish us, to punish me more like.'

'Punish? What are you talking about, Mrs Miller?'

Rose sighed and looked at his arrogant face with a swift and unexpected rush of compassion. Dorothy had

141

told her of his refusal to allow her a short time with the typewriter each day and about her removal to the packing section, away from her friends, and these things should have increased her feelings of coldness towards him rather than the reverse. In fact she had wanted to blurt the whole story out to Dorry, to reveal the identity of the baby's father, and to tell her to use the knowledge in any way she pleased. But she had resisted the temptation so far. If Dorry were a few years older, she decided, then she certainly would have done, but now here was Geoffrey Buxton standing before her looking almost vulnerable. She was glad she had kept his secret to herself.

Geoffrey became more and more uneasy as he stared at the troubled features of the woman who was looking at him so intently. Yet as he watched her he thought he saw a glimmer of the old kindness too. He hoped it was not merely wishful thinking. He couldn't do with her anger.

Finally, she answered his question. 'Well, we done wrong, didn't we, and the Almighty has sent us a trouble,' she said.

'A trouble?'

She turned away from him and he felt his body jolt with alarm. Oh dear God, not that, not a child!

'Rose,' he said sternly. 'Do you mean that you are going to have. . . .'

'Yes, Mr Buxton, a baby, a punishment.'

For the first time in his life he thought he was about to faint with shock, yet it was she who needed comforting surely! He tried to rally his failing shreds of humanity and common sense. After all he was a successful industrialist, a man who was used to taking responsibility for the lives of hundreds of his employees. Surely he could manage this situation.

'You must not think of it like that, Rose,' he said at last. 'It is no punishment from God, merely a consequence of my thoughtlessness.' He tried to think quickly, to decide what to do. 'I shall help you. Of course I shall help you,' he added bleakly.

'How, Sir? How can you possibly help me?' The habit of years remained and he was still 'Sir' to Rose in spite of what had happened between them.

He felt uncomfortable as he met the frank questioning in her blue eyes. 'With money of course,' he said. 'You can have something done about it. I shall pay. You must know about these things, who to go to.'

There was a moment of silence and he was aware of a sudden change in her. Her previous fear gave way to something like anger and he winced as he saw the disgust that was clearly written on her face.

'You, a man of God,' she said at last. 'And you can suggest a thing like that? Murder, that's what you'm telling me to do, and to your own baby too. 'Tis likely I'd not survive either. Do you know anything about it? What they do to you . . . ?' She said no more but flopped down into the large shabby chair and stared into the fire.

Geoffrey continued to stand and he looked down at her slumped figure. He had heard tales now and again about the goings-on in the back streets, had sometimes been asked to conduct a funeral, but he usually chose not to enquire too closely, not to concern himself with matters that were never likely to impinge on his own life. Now he shivered with apprehension and also with an element of pity for the woman before him. The shame of what he had brought about overwhelmed him. And Felicity would surely be released one day soon. The thought which, a few moments before, would have brought intense joy, now seared through his brain like a physical pain. How would he ever tell her?

Then suddenly he remembered that Rose was not a widow as he had once imagined. He'd heard it mentioned that she had a husband abroad. He stood still as an idea began to take shape in his mind and he grasped it as a drowning man would grasp at a precious lifeline.

'Your husband is in Canada isn't he, Rose?' he asked slowly.

'What of it? He left me here didn't he. He writes and sends me dollars now and then but I ain't seed'n for so many years that I've lost count.'

Geoffrey winced at her accent. It seemed to be more intrusive than he had noticed on his previous visit.

'Would you like to go there, now, immediately, for a visit? It would have to be straightaway. There are ships sailing for Canada every week from Bristol. You could return whenever you wanted to and everyone would think the baby was his. There would be no questions asked and your good name would remain intact! I am willing to arrange everything, pay your fare, and even that of Dorothy and your son as well if you wish them to go with you.'

He watched her as she slowly began to understand the full import of his suggestion. He had to admit that it was a clever idea. It would cost him something, a lot, but it was worth it.

He saw her grasp the worn arms of the chair and rise to her feet. She stared at him with blazing eyes and he took a step backwards, his self-congratulation vanishing as quickly as it had come.

'How can you dare say such things to me?' she said quietly but with a deadly calm, and he had never heard such contempt in any woman's voice. 'How can you push me off to Canada like that and make me tell lies, lies to everyone, use me and Frank like your underlings?' She pulled herself to her full height. 'No Mr Buxton. I have decided what to do. Just in this minute I've made up my mind. I shall have the babe and bring 'en up here in this house. I've got a trade. I can sew and keep 'en and I need no help from you. And never fear that I'll tell your secret. I'll not make your dear wife unhappy. As long as you keep faith no one'll know.'

She turned away from him and was about to go out to the scullery. He wasn't immediately sure what she meant by 'keep faith' but he knew, deep down, she was right. He put a hand on her arm and stared down at her. 'Can you forgive me,' he whispered. 'Can you ever forgive me, Rose? I underestimated you. I'm sorry.'

'Yes, I'll forgive you, Mr Buxton for the sake of the babe I carry, but I never want to see you again, never.' She shook off his restraining hand and went to the door. 'Go now and forget about me. We'll manage all right, Dorry and Franky and me and the little one when he comes.'

Suddenly he thought of Amy. 'We must keep faith with each other then, Rose,' he said repeating her words and giving them an additional meaning. 'We each have a secret now that belongs to the other!'

'What do you mean?' There was alarm in her voice as if she caught some veiled threat and he realized too late that he had made another mistake, was about to betray a friend, divulge a confidence.

Her face which had regained some of its colour was drained of it again. 'You'm not speaking just of this trouble are you? I can see it in your face.'

It was too late now for him to retract. There was a long silence and he took out his handkerchief and mopped his brow. 'Nothing, Rose. Just . . .'

'Yes. I think I can guess. You'm the Hardings' friend aren't you?'

Geoffrey looked down at his feet and appeared to be studying his shining boots and grey spats. At last he spoke.

'I've known about Amy for a long time. Ever since

Dr Harding first took her in fact. He asked for my advice and this is the first time I've mentioned it to anyone.' He realized that he was making excuses and he longed to escape, to be out of this small hot room. 'She is a lovely girl,' he went on desperately. You must be proud of her. She is my daughter's best friend.'

He paused, and still Rose said nothing. She was staring at him, her blue eyes inscrutable. He longed to know what she was thinking, but he could find no way to minimize the further hurt which he felt sure he was causing or to make amends for his insensitivity. 'Perhaps this baby will make up to you in some way for the loss of your daughter,' he went on recklessly. The words tumbled out, falling over each other, every one of them regretted as soon as he had spoken. He was at a complete loss, all his usual composure and self-confidence totally deserting him.

As she listened to his painful excuses, Rose felt compassion once more. She suddenly saw the real man behind the mask. He was like a child to her, and desperate for someone to believe in him, to need him. Yet he was not a small boy, he was a tall handsome man who had made love to her and whose child she carried. She grappled with her rising sympathy, trying to hold on to her hard-won serenity. She had come to terms now with her wrong-doing and the results of it and she wanted no further complications, no feelings of tenderness for this man. He was looking at her with eyes that seemed to beg for forgiveness and she steeled herself to remain firm. Forgiveness was one thing, and that she would gladly grant, but any fondness must be firmly stamped upon.

'Maybe the child will be a comfort to me. That remains to be seen,' she said quietly. 'Yes I miss Amy, but she'm happy. I know that, and Dorothy is a good girl.'

He continued to stare at her as she fell silent, her

last words making him even more ashamed at his lack of concern for her other daughter. He resolved to make another attempt to see what could be done. But would Rose forgive him? He desperately hoped so. His behaviour had been unspeakable. It must now seem that he was blackmailing her. That had not been his intention at all. He was failing. He was no longer the confident stern preacher, the rich factory owner, the strict parent. Slumping on to one of the hard chairs at the table, he covered his face with his hands.

Suddenly he was aware of Rose standing close to him. When she spoke at last her voice was softer than it had previously been and the anger was almost gone.

'Never fear, Mr Buxton,' she said. 'I suppose I was as guilty as you, but we'm not for each other, you and me, and it mustn't happen again. Maybe that one time'll be forgiven though. I'm thinking perhaps the Good Lord wants this baby for something special. I'll look after 'en anyway. And we've got each other's secrets sealed away in our hearts.'

He looked up at her and smiled a little. 'Thank you. Thank you, my dear,' he said. Then he got up quickly, adjusted his rumpled jacket and straightened the cravat at his neck. 'You will not want for anything, Rose,' he said firmly, regaining a morsel of his old assurance. 'I promise that I shall find a way.'

She said nothing and when he saw the tears in her eyes he was filled with a great sadness for this brave woman who was to bear his child, who would suffer all the jibes and insults and would leave him to enjoy his wife, his luxuries and his freedom. As he walked away down the dismal little street he pondered that perhaps his feelings about women might have been misguided after all. Maybe mankind had been wrong all down the centuries! For Geoffrey Buxton it was not a comfortable thought.

CHAPTER SEVEN

March 1912 had not been a happy month for Amy and the first wet-bright days of April promised to be no better. Laura was constantly preoccupied, always worrying over her mother's fate in prison, and each time the news of yet another episode of force-feeding reached them, a great blanket of gloom descended over both girls.

'It seems awful that my mother should have to go to America while yours is still in prison,' Amy said one day on the way home from school. 'I wish it wasn't necessary.'

'Well there's nothing she can do to help Mama at the moment,' Laura replied. 'But I shall miss her. She's a great comfort.'

'She doesn't want to leave us all just now, of course, but Grandmama refuses to go alone and my uncle is very sick, so she really has no choice.'

'Well perhaps Mama will be released soon,' Laura observed. 'But Papa said that she'll be weak and will need a lot of care and nursing.' She shuddered. 'How can they do such things to a person like Mama, treating her worse than a criminal, and just because of her beliefs?'

Amy shook her head and frowned at the unspeakable pictures that Laura's words produced. 'I don't understand it at all,' she said.

'Neither do I. I lie awake thinking about her every night, and then when I do manage to go to sleep I dream about the terrible things they are doing to her.'

Amy looked at her friend with sympathy and wondered how she would feel if it were her own mother. Laura was staying with her for much of the time lately and the two girls derived considerable comfort from each other's company. Every morning Ralph drove them to school in Clifton, and at the end of each afternoon the Buxton car, with Arthur Price at the wheel, waited for them in the school drive.

'I feel very guilty,' Amy said, 'because I moan about Mama going to America. At least I know she'll be living in luxury on that great liner. Apparently it's the most modern ship in the world. I should like a trip on her myself.'

'Perhaps you'll go one day?'

'Maybe. Papa promised that he would take us for a holiday in a couple of years' time. I have some cousins over there I've never met.'

'Wonderful. I should love to see America.'

'I'd certainly like to get away from here.' Amy's tone was full of distaste as she stared around at the squalid little shops that lined the busy street through which they were driving. 'Perhaps I'll go to live there!'

'I don't think Clifford has any ambitions in that direction,' Laura teased.

'Shut up, Laura Buxton.' Amy's spirits rose a little and she laughed. Every time she thought of Clifford she was cheered. 'If you let your brother hear you say things like that he'll take fright and never speak to me again.'

'No fear of that. I'm afraid that I am doomed to have you for a sister-in-law one day. How shall I put up with you all my life?'

Amy could not think of a suitable reply and anyway the car was turning into the driveway of her parents' home.

Arthur Price opened the door of the motor and

politely helped each girl out and Amy looked at him as she put her hand in his leather-gloved one. She always wondered why he stared at her in that strange way every time they saw each other, and she suddenly felt the need to say something to him.

'Thank you, Price,' she said. 'It must be wonderful to be able to drive a great big thing like this.'

'It is, Miss. 'But it's not too difficult.' Then he stood a little awkwardly, obviously wanting to say more. 'I hope you won't mind Miss, but I overheard you saying that Mrs Harding was going to America on that new ship.'

'Yes, that's right. You've heard of it then?' Amy's tone was suddenly remote and a little forbidding. She knew she must not encourage conversations with young men who were not of her own class.

'Everyone has I suppose, and I've been reading a bit about her. She's got all the latest engines and equipment. That's what I'm mostly interested in, how everything works! A floating palace they do say she is though.'

'Yes, so I believe.' Amy looked at him in some slight surprise and then she blushed beneath his gaze, for he continued to stare intently at her. She saw for the first time his good looks, the fair hair and blue eyes and the sensitive intelligent face.

'Do you read a lot then?' she enquired. It was strange to find a chauffeur who read books.

'Yes, as a matter of fact I do. The classics mostly, and things about mechanics.'

'Well that's good,' she said lamely.

'Sorry to stare, Miss,' he said suddenly. 'It's just that every time I see you, you do remind me so much of a friend of mine. She reads too, poetry mostly.'

Amy was aware now of Laura who was standing at the front door listening with obvious amusement to this conversation. Suddenly she broke into it.

'And do you read poetry Price?' Laura asked. Her tone was slightly condescending.

'No, Miss. Not poetry. Can't seem to get into that,' he answered, and then he saluted smartly and settled himself into the driving seat of the Rover again. 'I must get back. I'll be at the school tomorrow at the same time.'

Both girls watched him manoeuvre the great vehicle round the circular drive and out of the gates.

'Well, what do think of that then?' Laura commented. 'He's been working for us for ages now and I've never managed to get anything out of him. I didn't know you had it in you, Amy! He obviously appreciates your feminine charm!'

Amy grinned at her friend and they went together into the house where Myrtle was waiting for them. They gave her their coats and ran up the wide staircase to wash before going into the dining room where Cook always laid out cakes and scones to sustain them before evening dinner. They were both feeling more cheerful.

'I wonder who he means when he says you remind him of someone. How exciting to have a double,' Laura commented.

Suddenly a chill swept through Amy and she remembered the girl whom she saw now and again, the dressmaker's daughter, the girl who had come to the front door so long ago with that defiant look on her face. She did have an uncanny resemblance to herself. Could it possibly be her of whom Arthur Price had spoken? She shivered. 'Not exciting at all,' she said. 'In fact I find it rather frightening.'

'Don't be a goose,' Laura commanded. 'Come on let's hurry. I want some of those cakes!'

Both girls pulled off their school clothes and heaped them on their beds for Myrtle to put away and Amy went to the wardrobe to select a dress. The one she chose was a bright shimmering blue that set off her fair hair. 'I shall wear this,' she said to Laura. 'It's my newest one. Mrs Miller brought it round a few evenings ago.'

'She's brilliant, that dressmaker of yours,' Laura said enviously. 'I wish my mama would employ her.'

'Nice, too. It's just the daughter I have a funny feeling about.'

'What do you mean?'

'Well I think it's her that Price was referring to. She does look a lot like me and I hate the way she stares.'

'How often do you see her then?'

'Only from the motor usually. Sometimes when I'm coming home later than usual we pass her. I think she must go to the shops or something after work. Of course she always knows it's me because there aren't any other motors around. And she always looks at me with a sort of insolent expression.' Amy stood in her dainty chemise with its rows of frills and tucks, each one hand-stitched with loving care by Rose. She poured warm water into an elegant china bowl from the large matching jug that Myrtle had just placed on the washstand and proceeded to lather her hands and face.

Another array of toilet necessities had been laid out on a marble-topped table at the opposite side of the room for her friend.

'Perhaps she's jealous of you,' Laura said. 'After all you do lord it a bit over the locals down here, don't you.' She wiped her face in the soft white towel and grinned at Amy.

'Whatever do you mean, *lord it*?'

'Well, riding around in the motor all the time, and I bet you never smile at her or at any of them.'

Amy was indignant. 'Why should I? They don't smile at me.'

'They smile at your father though!'

For a few moments Amy was inclined to be cross

with Laura. But she had to admit to herself that it had occurred to her how unpopular she was around St Paul's compared to her father. He had such easy relations with the lower orders, but she found it incredibly difficult.

'You seemed to get on all right with the chauffeur just now,' Laura teased. 'Perhaps you'll improve from now on.'

Amy wanted to change the subject. She felt decidedly uncomfortable with this conversation and the slightly humorous tone of Laura's voice made her think that she was being laughed at. 'He's different,' she said.

'How different?'

'He reads things.'

Laura laughed aloud. 'You're priceless,' she said. 'What about your . . . what is she called . . . your Miller girl? Doesn't she read things?'

'How should I know? Probably some cheap weekly, but nothing else. Those types don't.'

'I thought I heard Price saying that she read poetry, or was I mistaken?' There was definite amusement in Laura's voice now.

'He must have meant rhymes, nothing serious. She wouldn't understand Keats or Shelley for example, would she?'

'You're just a snob, Amy Harding,' Laura said. 'Don't underestimate the working classes. You might get a shock!'

Amy saw the funny side and grinned at her friend. 'You are probably right,' she said. 'You nearly always are!' She had finished washing and she pulled the new dress over her head. 'Anyway, I'm going to ring for Myrtle now to brush my hair so please don't let's talk about it any more. I don't like having to think about Dorothy Miller. And I don't want to be gloomy for Mama's last few evenings at home.'

As soon as the words were out she realized that it was a tactless thing to say with Laura's mother in prison and suffering unknown indignities. But Laura was laughing again and Amy reflected that at least her own discomfiture over the Miller girl seemed to give her friend some amusement. Laura had so much to worry about, real things, not silly imagined problems. She was being stupid and self-centred she told herself. She should think more about Laura, try to give her some support. Yet as she looked at her friend she envied her a little, envied the independence and confidence and the bright determination with which she faced every difficulty that came her way.

At last, with their long hair brushed and shining, and their bright clean dresses each tied tightly at the waist with a wide sash, they went down to the dining room. Patricia was there to greet them.

'You both look charming,' she said as she kissed each girl gently on the cheek. 'Have you had a pleasant day at school?'

Amy looked at her mother and wondered if she could ever be as lovely as that. Her dress was long and elaborate, right down to the ground, even though some of the latest fashions were simpler with their hems above the ankles. It was made of a soft rich cream-coloured satin and the neck was scooped and decorated with flounces of lace.

'Just a usual sort of day, Mama,' she answered. 'What about you?'

'I've been packing,' Patricia said. 'And making arrangements for the journey to the port.' She turned to Laura. 'Your dear father has offered his splendid motor car to take us. We should never get all our trunks and boxes in our little one.'

'Then you'll enjoy the ride,' Amy stated. 'Arthur Price is an excellent driver.' She was suddenly aware of Laura looking at her with amusement again and she wondered why she had mentioned the chauffeur. 'And it's a lovely comfortable motor car,' she added hastily. She went to the table and selected a large piece of fruit cake. 'I wish you hadn't to go though,' she whispered. 'I shall miss you so much, Mama.'

Patricia smiled at her, that serene smile that had always cheered and comforted. 'It won't be long, darling,' she said. 'Just a little while and then I shall be back. And think of Laura with her mother in prison.'

'Yes I do think of her and I'm ashamed.' Amy ate her cake and then took another piece. 'I'll count the days until you come home, and by then Aunt Felicity will be back too. Perhaps we could have a party to celebrate.'

With the arrival of brighter April days, Dorothy tried to shake off the gloom that had shadowed her ever since she'd heard about the coming baby. But it was too big a worry to bear alone and she decided eventually that she must tell someone. Vera Price had kept her other secret. Perhaps she could be trusted with this one? Everyone would know soon enough anyway! She decided to risk telling her friend.

'So you don't know who it be then,' was Vera's down-to-earth and unsurprised comment. 'Is it some bloke she likes, some one she been seeing regular?'

'No. I'm sure not. There's never been anyone that I know of and we're together most of the time. She never goes out at night.'

'What about the day then? When you're at work?'

'It couldn't be then. She sews all the time and the neighbours would know. She'd never let that happen.' Tears sprang to Dorothy's eyes. 'Oh, Vera. However are we going to manage? I don't really mean about the money. I expect that'll be all right. She'll still sew. But everyone'll talk so, and she'm sensitive is Ma, proud

156

of her good name and going to the Chapel and all that. It'll half kill her.'

'No it won't,' Vera comforted. 'And folks aint so bad as you'm making out. Most are kind. If they likes you they'll be all right, and your Ma is a good sort.'

Dorothy sniffed and groped for her handkerchief. 'It's horrible, Vera, just horrible. You don't know how awful it is to think of Ma . . . like that . . . with a man I mean.' She felt colour rushing to her cheeks and she stared down at her black well-polished boots. 'What do go on . . . I mean . . . what really happens to make a baby start? I feel so foolish not knowing about it.'

In spite of Dorothy's embarrassment or perhaps because of it, Vera looked at her and grinned. 'Well, I'm not going to tell you all about that just now,' she stated. 'And I don't know too much, only what I hears from Ma's bedroom at night. Sometimes they seem to be enjoying theirselves and other times I just want to rush in and pull Dad off her. Then I puts my hands over my ears and tries to go to sleep and not hear.'

Dorothy shuddered. 'I'll never let a lad near me,' she said. 'And I'll not get married either.'

'Don't be so stupid, Dorothy Miller,' Vera scoffed. 'Of course you'll have someone one day, and marry him too I hopes. If you get a good one I think it must be nice, else why would all the girls keep on looking at the lads?'

It was the short afternoon tea-break and a young man from one of the offices passed the door of the room where the girls were standing. He glanced in and gave them a bold wink.

Dorothy looked him squarely in the eyes and turned to Vera when he had gone. 'And the other way round more often,' she said.

'Well there you are then. Most of them's nice. And you shouldn't do too badly with our Arthur neither!'

'No. I shouldn't do too badly with Arthur,' Dorothy

repeated thoughtfully, and she didn't add, 'nor with Clifford Buxton,' although the words flashed unbidden and unwelcome to her mind.

'You are to go at once to the supervisor's office, Miller!' Half an hour later, these abrupt words cut into Dorothy's thoughts as she mechanically packed yet another box of chocolates for the rich and pampered folks who could afford them. She looked up into the unfriendly face of Miss Jenkins. She seldom came into this part of the factory and her presence was far from reassuring. 'I don't know why you are wanted, but you had better hurry.'

Dorothy jumped up from her seat at the long, slowly moving belt and the girl next to her grinned in sympathy. 'Hope it's nothing bad,' she said.

'Shouldn't think so. I don't think I've done anything I shouldn't.' Her words sounded more confident than she felt and she brushed down her overall and patted her hair nervously into place. Her fair curls were forced into a tight bun at the nape of her neck in a perfect imitation of her mother's, and she knew that the severe style gave her a much more grown-up appearance. She walked quickly to the door and was aware of the stares of her fellow workers. A summons to the office sometimes meant dismissal for any girl who had displeased one of the bosses. Then poverty loomed, and often hunger, for jobs were difficult to find if you had been sacked. Dorothy felt fairly sure that this was not to be her fate, but she was scared nevertheless. With her mother's trouble ever present in her mind she knew that she would have to shoulder even greater burdens in the future.

She tapped on the office door and entered hesitantly, remembering her first interview in this intimidating room. To her surprise Geoffrey Buxton was sitting behind the desk. He usually did not bother himself with the smaller affairs of the factory, and since his wife's imprisonment in London he was seldom seen there, leaving the day to day running of the place to his underlings.

'Sit down, Dorothy,' he said, and she was surprised at his use of her first name, and at the kindness in his voice. It was so different from the last time she had spoken to him.

'I have enquired about your general abilities,' he continued, 'and I am told that you show above-average intelligence. This is shown in your writing successes of course, but also in the way you do your work here. I think that your talents are wasted in the factory.'

She sat on the edge of the chair that had been placed for her and held her hands tightly clenched in her lap. 'Thank you, Sir.' Her words were hardly audible above the loud ticking of the ugly clock on the wall behind his head.

'I am proposing that you should work in the office instead,' he continued. 'We need someone bright and efficient to take charge of the cards of all the girls in the factory. It will be a responsible job. You will be given a sum of money each week and you will have to take it to the Post Office to purchase their insurance stamps. Then you will have to stick one on each card and file them away. You will need to visit the factory frequently in order to interview any girl who has an enquiry about her card. You will also have the unpleasant task of returning their cards to those whom we sometimes find it necessary to dismiss. And of course you will see that all new workers are listed and have a card. Do you think you would like to do this?'

Dorothy was rendered almost speechless as he finished his description of what would be required of her. He was staring at her, his brown eyes so piercing that she lowered her gaze to the desk in her anxiety not to do or say anything that should betray her intense excitement. It was the kind of position she had dreamed about, a job that would need her brain as well as her hands! More money in her pocket each week would be wonderful too, but that was not the only attraction.

'Oh yes, Sir. I should love to do it. I know that I could. I've been going on with learning ever since I left school, reading and improving my arithmetic and all.'

'I know that, Dorothy. I make it my business to find out all about my employees, at least those to whom I intend to give greater responsibility. Your trustworthiness I have investigated, too, as you will have a considerable sum of company money in your possession each week. I am satisfied on all counts. You may start in the office next Monday then. He smiled at her and she wondered if she should leave. There was a moment of silence and the ticking of the clock matched the thudding of her heart. 'Your mother?' he enquired. 'Is she well?'

Amazed, Dorothy stared at him and wondered for a sickening moment if he knew that Ma was going to have a baby, and if he did, whether he would change his mind about the job. Her hands felt suddenly clammy with fear and shame, and she remembered the uncompromising words that he frequently thundered at his small congregation when he was preaching in the Chapel. 'Yes, Sir. Quite well, thank you,' she said faintly.

'Then give her my regards when you get home,' he said. He stood and nodded briefly, obviously dismissing her. 'You may go now, Dorothy, and I hope you are happy in your new job. Your wages will be increased in proportion to your new responsibilities. Miss Jenkins will see to it.'

This last piece of information was the only flaw in the arrangement. Miss Jenkins had become her enemy

160

it seemed. She wouldn't be pleased about the promotion!

As she stood up and turned to go he spoke once more. 'You may go straight home now. You need not return to your packing this afternoon. I should like you to give your mother the good news as soon as possible!'

'Thank you, Sir,' Dorothy murmured again breathlessly. She wanted to smile, to say something more, but no words came and she knew that she was trembling. She wasn't sure how she managed to get to the door, but when she found herself on the other side of it she stood still for a moment wondering if she had dreamt the whole episode. Then as she saw that the corridor was empty, she skipped for joy all the way down it, rushed back to her place in the factory and took off her overall. She put it carefully on its appointed hook, imparted her news to the startled supervisor and walked, slowly now, out of the building, along the sunny April streets to her home.

She pondered the boss's words all the way and could come to no believable explanation of his decidedly odd behaviour. The only thing she could think of that might possibly account for it was that his wife had been released from prison a few days before. Could that be the reason for his good humour, and the totally amazing offer of the free afternoon? She decided that was it. He was doing it as a kind of thank-offering, but even so it was strange. But any misgivings she had were quickly overcome by the anticipated pleasure of telling her mother, and by the time she reached her front door she was bubbling with excitement.

'Ma, Are you there, Ma?' she shouted as soon as she had pushed it open. 'Ma. You'll never guess. That hoity-toity Mr Buxton has given me a new job, the afternoon off, and he asked me to give you his regards! Can you believe it?'

Rose looked up from her sewing, but Dorothy was

hanging her coat on the hall-stand and failed to notice the strange look on her mother's face.

'Oh, yes. I can believe it,' Rose said. 'I can believe it very well. I can believe anything of Mr Buxton!'

Dorothy went into the back kitchen and stared at her. 'What do you mean by that, Ma? I thought you'd be pleased. It'll mean more money for us. You won't have to work so hard.'

'Sorry, love. Of course I'm pleased. There's bad news though. I haven't been able to think of anything else.'

'Bad news. What bad news?'

'The *Titanic*. It's sunk.'

Dorothy was so full of her own good fortune that at first the full import of the words failed to reach her. She had vaguely heard that the great ship had sailed a few days before, but it was of little interest. She kissed her mother and then bent to put the kettle closer to the flames of the fire. A thin curl of steam was winding upwards from it and the teapot was, as always, ready on the hearth. Then she looked at her mother again and was immediately concerned.

'That's awful, Ma,' she said. 'It was unsinkable they said. Whatever happened?'

'Hit an iceberg.' Rose stopped her sewing machine in the middle of the seam that she was stitching and the noise of the treadle beneath her feet was suddenly stilled. 'Ever such a lot of the passengers drowned the newsboys do say.'

'Are you sure, Ma? I didn't see anything about it on the way home.'

'You was in too much of hurry I suppose. You know who was on it don't you?'

'No. Should I? They're not our kind of folks are they?' A boat like that is only for the rich!' Even at a moment like this Dorothy could not prevent the touch of envy in her voice. Realizing it, she was slightly amused at herself. Well, she should be glad for once that she wasn't rich if it meant drowning like that. She had only seen the sea once, at Weston on a Sunday school outing, and then the tide was right out and the resulting mud hadn't been very frightening, just ugly. Icebergs and seas that could swallow up the greatest ship in the world were right out of her experience.

Then suddenly her mother was shouting at her. 'Mrs Harding was on it, that's who! Mrs Harding, Amy's mother. She was going to America with her mother. They was to spend a few weeks with some relations over there.'

All at once the full horror hit Dorothy and the terrible implications of the words fell like some icy hand on her heart. Amy's mother. Amy's adopted mother. That meant . . . the colour drained from her face and she was suddenly aware of how her own mother must be suffering, what she must be thinking. And then she knew that she must tell her about Vera's revelation that day in the playground so long ago, the secret knowledge about Amy that had been poisoning her ever since. There could be no more barriers between them. This new baby that was to come was problem enough.

'Oh, Ma, that's terrible. Too terrible to think about.'

The kettle was boiling now unheeded on the fire, filling the room with steam. Dorothy gripped the edge of the sturdy table in both hands and stared into her mother's eyes.

'Ma,' she whispered, 'I know about Amy. I know who she really is.'

The words cut like a knife across the quiet room. Neither of them spoke. Dorothy could feel the tension almost suffocating her. She wanted to cry out that she loved her mother and that nothing mattered except that fact, but the words refused to come, refused even to form themselves.

Rose got up stiffly and walked the few steps to the hearth. She took a thick knitted pan-holder from its nail on the wall and wrapped it around the hot and sooty handle of the kettle. Then she carefully lifted the kettle with its boiling water from the glowing coals, and placed it on the black stand in the grate. Each movement was slow and deliberate as if she needed time to marshal her thoughts, to choose her words, and Dorothy watched her, mesmerized, as a rabbit watches a stoat.

At last Rose spoke and there was no emotion in her voice, just emptiness. 'How long have you known?'

'A long time, two years. Vera told me.'

'Of course, Vera Price. The midwife's grand-daughter.' Rose went through into the scullery and Dorothy could hear her washing her hands in the enamel bowl in the sink. Then she returned and sat down again at her sewing machine, smoothing the shining blue velvet that lay on the table. 'I didn't want you to find out, Dorry,' she whispered. 'I've always feared what you'd think of me if you did.' She paused and when she spoke again her voice seemed to be pleading for understanding. 'I did it for both of you. Two babies and your dad out of work, and more and more babies to come, perhaps more twins. I did it so's one of my little ones would never want for anything; and for the other, for you, Dorry, so that there'd be more for you with one less mouth to feed . . .'

It was the first time she'd ever given full voice to the need to explain her action, an action that had troubled her ever since that dark January day when she had kissed the tiny scrap to whom she had just given life, and let the midwife bear her away. 'If I'd known that there'd only be you and Franky, if I'd known that my Frank was going to take himself off to Canada, I'd never have done it. My mother had sixteen children, Dorry!' Rose looked at her daughter with anxious,

164

pain-filled eyes. 'Amy doesn't know, must never know. I promised.'

Dorothy continued to stare and, as she watched her mother's hands lovingly stroke the half-made dress that was probably for Amy, she felt all the pent-up jealousy of the past years creep up from deep inside her. A shiver of treacherous anger ran through her body. Even now, even in this precious moment of her pleasure in the new job, her mother was thinking of Amy and not of her. There had been no word of praise, just concern for Amy. Then another thought crossed Dorothy's mind. This new baby, would it take her mother's affection too, take it away from her as Amy always had?

'Oh yes, you promised,' she taunted, her anger bursting out at last. 'But what about me? Did you ever think about me? Her words were icy cold. 'But you don't need to worry about your precious secret. Vera won't tell. You don't have to worry that anyone'll get to know that way. I've trusted Vera ever since, and she's never let on to anyone, not even to Arthur or any of her other brothers and sisters.'

She couldn't hide her hurt any longer, and as she spoke she felt tears beginning to threaten. 'Why though, Ma,' she went on relentlessly. 'Why is it so important that Amy shouldn't find out? I suppose she'd be ashamed of us wouldn't she?' Her voice was becoming more shrill with every sentence. 'Dear Amy with her hoity-toity ways, her posh way of talking and those clothes you're always slaving over.' She looked scathingly at the frock on the table. 'Oh yes, I've watched you, Ma, watched your face when you were sewing all that beautiful material. And I've envied her, more than you'll ever know.' She was shouting now, 'I just *hate* Amy Harding. I *hate* her, do you understand, Ma?' she screamed. 'Amy Miller is what she should be called, isn't it? My twin sister. Well I wish it'd been me you'd given away. Then *I'd* be sitting in that posh motor car, going to that posh school, wearing them posh clothes. And maybe you would've loved me like you love that Amy!'

She ran out of the kitchen and up the creaking stairs to her bedroom, flung herself on the old bed and thumped it angrily again and again. Even the bed wasn't her own, had to be shared with her mother. She had nothing, nothing, while that girl had everything.

There was no sound in the old house except her sobs and when they eventually ceased she was aware of Rose standing in the room holding a cup of tea. When she spoke it was in a calm, quiet voice.

'Dorry,' she said gently. 'Of course I love you. I've always loved you. But words don't come easy to me. I love Amy too but I can't show it can I, only on her clothes. I can make them a bit special because she's my lost baby.' She put the cup down on the small bedside table and sat on the bed.

Dorothy didn't look at her. She still felt angry, and suddenly there was another weapon she could use.

'This new one, then. This baby you're going to have. Are you going to give it away too? Is it going to come before me?'

The words were the cruellest she had ever uttered and she was immediately ashamed. Rose got up slowly and went to the window. She stared out of it and spoke without looking round.

'No. I shall keep 'en. I shall keep 'en and bring 'en up the best way I know. But no one will ever take your place, Dorry. No one, ever.'

Dorothy slowly sat up on the bed and stared at her mother's straight back. She felt so sorry for her all of a sudden, but then she knew she must ask the question that had been tormenting her. 'Ma,' she said, 'Please tell me who . . . I realize that I'm not supposed to know about things, but the girls talk and I do know a bit. Please tell me who it was, Ma.'

166

She held her breath watching the still figure by the window. Then Rose turned round and came back to the bed. Her eyes were full of tears.

'I can't tell you that, Dorry. I can't never tell you that. But he's a good man.'

Slowly Dorothy sat up and took the cup of tea from the table forcing herself to be calm. Tea in the bedroom was a luxury kept for when you were ill. She was grateful for it and she drank a little, its creamy sweetness comforting her. At last only the tea leaves were left in the bottom of the cup. Then she looked at her mother's troubled face and felt ashamed.

Rose spoke again, 'Don't say you hate her, Dorry. Please don't hate. It's a terrible thing. And if she've lost her mother . . . Mrs Harding may be one of them as is drowned. Think of it, Dorry.' She groped for a handkerchief in her capacious apron pocket and wiped her eyes. 'I don't never want any of my children to hate.'

The words were gentle and quiet, so unlike her own abrasive ones and Dorothy suddenly realized that everything that her mother did was always for others. Her caring was for her children, all three, and the new one would be loved too, whatever suffering it might bring. Her shame deepened and she wished she could take back some of the things she had said.

'I'm sorry, Ma. I'm sorry,' she whispered. She put the cup back on its saucer and took her mother's hand, feeling in that precious moment that, although her mind would go on asking for answers and reasons, her heart was satisfied and at peace. 'I'll try,' she said. 'That's all I can say. I promise I'll try.'

Dorothy's life as a lady clerk started the following Monday. She was extremely nervous when she arrived at the office entrance at the front of the large building. Factory girls had to go round the back. 'You're still going to be my friend aren't you, Vera?' she said as the younger girl waved to her and prepared to walk on.

'Of course, you ninny,' Vera said. 'We'll always be friends unless you become too much of a swell to have anything to do with me.'

'I'll never be that, Vera,' Dorothy said, unwilling to let her friend leave. 'Will we meet for our dinner hour like we always do?'

'No,' said Vera. 'You get to know your new cronies. You can tell me all about it tonight.'

With that she was gone and Dorothy found herself standing alone, frightened and unsure of herself in spite of her initial elation.

'You the new clerk?' A tall girl wearing a tailored costume in the latest style pushed past her. 'Follow me,' she directed. 'I'm Emily Harbottle. You're in my office.'

Timidly Dorothy followed her along endless corridors and at last reached a large airy room with big windows and four separate desks.

'Ah, you're Miss Miller. Welcome to Insurance.' The speaker was the fearsome, angular individual Dorothy remembered from her first interview more than a year ago. Now however, she was smiling and not fearsome at all. 'I'm Miss Enderby,' she said. 'I shall show you where to put your coat first of all and then give you a desk.'

Dorothy was allocated a wide desk complete with a vast number of lockable drawers, an inkwell with an array of pens, and a comfortable chair. She was immediately overcome with the glory of her new job. It was going to be every bit as grand as she'd hoped.

'You are in charge of all these insurance cards,' Miss Enderby explained. 'You will stick the appropriate stamps on them each week, you will eventually get to know the girls in the factory whose cards you have, and you will be responsible for any queries they may wish to ask you about. You will have to go to the Post Office and buy the stamps.' She indicated a sturdy cash box. 'This is where the money will be kept for the short time that it is in your care.'

When the instructions were complete she bustled out and Dorothy was left with the smart Emily Harbottle. She had enveloped herself in an overall which covered her elegant two-piece. Dorothy looked with some misgiving at her own shabby outfit.

The girl obviously followed her glance. 'No need to worry about what you wear in here,' she said cheerfully. 'We all have these overalls. Can you sew?'

Dorothy was surprised by the question. 'No, not really. My mother can. She's a dressmaker.'

'That's all right, then. You'll be given some material and told to make your overall. They seem to think that we're smart enough in the office to choose our own designs, so they leave us to it.'

This small thing, together with everything else that happened to her that day, confirmed Dorothy's pleasure in the new job. She left at the end of the afternoon clutching a parcel of bright shining material that would gladden Ma's eyes. She thought of the dull factory uniform and was glad that Vera wasn't anywhere to be seen. It wasn't that she didn't want to walk with her but she knew that she would have great difficulty in keeping her enthusiasm within bounds.

To her delight Arthur Price was in the back kitchen talking with her mother when she arrived home. He would be just the one to share her excitement. She didn't notice his gloomy face and plunged in with her news, regardless.

'Lovely to see you, Arthur?' she said. 'Have you heard about my new job?'

'Your Ma's been telling me. I'm very glad for you, Dorothy.'

'I'm in charge of loads of insurance cards and lots and lots of money, and I have a desk of my own, and there's a tennis club I can join!'

'A what?' Rose handed her a cup of tea.

'Tennis club, Ma. Tennis. You know, hitting a ball about.' She teased her mother gently as she sipped the tea and looked at Arthur Price's handsome face. 'Everyone in the office has the use of the courts up at the County Ground, free, and we can get free lessons too after work in the summer. Wimbledon, here I come!'

'Hush, Dorry. You only been in the office one day and you be talking like the nobs already!' Rose sounded indignant and slightly worried.

'I'm going to be one, Ma,' Dorothy said. 'I'm going to be a *nob*.' She looked at the startled faces of her audience. Then she went over to her mother and kissed her on the cheek. 'Never fear, Ma. I'm just joking. But you will make me a white tennis dress, won't you, for the summer? They're just the thing now.' She had dumped the parcel on the table and went over to it to pull at the string. 'And this too, Ma. Will you make me two really smart overalls as soon as you can?'

Rose gasped at the sight of the shining material. 'You been given this?' she said in wonder. 'This is expensive stuff.' She fingered it lovingly. 'When we'm all cleared away I'll get the machine out again and start on it. You shall have them as soon as I can do them, Dorry. I'm proud of you.'

'Thank you, Ma. I told the girl in the office that I wouldn't have any trouble getting them made. I told her I had a clever dressmaker for a mother. See, I'm proud of you too.'

Rose glowed at the unexpected compliment. Since their confrontation on Friday she had worried about her relationship with her daughter. Now things seemed to be getting back to normal.

170

Arthur was still pondering on the surprising idea of Dorothy playing tennis. No one from their class did so. 'What about a racket?' he asked in a down-to-earth and slightly doubtful voice.

'I'll look out for a second-hand one. I shall have to save up.' Dorothy was not to be put off.

'You won't have any time to write, I'm thinking,' said Rose.

'I most certainly will, and read too. I'm not letting all that go, Ma. This job will give me more experience, won't it. I'll meet more people, have more folks to write about!'

Since the weekend, since that painful talk with her mother she had gradually come to terms with her unrest. Her inability to write seemed to have departed and she was brimming with ideas once more. She turned to Arthur. 'I've just read a very funny book. I'll get it for you. You'd like it.' She put her cup down on the table and ran out of the room, returning a few minutes later with her hair loosed from its constraining bun and brushed so that it fell in luxurious waves over her shoulders. Her cheeks were glowing with colour and her eyes sparkled with the new confidence she felt. 'Here you are,' she said. '*Three Men in a Boat*. It made me laugh and laugh.'

'We need something to make us laugh up at Mr Buxton's house,' Arthur said taking the small volume and flicking through the pages. 'Miss Amy been staying there for a bit since we heard her poor ma got drowned. Everybody's all full of gloom.'

Dorothy clapped her hands over her mouth and was at once contrite. 'Oh gosh,' she said. 'Here I've been, carrying on about myself and forgetting all about that. What a selfish creature you must think I am.'

Arthur smiled at her a little sadly. 'Not selfish, Dorothy. We've all got to make the most of what we have and be happy when we can.' He stood up to go.

171

'I just popped in for half an hour while Miss Amy goes back home to fetch some things. They asked me to drive her. I got to be back there in five minutes.'

Dorothy walked with him to the front gate. She was full of self-condemnation, but also into her mind there flashed the sudden unwelcome thought that Amy had once more spoiled her moment of triumph. 'Where's that great motor you drive then?' she asked.

'I left it at the Hardings'. Couldn't park it in this street, could I now?'

The remark saddened her, annoyed her almost. 'No of course you couldn't. It's much too grand.'

He looked at her critically. 'What d'you mean by that?'

'Nothing. Just the truth. I've never been in a motor, Arthur.'

'Wish I could take you for a drive,' he said. 'Perhaps one day I'll have one of my own.'

'Pigs might fly,' she remarked with an effort at flippancy.

Arthur's reply was stern. 'You're jealous aren't you, and you with a kind lovely ma and a nice job and on the way to becoming a writer. I'd be ashamed, Dorothy Miller. Miss Amy hasn't got any of those things.'

Dorothy was angered at his tone. 'She've got money though, and that counts for a lot.'

'"Tisn't everything.' Then he added as an afterthought, 'You and she are so alike to look at. It's strange.'

'No it isn't,' said Dorothy hearing warning bells ring in her mind. 'It isn't strange, I mean. We're both fair, and we both got curls. Lots of people got those things.'

'I suppose so,' Arthur said doubtfully. 'Anyway I must go. Best wishes with the job and the tennis and all.' He bent and kissed her swiftly, not on the lips but just a peck on her cheek and she blushed. 'I reckon you'm the prettiest,' he said and he winked at her. 'I'll come and see you again as soon as I can,' he added and then he strode off down the street in the direction of Amy Harding's home.

Dorothy stood for a long time before going in and she put her finger thoughtfully over the place where she could still feel the touch of his lips. She liked Arthur Price. He was good and he was honest. And he was far from stupid. She'd be silly to let him go just for the sake of a dream! Slowly she went inside.

To Clifford's surprise and embarrassment it was to him that Amy turned most often in those difficult days just after her mother's death. Her father was too deeply immersed in his own grief to be of much help to his daughter, and although Laura attempted to give some comfort she confided to her brother that she found it incredibly difficult. Felicity Buxton, too, was unable to do very much. Her health had been severely damaged by her recent ordeal and she could do little more than lie in bed or on her sofa, and allow others to minister to her. So it was on Clifford that much of the burden fell.

At first Amy had totally refused to believe the news. There were survivors, she insisted. Her mother must have been given a place on one of the boats. But it wasn't until all those who had been rescued arrived at New York, not until the official lists were made known that the full measure of her loss finally began to make an impact. And then she took to her bed and refused to be comforted. Except by Clifford.

At last, after many weary days she was beginning to face life again but it was still Clifford to whom she turned whenever she felt completely overcome with despair.

'What am I going to do?' she said tonelessly one day when he had called to see how she was. 'How can I ever go on living without Mama?'

They were sitting together in the window seat of the beautiful drawing room, the room that Patricia had planned, the place where Amy loved to be, and which held so many memories of her mother.

Clifford impulsively took her hand in his and smiled at her. 'You will go on living, Amy,' he said. 'You will go on because you're brave and because your papa needs you.'

'But you don't understand,' she said. 'Without her I'm nothing at all. She was all the things I long to be, and now there's no reason to try any more.'

Clifford sighed. He sometimes felt the stirrings of protective love for this girl. She was so young and so vulnerable, not bright and confident like his own sister. It would take a brave man to try to protect Laura he reflected, but Amy was different. He looked at her fair curly hair, dishevelled now as he had never seen it, and at her solemn face. She was staring at him with hopeless tear-filled eyes and suddenly he wanted to take her into his arms, to press her slight body to his own and to comfort her with all the warmth and strength of which he was capable. But he held himself back. He knew that now was not the right time. She would retreat from him like a small frightened animal.

'There is every reason to try,' he told her gently. 'But not to make yourself into a copy of your mother, lovely though she was. You must be yourself, Amy, just yourself.'

He heard her small intake of breath and felt the tremulous flutter of her hand in his.

'What do you mean, Clifford?'

He hesitated, not wanting her to read into his words more than he had intended. 'You are very precious to a lot of people,' he replied. 'We need you Amy, just as you are.'

She withdrew her hand and stood up, turning to look at him as she did so. He tried to read the expression on her face. There was a sudden bravery there and determination too, but more that he could not decipher.

'That's a very nice thing to say to me,' she murmured. 'And I shall try to do as you suggest.'

'Are you ready now then?' he enquired. His mother had asked that he should bring her to tea. Felicity was still weak, but improving every day and he knew that the tea-party would be good for both of them. He hoped he had not been harsh with Amy but it was difficult to find the right things to say. He was beginning to find it quite a strain. He was not totally sure about his feelings for her either. He had to keep reminding himself how young she was. If she were to become more to him than just his sister's friend then they would have to wait for a long time. He sighed. He often felt bitter about all the constraints of his strict upbringing. Even now he couldn't drive Amy to his home. His father would not allow him the use of the motor car although he knew he was just as capable as the chauffeur.

'Yes, I'm ready. I shall just go and make myself respectable,' she said.

Arthur Price was waiting for them. He stood beside the gleaming and resplendent Rover, and Clifford saw him glance appreciatively at Amy as he helped her into the seat. She had changed and brushed her hair and he was obviously taking in the long fair waves falling in shining abundance down her back, and her neat figure, too, with its tiny waist circled by a tight satin sash. The shape of her small breasts was clearly visible, and Clifford suddenly felt enormously protective. He had no wish to see her hand in Arthur's as she stepped into the vehicle or the smile of thanks that she gave him. His jealousy startled him.

'You told me it was unsinkable,' he heard her say to the young man. 'That day you took my mother and

175

Grandmama to the docks. Do you remember?' There was a slight reproach in her voice.

'I am sorry, Miss Harding, very sorry indeed.'

'You were trying to be kind,' she whispered. Then she smiled at him. 'You cheered me. You really cheered me on that morning.'

Clifford looked from one to the other and felt left out. 'Hurry up, Price,' he said irritably.

The chauffeur looked at him in surprise. 'Right, Sir,' he said. 'Where do you want to go? Home is it?'

'Yes,' Clifford directed, settling himself in the back beside Amy. 'Straight home, now.'

When they left the streets of St Paul's behind and were climbing towards the more leafy suburbs, Clifford felt Amy shiver. He suddenly ceased to envy Arthur Price sitting in front of him, so competently handling the great motor car. Instead he slid his arm round Amy's slim shoulders and pulled her towards him. He felt her settle comfortably into his side and he was content. Perhaps the brotherly feeling he had always felt for her would develop into something deeper after all.

CHAPTER EIGHT
1915

Ralph Harding bought a copy of *The Times* and tucked it under his arm. The latest news could wait until he reached home: it was almost always gloomy. Three years had passed since Patricia had been lost at sea, three years of great change both in his own life and in that of almost everyone in the country. Britain was at war now, a terrible soul-destroying war with Germany that had already taken its toll of many of the young men he knew. Zeppelins had recently rained death and terror from the sky on to English towns; poison gas had been used on the Western Front, and women were working in all sorts of unsuitable jobs, taking the places of the many thousands of men slaughtered in the trenches.

On his way out of the shop he glanced at the board propped against the wall. At first he stared at the large scrawled words without any real comprehension. 'Cunard Liner lost,' he read. 'The *Lusitania* torpedoed by German submarine.'

Quickly changing his mind he opened his newspaper and read the details. Over a thousand men, women and children were believed drowned and in only twenty-one minutes the great ship had disappeared beneath the waves. An awful blankness swamped his mind as he stood there and, instead of this latest tragedy of the war, he saw the *Titanic* pictured before him. He stood quite still in the street and read the account through to the end but he was not concentrating on the words. All the old memories of his own personal tragedy returned once more to haunt him, memories that he tried constantly to push away from the threshold of his consciousness. Through all the years that had passed since Patricia had been drowned he had mourned her loss. He could still see a vivid picture of her as she'd been on the day she'd left. She had been so worried because she was leaving them all at a difficult time, and she was apprehensive about the long sea voyage with her mother. He remembered how infinitely desirable and how very beautiful she was, waving to him, blowing him kisses from the deck of the great unsinkable ship.

He walked the small distance to his home and eventually settled himself in his comfortable armchair, his pipe in his mouth, a small whisky in his hand, and a great emptiness in his heart.

'Would you like me to light the fire, Sir? 'Tis still a bit nippy in the evenings even though 'tis May.'

Ralph looked up vaguely at the maid, his face expressionless. 'No thank you, Myrtle,' he said. 'I'm going out to dinner later. No need to give you extra work.'

She put the box of matches she had been holding into her apron pocket. 'No trouble I'm sure. But if you'm warm enough then I'll leave 'en be.'

'I'm warm enough,' Ralph repeated, and as he spoke he made an effort to pull his thoughts back to the present and especially to the girl standing before him. She looked pale and drawn. 'You get along home to that husband of yours,' he said gently. 'His time on leave must be precious.'

'Yes it is, Sir. He do go back the day after tomorrow, to France, to them awful trenches that I've heard tell about. I can't bear to think of it.'

'As it's his last day at home you are not to come in

tomorrow then,' he instructed. 'Take the day off and I will pay you as usual.'

'Oh, Sir that's wonderful. Do you really mean it? But what about Cook?' she added doubtfully.

'Don't worry about a thing. I shall make it right with Cook. We can't have you wasting your last day together.' He paused for a moment suddenly realizing what he had said and wishing that he could take back those latter words. But she was smiling and he thought with relief that she had not registered his doom-laden implication. 'Go on to the Downs or somewhere,' he added quickly. 'The weather looks as though it will be good. Enjoy yourselves.' He returned her smile and was heartened by the look of pure joy that crossed her plain features. But, as she walked out of the room, closing the door quietly and carefully behind her, he felt a sudden stab of pain for her and for the young man who seemed to him little more than a boy. They had married just a few months ago and Ralph wondered how long Myrtle's husband would survive in 'them awful trenches' as she put it. His thoughts wandered to all the other young people he knew, to the generation on whom the burden of this seemingly futile war fell. He knew that his feelings about the war were slightly revolutionary, that his apparent lack of patriotism would be roundly condemned by all who knew him and so he kept his thoughts carefully to himself.

He was constantly worried for Geoffrey and Felicity now that Clifford had his commission. A second lieutenant seemed a good and honourable thing to be until you read the reports of what was happening in France. And there was Geoffrey's chauffeur, that pleasant young Arthur, he reflected. He had managed to get into the Royal Flying Corps. Ralph sighed and gave thanks, as he frequently did, that Patricia had wanted to adopt a girl all those years ago, and not a boy. At least he would not be faced with the agony of losing a child to the war.

Amy was away at school now but her letters kept arriving regularly and he was always cheered by her growing maturity and by her obvious happiness. Felicity had suggested the move a few months after Patricia's death, for at that time Amy had sunk into a frightening apathy.

'The child needs a complete change of scene and the school is one of best in the country.' He remembered Felicity's words clearly. 'I have persuaded Geoffrey to let Laura go as well,' she told him. 'It will be wonderful for them to be together.'

Although he knew that he would miss his daughter greatly, it seemed the best solution. He had heard glowing reports of the school and the fact that both Patricia and Felicity had been students there for a time finally broke down Amy's initial resistance and she had agreed to go. And the experiment had been a great success. Now, at eighteen and almost ready to leave she was confident and sure of herself, no longer the shy, diffident girl who had cried for so long and so desperately on that terrible April day three years ago.

Ralph finished his whisky, tapped out his pipe on to the unlit coals and stood up. Feeling somewhat cheered at the thought of Amy he smiled a little to himself. The change in her gave him great satisfaction and there was the coming summer to think about. Perhaps he would take her on a long holiday somewhere. He had not had one himself for years. For a moment a frown crossed his features. If only this lunatic war wasn't happening he could take her to France, to Italy, to Venice. And Laura could come too. His thoughts ran on in disarray and he wondered what his daughter would eventually want to do with her life. She certainly wouldn't wish to settle down in this great empty shell of a house here in St Paul's. He had thought of it like that ever since Patricia's death and he knew that Amy felt the same. And only Cook and Myrtle were left to run it now, along with an old man to do the garden. The others had left months ago to help the war effort. Perhaps he should sell the place, leave, do something else with his own life, even volunteer for the army as a doctor in some field hospital.

He sat there in the stillness and it seemed for a moment that Patricia might at any moment come into the room, bright and smiling, telling him that dinner was served.

Dinner! He stood up purposefully and folded the newspaper placing it carefully into the wastepaper basket. Then he strode quickly up the wide staircase to get ready to go out. Tonight would be good. There was no surgery and he had been invited to have dinner with Geoffrey and Felicity. The problems of his life could be set aside for another day.

'So you've got yourself transferred then?' Dorothy looked with renewed interest at the young man beside her on the park seat. Arthur Price had been her friend for years. Just a friend she firmly told him, and told Vera Price too. Vera had ideas. Vera was always making embarrassing remarks and she wished she wouldn't.

'Transferred to the Royal Flying Corps, yes. Didn't I tell you that I'd fly aeroplanes one day?'

'I never believed you!'

'No one did. They still don't. But I've made up my mind, and learning about cars and then being in the Royal Engineers was a sort of jumping-off ground.' He grinned.

Dorothy failed to see the pun. 'You haven't really been up in one of those contraptions yet have you?' she asked dubiously.

'A few trips, yes. But mechanics sometimes get

trained as pilots if they're good. That's what I'm aiming for.'

'Isn't it dangerous?'

Arthur laughed. 'Of course, but not so awful as them terrible trenches. Those trenches,' he corrected himself quickly.

'I don't know how you can like engines so much. Noisy dirty things I think they are.'

'So you've said before! Why do you think I got a job as a chauffeur then? Nothing like engines. They're wonderful, like that poetry you're always telling me to read!'

'You're laughing at me, Arthur Price. And you'd not do better than to read those books I gave you.'

'Not my kind of stuff, all that romantic rubbish, but I do read, Dorry. I've still got that one you gave me years ago. *Three Men in a Boat*. Do you remember? I still look at it now and then when I want a laugh. I read quite a lot. In fact I think I'm doing well with trying to educate myself. I finished one called *Tale of Two Cities* last week. Took a lot of getting through, but it's exciting, a man's book.' He pulled a battered volume from his coat pocket. 'I enjoyed this one, too. In fact I brought it for you if you want it.'

Dorothy took the book from him and read the title. '*Westward Ho!*' she said. 'That's a funny thing to call a book.'

'It's about a place down in Devon. I should like to go there one day, see the sea and all that. Perhaps we can go together when this old war's over.'

Dorothy handed the book back. 'I don't think I'd like it,' she said. 'The story I mean. And I'll never have time to take a holiday. I've got to write my own books in every spare minute I can manage. I've heard Ma talk about a relation of hers who lives in Teignmouth. That's in Devon I think. We've always known her as Aunt Elsie. She keeps a little shop or hotel or something by the sea. It sounds nice but I can't see myself getting there, so don't get any ideas.'

'Is the writing still going well?' Arthur enquired. 'I'm proud to know an author!'

'Not too bad. I'm still mostly doing short stories but *Woman's Weekly* have just taken a serial. That's longer. A proper book is my real ambition. Ma says that I can't expect to do that though until I'm a grown woman. She thinks that eighteen is still too young.'

Arthur looked at her with some awe. 'I shouldn't think so. You ought to have a go. I'm sure you could do it. Mothers never think you're grown. You'll be successful and you'll get rich, Dorry. Authors are rich!'

She laughed at him. 'That's not true,' she said. 'Most writers starve in attics unless they have rich husbands!'

'Are you looking for one of those then?'

'No,' she said quietly. 'I'm going to stay on at Buxtons. It's a good job. At least it is now that I'm in the office. I really like it there especially since old Jumpy Jenkins left. Some say she got the sack but no one knows for sure. She was just too awful. Since she went I've managed to teach myself to type on her precious machine. I'm allowed to practise in my dinner hour. She'd have hysterics if she knew.'

'I've heard Vera mention her. She was a supervisor or something wasn't she?'

'Yes. She was awful to us, Vera and me.'

'Our Vera's happy enough now,' Arthur said. 'She hasn't any ambitions. She'm quite content now that she'm walking out with someone.'

'I know. He's nice. She's still my best friend.'

'Funny that, with you two being so different. What about Franky by the way? He wasn't keen on getting more learning either was he? Seeing he's your brother I should have thought he'd have had some brains.'

'Still at Jennings selling candles and paraffin and things. He's keen on horses. He wants to go in the

Cavalry when he's eighteen. I don't suppose he'll manage that, but he's got a special feeling for animals. He'll probably get some job with them when he joins up.' Dorothy paused and looked at the fresh green leaves on the trees, the blue sky and the tiny scudding clouds. It was so peaceful. 'I can't think that there's a war on,' she said. 'I feel especially sorry for all the horses out there. They can't help it can they, and they get shot and wounded, too. It's terrible. I like to think of Franky helping them somehow. He's seventeen now. He's anxious to get into the army as soon as he can.'

Arthur grinned at her. 'How like a woman,' he said, 'to think more of the horses than the men. By the way,' he added. 'Did you know that Clifford Buxton is an officer now, a second lieutenant apparently?'

Dorothy's heart jumped warningly and colour flamed in her face. She had seen Clifford again from time to time at Buxtons when he visited with his father and sometimes in the Chapel where she still went every Sunday night. On each occasion that same strange attraction had overwhelmed her and at the mention of his name, it returned, flushing her with both pleasure and embarrassment. She moved restlessly further along the uncomfortable seat, further away from Arthur. She still felt that in some way her life would be affected by Clifford Buxton, that their paths would cross. It was not altogether a happy feeling. There was a strange heaviness that seemed to sweep over her mind when these thoughts came. She tried to convince herself that it could not be, that it was all in her imagination. He was far above her, one of the gentry. Yet perhaps she could bridge that gulf between them. She had tried so hard and had achieved so much. Even on the tennis court she worked hard to improve her game. Most evenings she walked all the way to the County Ground and played with the bright Emily Harbottle. There were usually a couple of lads, too, to make up a four.

She wondered for a second whether Arthur played tennis. She couldn't imagine it somehow and she dared not ask him. She acknowledged that she was very fond of him and that he was important to her. As he sat companionably beside her on the park seat, she had to admit that he was a much better proposition than Clifford Buxton: Clifford the dream, the fantasy. Yet however hard she tried she couldn't get excited over Arthur.

She turned to look at him and she felt ashamed. He was wearing his new uniform and it made him look even taller and more attractive than before. It set off his fair good looks and sensitive blue eyes to perfection and she knew that there were plenty of girls who would give anything to be sitting here with him as she was. To become a flier one day too! That showed initiative, immense courage and brains as well. Arthur Price had all three, so why did she still reject his advances?

She saw that he was watching her and she wondered how much of her heart he could read, how much he guessed, but his face gave nothing away. Suddenly sad for him, sad for the war, for the danger and death, she jumped up and took his hands in hers, pulling him up beside her. 'Come on, Arthur,' she said brightly. 'Let's go home and I'll make you something to eat. There isn't much but I think there might be an egg or two. Did I tell you that Ma keeps hens in the back yard now?'

Back at the house, Christabel was playing with some sand that Rose had managed to get for her. It was in an old wooden box beside the hen hut. At almost two and a half she was a bright intelligent child with straight brown hair and brown eyes that surveyed the world with friendship and interest. Rose had always expected Geoffrey's child to be a boy. Why she couldn't tell, but her surprise when the baby was female was as great as her pleasure. She had secretly felt a little daunted at the prospect of bringing up another son, and a son of the strict, autocratic preacher too! Even Franky had caused her some heartache recently. She could never seem to talk to him, and he was always out somewhere or other, not telling her where he went or what he did. She worried sometimes about him. A lad needed a father. She thought now and then about her husband. The letters still arrived regularly and she sometimes remembered those early years with nostalgia. He had been a handsome man then and he had swept her off her feet. She frequently looked at the photograph of the portly stranger he had become, which she kept on the mantelpiece, and wondered whether she was still glad that he'd gone away. Well, she couldn't truly answer that. All in all it had probably been for the best and her life was full again now that she had Chrissy.

She remembered holding this new little daughter in her arms when she was first born. It had been an easy birth and she had cuddled the fragile little scrap to her ample breast and loved her with a fierce protective love from that very first moment. Geoffrey had never seen her. A postal order arrived on the doormat regularly every month. There was never a letter or any indication from whom it came but Rose was grateful and she always took it to a Post Office some streets away from her home. Gossiping tongues were too keen to wag. It was better not to give them any ammunition.

She had told Frank about Christabel. It had been a difficult letter to write but she knew she had to get it done. It was the right thing to do and after all he might come home all unexpected one day when this war was over. She wanted to get it off her mind anyway. So her careful copperplate handwriting had covered two complete sheets of the thin crackly paper that she always posted regularly to Canada. She had waited in some suspense for his reply, but when it eventually came some extra dollar notes had fluttered out of the envelope and he had not been angry. She often remembered that day. She had suddenly known that he had another woman to occupy his bed and satisfy his needs. That must be the reason for his good humour. But it was natural wasn't it? She had refused to go, refused all his pleading letters. But the dollars kept arriving, and along with the postal orders that could only be from Geoffrey, an added prosperity had come to the little house. There was some fresh paint on the windowsills and always enough food in the larder. She had bought the day-old chicks and Franky had managed to make a ramshackle hen house. The cockerels had gone into the pot and the remaining six hens laid obligingly and regularly. That her marriage was finally over she minded not at all. In fact Rose was completely happy and fulfilled. In spite of the occasional snide remark from neighbours, Christabel had brought her nothing but joy.

She looked up with pleasure and with her customary good humour when Dorothy and Arthur came in. 'Hello, you two. Had a nice walk? Come and have a cup of tea. The kettle's just boiled.'

Whenever Amy thought about the war, whenever she read accounts of the men killed and of ground painfully gained or lost in France, she thought of that night ten months ago – when war had been declared. She felt that she would never forget it as long as she lived.

She had been to the theatre with her father. He had taken her to the old Theatre Royal to see a military drama called *Under Two Flags* and although secretly she would have preferred to go to the Hippodrome to laugh at the musical comedy that Myrtle was so enthusiastic about, it had still been a treat. In fact the slightly grim Anglo-French drama had seemed apt at such a time and her father had thoroughly enjoyed his evening.

Afterwards they had decided to walk through to the Tramway Centre before taking a taxi-cab home. She remembered vividly the crowds gathered outside the newspaper office. A strange and ominous silence had filled the still air. It had been frightening, unnerving, and then suddenly with a great rush, newsboys came racing out of the building brandishing placards announcing that Great Britain was at war with Germany.

She recalled the fright and the terror as she gripped her father's arm tightly and then her incredulous amazement as she heard the cheers. They started slowly, tentatively, until at last there was a great chorus of joyous sound that echoed round and round the streets. It struck her as totally out of place until some young men close to her started singing the National Anthem. Other patriotic songs followed until gradually her panic gave way to a sudden pride, and she was singing along with them all.

The war had not impinged too much on her life since then. She had been busy with all the activities that she was forced to cram into each school day, but now that the final examinations were over she knew that she must come face to face with reality once again.

'If we were boys there would be no choice,' she said thoughtfully to Laura on one golden July day in the summer of 1915. 'I'm not looking forward to the end of term very much.'

They were on their way back from the tennis courts and she swung her racket from side to side, carelessly swiping at the occasional bush beside the path. 'Do you wish you could go into the army or something? Women seem so useless in this war.'

Laura was silent for a moment. Amy knew that she was fairly sure of a place at Cambridge. She had been the most brilliant student of her year right through school and for her there would be no empty years ahead. Her path was clear and straight before her.

'At university I shall try to be single-minded and not think about the war,' Laura said. 'With so many men being . . .' she couldn't say the word. 'There are bound to be lots of jobs, lots of opportunities for women later on. We shall definitely be needed. We might even get the vote. Perhaps I shall go into Parliament.'

Amy's heart sank a little in spite of Laura's optimistic words. In fact she totally failed to share her friend's enthusiasm. Instead she thought of Clifford as she had last seen him, so proud in his uniform, so anxious to go to the Front.

'I wish you could come up to Cambridge with me,' Laura continued. 'I'm going to be jolly lonely without you.'

'Not clever enough. I should hate it.' Amy shuddered at the thought. 'I've been wondering about the future a lot recently though. It's so different at home now with only Papa there and just a couple of the staff left, so quiet. Even Tobin has gone.'

'Tobin, what happened to him?'

'Oh nothing awful. I thought you knew. He was miserable without me and Mama. Papa sent him to live with my aunt in the country. He's happy there apparently, chasing rabbits and things.' She smiled but there was a bleakness in her words as she thought of her little dog, her constant companion during those bitter weeks after her mother's death.

'What are you going to do then?'

'I suppose that I ought to do something to help the war effort. I wondered if I could drive ambulances. I've heard that girls are doing that sort of thing now.'

'Terrific idea,' Laura said enthusiastically. 'If Arthur Price still worked for Papa I'm sure he would have taught you. You remember our chauffeur? He's joined up like all the others. Went into the Royal Engineers first and in the last letter from Mama she said that he had managed to get a transfer to the Flying Corps. He was very proud of himself I believe.'

'I liked him,' Amy said. 'He was kind to me on the day Mama left. I remember it so clearly. I was upset about her going. He tried to comfort me. He told me that her ship was unsinkable!'

'Don't hold that against him, will you?'

Amy realized that Laura was trying to be cheerful, trying to lighten the conversation, and she felt immediately guilty. She was frequently depressed lately and not very good company for her friend, but Laura put up with all her moods. Suddenly she smiled. 'No of course I won't. And I think I really will learn to drive. I don't know how to go about it, but Papa will help me I'm sure. In fact he is probably the best person to teach me. He's a very good driver. I should feel safe with him.'

'How about becoming a nurse of some kind?' Laura suggested. 'There's the VAD of course, and the Queen Alexandra Nursing Corps if you really wanted to make it a career.'

'Who said anything about a career? I still hope to marry.' Amy's words carried a mild reproof and Laura laughed at her.

'Here we go again,' she said. 'You haven't *any* ambitions have you, Amy.'

'Ambitions? Yes of course I have. I want four children and a nice rich husband.'

Both girls laughed and linked hands and quickened their pace towards the large building that they could now see before them. It had been their term-time home for the past three years and they each had a remote sort of affection for it. Amy was feeling a little cheered. She squeezed Laura's hand in gratitude. Without her friend these years would have been bleak beyond endurance.

'What shall I do without you?' she said. 'Whatever shall I do when you aren't around to listen to all my moans?'

'You'll be fine. Absolutely fine. I just know it.' Laura's words were full of bounce and assurance. 'There's a whole world out there waiting for us, Amy. We're the new women, a new generation. We're going to take life in both hands and make something of it.'

'I wish I had your courage.'

They reached the school building and ran up the wide stone staircase two steps at a time and then paused, and in case they should be observed, walked decorously into the hall.

There was a letter on the wall rack for Amy. She took it and stared at the thick black writing on the envelope and her heart raced with pleasure. 'A letter from your brother,' she said. 'From Clifford.' She didn't open it at once but put it carefully into the pocket of her white tennis dress. 'I'll read it later.'

'Perhaps you have the right ambitions after all,' Laura commented drily. 'Anyway let's hurry and change. I'm starving.'

'Do you really have to go, Papa?' A few weeks later Amy was sitting white-faced in the quiet drawing room of her home. She stared at her father as though he had suddenly become a total stranger to her, this tall quiet man who was calmly telling her that he had volunteered to serve as a doctor, that he would be going to the Front some time soon.

'No, Amy. You know that no one is forcing me. It's something in me that makes me want to go. And our men are dying out there because there are not enough doctors in the field hospitals. They are lying unattended for days sometimes. From what I hear our medical

191

services are totally inadequate.'

She was silent. Reeling at the shock, she felt completely abandoned. Never in her whole life had she seemed so alone. There had always been the security of home, a safe haven to which she belonged and where those who cared for her could be found. She had blithely supposed it was a state of affairs which would always continue whatever she did and wherever she went. Now, without warning, it was being withdrawn. She was vulnerable and unprotected in a suddenly hostile world.

'I shall make adequate arrangements for you, you know that,' her father continued. 'You may go and live with your aunt if you wish. I have already written to her and she would be delighted to have you. And so would Tobin,' he added, obviously hoping for some response at the dog's name. 'Another possibility is that you should stay with Geoffrey and Felicity. You only have to choose.'

Amy had never really considered her father as a separate person before. He had merely been her father, existing in her mind only through his relationship with herself. Although in many ways they had been close, she had never looked beneath the surface to see the man behind the loving parent and the conscientious doctor. Now she forced herself to see him as a person with wishes and needs and suddenly understood the loneliness he had suffered since the death of her mother, and the bravery with which he was facing this difficult decision. When she spoke at last her voice was quiet and measured, and she hoped that he would not see the tears that sprang to her eyes.

'I wish you wouldn't go, Papa, but if it is really what you feel you must do, then I certainly could never stand in your way.'

'That's my girl,' he said and he came over to where she sat stiff and tense in the brocaded chair. He took her cold hands in his and looked down at her. 'I knew you'd understand, Amy. It won't be long. This war cannot go on for too long. Then we'll travel. I've dreamed of showing you Venice and Florence and Rome. There are so many things to see and do when the world comes to its senses again, and it will do so soon, I promise you!'

She smiled at his enthusiasm and tried to share it. 'I'll look forward to it,' she responded. 'I have always wanted so much to see Venice.'

'So what will you do in the meantime?' His voice had lost its sudden eagerness and resumed the careful businesslike tones that she was used to. He smiled at her. 'How will you spend these tiresome war years?' he asked, then added, 'I'm so sorry, my dear, so sorry to have to leave you and to ask you to change your life.' He dropped her hands and went over to the window and she stared after him, looked at his drooped shoulders and the set of his head as he gazed at the rain slanting down from the grey September sky. A great shaft of love for him shot through her and pride too that she had a father like this.

'Change your life,' he had said. Maybe this was the time when she must indeed face things squarely and not hide any more behind the security of a safe and stable home. Other people, other women had to take responsibility for themselves and it was something that she had never done, never even thought about. There had always been someone else to make the decisions for her and she had been happy to let things remain like that. Every arrangement made had been for her good, her welfare always the prime consideration, and her wishes, when she expressed them, had always been honoured. She knew that she had been privileged and very lucky, but now it was over. What could she do though? How could she start on this adventure of independent existence? For that was how she saw it. A new phase of her life was beginning, frightening it was true, yet a challenge also, and one that she would not shirk.

Perhaps the answer lay in her father's profession, of which she had always been proud yet from which she had remained remote. She remembered that Laura had mentioned the VADs. Nursing? It was the most honourable thing she could think of and would give her a link with her father, and with Clifford too for that matter – for she would be doing something to help with the war.

All these thoughts flashed through her mind as she sat in the quiet room. Her father had not moved either. He was still standing looking out of the window. Whether a minute passed or more she could not tell but eventually she spoke quietly, addressing his back.

'I should like to learn to be a nurse, Papa,' she said. 'Maybe a VAD eventually. But I've no idea how I go about it. Perhaps you could help me?'

As he turned round to face her she expected to see shock written on his features, to hear his refusal to allow such a thing. She sprang quickly to her feet, anxious to convince him. 'I'm no longer a child. I'm eighteen, Papa, and well able to take care of myself. A lot has changed since this war started – we've both seen it – but I've changed more than anything else!' Then she stared at him in bewilderment. The weariness she had grown used to seeing was gone. He was smiling.

'That's the most wonderful thing you could tell me, my darling,' he said. 'You just don't know how proud it makes me feel.' Then for a moment the old concern returned. 'But are you sure? It will be hard.'

She laughed and went over to him and laid her finger on his lips. 'It's decided,' she said. 'And I can't wait to get started. You'll come with me to wherever I have to go tomorrow to see about it, won't you, Papa!'

'Of course, and I shall be the most conceited officer

in the army,' he said, 'when I tell everyone what you're doing.'

Clifford was not so pleased when Amy told him, the following week, that she would soon be starting to work on the wards in a local hospital in order to get some experience.

'Suppose you catch some awful disease,' he complained. 'I don't like the idea at all.'

'You are so old fashioned, Clifford,' she scoffed. 'Why should I become ill any more than anyone else?'

'Because . . . because you've never been exposed to anything bad before,' he said lamely. 'You're too young.'

For reply she laughed heartily at him, pushing him playfully down the path. They were walking on the Downs above the Avon Gorge, for once alone together. That fact would be very much frowned upon by Geoffrey if he knew. He insisted upon a chaperone every time they went out, but Felicity had more advanced ideas, and she had deliberately looked the other way when she saw them leave the house.

Clifford turned and, catching Amy by the hand, pulled her towards a wooden seat nearby, tugging her down beside him. She looked around, anxious not to be seen in such a compromising position. Then she quickly released her hand from his and moved along the seat away from him leaving a respectable space between them. She fingered the loose bun of hair at the nape of her neck and tried to push the escaping curling strands back into place or fix them beneath her hat.

They sat for a few moments in silence. The sun was warm and the view of river and hillside very beautiful. Amy felt full of a new confidence and it gave her a different attitude to Clifford. She was no longer the little woman waiting to be gathered up in his arms and cherished for the rest of her life. Perhaps his sister's constant nagging through all the years of their long friendship was beginning to bear fruit. She hadn't had time yet to tell Laura of all her plans but she could just imagine her disbelief and then her pleasure.

But it was in her relationship with the man at her side that her new-found independence seemed to be making the most difference. It was not that her love for him was any the less, if anything it was enhanced. But she now felt that she was more his equal. She had something important of her own to think about, something to which to give her thoughts and her efforts. It was a totally new experience for her. Was it the war that had done it? Or was it because her father was going away? Or maybe because she was to be left alone? Yet perhaps the change went deeper than that, further back. Perhaps on that terrible day when the news of her mother's death had reached her, possibly then the first seeds of her new spirit of self-reliance had been sown.

Noticing that her thoughts had strayed away from him, Clifford tried to break into them again. 'I said I think you're too young to be a nurse,' he repeated. 'It's too hard for someone like you.'

'Rubbish,' she replied brightly. 'I don't want to spend my time sitting around knitting scarves for soldiers and waiting for the war to end.' She laughed at him. 'In fact I have no intention of knitting anything. I want to do something useful.'

'Yes, I can see that, but surely there are other jobs less dangerous. Women shouldn't be asked to do the awful things I've heard about. Some VADs are being sent to France. Please don't volunteer for that, Amy. You could be killed!'

'But why are we so different from the men?' she demanded. 'No one says that *you* shouldn't go because you might get . . .' She failed to complete her sentence and she stared across at the great span of the Clifton Suspension Bridge. She was suddenly horrified at the prospect of his death, embarrassed too. It was the first time they had talked seriously about the war. She realized afresh how precious he was.

'. . . might get killed you were going to say weren't you?' he finished for her. 'Well yes I might, but men have always taken those kind of risks. Women haven't.'

'Oh, Clifford,' she sighed. 'Please, please don't become like your father. Surely your mama has brought you up to understand that we're your equals?'

'Yes, of course she has, but equality doesn't go as far as dying on some filthy battlefield.' He looked sulky and upset.

Amy turned to him and suddenly her heart leapt. She realized that he was really concerned for her safety and her well-being. She blushed and stared at him, her whole body alive and pulsing in a way that she had never experienced before. Slowly he reached out for her and without caring now whether anyone should see she allowed him to pull her into his arms. Then he kissed her, the first kiss she had ever known, and the one that she would remember all her life.

'I love you, Clifford,' she gasped when he released her. 'I think I have always loved you.'

'And I you,' he said gently.

They walked back in a glorious daze. Surreptitiously they held hands whenever no one was in sight and, by the time they reached the tall imposing house that was almost as much home to Amy as her own, it seemed to be understood by both that should their parents agree they would become engaged before Clifford went to rejoin his unit. They were already talking excitedly about their future together. Any misgivings that they had about the haste of it all were swiftly banished. The war made a nonsense of waiting.

* * *

197

The first days in hospital were long and hard for Amy. She was to spend some weeks of initial training at a large Infirmary in the city before being drafted to an army establishment and she was secretly a little relieved at this arrangement. She would be living at home for a time: her father informed her that he considered this a far better arrangement than staying in some disagreeable and spartan nurses' hostel.

In spite of his enthusiasm for her decision she knew that he was a little worried too, and she unwillingly allowed him to drive her to the hospital gate on that first morning. 'I shall walk in future, Papa,' she told him. 'It isn't far from home, and I shall have to get myself back at lunch time anyway.'

But she was nervous and apprehensive as she stood and waved goodbye to him. She watched the motor until it was out of sight and then she turned and went up the broad steps towards the biggest adventure of her life so far. For the first time in all her eighteen years she was about to do something to help other people, and she would have a responsibility to do it well. Until lately the notion of serving others had never, in all those years, occurred to her at all. Her parents had made her the centre of their lives, the house had run smoothly with never a ripple of discord, meals had appeared at the appropriate times, at night she had always dropped her clothes on a chair or bed and expected them to be gathered up and returned to her clean and pressed. How all these things happened had never concerned her, and even after her mother's death there had been little outward change. At the beginning of the war servants had disappeared but most of the time she had been away at school or staying with Laura. She had never needed to make even a cup of tea. On this first morning of her new life she realized how little she'd ever had to worry about, and she was ashamed.

The day seemed endless. She was given a uniform that felt stiff and unyielding and before long her back ached and her head spun, yet she refused to be daunted. It was her ignorance of the simplest of domestic tasks that troubled her most. She had never even washed any crockery more onerous than the odd cup. Was hot water necessary? How did one remove grease and stains?

She was not allowed near the patients but was given the most menial of jobs, jobs considered simple enough for the most stupid of volunteers. When faced with her first bedpan she clamped one hand over her nose and mouth and prayed that she wouldn't be sick.

The morning started at eight o'clock and it was not until one o'clock that she was allowed to leave. No meals were provided for probationers or volunteers in the hospital. She was expected to make her own arrangements.

'You will be back at five for the evening shift, Nurse,' she was told. 'And you will work until nine-thirty. Those are your hours for the first month here. After that they will change.'

Amy looked meekly at the trim starched figure of the woman in charge and nodded. 'Yes, Sister,' she murmured, and she pulled on her coat and stumbled out into the sunshine wondering how she would ever manage to walk the mile or so home, to the blessed haven of her room, to Myrtle who would minister to her. And how would she get back here for another four and a half hours of back-breaking toil?

On the way home she saw a figure coming towards her, a figure with blonde hair like her own fastened into a neat bun at the nape of her neck, a girl hurrying like herself but in the opposite direction. Colour rushed to her face as she realized who it was and then she forced herself to smile a brief greeting. The other girl stared at her, disconcerted it seemed, and then she too smiled, a frozen half-smile, and then hurried on.

No word passed between them, but Amy felt a coldness creep through her body. Why did this girl affect her so? She was dressed more smartly now and it emphasized the likeness between them. Gone was the shabby coat and general air of poverty that she remembered. She was carrying a tennis racquet too. That surprised her. Did people from that class play tennis? She remembered hearing some mention of Dorothy Miller having stories published. The information must have come from Laura, or perhaps from the Buxtons' chauffeur, Arthur Price. That was it. He knew the Millers. Amy thought briefly and a little sadly of Price. She remembered his bright face when he drove her and Laura from school each afternoon before the war. She had liked him, been vaguely impressed by his intelligence. He had left to join up like most of the other young men, and Laura had said that he had eventually got into the Flying Corps. She wondered for a moment what had happened to him, and then her thoughts drifted to Clifford. She briefly pressed the precious engagement ring that was tied safely around her neck and lay next to her heart. She gave a little satisfied smile as her fingers located it beneath her uniform and it seemed to impart a new strength to her weary feet as she walked along the hot dusty pavement. Clifford's last leave had been short and he had been quiet and thoughtful for much of the time. He had not been drafted to France yet, but the newspapers had been full of the battles in Flanders, of the infantry engaging in fierce hand-to-hand fighting and he was obviously thinking of his imminent call to the Front. If he could risk everything for his country, then surely she could do something as small and insignificant as emptying a few bedpans!

The first weeks passed and she did not give up and eventually she was allocated to a male ward full of war-wounded casualties. The men were all young. Some were frightened and vulnerable, and others who were getting better were full of jokes and banter, some of which Amy found embarrassing.

'They joke because they're scared,' one of the nurses told her after one particularly cheeky sergeant had badly flustered her.

'Why scared when they're getting better?'

'Because they're frightened of going back of course. The thought of them trenches just frightens the life out of the poor things. If they've been in them once they don't want never to be forced into them again.'

Amy had not really thought about this, but afterwards she looked at her patients with more compassion and understanding. The winks aimed in her direction and more especially the frequent crude remarks no longer disturbed her. Their bodies too, at first a source of deep embarrassment, now became objects that needed her careful ministrations. With every day that passed she became more competent, more wise, and less liable to be shocked or disgusted at some of the things she had to do. She frequently had to wash the men, sometimes wash every part of a sick, suffering body and clean wounds that were suppurating and smelt so foul that she thought she would never forget the clinging sickly stench. But her hands were gentle and she always managed a smile of encouragement and a reassuring word. After a time she didn't even have to try to be cheerful. She was actually feeling fulfilled.

When she had time to think of herself Amy longed to see Laura again. She had only been home once during her first term at Cambridge and then Amy had been on duty most of the time. Now Laura was home for the Christmas holidays, and on one of Amy's rare evenings off Felicity had arranged a dinner party.

It was her father's last evening before he left to join his regiment and they had driven over together. Now the two girls were having the rare pleasure of a gossip in Laura's room while they waited for the gong to summon them to the dining room.

'So you're really enjoying all the hard work?' Laura asked in some amazement.

'Not every last bit of it,' Amy confessed. 'But our lads are terrific you know. I've been nursing mostly privates and it's been quite an experience. I can't think of them as "lower orders" like we used to call them. In fact I'm really ashamed that I ever thought that way. They're people like you and me. And they're amazingly brave.'

'My, you've changed haven't you,' Laura said. 'I can't believe I'm talking to the same person.'

'War changes everyone I suppose,' Amy replied. 'I sometimes wonder if any of us will be the same when it's all over.'

'It isn't making much difference to me at the moment, the war I mean. At university life goes on much as usual. I feel that I have to work hard to justify the luxury of being there when all the men are getting . . .'

She stopped in mid-sentence and Amy felt the colour rushing from her face. She twisted Clifford's ring round and round on her finger.

'There'll be a lot of work for us to do when the war ends,' Laura continued, trying to cover up her thoughtless remark. 'I'll be needed. We all will. I must get my degree.'

'You don't have to make excuses,' Amy told her. 'If I had your brains I'd be there too, with you. All I can do is scrub floors, empty bedpans and administer tender loving care.'

Laura looked at her friend and then stared at the large diamond which sparkled incongruously on her work-roughened hand.

Amy followed her glance. 'Yes my hands are a mess

aren't they,' she said. 'They seem to be constantly in hot soapy water or disinfectant – or more revolting things. I wear the ring on a ribbon round my neck at work.'

'You poor thing,' Laura said. 'I can't believe it. I just cannot believe that you actually enjoy doing all those horrible jobs.'

'Well, enjoy isn't quite the word,' Amy confessed. 'But perhaps for the first time in my life I feel that I'm doing something worthwhile, or learning anyway. I shall persevere with the training and one day I might get to France. Then I shall know I'm really of some use to someone.' She smoothed down the glowing blue silk of the dress she was wearing and her rough skin caught in the soft thread. She laughed. 'I shouldn't even wear good clothes now,' she said. 'I think it'll have to be tough serge when I'm off-duty in future.'

She had really felt almost too exhausted to make the effort to change, but she had known that she must and she wanted her father to remember her looking her best before he went to France. The effort felt worth it when she saw the proud expression on his face as she came down the wide staircase. He had helped her into the car with almost exaggerated concern, treating her as a woman, no longer a child. She was anxious for him, worried about the dangers he would be facing, but there was a new lift to his shoulders and a fresh enthusiasm about him that had not been there for a long time. She was sure that for her father the decision to go to France had been absolutely right, and her determination to follow, to some extent, in his footsteps, had been just as fitting. A glow of satisfaction filled her, for she had the joy of knowing that for the first time in her life she had made a choice about what happened to her, and that it was completely right.

Only Clifford's absence marred her evening. He had rejoined his unit a few days before and, despite her own satisfaction in her new rôle, she felt a constant nagging worry for him. Sometimes in her worst dreams one of the wounded patients before her became him and the face looking into hers with pain and pleading was his. She was always glad to wake up, glad to splash herself with cold water and to realize with immense relief that it was only a nightmare. Yet when it happened it seemed to cloud her day and the feel of his ring against her heart was like a talisman against disaster.

Tonight the ring glowed on her finger reflecting the glittering candles on the Christmas tree, and her conversation glowed too. Resolutely she put her fears aside, refusing to let anyone know of her anxiety. She concentrated firmly on being a bright and sparkling companion for her father and was rewarded by the pride in his eyes. She knew that at last she was truly growing up; her childhood insecurity had been vanquished.

CHAPTER NINE
1916

Amy scuffed disconsolately at the fallen leaves lying damp and soggy along the edges of the path as she walked back to her room. She held a letter in her hand, against her heart. She had not opened it yet and the brown stains on the envelope sent a chill through her, matching the dismal grey of the rain-heavy sky. It was the mud of the Somme, the red-brown mud that she knew about from the grim and dirty clothes of the battered men who had returned from it, the men whose torn bodies she was tending. Bristol was full of them, its hospitals reinforced by ordinary buildings taken over to give extra beds, extra places in which to die, or to be healed in order to go back again to the Front. She was no longer working in the big central hospital where she had been given her initial training, but had been moved out to a military hospital on the outskirts. Instead of the comfort of her own home every night she was billeted in an austere nurses' quarter, but it suited her, made her feel more a part of the war.

'I feel closer to Papa and to Clifford,' she had explained to Laura in a letter. 'The luxury of home was somehow obscene, too terrible a contrast to life here on the wards.'

Today, in spite of her weariness, or perhaps because of it, she hurried. It was good to know at least that Clifford was still alive, or had been when he sent this letter. He wrote regularly and he had survived the first horrors of the Somme. That had been in July when thousands of men had been killed in the first few minutes of fighting. Now, weeks later, it was still going on and Clifford was still there. Amy lived in constant fear of bad news and each letter was a small triumph.

When she reached the doubtful comfort of her small hard bed in the cramped cubicle that she shared with three other girls she slumped down wearily and opened the letter. She read it through, and then again, and twice more until every word was almost committed to memory. So he was well, he said, and happy. It couldn't be true of course. She had heard enough about the trenches to know that no one could be really happy, certainly no one like Clifford with his love of order and beauty. The trenches were chaos and noise and horror, and only the men who had experienced them, and to a lesser degree the nurses and VADs like herself, had any idea of the grisly reality. She often felt that even Laura had no concept of the appalling truth, the hideous face of war. Daily contact with the wounds of the patients in her care, watching their suffering, their courage – and at times their perfectly understandable cowardice – sometimes made Amy feel much older than her nineteen years. She frequently felt that she would never be young again.

She comforted herself with the thought that this personal experience of the war was making her a better person. She would be a more fitting wife for Clifford, and a better companion to her father when they both came home eventually. And she knew she would feel better about herself. It was this that often kept her on her feet when all her upbringing cried out to her to stop, to pamper herself, to give up.

At last she returned the letter to its grimed envelope and unlocked the wooden box she had brought specially from home. She placed the letter with the others, a growing pile of precious paper. Also in the box were letters from her father, from France too, for he had at last achieved his aim and been posted to a Field Dressing Station at the Front. Amy felt that all of her heart was there in that war-torn land.

She shivered in the cold dank room and thought for a moment of her bedroom at home with its cheerful fire tended by Myrtle, its rich silken drapes and soft carpet, and the large soft bed that had been her refuge ever since she could remember. But her work for the day was over and she must eat and sleep if she were to be capable of getting through another long day of endless toil tomorrow. There could be a further train-load of wounded arriving at Temple Meads any time, she thought hopelessly, and the small Red Cross Hospital to which she had been allocated would receive its share of suffering men to whom she must minister.

There was a basin on the old marble-topped table in the room with a cracked jug in it. She took the jug wearily and walked the length of the long cold corridor to the only bathroom in the hostel. There she stood impatiently while the ancient gas geyser trickled lukewarm water at a snail's pace and when the jug was only a quarter full she could wait no longer. She put it down and carefully turned off the gas tap on the fearsome contraption. Then she carried the precious water back, and stripping off her clothes, tried to wash some of the sickly smell of the wards from her body. When it was done to the best of her ability she pulled on a warm and serviceable woollen dress and stowed her uniform neatly on the chair beside her bed. She had only brought this one garment. It was long enough to hide her ankles, often swollen now with so much standing, and its cheerful but practical red-gold colour usually rallied her spirits. She pulled its shiny belt tightly round her small waist, brushed out her long hair, and as a change from the restricting bun, coiled it into two plaits round her head, and went into the dining hall for the usual indifferent but ample meal.

In spite of her tiredness she had determined to keep to the ritual of making herself clean and fresh each evening, and so far she had managed to keep to the self-imposed standard. It always cheered her, and tonight as she stared at herself in the only long mirror in the building, she felt better, felt that perhaps there was a hope after all for some sort of normality in a world gone mad.

It was late, almost nine o'clock by the time she had finished eating and she could think of nothing now except bed. She certainly did not expect to see both Felicity and Geoffrey Buxton standing in the hall as she hurried through!

'Why, Aunt Felicity,' she gasped. 'What are you . . . ?'

Then suddenly she saw the ravaged expression on the older woman's face and the tears, and Felicity was holding out her hands to her.

'My dear child,' she said. 'My dear, dear child.'

Amy stared at her in a cold numbing horror and she knew that it was Clifford. Clifford was dead!

She was unable to move, unable to speak. She just stood there, and Felicity came towards her and wrapped her arms around her.

'A shell on the tent where he was working,' she said. 'He was killed instantly.'

For a moment her mind would not focus on the words, and then realization broke through. 'You mean . . . ?'

'Your father, my dear.' The words were Geoffrey's and Amy was aware of him looking at her with a rare pity. 'He was actually performing an operation. The hospital had a number of hits. Despicable of course. You must come home with us. I've told Matron. You are to be given leave straightaway.'

After the first relief that Clifford was still alive Amy tried to register the devastating blow that had fallen upon her and she could not. A world that did not contain either her father or her mother was too terrible to contemplate. Felicity's arms were comforting and then there was the strength of Geoffrey, too, but after that just a great cloud of nothingness.

She awoke the following morning in the luxurious comfort of the great four-poster bed the Buxtons kept for guests, and for three full days she lay there refusing to speak or eat. She lay in total apathy and even Clifford's letters failed to rouse her. At last on the fourth day she sat up, and was persuaded to eat a softly boiled egg and a thin slice of white bread. And it was then that the full awareness of her loss struck her and she began to cry. She wept bitterly, on and on and would not be comforted. She felt anchorless and alone, as though the very fabric of her life had been wrenched away, leaving a hollow, meaningless, void.

She had hardly been aware of the rain or of anything outside of the room. The all-prevailing gloom of the weather during the past few days had matched her feelings. But on the fifth day the grey skies gave way to bright sunshine that forced its cheerful way between the thick curtains and shone right across the bed. When Amy awoke she resented its intrusion, wished the storm clouds had remained, but she was incapable of movement, incapable of getting up to pull the heavy drapes over the window and return the room to welcome darkness. She lay completely still, gazing up at the ceiling with its moulded plaster angels around the edges and its thick white bunches of grapes, yet she saw nothing but her father's face full of the enthusiasm and energy she remembered on the day he went away. A gentle tap on the door brought her back to the present.

It was Myrtle who appeared, her kind face full of concern and pity. 'Oh, Miss,' she whispered. 'I'm so sorry.'

'Myrtle!' Amy's surprise at seeing the maid overcame her misery for a moment. 'How did you get here?'

'Mr Buxton came over last night and he bid me bring some of your things and to come and look after you for a bit. He drove me.'

'That's the most wonderful thing he could have done. I'm so pleased, Myrtle. There's no one I'd rather have had.'

'I loved him too, Miss, your papa I mean. Loved him like my own father really. He were that good to me, and when the news came through about my Bill I can't tell you how understanding he were.'

Amy was suddenly jolted out of her own misery and her eyes filled with fresh tears as she looked at this girl, just two years older than herself, who had already been married and lost her young husband in the trenches. Myrtle had been part of her life for a long time, part of the background, someone whom she seldom thought about as a person. In a strange way, she reflected bleakly, even her parents had been like that to her, characters in a drama revolving always around herself. It was not until her father went to war that she had acknowledged him as he really was, appreciated him fully. Now for the first time she saw the maid, too, as a flesh-and-blood woman, a person of feelings and consequence.

And Myrtle was crying now. She was sobbing into the big handkerchief she had pulled from her gleaming white apron pocket. Suddenly Amy knew that from the depths of her sheltered upbringing she must pull some reserves of strength and comfort. It was of Patricia she immediately thought. Her mother had appeared to be delicate and gentle but beneath the light-hearted serenity she always presented to the world, there was a resolve and fortitude that Amy had sometimes detected, and this she must emulate. So she gingerly threw back the covers of the bed with a fresh determination and put her feet shakily on to the thick carpet. She held out her arms to Myrtle and hugged her. 'We must be brave,' she whispered. 'For their sakes we have to carry on.'

For a few seconds the two women held each other, their shared suffering breaking down the previous barriers between them. Eventually Myrtle drew away, obviously embarrassed, and went over to the windows to pull the long curtains back so that sunshine flooded the room. 'I was to bring you a cup of tea, Miss, if you was awake,' she said. 'And Mrs Buxton bid me to tell you that your clothes are all here in two trunks downstairs. I'm to put them in the wardrobe over there.' She indicated the enormous walnut cupboard that stretched from floor to ceiling. 'I packed up all your lovely things yesterday when Mr Buxton told me I was to come.'

'Thank you, Myrtle. Thank you very much for all your hard work.' It had seldom occurred to her in the past to feel gratitude to any of the staff who had previously laboured long hours to see that her every need was fulfilled, but now everything was different. The war, and the months she had spent scrubbing and cleaning in hospital had changed all that. She was surprised to find herself slightly shamed at being waited upon.

'If you're well enough to have a bath, Miss, I'll run it for you. The housekeeper here have showed me how to work the geyser. It do take about twenty minutes to fill.'

'I think I could just manage a bath,' Amy replied, grateful for Myrtle's care. 'But don't bother with the tea. I'll just stay here and be quiet until it's ready.'

When the maid had gone she sank on to the bed again and felt a great emptiness all about her. Her tears began to flow in abundance and she buried her head in the softness of the feather pillow and wept. She was not sure how long she stayed there, but when eventually her sobbing ceased and she raised herself from the bed, she could hear in the distance the sound of slowly running water. It brought a momentary sense of peace and stability. A bath would be a wonderful luxury! For an unwelcome second or two she remembered the one chipped bath at the hostel shared by all the staff. She shivered at the thought and got up shakily, pulling on the wrap that hung on a thick padded wooden hanger behind the door. It smelt delicious, of some heavy fragrance that reminded her of Felicity, and its luxurious warmth comforted her.

Later, lying in the abundant scented water, Amy began to wonder how she would cope with the future, whether she could bear to go back to the hospital, but eventually she closed her eyes and gave herself up to the sensual pleasure of the bath and to her grief, in equal measure. But then, as the water cooled and as she rubbed her body with the invigorating harshness of the loofah that Felicity had provided, her determination returned and she knew that she could not fail her father. By continuing to battle with the appalling suffering she saw every day on the wards she would be maintaining his work. In a very small and humble way she would be part of all he had wanted to do.

She stood up and pulled an enormous white towel from the wooden rack. It was warm and comforting and she felt a slight surge of energy and strength as she hugged it closely around her body. Then she thought of Clifford and shivered in spite of the steamy warmth of the room. 'Please, please, God,' she whispered. 'Don't let him die too. Please!'

Rose Miller sat in her back kitchen and stared at the letter in her hand. She had been enormously frightened half an hour earlier when a great black motor car came to a stop just outside her front door and her fright had increased when a soberly suited elderly gentleman alighted from it and rang the door bell. He had asked her name and when she assured him that she definitely was Mrs Rose Miller, he'd handed her a large envelope, commanded her to read its contents and then told her firmly that she was to come to the address that she would find inside, on the date and at the time indicated. After that he had departed in state, and she was aware of her rapidly beating heart as well as the flutter of lace curtains in many of the windows in the street.

There were in fact two letters, one from the solicitor and the other from Ralph Harding. She read them a great many times, especially the one from the doctor, and then she folded them carefully and put the envelope behind the clock. She would let Dorothy read them before she could even begin to think what to do. She returned to her sewing reluctantly. There was only an hour and a half to wait. Dorry would be home at half past six. She was never late.

Nevertheless it seemed an age before Dorothy held the letters in her hand and looked down at her mother. 'Well, Ma, what are you going to do then?' She had not even stopped to take off her coat. Rose had called her the very minute she opened the front door.

'I can't think straight, not yet anyway. For a wonderful gentleman like that to get killed in them trenches. Seems too terrible for words after all the good he done around here.'

'It wasn't in the trenches, Ma,' Dorothy corrected. 'He was in a hospital behind the lines.'

'Well, wherever he were he's dead and that poor girl an orphan!'

'Aren't you forgetting something?'

Rose looked up and Dorothy realized that her words sounded unnecessarily harsh.

'Forgetting? You mean that she still have got me

and Frank? Well that's not much, is it. I mean she don't even know.'

'And these letters say that you may tell her, but that you have to go and see Mr Buxton first because he's the only one who knows.'

'It's like a letter from the dead,' Rose said staring across at the sheet of thick vellum with its careful lines written in Ralph Harding's stylish loop. Dorothy was still holding the pages gingerly in front of her. 'Fancy him sitting down and writing all that before he went away and leaving it with that solicitor or whoever he was. It seems that he knew he was going to get killed.'

'He was just being sensible. I mean it was very possible wasn't it!' For a moment Dorothy thought of all the women she knew who had lovers and husbands at the Front. The terrible telegrams were arriving everywhere with an almost monotonous regularity. It made you hard, made you grow a shell of insensitivity, a kind of unfeeling that you wanted to discard but dare not. 'Well, are you going to talk to Mr Buxton then?' she asked her mother. 'I don't think you should say anything to Amy for a long time. She'll need to get over the shock of her pa's death first.'

'That's what Dr Harding do say in the letter. That she'll know that she weren't their true-born daughter when the will is read, or before if them Buxtons decide to tell her, and then I can go to see her.' Rose's hands were clasped in tight agitation and her usually cheerful face was pale and tense. 'But I'm just her dressmaker, and I haven't even been that for years now, not since she went away to that posh school. I haven't seen her for a long time either. I don't think I can do it, Dorry, tell her I mean.'

'Then you don't have to, do you.' Dorothy looked down again at the letter in her hand. 'It don't say that you must, just that you'm released from the promise that you made when she was born. Perhaps the right time isn't yet.' She was surprised at herself, at the cold calmness of her words and at her lapse into a way of talking that she tried desperately to reject.

The fierce jealousy she'd felt on that memorable day in the playground nearly six years ago when Vera had blurted out the truth about Amy Harding had not diminished as she grew up. There was still a depth of resentment that frightened her sometimes. Resentment that she was having to struggle so hard for all the advantages that money and position could bring, while her twin sister had everything that she could possibly desire. Even learning to play tennis had sometimes been an effort, for it meant a long walk each day after work during the summer and she had frequently been almost too tired to face the trek home again. But she had battled on, mostly enjoying it and imagining each improvement to her game as yet another step out of the rut into which she had been born and raised. During each dinner hour she worked too. There was no gossiping now with Vera or Winifred, instead she tapped away relentlessly on the typewriter that was hers just for that precious time. The stories flowed from her, many of them published, and her small bank balance was beginning to grow, but the struggle was long and hard.

And now like a further numbing blow came the thought of the will that was mentioned in the letter. Amy would get everything. She would be a rich woman in her own right. Dorothy felt her whole body react in a shiver of sudden anger. Power! That was what money gave you. Power and freedom to do whatever you wanted, and that was what Amy would get and all for doing nothing.

Dorothy felt tears of frustration in her eyes as she glared at the letter in her hand. She put it down quickly on the table beside her mother's silent sewing machine.

Rose picked the letter up and read it over again. 'I

can't go and see Mr Buxton, Dorry. It's something I just can't do.'

'But you have to. Dr Harding expressly says that it is the one thing he wishes you to do. He wants you to talk to both of them, Mr Buxton and his wife, because they must be the ones to advise.' Dorothy was impatient, wondering at her mother's reluctance to seek advice from these two.

'Do she know too then? Mrs Buxton?'

'I think he must have left instructions that she should be told before the news gets to Amy.'

Rose shuddered and Dorothy stared at her without understanding. Christabel was playing outside in the yard where she spent a lot of her time. At that moment she came into the room and Dorothy gathered her up in her arms. 'Who's a dirty girl then,' she said glad of a diversion. 'Come on my darling. Let Dorry get you clean.' She carried her through to the scullery and poured some water from a large white jug into the enamel bowl that stood on the rickety wooden table. First soaping the tiny hands and face, she then dried her small sister gently.

Christabel submitted to these ministrations but when they were done she struggled free from Dorothy's restraining grasp and ran into the back kitchen. 'Want tea,' she said. 'Want bread and jam.' Dorothy followed her little sister through, ready to take her coat off and sit down at last. From the doorway she saw Rose pull Christabel on to her lap and, to her surprise, burst into tears. 'Oh my precious baby,' she sobbed, burying her face in the soft straight hair. 'How am I going to do it? How can I possibly go up there and talk to your pa.'

Dorothy stared at her mother, paralyzed with shock and, as the full meaning of Rose's words began to penetrate, she could feel her face going a deathly white.

216

'What did you say, Ma?' she said. 'Did I really hear right just then? Did I?'

There was a menacing quality about the words and she stared at Rose over the top of Christabel's head. Her mother was rocking herself and the child nervously backwards and forwards, refusing to look up at her.

'Yes you heard. I've been thinking that you must know although I told him it would be a secret for ever. I can't keep it from you any longer, Dorry. Now you know. It was him. It was Mr Buxton.'

Dorothy's world fell about her in shreds. Her first thought was of her job of which she was so proud. It must have been given her because of this. Her mind reeled as other implications of her mother's words gradually achieved their full meaning. Clifford! Geoffrey Buxton's son! Her feelings about him seemed to be almost obscene now.

She pushed roughly past Rose and the child and her heart thudded violently as her little sister looked up at her with her baby-brown eyes. Christabel was Clifford's half-sister as well as her own!

She rushed upstairs and into the tiny room that had been Franky's and was now hers since he had joined the army on his recent eighteenth birthday. She didn't throw herself on to the bed as she would have done in the past, but she stood straight and still, staring out of the window down into the yard and across at the row of dismal, back-to-back houses, row after row of them as far as she could see. And then she laughed, bitterly at first and then with a strange intensity. So her mother had given herself to Geoffrey Buxton! Geoffrey Buxton with his high ideals and the fancy words he boomed forth from the pulpit! It was the most amazing, unbelievable thing she had heard in all of her life, except that she had a rich sister of course. And there was an irony about it all too. One sister adopted into

217

riches while this little one with the infinitely wealthy father was denied them.

Now she realized where all the postal orders were coming from! Giddy with the shock, she grasped the windowsill for support. Standing rigid at the window, she tried desperately to make sense of it all and after a time – it could have been a few minutes or half an hour – she forced her common sense to reassert itself.

She walked slowly across the room and stared at her small bookcase with its rows of battered and well-thumbed volumes of poetry and classics. They were her greatest pride, one of her ways to education and everything that Amy had without making any effort. She ran her fingers thoughtfully and lovingly along the backs of the books on the top, and then she moved to the old dressing table and looked at herself in its chipped and worn mirror. She pulled out the pins that held her long hair in place and started to brush the fair waves that fell now almost to her waist.

She brushed steadily, taking her time and with each stroke her determination and her courage grew. She would be strong and support her mother, and this new piece of staggering information would not alter her love for her baby sister. Chrissy was still Chrissy, whoever her father might be. It didn't matter how the Buxtons – or the Hardings for that matter – interfered in their lives. They were their own people.

When the brushing was completed to her satisfaction she took a ribbon and tied her hair with a large bow at the back of her neck as she used to do, and then she went slowly down the creaking wooden stairs and kissed her surprised mother on the cheek.

'Don't worry, Ma,' she said gently. 'I absolutely promise that no one will ever know your secret from my lips unless it's to our advantage and unless you agree. We'll decide what's the best thing to do about the letter after we've had something to eat. I'm hungry.'

Rose had cleared away her sewing and was laying the table for their tea. She looked up at Dorothy and the relief and gratitude in her face was clear. 'It seems that I'm always giving you surprises, Dorry. What with Amy and all! she said.

'And I think that I've got a wonderful mother,' Dorothy declared suddenly and with conviction. 'With you, Ma, life is never dull.'

'So it's all right then, Dorry? You don't mind too much about . . . about Mr Buxton?'

'It's all right, Ma. It's quite perfectly all right. I'll make a pot of tea, shall I?'

'Tea,' repeated Geoffrey's child, and Dorothy picked her up and held her high above her head.

'Bread and jam, my precious little Chrissy,' she said. 'And one day I just know that you'll be sitting down to better than that!'

Myrtle was a great source of strength to Amy during the grey November days of 1916. A slightly self-conscious friendship had developed between the two girls, their shared suffering bridging the gap in their social standing.

'It do get better,' Myrtle said one evening. 'I know because of my Bill. I still thinks of him a lot of course, but I ain't so down as I was at first. Life got to go on.'

Amy smiled at her. 'I know it has, and I'm trying to be sensible and plan a bit.'

'Are you going back to that hospital then? Sounds like hard work to me.'

'Yes I am, Myrtle. I've been lazy for too long. See, my hands are getting soft again!' She held them out for inspection. The harsh roughness had vanished, and Clifford's ring, sparkling with many reflected colours, set off the smooth white skin.

Myrtle looked at them carefully. 'That's what they ought to be like,' she said. 'A pity to get them all red again, but I suppose it can't be helped. I never seen a lady with hands like yours were two weeks ago.' She gathered up the cup and plate from the small table beside the fire, and then, pausing for a moment, she stared thoughtfully into the glowing coals. 'What shall I do then, Miss, when you leave here? I mean you won't have need of me, will you?'

Amy dragged her thoughts away from her own confused plans and tried to focus her mind on the girl standing before her. She noticed that Myrtle looked pale and worried and she suddenly realized that, now her father was gone, she was responsible for others as well as for herself.

It was a daunting thought. She had no idea what to do about the house in St Paul's. It held endless happy memories as well as the sad ones, but that part of her life was all in the past now and to go back and try to live there again permanently would only revive the grief, would make it much more difficult to try to forget. She knew that once more she must try to remake her life. Geoffrey Buxton was her guardian now but she was sure he wouldn't force her to take any action that she did not wish. She would have to make some decisions herself.

'What would you like to do?' she asked Myrtle, hoping that the girl had some suggestions, something that might push her in one direction or another.

'Well I don't rightly know. I could go and live with me ma again and get a job in one of they munition factories I suppose, but I'm not over-anxious to do that. There's not much room in her place and I'm used to houses like this now.'

Amy sighed, 'I'll talk to Mrs Buxton. She'll know what to do.'

'I'd be glad if you would, Miss. She's a lovely lady.

I don't suppose that there'd be a position for me here?'

'Would you like that?'

'Only if you was closing up the house. I'll go back and keep Cook company else.'

Amy put a weary hand to her forehead and smoothed back the straying curling tendrils of hair that would never stay in place. 'I'll really try to decide about things,' she said. 'Tomorrow, I'll put my mind to it, I promise you, Myrtle.'

The following morning Amy selected her most becoming dress from those that had been brought over for her. Perhaps it would cheer her a little. It was made in a warm but soft blue wool and the neckline, although fairly low, was bordered with a narrow band of fox fur. It was short too, well above her ankles. She belted it tightly round her waist and then brushed her hair strenuously. Since working in the hospital she would not consider asking anyone to do it for her. The days of having a maid to attend to every detail of her appearance had long gone.

She glared at herself in the ornate mirror on the dressing table and then smiled a little ruefully. It was a mature face that stared back. The careless flippant creature of former times had vanished for ever. Gone too was the helplessness and the timidity. She took her comb and drew it carefully in a straight line over the top of her head to make a parting and then gathered her hair into two equal sections one on each side. She looked in the mirror again, considering. Then she started to plait, first one side and then the other until two long braids hung down over each shoulder. That done she carefully wound them one each side of her head, skewering them into place with large brown hairpins and finally with a tortoiseshell comb at the back.

Satisfied with her appearance at last and determined that she would put an end to her time of apathy and listlessness, she went down to breakfast.

Arthur Price was home on leave. Dorothy heard his old motor bike rattle and roar along the road and she flung the door open as soon as he knocked. 'Arthur,' she said, delighted, 'I heard you were home.'

'Just ten days,' he told her. 'Then back to France.'

She looked at his tall figure and wonderfully broad chest and in spite of herself her heart missed a beat. 'Come in,' she said. 'It's really lovely to see you.'

He followed her through the narrow passage and into the back kitchen where Rose was sitting by the fire. Sunday was a day of rest never to be violated. Chrissy was on her mother's lap looking at a picture book.

'Hello, Arthur,' Rose said. 'Your ma tells me that you'm very grand now.'

Dorothy, watching, saw the colour flush his fair skin, and she knew how much the latest promotion meant to him. His sister had told her that he was now a sergeant. 'In charge of all the engines on his flight,' Vera had said proudly a few days ago. 'He do get to fly sometimes too.'

'I wanted to keep it a surprise,' he said. 'But Ma and Vera have told everyone.'

'No wonder,' Rose commented. 'So should I if you were my boy.' She set Chrissy down and poked the fire. 'We'll have a nice cup of tea and then I expect that you and Dorry want to go off for a walk.'

Embarrassed but pleased, Dorothy laughed. Her mother did not often encourage her to be alone with Arthur or any young man. 'Thanks, Ma,' she said gratefully. 'You're a dear!'

They decided to walk into town instead of up the hill to the park as they usually did. 'Brandon Hill,' Arthur suggested. 'Can you walk as far as that?'

'Of course I can,' Dorothy replied. 'I'm not that feeble!'

They stepped out briskly, not saying much at first,

and by the time they reached the steep slope of Park Street, Dorothy could feel her cheeks glowing in the crisp air. The clouds had gone for a time and a wintry sun was shining. She was proud to be with Arthur. His uniform drew respectful interest from every passer-by and she was aware of the envious glances from other girls as they stared at him.

'What's it like then, being a sergeant?' she asked. 'Tell me all about it – and your flying.'

'Well I don't get up as much as I'd like. I want to be in the air every day! When I watch the pilots take off I'm that jealous, I can't tell you.' He grinned. 'They take me up frequently though and I've even been allowed to hold the control lever now and then, all unofficial of course.'

'Will you get to be a pilot do you think?'

'That's what I'm aiming for. Perhaps one day. I shall probably fly as an observer first.'

'What about the Germans? Have you seen any?'

'Their planes? Yes of course I have. I was up recently when we met some Fokkers and had a few shots at them.'

'Fokkers?'

German fighters. They can do over ninety miles an hour, but they're not so good as our Bristol Scouts. They'll do a hundred!'

Dorothy shuddered. The words meant nothing to her at all. She had no way of imagining a hundred miles an hour and it all seemed so dangerous, barbaric even. Thoughts of Clifford Buxton flashed into her mind as they frequently did. From what she heard and read, it was much worse in the trenches. There the men had to go over the top right into the enemy gunfire. 'I'm glad I'm not a man,' she said.

Arthur laughed, and with a quick look around to see that no one was looking, he took her hand in his and squeezed it surreptitiously. Dorothy blushed and felt herself respond but she pulled away quickly. It wasn't likely that there was anyone she knew here in Park Street, but she was certainly not willing to risk it.

They were walking up towards the university buildings at the top of the hill, and Arthur turned and looked at her.

'You still prefer to be a woman even though you haven't got the vote and all that?' he teased.

'Even though we haven't got the vote,' she repeated. 'But just you wait. We'll get it. You mark my words.'

'No more stone throwing, I hope?'

'We don't need violence any more. Do you know there are over three million women in work now?' Dorothy said proudly, quoting something she had read recently. 'If that's not a reason for giving us the vote I don't know what is. Women are as good as men any day! And at anything,' she added triumphantly. 'In the career I've chosen there's no difference at all. I just wish I'd been able to get some more proper education though. It would have been a help to study at a university like that one!'

They both stared up at the imposing building.

'I should like that too, remember,' Arthur said, 'To get educated I mean. It's the door to everything.'

For a moment she felt ashamed. At least her life was not in constant danger, at least she knew that she had a future. For the man beside her, and for thousands like him, there was probably not much hope of living to enjoy one. It was a chilling thought. She held herself back from mentioning the latest numbers of men killed. She had read the terrible total somewhere recently. Five hundred thousand altogether on the Somme alone, it had said. She shivered.

He suddenly turned to her and she wondered if he could read her thoughts for he was drawing her attention to a draper's shop window as if trying to divert her. In spite of all the shortages it held some bolts of shining material displayed invitingly in the centre.

'Look,' he said. 'I'll buy you yards and yards of lovely stuff like that after the war. Your ma can make wonderful dresses for all three of you!'

'Three?'

'You and Chrissy and herself of course!'

'I'm always telling you, you've got big ideas, Arthur Price,' Dorothy scolded, but his mood had cheered her and she looked up at him gratefully. 'It's nice to dream a bit though.'

Eventually they turned away from the shops up a side street that led directly to the green oasis of Brandon Hill and there Arthur found a seat and pulled Dorothy down beside him. There was no one else in sight and suddenly his arms were round her and he was kissing her. She could feel her lips parting beneath the strength of his and she was helpless to stop, wondered if she even wanted to. She sensed that all the insecurity of the future was in the intensity of that kiss.

Eventually she managed to struggle free, and breathless, she looked up and grinned at him. 'You'm pretty sure of yourself, ain't you, Arthur,' she managed, lapsing into her old way of talking. 'I've never been kissed like that before!'

'I'm glad of that,' he laughed. 'Very glad. And now Dorothy Miller, will you be my wedded wife, to have and to hold, etc, etc . . .'

Dorothy had never been so astonished in her life. She had certainly not expected anything like this so soon, yet as she sat there looking at him the idea seemed suddenly to be not so preposterous after all. She was silent for a long time and she held his large square hand in hers. She held it on her lap as though it were some inanimate thing, turning it over, studying the broad strong fingers, mechanic's fingers, scrubbed and clean yet still stained faintly with grease and oil.

Then suddenly into her memory flashed a picture of

those other hands that she had watched mesmerized years ago when she first saw Clifford Buxton on the platform at the WSPU meeting. The recollection came unbidden, but it would not be banished. She had never seen hands like that on a man, long thin tapering fingers, artistic and gentle, the skin white and smooth. She had never forgotten them. The memory had been stored away until now, until this minute when it returned to disturb her. She felt almost angry with it.

At last she spoke. 'Thank you, Arthur. Thank you very much, but it's a shock and sudden too.' She gently lifted his hand from her lap, unclasping her fingers from his. 'I'll have to think about it. Give me time.' She felt cold and detached when she knew she should be thrilled and excited.

'There's not much time, Dorry,' he whispered. 'Not with this old war. That's why I asked you now.'

She jumped up, determined to talk of something else, to remove the seriousness of the moment, or at least to turn their thoughts away from themselves. 'I promise that I'll give you an answer soon, in a day or two,' she said. And then she turned her face to him and kissed him briefly on the cheek, a quick affectionate kiss. 'You'm jolly nice, Arthur Price. Do you know that?'

'If you say so!'

With the mood lightened, they walked hand in hand along the path, arms swinging for they still had the hillside to themselves. Then Dorothy, for no apparent reason, suddenly thought of Amy.

'You've heard about Dr Harding of course?' she questioned, wondering why the subject had not come up before.

'Yes. Terrible for Miss Amy.'

'Don't call her that,' she snapped with unintended irritability. 'She's just a girl like me. Why the "Miss"?'

Arthur grinned at her in obvious surprise. 'Just that

226

I always knew her as that when I was chauffeur to the Buxtons. I drove her and Laura Buxton about a lot.'

They walked more slowly now up towards Cabot Tower on the top of the hill. 'She was a nice girl,' he continued thoughtfully. 'In fact they were both pleasant. Miss Laura was different though, sort of bright and sure of herself. Amy was shy. I liked her the best I suppose.' He paused and turned to stare at Dorothy. 'In fact I always thought how like you she was in her looks. It was her hair and eyes and the way she moved her head sometimes. It often gave me quite a turn, and once I almost forgot myself and was just about to call her Dorothy!'

For a chilling second Dorothy wondered if he knew. After all, it was his sister, Vera, who had first given her the news, and his own grandmother who had brought herself and Amy into the world. That grandmother was the one who was to blame for everything! She stared at him questioningly but from the innocent look on his face it seemed she was wrong. She breathed a sigh of relief.

'Well, she'll be a rich woman now by all accounts.' She couldn't keep the bitterness from creeping into her voice. 'She'll get everything, I suppose, that great house in City Road and all the money and things!'

'The money don't necessarily mean she'll be happy,' Arthur said. 'And I don't suppose she's very happy right now either. I feel sorry for her. I remember when her poor ma went away. I told her that the ship was unsinkable. I could have bit my tongue off when I heard what had happened!'

'You seem to be jolly concerned about her,' Dorothy said. 'She's engaged to Clifford Buxton you know.' It pained her to say it. Ever since she'd heard the news her jealousy had increased.

'Yes. I know. A nice bloke, Mr Clifford. In France I believe, in the trenches.'

They had reached the path round the Tower itself and they stopped to lean over the wall and to stare at the city of Bristol stretched out before them.

'What a lot of churches,' Dorothy said, deliberately changing the subject again. 'Lots of churches, yet we don't seem to be a very religious city.'

'It depends what you mean by religious,' Arthur replied, 'And now can I kiss you again? There's no one for miles.'

Before she could protest she was in his arms. Pressed close, between him and the wall, Dorothy could feel his strength and hear his heart beating furiously against hers. At first her body responded to his, but then suddenly she felt a rush of doubt and misgivings. She wanted to push him away, yet she knew she shouldn't feel like this.

The unspoken message must have somehow communicated itself to Arthur, for he kissed her and then released her slowly, and she could feel him staring down at her without comprehension. His blue eyes showed hurt and disappointment. She turned away and gripped the top of the wall.

'I'm so sorry, Arthur,' she whispered. 'Just give me time, will you?' There it was again, the demand for time. She realized what she had said as soon as the words were spoken, and she remembered guiltily that he had already reminded her that time was not his to give!

'Let's get back then,' he said flatly. He looked at the darkening sky. 'I think its going to rain and we've a long way to go.'

Lying sleepless in bed that night she thought about Arthur Price and desperately wished to be in love with him. There was no reason why she should not be. She liked him, respected him. They had been friends for years and she had hoped the liking would grow into

228

love. Perhaps it still could? Perhaps if they waited long enough it might happen? Yet she so desperately wanted success, to *do* something with her life. Could she still have that if she married Arthur? Wouldn't he hold her back somehow? And there would be babies. How could she make something of herself, her talents, if she was burdened with a string of babies? But that would apply whoever she married.

The longer she thought about it the more sure she became that all these other considerations would not matter at all if she were really in love with him. Maybe love would come? What was it anyway, this special something that she had heard about, read about, but didn't understand?

She tossed and turned on the feather bed until it became lumpy and uncomfortable. When she eventually slept it was to dream of Arthur in one of those flimsy Scout aeroplanes he was so proud of it, but he was spinning in violent circles to the ground, and she heard his voice clearly as he fell. He was calling her name over and over again.

CHAPTER TEN

Amy sat on the settee in the beautiful Buxton drawing room and stared at the vases of glowing chrysanthemus that Felicity had placed in strategic places to catch the eye and lift the heart. She was recovering slowly from the stupor that had engulfed her after the news of her father's death. She still felt numb, but no longer totally without hope.

November was a gloomy month and so far had matched the deadness of her spirit. She glanced at the newspaper that Geoffrey had left on the small table beside her. In France five hundred thousand men had been reported killed in the ever-continuing battles that raged around the Somme, most of them British, it said, and at Verdun unofficial estimates were around seven hundred thousand dead. She turned the paper over so that the report was hidden. She couldn't envisage such numbers. To cope with facts like that you had to close your mind to the reality and, while she mourned her father, she found herself clinging desperately to the fact that Clifford, so far, was not one of that number. In many ways she longed to return to her work at the hospital. In the wards she had found that the terrible statistics could be pushed to the back of her mind, for the men who had survived the slaughter demanded every ounce of energy and concern that she possessed. The vast numbers of the dead seemed to fade, or at least were encompassed in the suffering of the few in her care.

She thought of the hospital tonight as she looked at the expensively furnished room in which she was sitting and decided that she would ask the doctor who had attended her if she could go back to work next week. She felt ashamed to be surrounded by so much luxury, luxury that she thought she had turned her back upon long ago. And although she was happy here she felt that she needed some young companionship. She had become friendly with two or three of the other nurses, girls whom she had never thought to have as friends. They came from working-class families, and she missed their jokes and their earthy conversation. It had been a revelation to her and she found that she enjoyed their company. She and Laura still wrote frequently, but that was not quite the same.

The gas lamps glowed comfortingly, flooding the room with light, and long velvet curtains hid the rain and darkness outside. Yet there was something wrong, a feeling that Amy could not identify. Geoffrey was standing nervously in front of the fire successfully blocking its heat from warming anyone else, and Felicity was sitting with her hands tightly clenched in her lap. She had not been well lately but the pallor in her cheeks was more noticeable than usual.

Amy looked anxiously from one to the other. There was obviously something amiss and her whole body was suddenly icy cold. She lived in constant fear of news of Clifford's injury or death, but surely they would not have kept that from her until now?

Felicity had asked her to come down half an hour before dinner. There were some important things to talk about she had said. Amy calmed herself a little, hoping that it was just arrangements about her and Myrtle's futures to be sorted out. Yet she had never seen Geoffrey Buxton so ill at ease.

He cleared his throat and looked across at her. 'You know, don't you, Amy, that your father's solicitor will be here tomorrow afternoon to read the will,' he said at last. 'Well, there is something important you must know before he comes.'

So that was it! She wasn't going to get any money! 'I don't mind if there's nothing for me, Uncle Geoffrey,' she said quickly. 'I can earn my own living now. I intend to make nursing a career.' She gabbled the words. It was important not to be at a disadvantage, not to be a burden any more.

Felicity rose slowly and came over to sit beside her. 'My darling child,' she said quietly. 'It's nothing like that. You will be well provided for. You don't think your father would have neglected to arrange for your future do you?'

Amy felt ashamed and tears slid from her eyes. Of course she should never have thought that of Papa. And there was the money Mama had left her too. She knew that it had been safely invested some years before. 'Then what is it, Aunt Felicity?' she said. 'It's not Clifford is it?'

'No, dear. Nothing to do with Clifford,' Felicity's voice was a little odd, her manner tense.

There was an uncomfortable silence and Geoffrey went to the small writing table that stood in the corner of the room and unlocked the drawer beneath it. He took out a letter and held it in his hand for a moment. He stared down at it and then looked at his wife and finally at Amy. 'This is from your father, my dear,' he said at last. 'He left it for you if . . . He said that we were to talk to you first and then give it to you.'

She glanced at the slim cream envelope and longed to snatch it from him. She could just see her name written on the front in her father's large copperplate handwriting. For one agonizing moment it was almost as if he himself were standing there smiling at her.

Then Felicity took both her hands in her own. 'You know that your parents loved you very much don't you?' she said. 'You must always keep that thought foremost in your mind.'

Amy nodded dumbly. She was quite unable to imagine what was to follow.

'Your mama was unable to have any babies, Amy,' she continued. 'She was desperately unhappy. Then one day a beautiful little girl was brought to her and she loved her straightaway. The baby was only a few hours old.' There was another pause and Amy was aware of the anxiety in Felicity's eyes. 'That was you, Amy!' The words were gentle, full of compassion. 'You were as much her child as if she had borne you, and more loved than many true-born children ever are.'

For a moment Amy could not grasp the absurd and intolerable things that she was hearing. She stared at Felicity and gradually the words she had spoken, in spite of their gentleness, began to make a kind of horrible sense.

It was impossible to speak. Her throat and mouth were constricted and there seemed to be no words that she could find to embody the shock she had received. She got up and walked unseeing to the door. She couldn't even bring herself to take the letter.

'Let her go!'

She heard Geoffrey's voice through her pain, and she went out of the house into the cold street and, without her coat, walked until the bitter Clifton wind, the darkness and the drizzling rain, forced her return. It was an automatic response, nothing reasoned, and she was only vaguely aware, much later, of Myrtle helping her out of her wet clothing and piling warm blankets over her as she sank on to her bed. There were stone hot-water-bottles as well, each wrapped in a thick knitted cover, one at her side and the other at her feet. She was conscious of their hard but comforting heat.

At last she slept, a disturbed dream-filled sleep.

When she awoke Felicity was at her side. Gradually she recalled the horror, quite sure that it was all a bad dream.

'It's not true, Aunt Felicity. Tell me it's not true,' she pleaded.

'Their great love for you is true, my dear. Nothing else matters.'

'But it does. I'm not their child. It's all been lies. It was all a pretence. Everything, my whole life!'

Felicity sat looking at her with strained hurt eyes. Then she gently stroked the damp tendrils of hair from Amy's forehead. 'The one who brings a baby up is more important than the one who gives birth to that child,' she said. 'Amy, precious Amy, you have to hold to that now.' She rose quietly and fetched the letter from Ralph which she had brought upstairs. Without saying any more she placed it on the table beside the bed.

Amy looked at it with hostile eyes. 'Why didn't they tell me? Why did they leave me to find out this way?'

'Your mother could never bring herself to admit that she had not borne you. They didn't expect to die so early of course. I suppose she felt that you would be told one day in the distant future when you were married, probably, and with children of your own. But it was something we never talked about. You were her very own precious child, only that.'

Amy listened and tried to picture her mother, but the likeness would not come. 'Who else knows?' she asked suddenly. 'Does Laura? Does Clifford?'

'No, neither of them. You can tell them or not, as you wish.'

Then a new and infinitely disturbing thought flashed across Amy's mind. She sat up in the bed, her voice suddenly shrill and angry. 'My . . . my real mother. Who is she? Where is she? So I have a mother still!' She felt used, like a possession that had been tossed about carelessly. 'I have to know who she is,' she demanded. 'And my father too.'

She looked at Felicity expecting an answer, but the older woman was silent. 'Why don't you speak?' she sobbed. 'You know don't you? I can tell that you do!'

'I'm not at liberty to tell you, Amy dear. Not yet, but I promise that one day you shall be told!'

'Not at liberty! Not at liberty!' she repeated. 'This is my *life* you are talking about.'

'It's someone else's life too,' Felicity said gently. 'You must remember that.'

Amy was silent for a moment thinking about the words, and then another thought pierced her. 'She gave me away, didn't she, this woman you are protecting? She gave me away when I was just born!'

The bedroom suddenly felt suffocating, like a prison, and she pushed Felicity's arms aside and jumped out of bed, then ran to the window and wrenched at the catch. Eventually it gave beneath the pressure of her angry fingers and she slid the frame right up and leaned out into the cold November night. The sky was clear now and the garden moonlit. She stood there for a time, shivering in her thin nightdress, and then her anger gave way to intense grief.

'Oh, Mama, Papa,' she whispered to the silent sky. 'Why didn't you tell me? I could have borne it if only you had told me!'

'You'll come with me, Dorry. You will come?' There was panic in Rose's voice.

'Of course I'll come, Ma,' Dorothy replied. 'It's not a visit that I'll look forward to, but I'll definitely come.'

'How are we going to arrange it then?'

'Well the solicitor said that we'd be hearing, so we probably don't have to do anything yet. We must just wait until we get a letter I suppose.'

'What if Mr Buxton comes here himself when you're away at work?'

Dorothy sighed. Ever since her mother had heard the news about Dr Harding's death she had been in a state of nerves. She was quite unlike her usual cheerful self. 'You would cope, Ma. I know you would. Stop worrying so much,' she said, hoping her voice sounded full of an assurance that she was far from feeling.

Rose was obviously not comforted. 'What am I to say? Do you really think that she ought to know that I'm her mother?'

'That'll be up to Mr Buxton I should think. He'll advise you what to do.' In spite of her confident words Dorothy was worried. The thought of suddenly having a sister thrust upon her was infinitely disturbing.

'I shouldn't think we'd see much of her though,' she said hopefully. 'It'll be quite a shock won't it, to know that this is where she rightly belongs. She wouldn't want to come and live here.' Dorothy looked round the scullery with distaste. There was a large stone sink and two scrubbed wooden tables set along one wall, while open storage shelves and a small larder took up most of the remaining space. The door, which at the moment stood open to allow more light into the gloom, led into the yard with its outhouse and the tap which had to be shared with next door.

'Well of course she won't, not with all that money she'll have.' Rose emptied boiling water from the heavy black kettle she was holding on to the pile of greasy pans in the sink. She put a handful of soda with it and added cold water from the enamel pail that stood outside. Then she rolled up her sleeves and plunged her hands into the sink, wincing as she did so. She swished the water about to dissolve the soda and then started the laborious job of washing up. There was always extra to do when she had been cooking. She had baked some pies and yeast cakes, and a few potato cakes too while the oven was hot and they were spread out in appetizing rows on the table in the other room.

Dorothy looked at the mist and drizzle outside and shivered with the November cold. 'Come on, Ma, let's get this lot finished and then we can close the door and have some of those delicious pies you've baked.' She quickly dried the things her mother was piling on to the wooden draining board and put the plates away in their racks on the wall. Then she carried the few more delicate items through to the other room and put them in the cupboard out of reach of Christabel's inquisitive fingers.

Her small sister was playing with her doll, a sturdy wooden object that had been purchased second-hand from a market stall a few days before and which her mother had clothed with elaborate frills and left-over lace.

'Look, Dorry,' the child said, holding it out for her inspection. 'A queen. My baby is a queen! Queen Lucy!'

'Very pretty, darling. Would you like a dress like that?'

'No, too frilly,' commented the practical Chrissy. 'She couldn't run in this could she?'

Dorothy laughed. Here was another candidate for the women's cause, she thought. At nearly four her small sister was surprisingly bright and articulate. Dorothy had made up her mind long ago that she would do everything in her power to ensure that the child had every opportunity, and as often as she could she had taken over the bedtime ritual, always telling or reading a story to her. Sometimes she made the stories up to fit something they had done that day or perhaps read one of her own from the pile of exercise books that grew ever bigger week by week. If one had been published and had illustrations with it that was an extra pleasure. They both enjoyed this precious time together and Christabel could already read a few words.

Before Dorothy could further discuss the matter of the doll's clothes there was a knock at the door and she quickly untied her apron and glanced in the mirror before running to open it. It must surely be Arthur. He hadn't gone back yet and there was no one else who was likely to come at this time on a dark and dismal Saturday afternoon. Her heart jumped a little, not with any particular joy, but rather with concern. He was due to go back to France soon and she dreaded sending him away with no hope, no commitment on her part.

But it was a woman who stood there on the path just beyond the shining brass doorstep and there was a motor standing at the kerb. For a moment Dorothy could not make out who her visitor was. The dim light of the street lamp on the pavement edge gave little away.

'It's Miss Miller, isn't it?' the woman said, and Dorothy immediately noted the cultured voice. She was constantly trying to speak like that! Then, with a nervous thudding of her heart she recognized Felicity Buxton.

'Yes. I'm Dorothy Miller. I expect you want to see my mother,' she gabbled. 'Come in Mrs Buxton.'

She led the way inside and hoped desperately that Ma wouldn't be too fearful, too agitated to talk sensibly with Geoffrey Buxton's wife. The presence of Geoffrey Buxton's little daughter playing happily by the fireside with her doll was bound to make Rose apprehensive.

'Thank you.' Felicity Buxton followed her inside and as she walked through the narrow passage Dorothy turned to look at her visitor again. In the light from the open kitchen door she noticed the smart tailor-made suit devoid of all fussiness, the small hat perched on her head and the friendly smile. She looked thinner than Dorothy had remembered and her face was pale, but there was nothing about her to denote any hostility. Perhaps there was no need to be fearful. It was almost certain that she didn't know about Chrissy, after all.

'Ma, you have a visitor! Mrs Buxton is here!'

Rose came through from the scullery, her hands damp and red from the hot water and the strong soda, her hair escaping from its restraining pins. Dorothy felt for her, knowing she would be embarrassed by her appearance in front of this immaculate and self-assured woman. But Felicity drew off her tight kid gloves and clasped Rose's red and work-roughened hands in hers. And she smiled. 'How nice to see you, Mrs Miller,' she said. 'I've long admired the beautiful clothes you make, and have often wished to meet you. I see that you are an excellent cook too.' She glanced at the table with its trays of cakes and pies.

'Thank you,' Rose said in a surprisingly calm voice. 'I always enjoyed sewing for Miss Amy. I haven't made anything for her for a long time now though. But you and me have met,' she added. 'I don't expect you remember, but I was at a meeting when you spoke to us about women getting the vote.'

'I was too concerned about my talk to really notice who was there,' Felicity said with a laugh. 'But yes, I do remember coming down here to speak once. Though it was a long time ago. All our efforts have been set aside now of course, haven't they. We are all involved in trying to win this terrible war.'

'Do you think it was all wasted then?' Rose said. 'All that throwing stones and that terrible force-feeding that they did to you?'

'No I don't. Women are doing so many vital jobs now that the government is bound to listen to us soon.'

'I hope so,' Rose said. 'We ought to have the vote. I haven't done much for it, not like you, but I believe in it.'

Listening, Dorothy was amazed by her mother's composure. But she was also annoyed by that ridiculous expression, 'Miss Amy', that she had used just now. It reminded her for a moment of Arthur and his subservience. A little crossly she picked up the kettle and went outside to refill it before putting it back on to the flames. A cup of tea would certainly be asked for before long. It was the answer to almost every difficult situation!

There was a slight pause in the conversation and then Felicity said, 'You have probably guessed why I've come here to see you?'

'Yes. I have to see Mr Buxton,' Rose replied at once. 'The letter that Dr Harding left for me said that I was to see him as he's Miss Amy's guardian now.'

Dorothy poked the fire viciously as she heard the offending words again. 'Miss Amy' indeed. What a way to speak of your own daughter!

'Of course,' their guest replied. 'But I felt that we ought to talk a little first and, as I was coming to the Hardings' house to sort out a few things for Amy, I took the opportunity of coming here as well. I do hope you don't mind? My husband doesn't know that I am calling on you.'

'No. No, I don't mind. It's very good of you to come.' Rose turned to Dorothy. 'Dorry, a cup of tea for us all, please.'

While the two women talked Dorothy set cups and saucers on the table, arranged a selection of cakes on the best plate with the best lace doily, and kept a careful watch on her small sister. Christabel was unusually quiet, sitting quite still on a small stool and staring at their visitor. Dorothy devoutly hoped she would continue to be good.

The kettle boiled, the tea was made, and Dorothy poured it out carefully, handing the plate of her mother's freshly made cakes to Mrs Buxton. Then she selected one for Christabel and gave it to her with half a cup of milk. 'Don't make crumbs and don't spill your milk,' she whispered to the child. 'Watch what you're doing.'

Christabel ate the cake in silence, still watching and listening. She finally drank her milk and then asked for some more. When Dorothy poured a little into her cup, Chrissie asked in a piercing voice, 'Who's Amy? They keep on talking about Amy and you look cross, Dorry. Don't you like her?'

Suddenly there was an embarrassed silence in the room and the two women at the table looked at them. Dorothy laughed uncomfortably. 'Yes, of course I like her,' she lied. 'I don't know her very well.'

Felicity came speedily to the rescue. 'Amy may come to see you one day soon,' she said addressing the little girl directly. 'I'm sure that you'll like her.' Then she smiled. 'You'll be able to show her that lovely doll, won't you. What's her name?'

Christabel put her plate and cup down on the hearth and picked up the doll from the armchair. She stood up and moved over to Felicity's side. 'Lucy,' she said. She held her out proudly. 'Does Amy wear frilly dresses like my Lucy?'

'Sometimes,' Felicity replied. 'Your mama used to make very pretty dresses for her when she was small like you, but now she prefers simple ones and suits like mine.'

Chrissy stared at the grey suit and at the little hat that Felicity was still wearing. 'I should like a hat like yours,' she said.

They all laughed and Dorothy felt relieved that things seemed to be going well. Christabel was in one of her more charming moods and was, if anything, making the visit easier.

'Your Lucy is very splendid,' Felicity said. 'May I hold her please?' She held out her hands to the child and to Dorothy's surprise it was not just the doll that she suddenly held, but Chrissy as well. The little girl climbed into her arms so naturally as if they had always known each other. For a time they sat there talking about the doll, looking at her clothes and at the chemise underneath the dress. That, too, had been beautifully stitched by Rose. 'You have a very clever mama,' Felicity said eventually. 'I wish I could sew like that.'

When Chrissy jumped down Felicity turned to Rose. 'What a charming child,' she said. 'I didn't know until today that you had another daughter. And you have chosen a lovely name. Had I had a second daughter, Christabel would have been my choice too.'

'Yes,' Dorothy interrupted quickly, 'Christabel after Miss Pankhurst.'

Felicity laughed. 'Yes of course,' she said. 'She seems very bright. She reminds me so much of my Laura at her age!'

'Well it wasn't so bad was it, Ma?' Dorothy said when their visitor had left. 'I was so busy seeing to things and making sure our Chrissy behaved herself that I didn't hear half of what you were talking about. But Mrs Buxton said that she'd arrange for you to see Mr Buxton in the factory didn't she?'

'Yes. That'll be much better,' Rose said gratefully. 'She's a very nice person, isn't she. And she put me at my ease in spite of things. She'm a real lady. You can always tell someone who got breeding!'

Dorothy sniffed in disgust at this last comment.

'It weren't till she were about to go that I felt guilty. 'Twas when she said about Miss Laura looking like our Chrissy!' Rose continued, 'That brought it home to me. When I thinks about the poor soul in prison being force-fed while I . . .'

Dorothy sighed. 'Oh, Ma. You've got to put all that behind you. Her mentioning Laura was just an ordinary

243

thing to say. Nothing in it.'

'She didn't say nothing else about Chrissy though, so perhaps you'm right. I mean she didn't look at me all superior-like, as some folks do, counting years and months and things.'

'Well she doesn't know when Pa went away does she? I mean he could have come back couldn't he? She obviously thinks that he . . .' Dorothy broke off in mid-sentence and they were both suddenly aware of the child looking at them.

'She said I was like her Laura,' Chrissy interrupted. 'Who's Laura? Can I see her?'

Rose felt the colour flood her face for a moment and she got up and started to clear away the china tea-cups. Then she heard a chuckle from Dorothy.

'One day you might,' Dorothy said. 'But she's a grand young lady, away at a university learning to be very clever.'

'What's a 'versity?'

'A place for rich people.'

'Am I rich?'

'No, my precious. You aren't rich!'

'Is Amy rich?'

'Oh yes she is. Very rich.'

'Is she pretty, Dorry. Is she pretty like you?'

'Just like me, Chrissy. She's just like me!'

Rose turned to look at the two of them and her good nature suddenly deserted her. She heard the bitterness in Dorothy's voice as well as the hint of sarcastic amusement. It was all too much. What was to become of her three girls? Each one was so different and she loved them all, but differently. She couldn't bear to hear Dorothy's resentment whenever Amy was mentioned.

For once she wished for a man to share the burdens, to lean upon, someone strong and capable and with the brains to sort out the tangle. Her Frank wouldn't have been any good and that Geoffrey Buxton was too stern. Poor Dr Harding, now he'd have been able to manage everything! And him dead and all . . . Her thoughts were in as much of a muddle as her life. If she hadn't given Amy away none of this would have happened . . .

She piled the best china on to the tray without her usual care, almost breaking it. 'Be quiet both of you,' she said angrily. 'I've had enough for one day. Just be quiet.'

All the weekend Rose thought about the coming meeting with Geoffrey Buxton. Sometimes she panicked, sometimes she became angry, and now and then, to her own shame she thought of how tall and handsome he was. When these last thoughts persisted she would send up a quick and desperate prayer for forgiveness and for strength to resist such shameful physical desire.

Finally a message was sent through Dorothy that he would be in his office every afternoon the following week if she liked to call at her own convenience.

'My convenience,' Rose said when she read the brief note. 'That's a grand idea. I've never been asked to go anywhere at my convenience. What do it really mean, Dorry?'

'That you can go at a time to suit you. He's being thoughtful!'

'Pity he weren't thoughtful a while back,' she observed dryly. 'Anyway, I'll get it over with. I shall go tomorrow. And I think I'll see him on my own after all. That visit from Mrs Buxton have given me confidence somehow although I don't rightly know why. I won't need you, Dorry. Without Chrissy around I'll be all right.'

She was wearing her one best dress with the cameo brooch prominent at her throat, and a large unfashionable hat when she was shown into the rather drab office that Geoffrey Buxton kept for his own use at the factory. He stood as she entered and when the door had closed behind the perplexed secretary he came round the desk and took one of her hands in both of his.

'Mrs Miller! How nice to see you after all this time,' he said. 'Are you well, and is everything all right?' He lowered his voice. 'You get my . . . I mean you and the child are not in need of anything, I trust?'

'Nothing thank you, Sir. We manage very well, and thank you for what you do.'

'Then we must decide what is best to be done about Amy mustn't we?' he said with a change of tone. He pulled out a chair for her and held it as he would do for any lady; a fact that, to her own annoyance, pleased her greatly.

She sat, arranging her skirts and then she placed her trembling hands in her lap holding them tightly clasped together. 'I'm so sad for her, for Amy,' she said. 'Poor mite.'

Geoffrey laughed and the tension was broken. 'You haven't seen her for quite a time, have you? She's changed a lot, Rose. She is a very self-confident young lady now, and engaged, I'm sure you know, to my son.'

Rose was quiet for a moment. She felt slightly inadequate and useless. She knew that what he said was true so what would Amy want with her? 'Do she really need to know that I'm her ma, Mr Buxton?' she whispered. 'I mean she have got everything she needs, haven't she?'

A strange look crossed his face for a moment. 'Quite so. A child does not always need to know who his or her parents are, as you so rightly suggest. Sometimes it may be better for all concerned if the truth is hidden.'

He paused for a moment and Rose felt herself trembling again. Was he referring to Chrissy? Did he mean that she must never know that he was her father? It was a thought that frequently gave her considerable concern.

If there had been any such reflections in Geoffrey's mind he gave no sign, and Rose stared at him with a measure of resentment. Chrissy was intelligent and one day the questions would start. It was a day she dreaded. She felt suddenly dejected and her body seemed to sag into the chair. But she had come to discuss Amy she reminded herself fiercely. She tried to gather her thoughts together and concentrate on her older child.

'In Amy's case however,' Geoffrey Buxton continued, 'we really have no choice. We can't let her continue her adult life under false pretences. Dr Harding always felt that there would come a time when it was right and proper for her to know all.'

'Does she know already that him and Mrs Harding weren't her rightful parents?'

'Yes. We had to tell her before the will was read. We didn't want it coming out suddenly in front of other people.'

'And what did she say?'

'Well of course she was very shocked and upset and she demanded to know who her real parents were. We told her that she would know in due time, but that we had to protect others as well.'

'You mean me?'

'Yes Rose. You had to be consulted of course.'

'If you think it's right, Mr Buxton, then you tell her. My Dorry won't be pleased, but I think that Miss Amy ought to know. It'll be a shock to her, us being poor and all, but she got a right to know.'

Geoffrey coughed nervously. There was one more thing that he needed to say and it was the most embarrassing part of the whole sorry affair. 'All the money

247

is tied up, Mrs Miller. You do know that don't you? There are trustees.'

Rose felt herself flush with sudden indignation as the meaning of his words dawned upon her. 'Do you really think that I want a penny of hers, Mr Buxton? Is that what you think of me?'

'My dear Mrs Miller, please do forgive me,' he said contritely, using her full name again. 'I had to tell you, but of course I didn't think that you would be influenced by anything other than your love for Amy.'

Suddenly Rose felt tears creeping from her eyes and she hastily brushed them away. 'I do love her, Sir. I've always loved her and I just long to have her back. I know that can't be, but perhaps one day I might be able to help her a bit.'

'It will be difficult for her. You must appreciate that.' Memories of the woman whom Amy had always called Mama suddenly came to Geoffrey. He remembered the lovely Patricia with her aristocratic features and her beautiful clothes, and he looked with infinite compassion on the humble woman before him. 'Don't expect too much too soon, my dear, will you?' he said kindly.

'I don't expect anything, Sir. And I leave it all to you. If you think that she shouldn't know yet, you keep it from her a bit longer. You do just what you think is best.'

'Very well. My wife will know when the right time comes. I shall leave it to her. And as soon as Amy knows we shall tell you. You must be prepared for her to come and see you of course.'

Rose shook her head. 'I don't think she'll want to come for a long while.' There was great sadness in her voice. 'She's too grand a young lady for the likes of me.'

'Don't underestimate yourself. You love her, and we must never hold love cheaply.' Geoffrey looked

248

embarrassed by his own words. 'She is a fortunate girl,' he added. 'Very fortunate indeed to have had the love of not just two parents but three. Try to look at it like that.'

He smiled at her and then stood up, indicating that the interview was at an end. 'My thanks to you, Rose, for everything,' he said. 'I think of you often, you know.'

She couldn't look at him. More flustered than she had ever been she too stood, longing now to be outside, longing desperately for a cup of tea. 'Thank you,' she murmured. 'Thank you, Sir.'

He walked to the door and paused for a moment. 'You are a very brave woman,' he said quietly. 'Take care of yourself, my dear, and of Christabel.'

Then he opened the door and was once more the efficient businessman. 'Goodbye, Mrs Miller, and thank you for coming.'

'Will you be free to come to us for Christmas, my dear?' Felicity asked one bright December day when Amy, with a few hours off-duty, had come over for the afternoon and evening.

'Sorry, Aunt. I only have two days' leave due to me and I've said that I'll take them some other time. I shall work on Christmas Day so that someone who has a family can be free.'

As soon as she had spoken the words she realized that they sounded unkind. Felicity and Geoffrey were constantly telling her that she must regard their home as hers and that she was as good as a daughter to them. 'I mean,' she stammered, 'I thought that I'd save up a few days for Clifford's leave.'

Felicity smiled. 'Of course,' she said. 'He'll be home in the new year, I expect.'

Amy sighed and replaced her delicate china cup on its saucer. She paused for a moment and looked at

Felicity and then she stared unseeing at the glowing coals in the grate. 'Before he comes home I must know who my real parents are,' she said in a low hesitant voice. 'You promised me that you would tell me. Please, Aunt, can you not do so now?'

It was Felicity's turn to look troubled. 'If it continues to worry you, my dear, then perhaps the time has come,' she said. 'We both wanted you to be stronger and more able to cope with another new situation before we allowed you to know. And we had to see your . . . your mother and make sure that she was happy about it.'

'And have you done that?'

'Yes.'

'What did she say?'

'That she left the decision to us. She assured us that she loved you and has always done so.'

Amy took a deep breath. She had to come to terms with the fact that she had a mother again, an unknown woman, someone who said that she loved her. That she had a duty to meet her, even if only once. These were all deeply troublesome emotions. 'Do you think I should know, then?' she asked, suddenly unsure.

'I don't think you'll be at peace until you do know, until you have met her and I think that she too longs for it.'

She was reminded of the other and far more frightening thought. 'Is there a father? I mean do I have a father too?' A woman was a simpler matter to cope with, but her papa was too precious to be replaced. Amy had come to terms with Patricia's death. That had been some years ago now, but Papa was a very dear and living memory. She wanted no other man to call Father. And parents had control over you. Her heat beat furiously as she considered all the terrifying possibilities.

'Will my real parents have any rights over me, Aunt?

I'm not even twenty until New Year's Day and that leaves a whole year before I become of age.'

'Your papa thought of that, my dear. In his will, as you know, he specifically says that Geoffrey is to be your guardian until 1st January 1918. And all your money is tied up until then, so you need not worry.'

'But is it legal? I've been thinking about it and reading a bit about the law. There's no legal adoption in England is there, so I suppose that really my name is wrong. I should still have their name.'

'I don't think you need worry about that. When you've met the lady who was your first mother, your fears will all disappear. And as for your father, well he need not concern you at the moment. You have nothing to worry about there I assure you, Amy.'

'First mother!' Amy repeated the words. Suddenly she felt sick with apprehension. Yet perhaps it was better to know everything rather than to go on imagining all sorts of things. Nothing could be worse than the possibilities she'd been conjuring up for herself. Sometimes her mother was, in her mind, a criminal, a murderer even. Could that be why they were keeping it from her? Or was she mad, unable to raise her child? Had they told her that she was dead, perhaps it might have been more acceptable. A living flesh-and-blood woman whom she would have to confront was almost unthinkable.

She got up and went to the window. 'Could you tell me tonight before I go back to the hospital?' she said, not looking at Felicity as she spoke. She kept her eyes focused on the tall trees in the garden and she noticed the late afternoon sun shining through their bare brown branches and on to the wet grass beneath.

'I think we must. I shall talk to your uncle when he comes in, and . . . yes, my dear. I think we must.'

Suddenly Amy longed to be alone in the cold fresh air, to walk and walk until her brain cleared and she could make some sort of sense of all the traumatic events of the past weeks. 'I should like to walk on the Downs for a time, on my own if you wouldn't mind,' she said.

'Of course.' Felicity rang for the tea things to be cleared away. 'I have some letters to write. Don't go far, will you. It gets dark so quickly now.' Her voice was matter-of-fact, but underpinned with compassion and understanding.

Amy turned and kissed her lightly on the cheek. 'You are wonderful, Aunt Felicity,' she said. 'I could never have coped without you.'

'Fiddlesticks!' Felicity said brightly trying to dispel the gloom. 'Get along with you.'

Amy walked for more than an hour, deeply troubled by everything that had happened to her. She felt almost as if her parents had been taken from her twice over. And as if, having recently felt so much surer of herself, that had been taken from her too. She was not herself any more. Even her feelings for Clifford seemed to be undergoing a change. Amy Harding had been in love with him, but Amy Harding no longer existed. She walked to the great Suspension Bridge and stared down into the mud at the edge of the river far below. People had plunged to their deaths here. She shivered and turned purposefully away and started to retrace her steps back to the bright lights and the security of the Buxton home.

As she walked she thought of Laura. She longed for her friend. It was only to Laura that she felt she could really unburden all her worries. But she was away, unable to come home until the Christmas vacation and, although that was quite soon now, there were still many days before they could be together. She had poured some of her agony into the long letters that travelled regularly between Cambridge and Bristol but she was aware that her friend had her own life to lead now, an exciting life full of new experiences and new friends.

There were letters too from the Front, but Amy felt that Clifford had enough of his own worries without being burdened with hers. Perhaps when she saw him again she could talk to him about her problems, but she deliberately hid them from him at the moment. Each letter she wrote to him was full of false cheerfulness. She told him only the bare facts and allowed him to think that she was managing to overcome all her worries. And she resolutely managed to keep her secret dread from slipping into the pages. Would he still want to marry her now that she wasn't whom she had always claimed to be?

Tears filled her eyes as she turned the last corner on her way back to the house, and there, unexpectedly, was Myrtle hurrying along the road too.

'Good day, Miss,' the maid said cheerfully. 'I haven't seen you for a long time.'

'I don't get much time off. There are too many wounded soldiers coming into Bristol now. A hospital train arrives almost every night!'

Myrtle's smile faded. 'Terrible, ain't it. An' they said it would be all over by Christmas and that was more'n two years ago, and still there seems no end of it all!'

Amy pretended to blow her nose and surreptitiously wiped her tears away. She tried to put her own worries and griefs aside for a moment. She had long ago discovered that to think of others was sometimes a way of dealing temporarily with her own hurts.

'How are you liking it here with Mr and Mrs Buxton?' she asked.

'Oh, Miss, it's lovely. She's a lovely lady, Mrs Buxton, and so kind. Not that I weren't very happy in your house of course,' she added hastily. 'But after your dear mother got 'erself drowned in that *Titanic* and you went away it was a bit quiet like. Here there's

253

always something going on, and Miss Laura be fun too. She'll be home for the holidays soon.'

'Yes. I'm looking forward to seeing her again and hearing all about Cambridge.'

A dreamy look crossed Myrtle's face. 'I bet she'll be clever now, up there with all that learning!'

Amy smiled. 'Yes. I expect she will. We shall have to be careful not to say anything silly, shan't we, Myrtle!'

'Oh, you wouldn't say anything silly, not with all your schooling!'

'I'm not so sure. I was never very clever you know.'

The two girls had reached the house and Amy prepared to go to the front door, but then seeing Myrtle walk round the side, she followed her. 'I'll come in the back entrance,' she said a little embarrassed. 'I've got muddy boots.' She still felt guilty about all the differences there were between them, about the gulf that her position created.

Once inside Myrtle turned to her, 'I'll be happy to come back if you want to open up your own house again, Miss,' she said. 'I hope I didn't sound ungrateful when I told you how I liked it here.'

'Thank you,' Amy replied. 'But no, Myrtle. I don't think I shall live down there in City Road again. Well, not permanently. It has too many memories.' She didn't add that she had heard from Geoffrey that the house might not even be hers. A cousin in America was contesting the will. It felt as if every last shred of her former life were being taken away from her.

She could eat very little of the sumptuous dinner that had been prepared and she felt guilty once more, for there was little good food to be found in the shops now, and she knew that Felicity had asked Cook to make a special effort on her behalf.

'I'm so sorry, Aunt,' she said as her plate was borne away to the kitchen with half of the chicken and roast potatoes still on it. 'It was lovely, but I can't eat much lately.'

'Don't worry, my dear,' Felicity said. 'It will all be made into soup tomorrow no doubt!'

When at last the meal was finished and they were comfortably seated round a blazing fire in the drawing room, Amy glanced from Geoffrey to Felicity and she wondered if they were aware of the thumping of her heart and the panic that was beginning to rise in her chest.

Geoffrey coughed nervously and took another sip of brandy. Then he set the glass down and looked at Amy. 'I think the time has come to talk a little more, my dear,' he said. 'There are lots of things we have to discuss.'

CHAPTER ELEVEN

Amy awoke sluggishly on the first day of 1917 as though something deep inside her was loath to remember that it was her twentieth birthday. Each year since her mother had drowned she had thought about her on this special day, about the composed, beautiful Patricia she had worshipped. But now, this morning, there was a self-imposed blank where the precious memory had been. The silver-framed photograph was gone from beside her bed, put away in anger, just as she hoped to blot the likeness from her mind. For Patricia had deceived her horribly, allowed her to think that she was born the heir to gentility and privilege. Her life had been a lie!

Instead, now, she must think about Rose Miller, her dressmaker, the cheerful little sewing woman whom she had known for years. Rose Miller, her mother!

She washed herself briefly with cold water from the chipped jug on the washstand and pulled on her uniform. Another day of harrowing toil on the wards awaited her and she was glad of it, relieved because she would not have time to think, to consider what to do, and she could put off for a little longer the visit that must soon be made.

And Clifford was home. Just yesterday he had arrived for seven days' leave and he was coming to see her tonight. In spite of her agony of mind the prospect lent a slight spring to her step as she rushed over to the nurses' dining room for a quick breakfast before the long hours of work began. But thoughts of Clifford were also compounded with doubt and concern. Would he want to marry her now? And even more frightening, did she still want to marry him? The kernel of disquiet had grown gradually and surely in her mind ever since the day she had heard the full details of her birth. She had written to him, a long letter infinitely difficult to compose and there had been no answer, probably because the post was so erratic. She kept telling herself that was the reason. Tonight she would know.

Laura of course had been all common sense. She had declared that it made no difference at all to their friendship, and that the parents who brought a child up were more important than the natural ones. Amy wasn't too sure. And she understood at last why she could never attain the calm cool beauty of her mother . . . mother?

She had no true sense of herself any longer, let alone of her mother. It was as if she were someone else, some unknown girl with no roots and no true place in any sort of background. She stared at herself frequently now in the chipped mirror that was fastened to the wall in the comfortless shared bedroom, but it was not to check her appearance. It was to look critically at this stranger who peered back at her with the remembered eyes of Dorothy Miller, the girl whom she had long feared in an uncanny way, the girl who probably hated her, her twin sister.

The memory that had returned vividly with Geoffrey's words was of the fourteen-year-old Dorothy who had come to her front door demanding to speak with her father. Amy recalled, with intense shame, her feelings on that day, and the revulsion which Dorothy must have sensed in the spoilt child that Amy now firmly believed herself to have been. Surely there could be little understanding or love between herself and Dorothy?

She picked at her breakfast, forcing the thick lumpy porridge into her mouth, washing it down with cups of sweet strong tea. And when it was finished she went into the ward and looked with extra compassion at the rows of young men lying there waiting for her smile and her gentle ministering hands.

As each hour passed she became more nervous. Clifford had sent a brief message to say that he would call for her in the family motor car and they would find a small hotel for a birthday dinner.

At last it was time to get ready and she removed her starched white apron and took the outfit that she had selected for the evening from its wraps in the communal cupboard. She had brought a suit back from her last day's leave especially for this evening and she looked at it critically wondering if it would be suitable. The skirt was long and straight made in a thick amethyst-coloured wool, and the matching coat had a smart edging of slightly darker satin. There was a scarf to match and gloves, long warm gloves in soft leather. Her blouse was high to the neck and the only frills on it were small ones round the collar and cuffs. There was a hat too, small and neat, chosen for her by Felicity and far more expensive than its size warranted. She laid the things on the bed and after she had washed, she brushed out her hair and then pinned it up at the nape of her neck. She fixed it more loosely than usual so that it should frame her face, for she had lost weight and there were shadows beneath her eyes. The soft cloud of curls helped to hide the pallor and the signs of worry. Her roommates were on duty and she was grateful that she had the room to herself for once. She couldn't do with sly remarks and crude jokes just now.

When Clifford drove the Rover up to the entrance of the great house, he stopped it dramatically just as she opened the door. For a moment they were quite still looking at each other and then she was in his arms. 'You look beautiful,' he said.

She returned his kiss, but it was a formal embrace and there seemed to be an embarrassment between them. He settled her in the motor car, tucked a rug about her, and then they drove away to the small country hotel he had chosen. He concentrated on driving and there was little conversation between them. She couldn't bring herself to ask the questions that burned in her mind and he seemed to find it difficult to broach the subject they were both thinking about. Even over the meal they only talked about ordinary things.

When they arrived back at the hospital he pulled the motor into the shadow of a line of bushes well away from the light that shone from the windows. He took her cold hands in his. 'You were a goose,' he whispered, 'to think that it would make any difference to me. I don't care who your parents were. I love you and you are still you. You are still Amy Harding whatever you feel.' His words were troubled and he held her hands tightly. 'When I had your letter I couldn't believe some of the things you said. I wanted to rush over and tell you how precious you are, that nothing has changed.'

Amy shivered with the January cold and moved away from him. 'I don't feel the same,' she replied. 'Don't you understand? Whatever you say, Clifford, everything has changed, for me it has anyway. My adoption isn't even legal. There never was any adoption in fact. There is nothing in the law that says I am the person I believed myself to be. I am officially not me. I am Amy Miller and my mother is a sewing woman and my father works in a Ford factory somewhere in Canada. I have a twin sister who probably hates me and I possibly have no money. If I am not who I am then even my mother's money may not be mine.'

There was a silence all about them, broken only by the wind in the tall trees lining the long drive to the beautiful grey stone house. It had been requisitioned as an army hospital and the lights twinkling from each window only served to remind Amy of the men inside, most of them glad of their wounds, glad for a reason to be out of the trenches, to be safe whatever the suffering. She was suddenly full of fear for Clifford. Yet there was a coldness in her heart that she couldn't understand and that she wished was not there.

'The money means nothing, Amy. What you have or do not have is of no concern whatever to me.'

His words, meant to calm and reassure, made her suddenly angry instead. 'How can you say that, Clifford Buxton?' she demanded. Then she paused and with her free hand stroked the smooth leather of the car upholstery. 'Of course I know how you can say it. You've never been short of money have you, never wanted for anything? Well neither have I, but I've seen what the lack of it does to a person. You can't live in St Paul's without seeing that. To be poor is utterly degrading. Poverty destroys. Money is not nothing. Oh no. And I won't be dependent on anyone, Clifford, not even you. If I can't come to you on my terms then I won't come at all.'

She surprised herself with the words. They were not what she had intended to say and sounded more like Laura, more like his sister with her fierce independence. She could feel his shock.

Amy had always vowed that she wanted a rich husband. That had been the pinnacle of her ambitions. Yet of course she had always taken for granted the fact that she would be rich herself. Like her mother and her Aunt Felicity she would have means of her own and would never be dependent on any man. To have your own money meant power and freedom. Now that her father's will was being contested she feared she would lose her possessions in addition to her name, and she had come to realize that if she wanted independence she would have to work for it like so many others, like Dorothy Miller in fact.

Clifford was looking at her without comprehension. 'You've allowed all this to change you too much,' he said. 'I know it's been terrible for you, but I still love you, Amy,' he repeated. 'That hasn't altered.' He leaned towards her and kissed her gently on the lips, but there was nothing of passion in him now and she could not respond. She felt dried-up, shrivelled. She even doubted his words. For the first time she doubted his love.

'We've both changed.' There was infinite sadness in her words. 'We're not the same two people at all. You're different too. I can feel it.'

They sat side by side in the motor each aware of the other and yet not touching, both wrapped in the experiences of the past weeks. Their totally different sufferings seemed to have made a rift between them rather than drawn them together.

'Yes.' Clifford spoke the one word and it seemed to Amy to have some awful significance. 'Yes, I have changed. You can't spend months in the trenches and not come out changed.' He looked away from her across the peaceful lawn streaked silver now in the moonlight. 'I've seen my friends blown to pieces beside me, I've seen dead men left to rot. That's what happens every day out there.' His voice was hard and without feeling as if he had suddenly removed himself from her, as if he were not aware of her presence any more. 'And the mud,' he went on, 'can you imagine living in mud up to your middle and lice all over your body, with rats running over you at night? Great fat obscene creatures coming out of the darkness, feeding on the dead and just waiting for you to die too? There was one particular lad in my company, only just eighteen, he . . .'

'Stop it!' Amy screamed putting her hands over her ears. 'Stop it do you hear.' Then she turned to him and gripped his shoulders and started to shake him, anything to bring him back to her, back to the quiet night, to present reality. But he failed to react and when she looked at him in the bright moonlight she was frightened by what she saw in his eyes: a blankness that had never been there before, but which she recognized. She had experienced it in others, in shell-shocked men coming off the ambulance trains at Temple Meads, and in young soldiers struggling to cope with the terrible memories they could not banish either from their waking hours or from their dreams. She put her arms round him then and held him close to her and gradually she felt him relax, but there was no spark, and eventually she sat up desperate to get away, to be alone. Her relationship with Clifford had always been a strength. Now it had become a source of unrest. She tried to speak normally. 'I must go, Clifford,' she said. 'I've an early start tomorrow.'

'Shall I see you again?'

The question startled her. That he should even say such a thing was frightening. 'I . . . I don't know. Yes if you like.'

He was silent for a time, considering. 'I'll come over at the weekend,' he said eventually. 'You've got Saturday off I believe.'

'Yes. Just the one day.'

'Ten o'clock then.'

They both climbed out of the motor and stood facing each other. He took her hands in his. 'It'll be all right,' he said. 'You'll see. Everything will be all right in the end.'

Then he took her in his arms again and kissed her, but as before there was no flicker of emotion between them. She turned as he released her and ran back towards the house and at the door she stopped and raised her hand to wave. But he was not looking. He was cranking the engine, again and again, until at last the great vehicle groaned into life and she saw its brilliant lights pierce the darkness. She stood and watched as he turned the Rover expertly and drove slowly out of the gates. She remained there motionless until the noise of the engine had died away in the distance leaving only the spine-chilling sound of an owl hooting to its mate in the tall trees above her head, and the wind still blowing through the swaying branches. She shivered and went inside, closing the heavy oak door on all her dreams.

Clifford drove as fast as he dared. His father had at last allowed him to take the vehicle out on his own. There was no chauffeur now anyway. Even his mother drove herself. The Rover would do over forty miles an hour but on the long winding country road he only dared take it to twenty in spite of his mood. Driving still needed every ounce of concentration he could muster and released him a little from his thoughts. He eventually reached the streets of Clifton and parked in the drive of his parents' home, but it was still early and he couldn't face anyone yet. Without going into the house he started to walk down towards the centre of the town.

Park Street was fairly quiet at this time in the evening and he stared blankly at the shop fronts. There were a few couples strolling up the hill, most of the men in uniform, and as he heard their laughter, sensed their joy in each other, he felt a great sense of loneliness and discord.

He walked round College Green aimlessly and then on to the Tramway Centre where he stared at the steamer that was docked at the quayside. He was suddenly consumed with a desire to get away and disappear for ever, away from the war, away even from Amy. The thought disturbed him and as he walked bleakly towards the more doubtful streets around the Haymarket, he wondered for a moment if he should find himself a woman. It would be his first time. There were dire warnings about things one could catch, pass on to loved ones, and he had always thought of Amy and resisted. Now he found himself sweating profusely as forbidden thoughts and desires whirled round and round in his head and his loins burned with a fierce unrest.

He walked on with no real idea of where he was going and eventually found himself in Old Market Street. There he looked with distaste at the sleazy shops and the people standing round the pub. Some of them stared at him and he wished he were in uniform. It was a kind of safety.

'Want a white feather, sonny?' A tiny knot of fear gathered in Clifford's stomach as he heard the words thrown at him sarcastically from a woman who was draped round the brawny figure of a young man in a private's uniform. There was a threat in her voice and he shivered and turned down a side street that took him back towards the Tramway Centre.

Slightly out of breath, he stopped outside the Hippodrome and stared at the pictures displayed there. He had never seen a Music Hall performance. His father strongly disapproved of all forms of theatre and in his childhood he had not been allowed to go. On sudden impulse he strode up the steps and bought a ticket. At least this wasn't as open to criticism as finding a woman. He was saved. Saved from the need to prove himself! He slid into the anonymity of the nearest empty seat and thankfully gave himself up to the glitter and the noise.

For the next few days Clifford said little to his

parents. When it was necessary to be indoors he kept
to his room as much as possible and during the day he
walked miles in the winter sunshine. He noticed his
mother's worried face but was incapable of talking to
her as he used to do. Dreams of battle filled his unquiet
nights and frequently he would wake up sweating profusely, seeing in the moonlight that streamed through
his window the faces of dead friends or slaughtered
enemies.

Sometimes when he walked in the country he saw,
instead of the peaceful English fields, the mud of the
trenches. The graceful oak trees became the trees of
France, blasted and torn. And there were horses and
mules in the black places of his mind, too. He seemed
to see them there at the roadsides, scores of them with
great distended bellies and stiff legs pointing skyward,
their vacant eyes staring reproachfully.

Frequently he stumbled, for there had been gales
recently, bringing down trees and branches, and often
when he encountered such an obstruction he would
swear and curse – thinking for one panic-filled moment
that it was a corpse, tommy or Boche, no matter which.
Then reality would return and he wondered how he
could bring himself to live through the rest of his leave
in the bright brittle world of his parents' home. These
seven days had seemed so precious, so much longed
for, and now he actually wished them gone. The smell
of battle had got into his blood, permeated his flesh,
and the horror and the dying had become so much part
of life that to enter for a short space of time into an
environment of casual nothingness was just another
sort of hell.

One afternoon towards the end of the week, Clifford
had been out walking most of the day, not returning
for lunch, just walking blankly without plan or thought.
Only when the weak afternoon sun disappeared behind

the trees did he turn for home, as automatically as though he were a puppet propelled along without any conscious thought. As he entered the house he heard a Chopin nocturne being played very badly on the grand piano. The sound seemed to reach him as nothing else could. He threw down his coat and burst into the drawing room. 'What an awful row,' he shouted at Laura who was sitting there with a frown of concentration on her face.

She looked up at him and laughed. 'Come and show me how to do it then, brother dear,' she said. 'I need to have it perfect for next term.'

He pulled up a chair beside her and they sat for an hour and at the end of it he too was actually laughing, the mists were beginning to clear.

'And Amy?' Laura said gently as they closed the piano. 'Something is wrong isn't it? Can you talk?'

He was silent for a while, shocked by her question. Then he spoke slowly, considering each word. 'She needs time. Perhaps we rushed into our engagement. We had known each other for so long and subconsciously thought that it was expected of us I suppose. We both need time.' He wanted to say more, wanted to say that he loved her, that she was necessary to him, but the words failed to come and Laura smiled at him. She took his hand and squeezed it companionably.

'It'll come all right, eventually,' she said, echoing words he remembered saying to Amy. 'You'll see.'

The following day as Clifford walked down into town once more and through the busy streets of St Paul's, he wasn't sure what strange compulsion took him there. Perhaps he wanted to see Amy's roots, to try to help her come to terms with all that had happened. They were to spend the whole of Saturday together and he wasn't sure how he would cope, or how best to comfort her. He stopped eventually in front of the familiar house, her old home, shuttered and closed now, and he sighed a little, remembering the happy unburdened times.

'Mr Buxton, isn't it?'

He turned, startled, and then stared with amazement at the girl who was addressing him. It was Amy, another bolder brighter Amy standing there looking at him with obvious surprise and pleasure. Then recognition dawned and he smiled at her and held out his hand.

'You must be . . .' He realized that he had forgotten her name and hoped that she would quickly supply it.

'Dorothy Miller,' she said taking the proffered hand and shaking it briefly.

He noticed her embarrassment and the way colour flooded her face. 'Of course,' he said. 'Your mother is the dressmaker.'

'You mean Amy's dressmaker,' she replied. 'Yes, she used to make her clothes.'

They both stood awkwardly not knowing what to say, each wondering how much the other knew.

Clifford broke the embarrassed silence. 'Has Amy been to see you?' he asked.

Dorothy stared at him. 'So you know,' she said. 'I guessed you would. I suppose that's why you are down here, to have a look at her beginnings.' She couldn't help feeling a twinge of sarcasm, but she hoped that it didn't show in her voice. 'No, she hasn't called on us yet,' she continued evenly. 'Ma is hoping she'll come soon but I'm not too sure that I am. Having a twin sister thrust upon me isn't going to be easy.'

'No. I don't suppose it is. Not for her either. I haven't known for long. She wrote to me, to France.'

'I've known for years,' Dorothy said. 'But I didn't expect it all to turn out like this, her being an orphan, I mean.'

'That's an odd way to look at it.'

'What do you mean?' Dorothy's voice was sharp and anxious.

Clifford smiled at her and so dispelled her rising antagonism. 'I'm not really sure what I mean,' he said. 'It's all a bit of a muddle, isn't it?'

Dorothy glanced up at the tall handsome figure in the immaculate uniform, and realized that she had yet another reason to envy this sister of hers. She had fantasized about this man for years, but it had only been a sort of dream. There had never been any substantial hope in her feelings. Yet here he was standing close to her, talking to her, smiling at her. She felt the hot blood rushing to her face and her heart beat an unwelcome tattoo inside her body. She groped for something to say, something that would return her feelings to normal and make her capable of sensible conversation.

'It's terrible of course, Dr Harding getting killed like that,' she said faintly.

'Yes. It was a great shock. Somehow one feels that a doctor will be safe, even at the Front.'

There was a pause and Dorothy felt suddenly that she wished to get away. 'This is my dinner hour,' she managed, 'I don't have long. I shall have to go.'

For Clifford the encounter was a strange one. The two sisters were so alike that he almost felt that it was Amy to whom he was speaking and he couldn't help noting her twin's intelligence. Although he had not come to St Paul's for that reason, he wanted to find out more about this girl and her mother too. Perhaps he might be able to help Amy accept this strange background a little if he came to terms with it himself.

'May I walk a little way with you,' he asked. 'Do you live far?'

Dorothy was surprised at the request, and in spite of her need to compose herself she was, nevertheless, flattered. 'Just a couple of streets away,' she managed.

'And yes, of course you can walk along with me. I shall be proud.'

Clifford laughed. 'Of my uniform you must mean. I thought I'd better wear it. I was offered a white feather the other night.'

'How awful. Did you tell them you were a . . .'

'Lieutenant? No. I don't think the young lady and her friends were in any mood to believe me. I removed myself as quickly as I could. I went to the Hippodrome actually.'

They fell into step and conversation between them eventually became easy and spontaneous. Clifford found himself laughing at some of the things she said, and by the time Dorothy stopped in front of the small gate of her home, he was feeling better than he had done for some time.

'Would you like to come in and meet Ma and have a cup of tea?' Dorothy asked on impulse.

'Are you sure your mother wouldn't mind?'

The invitation had been speedily given and Dorothy suddenly had second thoughts as it dawned upon her that Clifford and Chrissy were half-brother and sister, but she couldn't change her mind now. 'Ma will be thrilled,' she said. 'We don't often get officers round here.'

He grinned at her. 'I can see that my uniform will get me all sorts of privileges!'

'It'll get you one of Ma's meat-pies for sure,' she declared. 'She was going to make some today. That's why I've come home for dinner. I often stay and work.'

Dorothy pushed open the front door and called loudly. 'Ma. Mr Clifford Buxton to see you.'

Clifford stepped carefully over the brass step and into the narrow hallway. He suddenly felt too big for such a small house.

'This is my mother,' Dorothy said, as a comfortable little woman appeared at the end of the passage. She was patting her hair nervously into place and he was immediately reminded of Amy. It was a gesture he had seen frequently.

'How do you do, Mrs Miller?' He drew off his gloves and held out his hand to her.

'I'm pleased to see you, Mr Buxton,' Rose said. She was obviously ill-at-ease and wondering what he was doing here.

'Mr Buxton met me on my way home,' Dorothy explained. 'He knows about Amy, Ma, and I thought that he'd like to come and meet you.'

'Yes, well. That was a nice idea. You and Miss Amy are engaged to be married aren't you?'

Dorothy felt a stab of pain at the words. She knew, of course, had known for a long time, but with Clifford standing right here in their little house just about to sit down and eat one of Ma's pies . . . it hurt her so much she almost wanted to cry out.

'Yes, we are,' Clifford said. 'We've known each other since we were children.'

'Are you to wed soon then?' Rose busied herself clearing the table as she spoke and Dorothy hated her mother for asking the question.

'There are no plans,' he replied. 'We may wait until the war is over.'

Dorothy was anxious to change the subject and she realized that she hadn't made her visitor very much at home yet. 'Shall I take your cap and cane and things,' she said nervously. 'I'll put them on the hall-stand. There doesn't seem to be much room in here. It's always cluttered when Ma's sewing.'

'It's very nice,' he said and he surprised himself by really meaning the words. There was a clean homely warmth about everything and he settled himself in the large chair which Rose indicated, and spread out his hands to the warmth of the fire. He watched Dorothy as she took off her coat and set the room to rights.

Her figure beneath the rather ugly outer garment was slim and attractive and he noticed her hands and the long artistic fingers. She should be a pianist he thought. There was a sensitivity about her that was wonderfully pleasing. Then he was suddenly surprised as a small child burst into the room. She stopped uncertainly as soon as she saw him.

'Come here Chrissy and meet Mr Buxton.' Dorothy spoke firmly to the little girl. 'He won't eat you.'

She turned to him to explain. 'She doesn't meet many men. My brother is away in France and Pa works in the Ford Motor Company in Canada. So we're an all-female household at the moment.'

Clifford tried to hide his surprise. He had no idea that there was another sister. Amy hadn't mentioned her. 'Hello, Chrissy,' he said, smiling.

Her eyes widened and there were tear drops on her long lashes. She looked at him for a moment and then ran to her mother. 'I've made a hole in my stockings, Mam,' she said pulling up her frock to show the damage. 'Look. I fell down.'

'Never fear, lovey,' Rose said gently. 'I'll mend it for you as soon as we've had our dinner. Are you hurt?'

'No, I'm not hurt.' The child lowered her skirt and peeped again at Clifford.

Suddenly she reminded him vividly of Laura. 'I have a sister who used to fall down and make holes in her stockings,' he told her.

Chrissy ventured a step in his direction. 'Was your mam cross with her?'

He laughed. 'Not usually. My sister is called Laura. She was always climbing trees and falling off.'

'Does she climb trees now?'

'No, not now. She's quite grown up.'

Chrissy stood still, obviously taking in this information and Clifford looked at her and turned to Rose.

'She reminds me rather of Laura, the same big brown eyes and straight hair.'

'Dorry puts my hair in rags sometimes,' Chrissy said, anxious not to be put at a disadvantage. 'Then I have curls like her and Mam.' She thought for a moment and then asked, 'Have you got any more brothers or sisters?'

'No. No more.' As he spoke smilingly at Chrissy he failed to see the look that passed between Dorothy and her mother.

He drank the tea and ate the delicious meat-pie that was offered to him and when it was time for Dorothy to go back to work, he said that he must go too and would walk with her to the factory.

'I like your mother,' he remarked when they were once more outside in the January cold. 'Shall I tell Amy that I've visited her?'

'If you think it will do any good. The meeting between them is bound to be difficult don't you think?'

'Of course. But life isn't easy anyway.'

'What do you mean, life isn't easy? For you, you mean, or for everyone?'

Aware of the poverty of the streets around him, he didn't answer at once and he sensed a bleakness in Dorothy's words. At last he said, 'It's hard for most people just now. I rejoin my regiment in two days' time.'

'I'm sorry. It's pretty terrible isn't it?'

'Yes. It's pretty terrible.'

'Are you frightened to go back?'

He turned to look at her. It wasn't a question many people dared to ask, but she met his eyes and he felt a concern in the words.

'Fear is relative,' he replied thoughtfully. 'Yes I suppose I am frightened, but once you're out there a kind of unreasoning confidence takes over. Everything is so monstrous that you almost stop thinking about it as

273

relating to yourself. It's like . . .' He groped for words. 'It's like being in a play.'

He was very much aware of her at his side. She kept in step with him and he felt a certain comfort in her presence. She demanded nothing of him and he felt relaxed and peaceful in spite of the subject of their conversation.

'I've read some plays, but I've never seen one,' she said.

'Nor have I, apart from those we did at school. I remember we did one of Shakespeare's in which the king says something about summoning up the blood and disguising fair nature with hard favoured rage. Going over the top is a bit like that. It's a quite irrational rage against the Hun that carries you into that gunfire.'

'That's *Henry V*,' she said. 'I know that bit.'

He turned to her in amazement. 'You read Shakespeare?'

'Yes. Is there any reason why I shouldn't?'

He was embarrassed by the rebuke. 'No. No, of course not but . . .'

'I work in a factory and live in the slums so I shouldn't know Shakespeare. Is that what you mean?'

'Of course I don't mean that,' he said hurriedly. 'And you don't live in the slums. You live in a very nice house. Yet . . . well, it is a bit unusual isn't it, to read things like that for pleasure?'

'I suppose so,' she admitted, softening a little. 'I was determined to get educated you see. I had to leave school at fourteen to earn some money. I had no idea how to start learning things. A friend gave me a copy of Shakespeare's Comedies for my birthday and then I found an old copy of the complete works in a pawn shop, and lots of other books too.' For a moment she thought of Arthur and that long-ago present. It was still precious to her. 'I don't understand a lot that I

274

read,' she continued. 'But some things are good, and I write too.'

'Write?' He looked at her with renewed interest.

'Yes, stories and things. I've started on a book.'

'You don't mean you're published?'

'I wouldn't waste my time writing for nothing,' she stated bluntly. 'I've had a lot of stories in magazines and a serial.'

'Gosh, I don't believe it!'

Dorothy laughed at him, all her nervousness gone. 'Well it's true. You're talking to a real live author!' Her voice was full of pride.

'What an incredible girl you are,' Clifford said. 'It's you who should have been educated, not Amy. She has no ambitions.'

'So I've heard. I wanted to be a teacher a long time ago.'

'Can't it be managed?'

'There's no chance now. But I'm happy, and I'd rather be a writer. People seem to think more of writers than teachers, and I might make more money one day.'

They both laughed and then walked in silence for a time, busy with their own thoughts. It was a comfortable silence. Neither felt the need for words.

Then Dorothy spoke. 'I shall think of you, and pray for you too,' she said, suddenly serious.

He turned to look at her but she was staring ahead and he could see the colour rising in her face. He was all at once startled by the dawning impression that this girl could become important to him. More than that he dared not acknowledge. He was overwhelmed and considerably shaken by the discovery.

'Thank you. I shall need your prayers,' he murmured. 'Will you write to me? Can you spare time from your other kind of writing? Letters are precious out there. And letters from "a real live author",' he quoted, 'those would be special!' He tried to make the words sound amusing and casual.

They had reached the factory. Dorothy walked past the main gate and he was aware of many pairs of eyes staring at them as countless girls streamed through. Seeing the boss's son with one of the clerks was something to be much talked about.

'I work in the office as you know, I expect,' she said. 'I don't use that entrance.' There was pride in her voice again. 'I like my job. It's fairly responsible. I'm in charge of all the workers' insurance cards. I have to interview the girls sometimes and I buy the stamps each week and put them on the cards.' Then she laughed, 'Why am I telling you this? You used to come round now and then with your father, didn't you, before you joined up. I saw you sometimes.' She hoped that he didn't realize how much those visits had meant to her in those early days, how much she had dreamed of him then.

They had stopped now at the main door to the office. 'Are you going to take over one day?' she asked.

A bleak look crossed his face. 'My father wants me to of course, but it's not my choice. I want to be a musician.' There was no time for more discussion and Clifford looked at the girl beside him and wondered for a terrible paralyzing moment if he would ever see her again. 'You haven't answered my question,' he said. 'Will you write to me?'

'You're engaged to Amy, my sister. It wouldn't be correct.'

'Please Dorothy. Just once perhaps. May I call you Dorothy?'

'Yes,' she said. 'Call me that, and I will write. Just once.' She stared up at him, locked in a precious moment of time.

He took her hand and pressed it in his and then he turned and walked quickly away and he felt that he had left his heart behind him. Yet his spirit soared with the joy of it. The complications, for a few fleeting seconds, meant nothing. That brief snatched hour with Dorothy had imparted a new and a strange sense of optimism. Instead of the blackness there seemed to be hope, a silver lining behind the dark clouds. He started to hum the popular song to himself as he strode back towards the Tramway Centre, back up Park Street, back towards tomorrow, tomorrow and Amy.

CHAPTER TWELVE

With Clifford away at the Front, Amy worried about him constantly and frequently pondered over their last day together. They had driven down to Weston-Super-Mare, stared disconsolately at the sand and the stretch of mud beyond it where the thin silver line of the Bristol Channel reached over to Wales, both trying to recreate something of their old feelings for each other. But he seemed to be far from her and she blamed herself. Perhaps she had been cold and distant when she should have been warm and loving.

'I'm worrying about going to see Mrs Miller,' she had said lamely in an effort to find some small excuse.

'You've no need to. She's a lovely person.'

'I know that. As a dressmaker she's nice, but as a new mother . . .' She had not been able to finish the sentence and he had looked at her strangely.

'When are you going? Don't put it off.'

'I don't know, and I don't want any lectures, Clifford. I'll go in my own time.'

She winced at the remembered sharpness of her voice. There were so many things she wished had not been said, and so many others that she knew would have eased the situation between them, but she had been silent about all the important things. And now he was gone. But there had been a letter from him that, in some ways, had cheered her, yet also made her feel more guilty. It was full of a tenderness and concern that twisted at her heart and made any thought of his loss more terrible.

Although she was almost totally exhausted at the end of each day, her thoughts frequently kept her awake. As well as her anxiety over Clifford there was the overwhelming sensation of being completely alone. It was always there in the back of her mind like a grey blanket that clouded her life and would not be dispelled.

She knew that she must visit Mrs Miller soon and this, too, was a source of utmost disquiet. She dreaded the prospect, and considered that it was probably the hardest thing that she would ever be called upon to do. Fragments of words and sentences that she would say constantly went round and round in her head, until eventually she decided to put it off no longer.

So, one morning in February she dressed herself in one of the two ordinary frocks that she kept at the hospital, leaving her uniform hanging in the small rickety cupboard. The dress was made in a soft woollen material in just the shade of pale blue that she loved. It was caught at the waist with a belt of darker blue and the skirt was fairly straight and simple, falling to a few inches above her ankles. She added a chain of bright coral coloured beads and a warm jacket, and then fastened her hat with long hatpins. She pulled on her gloves and peered at herself in the small mirror. She hoped she looked right. If you felt good it was easier to be confident. She thought that she would do, and reluctantly walked slowly down the stairs.

The sky was bright, the winter sun shining through the branches of the trees that lined the country lane, Amy's breath making steamy patterns in the air. She tried to enjoy the lovely freshness of the morning, but her steps were leaden. She walked to the outskirts of the city and was glad that it was a long way. Then she was in the city streets and there were trams.

She climbed up the little spiral staircase to the open top of one that was going somewhere near St Paul's and sat on the slatted wooden seat to stare down at the people in the streets below. She was glad that it was still early. She had decided to go at this time because Dorothy would certainly be at work.

When the trundling vehicle reached an area she knew, she left it and walked through the familiar streets with a heart full of painful memories. She paused before her old shuttered home and stared at its neglected garden and cheerless windows. There were mixed emotions in her heart. She never wanted to live there again, but she couldn't help wondering with a little shiver of fear if the unknown cousin would win his case and deprive her of this house in addition to much else.

She walked on eventually and stopped again outside the small house in Campbell Street. It took courage to ring the door bell, but at last she managed to do so and waited nervously, hands clasped tightly together.

'Mrs Miller? It's me, Amy,' she said as Rose opened the door to her.

For a moment they stood facing each other, neither knowing what to say. Amy stared at the cosy figure before her, at the long dress, too long now to be fashionable, the hair pulled into a neat bun, curling strands framing the face, and at the apron tied round an ample waist. Her heart thumped with panic. This was her mother. This woman had borne her, borne her and given her away.

'Come in, my dear,' Rose said at last. 'I've been hoping you'd come.'

Amy followed her into the house and registered the clean scrubbed smell, the unmistakable scent of carbolic soap. She couldn't remember ever having been in this house and it was a long time since she had seen Mrs Miller. After she went away to school, her clothes had been ordered by Felicity and just lately she had bought everything she needed from Bentalls' Ready-to-Wear catalogue. A private dressmaker no longer fitted into her image of the kind of person she wished to be. Long gone were the elaborate ball gowns, the frills and dainty materials that her mother . . . that Patricia had thought necessary.

'Would you like a cup of tea?' Without waiting for an answer Rose poked up the fire beneath the kettle. 'And I've got some little buns I made yesterday.' She was obviously nervous, making conversation.

Amy felt strange and ill-at-ease. Mama would hardly have known how to make tea, let alone little buns. She tried to stop making comparisons, tried to behave normally. 'Thank you. That would be nice,' she said. Then she looked at the doll sitting in the chair.

Rose, embarrassed now, took it up and indicated that she should sit here. 'Our Chrissy will leave her things all over the place,' she said.

As soon as the child was mentioned, Amy felt slightly better. It was a distraction, taking her thoughts away for a second from the strange new relationship that had to be forged. 'I heard that you had another daughter,' she exclaimed, managing to smile. 'Clifford told me. Will I be able to meet her?'

The knowledge that there was a little sister had at first been a shock, but as she became used to the idea it gradually began to intrigue her. A small child might be a help, someone who would relate to her without any preconceptions.

'She'll be in soon,' Rose said. 'She've just gone next door to play for a bit.'

'You called her Christabel after Miss Pankhurst?'

'Yes. Dorothy thinks she's a grand lady.'

'Did you know that Parliament has recommended giving the vote to women?' Amy was glad to have something impersonal to say.

'Yes. Dorothy tells me all about them sort of things.

Not all women though, not yet anyway. Older ones, or married ones or something.'

Amy flinched at the way she spoke. It was the language of the servants. When Myrtle talked like that it sounded right, but in her mother it was almost an offence. She tried to take control of herself once more, to accept and not to mind.

'I don't think anyone is sure just yet what they really are going to give us.' She tried not to sound too knowledgeable. 'It's because of all that we've done in the war of course. One day all women will have a vote though.'

'Well I just hope so,' Rose said as she took off her apron and set cups and plates on the table.

Amy watched her pour water out of the old kettle into a large chipped china teapot and tried to believe that this was her true background. She closed her eyes for a second, remembering: remembering the maid in her cap and apron; the tray brought into the drawing room in response to the bell; the sparkling silver; the beautiful china; Mama's soft white hands.

She took the cup and saucer from Rose and smiled. She drank the hot sweet tea, ate the cakes that were set before her and wondered what to say next. How could she begin to acknowledge this woman as her mother? The memory of Patricia Harding would not be dimmed. She saw the tall slim figure in the beautiful clothes, smelt the perfume, almost felt the comfort of her arms, and saw her lovely smile as she waved goodbye on that fateful day when she left for America. It had been the last time she had seen her mother. Her mother? Then suddenly she was crying. Her tears flowed and she could not stop them and she was desperately ashamed. 'I'm so sorry,' she murmured at last. 'Very stupid of me.'

'It's not stupid at all,' Rose said, misunderstanding. 'I feel like crying too. All those lost years!'

Amy found her handkerchief and mopped her eyes. 'I . . . I've been dreading coming here today. Yet I wanted to come.'

Rose didn't look at her. 'I just want to know if you'll ever forgive me for what I done?' she said humbly.

The words jolted Amy out of her self-pity. She stared at Rose, suddenly seeing her differently, as a person with feelings and emotions. It was almost as though the woman in front of her had come to life, had ceased to be merely an awkward embarrassment. She felt the first stirrings of affection.

'Forgive you? Of course I forgive you,' she whispered. 'There's nothing to forgive. You gave me a wonderful start in life. That's how I've tried to see it ever since I knew.'

'Then you're not angry?'

She was amazed at the relief in Rose's voice. 'No, I couldn't be angry. I have too many wonderful memories.'

'You mean of your dear Mama and Papa?'

'Yes.'

There was silence for a time, a difficult silence, and then hesitantly Rose said, 'I was so sorry to hear about Dr Harding. He was a wonderful man. Everyone hereabouts liked him.'

'Yes.' The one word seemed to be all that she could manage in reply.

'What are you going to do, my dear? Have you any plans?'

Amy turned away from the fire into which she been staring. She felt herself being wrenched away from the precious memories of the past. The innocent question was pulling her back to the uncertainties of today and the problems of the future.

'I shall go on working as a nurse until the war is over, and then I'm not sure,' she murmured.

'Aren't you engaged to be married to Mr Clifford Buxton?'

'Well, yes I am.' There was a hesitancy in her answer and she hoped Rose had not noticed it.

'That's nice then. Now I'll just go and fetch Chrissy so you can get to know her. You sit there in the warm.'

Amy did as she was told and held out her hands to the welcome glow of the coals in the grate. She thought about her small sister. Mr Miller, for she could never call him anything more personal than that, must have been home from Canada a few years ago. She decided that it wouldn't do to make any comment about it.

The door to the yard had been firmly closed against the cold when Rose went out of it, but eventually Amy heard the two of them coming back, sounds of splashing water and Chrissy being told to keep still while she had her hands washed.

After a few moments they came into the room and Amy saw a thin plain child with straight hair pulled back and tied with large red satin ribbons each side of her face. She was not a bit like her mother, and Amy immediately thought of Laura. This is just how she had looked years ago when they were both little, with big brown eyes that stared out at the world with curiosity and friendly interest. She warmed to the little girl at once.

'This is your new sister,' Rose said. 'This is Amy.'

'Hello, Christabel.' Amy held out her hands and smiled, but the child stood still for a moment.

'You've got pretty hair like my Dorry,' she said at last. 'You look just like Dorry.'

'We're twins,' Amy surprised herself by saying. 'Do you know what twins are?'

'Special kind of sisters. My mam told me.'

'Yes, a special kind of sister,' Amy repeated thoughtfully.

'Are you going to live here?'

'No. I'm a nurse. I help to make people better. I live in a hospital.'

This information was carefully absorbed. Then Chrissy ran out of the room and appeared later with two ancient and battered dolls. 'Can you make these better?' she asked. 'They want to be made well.'

The tension was broken, they all laughed, and conversation became easier. Amy eventually found, to her surprise and great pleasure, that she was actually beginning to enjoy herself, that she was more relaxed than she had been for a long time. In spite of her fears, the hour here was perhaps going to be a success after all. She felt warmth creeping over her that had nothing to do with the fire or with the tea and buns.

It was not until she was ready to leave that she realized that she still did not know what to call Rose Miller. What their future relationship would be she couldn't tell. They were standing at the front door and on a sudden impulse she stooped to kiss her. 'Can I call you "mother"?' she whispered. 'It couldn't be Mama or Ma, but Mother sounds right.'

It was Rose's turn to wipe tears from her eyes. 'I'd like that very much, my dear,' she said.

As soon as Dorothy entered the house later that day she was aware of her mother's happiness.

'She've been,' Rose said. 'This morning, and everything's all right.'

'You mean Amy I suppose,' she said and then was immediately ashamed of the coldness in her voice. 'How did you get on? What did she have to say?' She smiled, trying to sound kinder.

'Not much really. I gave her something to eat and Chrissy asked her if she could make her dolls better, her being a nurse and all that.'

'What's she going to do then?'

'Do?'

'Well yes. Is she going to claim us as her long-lost relations or anything?'

'I don't know what you mean, Dorry. You two must meet and talk about it yourselves. She'm living in the nurses' home and works long hours. She haven't got time to come here much, so you don't need to fear that she'll ever want to come and stay with us. When she'm not working she goes to Mr Buxton's house I think.'

Dorothy could feel the colour draining from her face at the reminder of her sister's relationship with Clifford. She went back into the passage and hung her coat carefully on a hanger on the hall-stand. Then she slumped into the armchair and gathered Chrissy in her arms and buried her head in the child's hair. She could feel tears gathering in her eyes and she tried to force them back.

'You all right, Dorry?' Rose sounded concerned.

'Yes, Ma. I suppose I'm all right.' She couldn't keep the misery from her voice. There had been a letter from Clifford. It had arrived yesterday and she had started to reply last night.

'What's the matter?' Rose continued to probe.

Chrissy turned to look at her and jumped from her lap. 'You're crying,' she said. 'Ma, our Dorry's crying.'

Dorothy was unable to keep the tears away any longer. She started to weep copiously and Rose turned to Chrissy.

'Go on up to your bedroom,' she told the child firmly. 'I want to talk to your sister. Go and get your new book and I'll read to you in a minute. You can come down again when I call.'

Chrissy looked from one to the other. It was cold upstairs, but she knew that this time she had better do as she was told. Reluctantly she left the room. Rose got up and closed the door behind her.

'Now, what's the matter? You've been peaky and

miserable-looking for days lately. Tell me, Dorry. I'm that worried about you.'

Dorothy took out her large handkerchief and wiped her eyes and after a few moments she stared up at her mother with a desolate look on her face. 'I can't stop thinking about Clifford Buxton, Ma. I can't get him out of my mind.'

Rose flopped down again at one of the chairs that was set at the table in the bay window and Dorothy could feel the shock waves that her news had caused.

'So that's it. Well, you'd better forget about him quickly then hadn't you. He's not for the likes of you, Dorry. He's from another class, an officer and all.'

'And what about him and Amy then? She's my twin sister, or had you forgotten?'

'That's different.'

'Different, *different*? How can it be different?' Dorothy's voice was heavy with self-pity and with anger too. 'And he likes me a lot. I know he does. The letter that came yesterday was from him.'

Rose's face was drained of all colour now. The happiness that had filled her had swiftly disappeared and she felt at a loss as to how to cope with this latest predicament. 'I thought it'd come from Arthur,' she said in a small flat voice. 'I hoped you and him had an understanding.'

Dorothy was silent. She had meant to keep her secret for much longer than this but Rose always sensed when her children were in trouble.

'Well, you can't let it go on can you,' her mother continued relentlessly. 'I mean if he and Amy are engaged then you'll *have* to put him out of your mind.'

The words could have sounded cold and heartless, but Dorothy heard the tenderness and concern behind them and her anger dissipated a little.

'I can't do that, Ma. I love him. I do truly love him.'

Rose shook her head in horrified disbelief. 'That's

the saddest thing I've heard for a long time,' she said. 'Both my daughters wanting the same man! As if you hadn't enough already to make you dislike each other!'

Dorothy stared at her. It would have been better if her mother had screamed and raged, shouted at her to stop behaving so badly, even turned her out of the house until she came to her senses and promised to forget Clifford for ever. An angry scene she could have coped with, but this quiet sadness was much more difficult.

Then another element in the complicated jigsaw apparently crossed Rose's mind. 'Perhaps he won't want neither of you if he finds out about our Chrissy,' she said. 'She's his half-sister and yours and Amy's. Mr Buxton don't want her told, ever, but how can we keep something like that a secret if Mr Clifford's to marry either one of you?'

'Oh, Ma. It's all so awful. What are we to do?' Dorothy had already thought about the problem of her little sister's birth. There seemed to be no solution.

'Just get on with our lives, my girl. That's what we are to do. This awful war don't seem to be coming to any kind of an end. Things might sort themselves out.'

'By him getting killed you mean don't you?' Dorothy's words were shrill now and accusing. 'That would be convenient wouldn't it. Oh Ma you can't mean that.'

'I don't mean nothing, Dorry. Just that it's all so uncertain. We must live one day at a time and not worry about tomorrow.' She got up from the table. 'We can't keep Chrissy up there in the cold any more. I'll go up and fetch her.'

When the child came back into the room she ran over to Dorothy. 'Don't cry,' she said, putting her little arm round her shoulder. 'We've got a nice new sister so you shouldn't cry. Mam told me that Amy is our sister. I liked her.'

Dorothy stared at the little girl blankly. Could she

ever like Amy? She had read Clifford's letter over and over again trying to find something special behind the words, something to give her hope. But she had to admit that it had been just a friendly letter such as he might have written to anyone. He had mentioned Amy, too, and when she thought about it she had to admit that he obviously cared a lot about her sister, about this sister whom she was supposed to grow to love, this girl who was going to marry the man she herself wanted – the girl who had everything, absolutely everything . . .

Winter gave way gradually to spring and then to summer. Amy had volunteered for service abroad, telling Rose that nurses were needed in France. There were plenty of girls willing to work at home but parents were usually reluctant to allow their daughters to face the dangers of the battlefield. She had no one to refuse her permission except Geoffrey and he had very unwillingly at last agreed to her persistent requests.

'She don't think of 'erself as belonging to us,' Rose commented sadly to Dorothy. 'She said that as she'd got no family she felt she ought to go. She were a bit embarrassed when she'd said it, but I understood. The poor girl feels all alone in the world.'

'Alone, my foot,' Dorothy replied crossly. 'She's got Clifford Buxton hasn't she, and his parents? Don't say she's alone! And she's got all that money as well. No need to be sorry for our dear Amy.'

Her mother said nothing, just looked sadly at her angry daughter.

Although the days were long and warm with roses blooming in the parks, and even the little front garden in St Paul's bright with wallflowers that Rose had planted months before, yet still there were few really happy faces to be seen. The war seemed to be no nearer its end.

'Them planes that your Arthur be so proud of,' Rose said, a few days after Dorothy's outburst. 'Well they been and gone and dropped bombs on London. The war's coming here, Dorry.'

'He's not my Arthur,' Dorothy said, 'And they were German planes, Ma, not ours!'

'I knows that, girl. Don't be so stupid. But it's frightening having Germans right up in the sky above our heads. Suppose they comes over Bristol?'

'I'm sure they won't, and if they do then Arthur might shoot them down!'

'P'raps he will and p'raps he won't, but I don't like it anyway.' Rose's voice was doubtful. 'I don't know what the world is coming to,' she said. 'If the Good Lord had meant us to fly He'd have given us wings.'

The remark made Dorothy laugh. 'Are you going to say that to Arthur when he comes home on leave?'

'No, of course I shan't. He's a good lad is Arthur.' She looked at Dorothy reproachfully. 'As good as you'll find, my girl, and just you remember it.'

'Yes, Ma,' Dorothy said agreeing wholeheartedly. She just wished how she felt could be ruled by common sense. It would make life much easier.

It was only Rose who gave much thought to Franky. He had survived the horrors of the Somme almost a year ago, had come home twice, boasting of his deeds, and had returned again to the Front. Now he was at some place with a name she couldn't possibly pronounce. 'Wipers,' she told her friends. They spell it Y – P – R – E – S. What kind of a name is that?'

When the telegram arrived the following Tuesday morning to say he had died of wounds in a field hospital, she shed copious tears for her only son and then went on stitching the sturdy material that lay on her sewing machine.

Dorothy shed a few tears but not too many. She had

never been close to Franky and she could not pretend otherwise.

'Amy never met him,' Rose said sadly when Dorothy came home that evening. 'He was her brother, but she never talked to him at all.'

Privately Dorothy thought that it was probably a blessing in disguise. She couldn't imagine what the gently reared Amy would have made of her noisy, often rather coarse, young brother. She felt desperately disloyal about such thoughts, but she had frequently wondered how Franky, brought up by Rose, could have turned out as he had.

'Amy's out there at the Front now, in a hospital. Perhaps she did meet him. Perhaps she looked after him,' Rose said.

'Not very likely, Ma. There are thousands of wounded and lots of different hospitals. They aren't proper hospitals. Some of them are just tents behind the lines from what I hear.'

The thought of Amy working in all that horror was almost unendurable to Rose, and even Dorothy had to admit to a reluctant admiration. Just lately she'd been feeling very guilty because she wasn't doing anything for the war effort. Trying to become a successful author, working every minute that she could spare to improve herself in all sorts of ways had seemed honourable aims, but now there was a hollow ring about them. She sometimes felt that the selfishness of her life was a reproach and the only excuse she made was the old one, that she had been born with nothing and therefore had to strive and strive for everything she wanted. She had achieved so much, publication and a good job, and she knew that she was articulate now and could hold her own in conversation with anyone. These things hadn't been easily achieved. There had been hours of reading and studying as well as her own writing and there were other things too. She had studied the latest fashions, not the ones followed by the factory girls, but the sort of clothes that Felicity Buxton wore. She could not afford to buy them, but she bought paper patterns at threepence each and because Rose had often been too busy to make them up for her she had taught herself to sew. The materials were often cheap, but the lines were right up to date.

When the letters arrived from Amy, as they did quite often lately, Dorothy recalled all her own achievements and persuaded herself that she was morally justified in her choices. Yet there was a worm of doubt always there and she knew that for her own integrity she must soon do something, however small, to help someone other than herself.

Amy's letters said nothing of the long hours she was working and the terrible conditions. They were usually full of small unimportant details and occasionally an account of the few hours, or even a day's leave, when she and one or two other nurses were taken back to one of the villages behind the lines for a short break, sometimes to the seaside. There was one special place that she especially liked she said. It was called Le Montaine and was on the coast.

Dorothy guessed that she made much of those times in her letters, saying little, for Rose's sake, of the more terrifying details of her life. She couldn't help but feel a grudging respect for her sometimes.

One morning Rose put down the letter that had just arrived. 'Fancy being over there near all them shells and things and going into a café and having a meal.' The two activities appeared to have no connection.

'Well, I suppose that she needs to get away and relax now and again,' Dorothy said, trying to be agreeable. Lately her feelings of guilt and uselessness had increased, largely because of her continued correspondence with Clifford. She tried to tell herself that they were merely pen-pals. Lots of girls wrote letters to soldiers to cheer them, but in her more honest moments she had to admit that her communications with Amy's fiancé were much more than that and had gone beyond the one letter she'd agreed at the outset. The letters had become longer and they were now an intense source of pleasure for Dorothy, and she knew that for Clifford, too, they were important. They discussed many things, books and ideas, plans for the future and sometimes impossible dreams.

She kept the precious sheets of thin paper locked away in a second little wooden box beside her bed. She had saved up for a long time for that box. It had ornate patterns on its lid, fashioned with different kinds of wood, tiny pieces inlaid elaborately; but most important of all it possessed a strong lock and two keys, both of which she carried safely tied on a long piece of ribbon round her neck and tucked down inside her blouse.

There were letters from Arthur too but those were usually read to Rose and kept on the mantelpiece along with Amy's. In the early summer he had spent some weeks in England training to become a pilot and there had been frequent short visits home. He had repeated his proposal to Dorothy and she had tried to put him off without being too unkind.

'You'm a very foolish girl,' Rose told her more than once. 'He be a jolly good catch, one you'll never have the chance of again.'

'But I can't marry him if I don't love him, Ma, can I?' Dorothy usually replied, and the answer was always the same. 'Love grows. You marry him and love'll just grow.'

Dorothy gravely doubted that that could ever be the case and she had no intentions whatsoever of seeing whether or not she was right.

And whenever Rose gave the advice she had to

admit to herself, if she thought about it at all, that she probably didn't quite believe that it was true either; but it sounded right, and with Arthur Price it might well work. He was a good lad with his head screwed on the right way, and he was clever and ambitious like Dorothy. With her Frank it had been different. Love had grown a bit in those early years, but she doubted if it would have gone on growing, especially when she looked at the latest photograph from Canada. He sent them regularly and in each one he was a little fatter, a little older, and as far removed from the dashing young man who had wooed her more than twenty years ago as it was possible to be. Well, she consoled herself, Arthur Price wouldn't let himself go to seed like that. Dorothy was a foolish girl.

In a base hospital on the Western Front, Amy was working harder and for more hours than she had ever thought possible. She worked until her mind and her body were almost incapable of any normal responses, until it seemed that the world could have no existence outside the walls of the long wooden huts that housed so much suffering and death. The noise of distant guns went on and on with little respite and even when they were quiet she was always listening for them to start again as if the incessant bombardment were some awful necessity to life.

After nearly five weeks with very little leave she was told to go for three days' rest.

'It'll be nice to feel a bit normal again,' her fellow VAD Iris Jones said as they arranged themselves in the truck that was to take them the few miles behind the lines to the relatively peaceful seaside town that was used to allow officers and nurses to recuperate from time to time.

'Will we ever feel normal again?' Amy repeated doubtfully. 'What is normal anyway?'

'Just to be able to spend a whole day thinking about oneself,' Iris said. She was a small pretty ginger-haired girl with whom Amy had formed a casual friendship. 'Perhaps we'll meet some nice officers.'

'Not allowed,' Amy remarked.

'Trust you to spoil the fun,' Iris replied with a laugh. 'I don't care what the rules say. I've seen enough wounded men to last me all my life. I want to speak to a few healthy ones for a change.'

At Le Montaine the sea lay sparkling in the afternoon sun. Tiny waves were breaking lazily on the beach, gulls wheeled and called in the sky and there was quietness.

They stared at it, hardly believing it to be real, as the truck set them down at the door of the small hotel where they were to be billeted during their precious three days.

'Just look at that,' Amy said. 'Just look at those waves. All I want to do is walk on the beach and to sleep in a room with only the sound of the sea instead of gunfire, and to eat good meals nicely served.'

For the first day and night that was all they did and as the peace and the beauty of the place began to take hold of them, so they felt their strength returning and with it some of the buoyancy of their youth.

Not until almost the end of their stay did the officers that Iris desired materialize. The two girls were sitting in a small café enjoying some enormous pastries, faced with nothing more demanding than deciding which creamy confection to try next, when three young men in uniform entered and sat at the next table. Amy nervously looked the other way, but Iris was more adventurous.

'They're fliers,' she whispered. 'Look at those wings on their uniforms.'

Amy took a surreptitious glance and was suddenly jolted out of her nervousness. She stared at one of the young officers who was staring back at her with equal interest and amazement. Suddenly he jumped to his feet to address her.

'Am I dreaming or is it Miss Harding?'

'Yes. Yes I am Amy Harding, and you are . . .' She was just about to say 'Price' but then stopped herself in time.

'Arthur Price,' he supplied. Then, obviously guessing at her surprise, he added, 'I'm a pilot now and I've just been commissioned in case you're wondering. Second Lieutenant Price, at your service.' He saluted and bowed slightly and then smiled and sat down in the vacant seat at her table. 'And you're a nurse I see.'

'Just a VAD she corrected. 'I've been here a couple of months now.'

After the initial shock Amy was pleased to see Arthur and introduced him to Iris. He was a link from home. 'What are you doing here then?' Amy asked.

'I'm stationed not too far away, and we're not usually up on patrol until the evening,' he explained. 'There's quite a bit of spare time.'

'And you really fly one of those flimsy things we see now and again up above us?'

'I'd not exactly call them flimsy things,' he said in mock reproof. 'I've a wonderful little plane.'

'He's downed five Huns in the latest one!'

The remark was made by one of Arthur's companions, and Amy looked with immense respect at the young man sitting beside her.

'You mean you've actually shot down enemy planes?'

'Just a few,' he said. 'Shall we go outside and walk a bit? If I eat another of those pastries my poor old machine won't be able to get me off the ground.'

'I'll stay here,' Iris volunteered with commendable tact. 'I couldn't walk another inch.'

'Come on then,' Arthur said. 'I want all the news from home.'

They walked along the beach in the afternoon sunshine. The waves were breaking gently on the sandy shore and a dog was barking joyously as he frisked in and out of the surf. Two boys were throwing sticks for him and they had taken off their shoes and socks to get themselves thoroughly wet as they chased the dog and each other. Their laughter and their shouts sounded strangely on Amy's ears.

'You wouldn't think that men are dying in their thousands not far from here, would you?' she said quietly. 'The war doesn't seem to exist in this wonderful place.'

'I can still hear the guns in the distance,' Arthur said. 'You can never get right away from that.' He turned sideways to look at her. 'I learnt of your sad news,' he added. 'About your father.'

'Did you hear the rest of it as well?'

'Yes. Dorothy told me. I don't know what to say.'

'You need not feel embarrassed. Everyone knows now. And I've been to see . . . to see Mrs Miller. She's a lovely person.'

'You're engaged to Mr Clifford aren't you?'

Amy smiled a little at the title. It was the name which the servants always used for Clifford at home before the war. But she felt that there was no truthful answer she could give to the question. 'He's out here somewhere,' she said, prevaricating. 'South of Ypres I think. I hear from him now and again, but our ways haven't crossed at all since I came from England.'

'He's in the trenches then?'

'Yes. So far he's been lucky.' She shivered thinking of the men she tended, of their horrific wounds.

Arthur wondered what to say. He was constantly glad that he had opted to be in the air rather than in the filth and the mud down below. PBI he thought,

Poor Bloody Infantry! Aloud he said, 'Try not to worry too much. Sounds trite I know, but we've all got to hope. That's all there is to do. Perhaps it'll be over soon, this stupid old war, and then we can go home.'

'You're going to marry Dorothy aren't you?' Amy remarked, trying to sound casual. She wanted to shift the attention away from herself and Clifford.

'It's not certain,' he replied and his voice was suddenly flat and cold. 'I asked her but she wouldn't give me an answer.'

'She's my twin sister of course.'

Arthur nodded. 'Yes. You're very alike. I noticed it even before I knew.'

'I don't think we shall ever be true sisters, become fond of each other I mean. She seems very jealous of me.' Amy kicked the sand unhappily as she walked.

'That's natural. But she's a good girl, is Dorothy. I hope you do become friends one day.'

They had reached the end of the beach. A stone wall jutted out towards the sea and Arthur stopped and leaned on it. 'I shall come back here one day, in peace time,' he said. 'I didn't know there could be anywhere so beautiful.'

Amy stared at him and for the first time she noticed his fair good looks, and the kindness in his blue eyes. She wondered why Dorothy had refused him. Then suddenly another and quite different thought struck her.

'Arthur,' she asked. 'Did you ever meet Mr Miller? My . . . my real father? He must have come home four or five years ago. No one talks about him much. I'd like to find out what kind of person he is.'

Her companion was jolted out of his reverie. 'What made you think about him just now?' he enquired.

She blushed violently. 'I suppose it's one of the things I dread knowing about. Papa was such a wonderful person, and to have to acknowledge suddenly that there's someone else, some unknown man who has a claim on me is rather frightening. I keep thinking about it. I wonder what kind of person he is to go and leave my mother and not want to see Christabel. She's sweet. He must have gone back to Canada before she was born.'

Arthur looked at her and his face paled beneath its summer tan. 'You mean you don't know?' he said slowly. 'They haven't told you?'

It was Amy's turn to feel suddenly cold as if a chill wind had swept over them. 'Told me what?' she asked fearfully.

'Your father hasn't been home for about eighteen years,' he said. 'I've never met him.'

'Then . . . Chrissy?' Amy felt faint. She gripped the wall for support as the full meaning of his words conveyed themselves to her. The facts of life had meant little until she became a VAD. After that she had quickly become acquainted with all the details.

'Who?' she gasped.

'No one knows except Mrs Miller and maybe Dorothy. It's a well-guarded secret.'

Amy bent her head and wept. It was the final blow. Her mother was . . . she couldn't bring herself even to think the word. Then suddenly she felt Arthur's hand clasping hers.

'Amy, please Amy don't judge her too harshly. She needs you, and she's still the same person now as before. I'm sorry you had to know, and even more sorry that it had to be me who told you.'

She leaned against him and took strength from his strength. He put an arm about her and she was a little comforted. 'I don't think that there is anything worse now,' she whispered. 'Perhaps this is as far down as I can possibly go, the last straw. Surely there can't be any more?'

'No more,' he said. 'So now the only way is up.' He

held her away from him and smiled into her tear-stained eyes. 'You'll be brave I know, and kind to her.'

'I shall try my best,' she said, strengthened by his confidence in her. 'Thank you Arthur for telling me. I'm glad you did, glad that I found out from you and not from her or from Dorothy. Don't be sorry about that. I shall be prepared now, and yes, I hope I shall be kind.'

They walked together back to the little café and by the time they joined the others she had regained some composure.

Arthur smiled at her as he left. 'Perhaps I shall see you around here some other time,' he said. 'Maybe our ways will cross again.'

'Maybe, and I'll wave every time I see one of our planes up there,' she said. 'Take care of yourself.' Suddenly it was important that he should.

It was not until she was in her narrow bed that night that she gave herself up to frenzied grief. Every blow that had fallen, starting with Mama's drowning came back to her in heightened clarity and she wept again.

At last Iris came to her and touched her gently. 'Anything I can do?' she whispered.

'There's nothing anyone can do,' Amy sobbed. 'My mother is a common whore. Go back to bed, Iris. I'm sorry I woke you.'

CHAPTER THIRTEEN

Clifford plodded through the mud, fell into it, cursed loudly, struggled to his feet and wiped the slime and filth from his hands. He heard the shelling ahead, the familiar gut-rending sound that terrified him. Visions of the wounds it inflicted swam before his eyes. Shells could rip off a hand, an arm or, much worse, half a face. He had seen men like that, still alive, still breathing. The dead were easier to pass by, easier to put out of your mind. There was nothing more to be done for them, they were just bodies, almost garbage, to be left where they lay until they could be disposed of somehow. But the living were a different matter. He couldn't get them out of his mind by day and they haunted his dreams at night.

But neither the dead nor the injured were his concern, he told himself angrily. They must be left to the stretcher-bearers and medics. He frequently thanked God that he was not a stretcher-bearer, for they were closer to the pain and the agony, and he saw them sometimes having to make choices – decisions about which man to take and which to leave in the mud – which Clifford could never imagine himself having the courage to make.

He tried to develop a hardness, almost a callousness. Without it he felt that he could no longer bring himself to direct his men towards the hell that he knew waited for them. The horror of it filled him with a monstrous disgust for everything to do with this war. Yet here he was, leading his platoon forward to the front line, forward to the slaughter when every normal human reaction told him to turn round and run. But of course you only ran over the top into the guns, into death, not away from it. Every step he made was unwilling. There was no sense in the war any more. The patriotism was gone, lost for ever months ago in the terror of the Somme.

This was the third battle for Ypres. At some time in the recent past he had seen it. The days seemed to run into each other and he couldn't remember whether it was last week or last month. He just had a vague recollection of a shattered and ruined town of no apparent use to anyone. Yet he knew, cynically, that he was wrong. This place was important, more important than the lives of the thousands who had already died on both sides as the armies advanced and fell back with repeated monotony. And now it was the turn of his company. The remorseless rain and the terrible Flanders mud were almost as much to be feared as the ceaseless bombardment he could hear from the German guns ahead.

'I was here before, Sir.'

Clifford looked at the sturdy corporal at his side. Jim Hardy was his senior by at least twenty years, a tough, thick-set man and as good a soldier as he could wish for. 'Happy memories, then?' Clifford's effort at humour was weak but the man laughed.

'You could say that,' he replied. 'I got a Blighty wound last time and had a few weeks home, but it wasn't bad enough so now I'm back and hoping for something a bit better this time.'

Clifford winced slightly. 'Just sufficient to last the war out?'

'That's it, Sir. That's what we all want.'

'Pretty awful place, this,' Clifford said with immense understatement as he glanced round at the countryside that lay spread out each side of the Ypres to Menin road. As far as they could see were stumps of shattered trees, corpses of dead and stinking horses mostly half-buried in the mud, and occasionally a heap of rubble that had been a house. It was a wilderness of soil – littered with abandoned trenches and shell holes, barbed wire, rifles, bayonets, shell cases, dirty blood-stained groundsheets and hideous pieces of torn uniform. 'At least there was a bit of greenery around the Somme,' he added. 'And the odd tree or two.'

'You were on the Somme?'

'Yes.'

Their conversation was interrupted by the drone of aeroplanes overhead and Clifford looked up, wondering if they were the Boche or theirs. He remembered the letter he had received recently from Amy. She had met Price, their old chauffeur and now an officer she said, a flier. For a moment he envied him up there in the wholesomeness of the blue sky, out of the mud, out of the squalor and foulness of the trenches. For once the sun was shining and it glinted on the squarish wings. He could see the welcome circles painted on them. Ours! Perhaps it was actually Price.

He shaded his eyes and stared upwards, fascinated. The sight cheered him a little, and then he saw other aeroplanes in the distance. They came on, two of them menacingly, and soon they were firing with no more than a few hundred yards between them. The fire was returned and Clifford held his breath. The men behind him had been singing as they marched, but now they stopped, enthralled. This was a new kind of fighting, almost a game. None of them understood it or how it could affect the war. Then one of the Boche planes was hit, started to wobble and pitch, and there was smoke and finally terrifying flames as it spiralled down-wards out of control. It crashed out of sight behind a small wood, and there was silence for a second followed by a great cheer from the men on the ground as the remaining Hun turned and headed into the distant clouds.

Clifford watched one of the small fragile-looking British craft circling above them and he waved, although whether the pilot could see them in the greyness of the mud all around he doubted. It eventually left and, as he watched it disappear, some of the hope and confidence that it had imparted receded too.

He shifted his pack and stepped out doggedly. With mixed feelings he saw that the mud was covered with narrow duckboards now stretching as far as he could see into the distance. At least it would make it easier to walk, easier to reach the front line, easier to get to the slaughter. Long ago robbed of any sense of the glory of their cause, he privately hoped, like most of the others, for a wound that would take him back to England, back to dear old Blighty, out of the war for good. 'Please God let it be a nice clean bullet wound,' he prayed with every step that he marched. He couldn't bear the thought of a slow terrible death from mustard gas or phosgene, couldn't bear to be crippled by anything disfiguring. 'Let me keep my face,' he pleaded with the Almighty. 'I couldn't go through life with half a face!'

The trench to which his platoon was assigned was worse than he had imagined, barely five feet deep and unlined at the bottom. His boots squelched into the mud and filth but the long march had taken its toll and any refuge was better than none. He ate the bread and beef handed to him on a tin plate and thankfully downed two mugs of hot strong tea liberally sweetened with condensed milk. There were others to keep watch for a few hours, and gratefully he and most of his men slept. It was all they were capable of. Tomorrow they must improve the trench, reinforcing it, acquaint themselves with their exact position, and try to get rid of the maggots. Clifford removed some of the fat obscene creatures that were crawling from the wall of the trench. Maggots which had fed on the dead, he reflected in disgust. But at that moment the guns mercifully ceased and in the uncanny silence that followed, he slept.

In his unquiet sleep he sometimes thought he was in his soft bed at home but then he would wake with cold fear as the foul smell of his surroundings penetrated his senses. Then reality would dawn and with it a deadening dread. But aching tiredness allowed him to sleep again and it was Amy who filled his dreams. But she became Dorothy, the two mingled into one girl holding out welcoming arms to him, but always out of reach, distant.

A young private, bearing a mug of steaming tea, finally brought him to full consciousness. 'Time to be up, Sir,' he said, and the next horrific day was beginning.

It was raining again. It was always raining. They tried to fix tarpaulins overhead in some parts of the trench but the rain merely found its way in rushing torrents into those places not protected.

Two days later they knew that their turn to go over the top was close. At first there was a tenseness, almost an excitement, but as zero hour approached Clifford sensed that his men were beginning to show fright. Most of them tried to keep it hidden but as he looked at them he was aware of the signs, the silence, the way they sat waiting for the final command. He knew that some were praying, some cursing the Hun, some thinking of home and removing themselves in spirit from all this. The fearful things they had seen on the way up here must be filling their thoughts now.

As he looked at them he prayed. The habits of his upbringing took precedence over everything else and silently, with his eyes wide open and his hands grasping his revolver, he prayed as he had never done before. He thought of Dorothy safe at home, and then he included Amy in his prayers. She was out here too. God only knew in what similar bit of hellfire she was labouring and he couldn't bear to think of it. Visions of her as she used to be in dainty frilly dresses and long flowing hair seemed to dance before him. All that seemed like a fairy-tale now.

Corporal Jim Hardy was of a more earthy calibre and he strolled along the trench in a deliberately calm manner. He smoked a cigarette and joked and laughed. Clifford looked at him with respect and was jolted out of his reverie. Suddenly the jokes became more crude and the laughter spread. Then the command came and the long waiting was over. They were still laughing as Clifford shouted at his men and led them over the top into the mud and the horror. He was aware of the corporal beside him and of his frantic shouts of encouragement to those who followed. It was like Dante's *Inferno*. There would be no need to wonder what hell was like after this. The air was filled with the acrid smell of smoke and the ground was littered with the dead and wounded from the first wave that had gone before. He ran forward over them unheeding, jumping the clutching outstretched arms and stumbling over bodies which were rapidly sinking into the mud where they had fallen. Shells were bursting all around him and he was still going on. A fierce jubilation filled him, together with a hatred for the Huns over the rise who were responsible for mowing his men down. He turned and saw some of his troops holding their rifles and bayonets at the ready.

'Come on,' he yelled. 'Go for them.'

But they fell, one by one, bemused frightened expressions on their young faces until only a few were left. Corporal Hardy was still there, just in front of him now and still unbelievably laughing, though at what sick joke Clifford had no idea, and then the top of his head was blown right off and the laughter fell into the thick sucking mud and was gone. There was no time to stop, no time to think. Clifford went on right into the worst of the machine-gun fire, and then he heard the call to retreat. He rallied the few men he had left and they blundered back the way they had come, stepping on the dead and sometimes noting someone living needing a stretcher.

It was clear that the German lines were still in place. The sacrifice had been to no avail at all. The only difference was in the appearance of the land in between. It was full of still and silent shapes and the mud had lost its dismal colour, running red now, endless red streaks and pools that mingled with the grey.

Clifford crawled the last few yards back to the trench. He slid into it and the slime and the mud embraced him. He vomited over himself and over the mess that was his right arm. He looked at it and felt the whole world spin and revolve until a blackness swept him into blessed unconsciousness.

Amy wondered if she would ever feel clean again. For weeks, since the latest offensive she had been working long hours, frequently both day and night. Each time a convoy of ambulances arrived from the Front there was hardly time to eat, and almost none to bath or rest. The smell of death, and of the blood, vomit and excreta with which many of the pathetic wrecks of men were covered, was with her all the time. They arrived with the most horrific wounds, some of them already dead, others so near death that she knew there was little to be done except make them relatively comfortable in a makeshift bed, probably on the floor. She felt she would never forget the sickening stench or the sight of lice crawling all over raw flesh and exposed bones.

She thought frequently of Arthur and Clifford and

prayed fervently that if either should come here, then their wounds would be simple ones, bad enough to take them out of the war but not too terrible. She sometimes smiled with young men who greeted her jubilantly, displaying a wound in a leg or an arm. 'It's a true Blighty,' they would say. 'No more war for me.' It was the ultimate pleasure, the ultimate irony here in this terrible place.

'Not much chance of the fliers getting those sorts of wounds,' Iris commented with blunt truthfulness. 'If they're shot down, then they've had it I should think. It's not like the others on the ground.'

Amy shuddered. She saw fights between aeroplanes frequently now that she had been moved to this field hospital close to the front line, and always she prayed silently for the pilots up there. Secretly she prayed for the Germans as well. It seemed so frightening to be in the sky and to be shot at, to face burning to death in a twisting plummeting craft. But it was always Arthur who benefited from her longest and most fervent prayers.

The wounded were brought straight to the temporary buildings and tents of the hospital from the trenches where they had been briefly patched or bandaged, sometimes in a Casualty Clearing Station. They came in rickety ambulances driven by girls like herself. Once they had arrived they would be cleaned up, their terrible wounds dressed again, and if they were lucky they would be sent on after a few days to the larger safer hospitals further away, or best of all, back to England. But frequently it was necessary to take them to the makeshift operating tent straightaway. Here, doctors worked right through the hours of daylight and then all night, too, beneath a swinging lamp strung to the uncertain roof above, and to the accompaniment of shelling that hardly ever stopped. Amy thought frequently of her father. Being here brought vividly clear memories of him back to her for it was somewhere like this that he had died. Sometimes she cried out for him in the night as she had done when she was a small child.

Clifford arrived there on a day in September when the rain had at last eased a little and the sky was showing glimpses of blue between heavy clouds. He was aware of none of it. He had lain, frequently semi-conscious, in the bumping ambulance and groaned each time it lurched over the uneven road. The pain in his arm had become steadily worse, the swollen mass of poisoned flesh was fixed in a kind of sling and every time the side of the vehicle pressed upon it his body became one great agony.

Amy had just finished the night shift and was about to climb wearily into her bed when Iris rushed in. She stood there in the doorway, her face pale and her eyes full of fear.

'They've just brought a Captain Buxton in,' she said. 'It might be . . . Clifford.'

Amy pulled her frock back over her head again and didn't stop to add her cap or apron. 'Where is he?' she said, her heart thudding uncontrollably. 'How badly is he injured? Have you seen him?'

'It's only his arm,' Iris replied. 'Yes, I've seen him. He'll be all right. It's just his arm. He's in the arrivals tent.'

Amy ran through the rows of stretchers searching each pain-filled face until she found at last the one she sought. She knelt beside him and taking his uninjured hand in hers, she caressed it gently, tears pouring down her face as she looked at the place where the other should have been. 'Your beautiful hands,' she murmured so that no one could hear, and then she bent and kissed him gently on the lips.

For a second he opened his eyes and stared at her.

311

'Dorothy,' he said, and then he groaned again and was silent.

'He can't be sent on. We'll have to operate here.' He heard the voice through mists of pain and he could see the red cross showing through the canvas roof above his head. He wondered where he was and what they were talking about, but before he could sort out the meaning of the words he sank again into a blackness. Only the faces of Dorothy and Amy, combined into one in his dreams, made any sense.

When he came round from the chloroform he thought he must certainly have died. Bending over him once more was a girl he recognized, the fair hair curling round her face and the blue eyes full of concern. 'Amy,' he muttered, and then as the face receded out of his reach he called again, desperately, 'Dorothy!'

Dorothy, at home and enjoying the comparative peace of Bristol, continued to feel guilty about her life and her job. She seemed to be doing nothing brave or useful. 'Just helping to make chocolate!' she said in disdain one day to her mother. 'And write silly little stories. I ought to be driving an ambulance or something. The thought of Amy out there at the Front makes me feel ashamed.'

'Your stories cheers people up, and the factory makes all them lovely little tins of chocolates for the troops,' Rose said consolingly. 'Think what it must be like to be given one of they before you got to go and fight!'

'Wonderful,' said Dorothy scathingly. 'I expect it gives them a bit more energy to kill another Hun.'

Rose sighed. 'I don't rightly know what be the matter with you lately, Dorothy. You seldom got a pleasant word for anyone.'

Dorothy felt immediately contrite. 'Sorry, Ma,' she

replied. 'I don't like myself very much at the moment either. I suppose I'm worried for Clifford and Arthur, and the war just drags on and on. If I could do something positive I might feel better.'

'Go and visit our lads in hospital then,' Rose suggested. 'I don't know why you don't join one of they groups of girls who go regularly to take them presents and cheer them up.'

'I don't think I'd be very good company, would I?'

'Of course you would. You can do anything you want to if you'll just try a bit harder.'

'All right, Ma,' she said resolutely. 'I'll do it. Some go regularly from work. I'll see if I can join them.'

The last letter from Clifford had been brief. He was going up to the front line again he said and he asked for her prayers and her love. She had given him both liberally but her heart was full of fear.

'I shall do more than visit those who are convalescing,' she said on sudden impulse. 'I shall volunteer to work at the railway station. They need tea-ladies I'm told, for when the ambulance trains come in. I could work two or three nights a week couldn't I? It's not much, but more useful than just visiting. That's too easy.'

So she became one of the workers manning a refreshment stand, ready with tea and coffee as each trainload of weary battle-scarred men arrived in Bristol. She persuaded Vera Price to join her and on their first night the two of them waited nervously behind their laden table. They had both seen plenty of wounded soldiers in hospital blue around the city streets, but those had been relatively cheerful, most of them well enough to walk or hobble, and all were on the way to recovery.

'This is going to be different,' Dorothy warned both herself and Vera. 'We shall see some pretty awful things I expect.' But nothing in her experience or her

313

imagination had prepared for the horrifying reality.

The first train pulled in slowly and chugged to a shuddering halt. They could see faces at the windows and they felt their throat muscles tightening. The doors were flung open and the first men stumbled out. These were the walking wounded who were gently helped to chairs which had been set out along the platform in readiness. Dorothy and Vera had been told not to leave their place behind the table but to make sure that the water was hot and the tea and food ready. They poured and stirred and handed the brimming cups to other helpers who carried them to the bemused and grateful men.

When there was a moment's respite Dorothy glanced up and saw the more seriously wounded being taken from the train with great care and gentleness. They were placed on waiting stretchers and each was given cigarettes and a clean handkerchief. She wondered about the handkerchief but was told later that it was considered one of the most precious things, a symbol of home and comfort and cleanliness.

Some of the men were not capable of lighting a cigarette for themselves and she watched as this was done for them. She shuddered as she saw a stretcher here and there, the blankets completely flat where the legs of its occupant should have been, and there were others more sinister still with no limbs visible at all. They all looked alike, each one just a swathed torso lying still and helpless with a pale face and staring eyes full of a fear Dorothy knew she could barely comprehend.

When no more tea was needed she was asked to collect up the postcards from the more able men. They had all been issued with stamped cards to write to relatives or friends to say that they had arrived safely in Bristol. These would be posted for them straightaway. Dorothy was embarrassed at this first close encounter with so much suffering. She approached the men diffidently and she smiled as she had been instructed to do. 'Listen to them, let them talk to you,' she had been told, and as she did so, she gradually overcame her first nervousness and eventually shared in their joy at being home.

'Look Miss,' one of them said to her happily. 'I've got a real Blighty wound,' and he pointed to his left leg that ended in a bloody bandaged stump. 'They can't send me back without a foot can they!' Dorothy, to her amazement, found herself laughing with him.

On their way home in the early hours of the morning she turned to her companion. 'That's my first real taste of war, Vera,' she said. 'I've lived in a kind of fool's paradise. I didn't know it was so terrible. At least,' she added. 'I suppose we all knew, but knowing isn't the same as experiencing, is it.'

They were both silent for a long time. They walked speedily through the eerie and dimly lit streets towards St Paul's.

'Them with no legs and no arms. Them's the worst,' Vera said at last. 'Just thinking about it makes me feel I want to be sick.'

'We *haven't* seen the worst,' Dorothy contradicted grimly. 'I've heard that some haven't got faces any more.'

'They'd be better dead, wouldn't they!'

There was no answer to that and later when Dorothy at last climbed wearily into her bed for a couple of hours' rest before she had to get up for work again, she felt quite numb with horror. Tired though she was, a long time passed before she slept and then her dreams were so terrible that she was glad to be wakened in the morning by Rose standing at her bedside with a welcome cup of tea.

'Thought you deserved it, Dorry,' she said. 'After seeing all them soldiers I thought you'd need a cup. I heard tell it's not very nice when they first comes in with all them wounds.'

'No. It's not very nice, Ma,' Dorothy said, 'but I'm glad I've volunteered to do it. It's not really enough though is it? I still feel guilty sitting here just writing and sticking stamps on cards while everyone of my generation is dying?'

'You'm exaggerating as usual,' Rose said. 'Now come and have some breakfast and hurry, or else you'll be late.'

'Perhaps I could work in a munitions factory,' Dorothy called down the stairs after the departing figure of her mother.

Rose turned at the bottom and looked up. 'Now I know you'm proper daft. You'll turn yellow. They all go yellow in them factories!'

Clifford was eventually sent back to Bristol but his wound was gangrenous and he hovered between life and death for a long time in the beautiful house at Ashton that had been turned into a hospital for officers. Felicity sat at his side each afternoon and Geoffrey visited every evening. He gazed frequently at the thickly bandaged stump lying on the sheet and although he was not a swearing man he silently cursed the war for the terrible havoc it had wreaked on all his son's generation.

The news did not at first reach Dorothy. She heard it one afternoon when she had to go into the factory to see a girl who was leaving to work in munitions. As she entered the large building she was thinking of her mother's words about turning yellow: she had heard that it was something to do with the chemicals that were used for filling the shells. Did the girls do it for more money or for reasons of patriotism, she wondered? She stared at the pretty dark-haired girl whom she had come to see. She was sitting at the long moving belt of chocolates and Dorothy thought that it seemed much more preferable to be in here than in one of those awful munitions factories she had heard about. But at least women had a choice now, she reflected. At least they were comparatively free to decide for themselves. Suddenly her thoughts were interrupted.

'Heard the news, Miss?' the girl said as Dorothy handed her the insurance card.

'What news is that then?'

'Mr Clifford. Well, Captain Clifford he is now of course.'

Dorothy gripped the table and felt herself trembling. From the girl's tone it could only be bad. 'Tell me then,' she said sharply.

Two or three faces turned in her direction but she was only vaguely aware of their sudden curiosity.

'Wounded bad, they say. Lost an arm and it's poisoned. He don't stand much chance.'

Dorothy didn't wait to hear more. She turned and walked steadily out of the noisy room, trying desperately to control her racing heart. The only one who could give her accurate information was Mr Buxton himself and she cared not one jot what his reaction might be to her enquiries. She tried to assume a suitable decorum, but failed and only when she found herself outside his office door did she pause and nervously adjust her blouse and pat her hair into place.

She entered in response to his loud 'Come in' and stared at him, this man who was Chrissy's father, and the father of the man she loved.

He looked up in surprise. 'Miss Miller? Can I help you?'

'I'm sorry to disturb you, Sir,' she murmured. 'But I just heard that Captain Buxton has been wounded and I should like to know how he is?'

'Thank you,' he said slowly. 'Thank you for your concern. He has been very ill, but they think he will

317

pull through. He lost his right hand, and then the wound became poisoned and they had to amputate to the elbow. However he has regained consciousness once more and when I saw him last evening we managed to talk a little.'

The relief was tremendous and Dorothy felt the room spin around her. She clasped her hands tightly together and tried to regain control. 'I'm so glad,' she said at last. 'I'm so glad he's going to get better.' She couldn't help the relief showing in her face and in her voice. 'Could you give him my . . . my very best wishes please?'

'I will certainly do that. Do you know each other?'

'He came to see my mother before he went back the last time.' As she spoke Dorothy thought she saw a flash of fear pass over Geoffrey Buxton's face. But it was gone almost as soon as it had come and the self-confidence seemed to return.

'Of course,' he said. 'I suppose he wanted to make your mother's acquaintance because of Amy. Very natural.'

He paused and adjusted his cravat and Dorothy wondered if he was not quite so assured as he wished to appear.

'Amy saw my son in France, you know,' he continued. 'Clifford was taken to the field hospital where she is working.'

Dorothy felt her spirits suddenly fall and she looked at Geoffrey hoping he would not go into long descriptions of Amy nursing Clifford. The picture it conjured up in her mind was too painful and she felt again the gnawing of the fierce jealousy that was so much part of her life.

'He hardly remembers seeing her. It was there that his arm was amputated and he was delirious much of the time. It seems a great pity. Apparently she sat at his bedside for hours waiting for some response. Now of course she can't be spared any leave to come and visit him here.'

Dorothy felt relieved at this last piece of news. 'Perhaps I could go to see him when he's well enough to receive visitors?' she queried.

'Probably, my dear,' Geoffrey Buxton said. 'You would remind him of Amy. I will send a message to your office and let you know when that time comes.' He stood up and Dorothy gulped and turned to leave.

'Is your mother well,' he enquired as she was about to open the door. 'And your little sister?'

'Yes. Both are very well thank you,' she said quietly, and then she let herself out and shut the door carefully behind her. She leaned on the wall of the corridor and closed her eyes for a moment to compose herself and then walked slowly back to her office and mechanically did all that was required of her for the rest of the day. It was not until she was mulling everything over in her mind as she walked home that she realized the full implications of what she had been told. His right arm! His music! She stumbled along the busy impersonal streets and all she wanted to do was to rush over to the hospital, to comfort him in any way she knew.

But it was to be three seemingly endless weeks before the message came that he was well enough to see her. She was summoned to the big office and told by a benign Geoffrey Buxton that Clifford was much better, was sitting out in a chair in fact, and that he had been asking for her. He was friendly, and smiled at her as he gave her the news. 'You will remind him of Amy of course,' he said as she was about to leave. 'And that will be good for him.'

It was not until some time later that Geoffrey felt the first stirrings of unease about Dorothy's desire to visit his son. He recalled her flushed face and then remembered Clifford's repeated requests to see her.

Suddenly filled with concern, he determined to write again to Amy and urge her to come home.

CHAPTER FOURTEEN

The letter from Geoffrey had its desired effect. Amy asked for special compassionate leave and it was speedily granted.

Her feelings about going home were mixed as she sat in the train which was clattering its way to Boulogne and she stared disconsolately out of the window at the devastated French countryside. The railway line was bordered by dismal army camps where thousands of enthusiastic tommies had been billeted over the past three years on their way to the Front. There were endless hutted hospitals built there too, conveniently placed to take the pathetic and disillusioned survivors.

Tears filled her eyes for the sadness of it all and she began to think of her life before the war, before all the horrors of the past few years. All those years, all those people, even her parents and Clifford, achieved an insubstantial quality in her mind as she sat on the swaying rattling train. Everything that belonged to those carefree years seemed to exist only in a bubble. For a second she remembered the little clay pipes that she used to play with as a child. Cook would make her up a bowl of warm soapy water and she would dip the pipe into it again and again and then set it to her lips and blow, and the kitchen would be filled with glowing bubbles, some small, some large, each one a perfect sphere of magic, a floating world of enchantment. She would watch them until they came into contact with any hard object and then there was the swift silent ending of their perfection, and only a circle of dampness remained. She felt it was an exact picture of her life.

She struggled to bring her reluctant mind back to reality, back to Clifford, and she thought with pain of those terrible days when he had hung between life and death. The time she had spent at his bedside during his long hours of delirium could have been precious even though fraught with anxiety, but his fevered calling of Dorothy's name had sent numb shock waves through her body time and time again. It was true that he had called her name too. 'Amy,' he said sometimes and then the tears would start to her eyes and she would press his hand with greater love and tenderness.

'Was it my fault?' she questioned herself repeatedly. 'Did my self-pity drive him away from me during that last leave, and how did he come to know Dorothy so well?' The misgivings that filled her mind would not be stilled and she could find no peace in her heart. She was filled instead with unceasing regret for her thoughtlessness. She had been selfish too and that compounded her self-condemnation.

She remembered again how he would stare at her without comprehension each time he awoke, and then would come the name whispered with an intensity that even now made tears fill her eyes again. 'Dorothy!' She could hear his voice and the way he said it, hear the longing that in his weakness he could not disguise.

There had been a letter too. A large fat envelope forwarded on and she had been told that it was from her sister. But Amy didn't recognise the handwriting and she refused to read it to him, leaving that duty to another nurse. She had deliberately been silent when Iris commented on it and her friend had looked at her strangely, obviously wondering who had written the five closely written pages. She had said nothing and the letter had been packed up with Clifford's other things when he left. Amy remembered that day vividly. The envelope had been on the table beside his bed and she had been careful not to touch it. He was still very ill then, hardly conscious, and she wondered if he even remembered who had written it. Had there been other letters though before he was wounded? Had he replied?

Mercifully there had been no time to stop and think during those nightmare times. Hundreds of men were constantly arriving and her own concerns could, with a little difficulty, be pushed to the back of her mind. Fortunately it was Iris who was given the task of preparing Clifford for the journey back to a base hospital. Amy had not needed to touch the letter and she was glad. Just seeing it lying there beside him was bad enough.

The journey to Boulogne was long and tortuous and Amy's thoughts were as dismal as the shattered countryside along the track. But in spite of the discomfort of the crowded compartment her weariness eventually overcame her unhappiness and she slept, a disturbed and agitated slumber full of dreams of unimaginable horror, a combination of all she had seen during the last terrible months.

With his strength gradually returning, Clifford tried to face the thing that had happened to him. That he was alive and likely to remain so was the first fact to be grasped. For two years now, ever since he joined up, he had tried not to think of the future. For most of the men who fought beside him there would be no future. He lay in bed and stared out of the window at the autumn sky, at the leaves that were falling gently from the big oak tree, and then he looked at his arm, or rather at the stump that still throbbed and ached. He was able to move it a little, for the shoulder had not been damaged. It was a useless appendage that angered him, that had to be carefully dressed and bandaged, a badge of his incapacity. And everyone told him he was lucky!

'Ready to get up are we?' The nurse was brisk and efficient. She stood and smiled at him. 'There's a young lady coming to see you after lunch,' she said. 'We must get you shaved and presentable.'

He stared at her with slight hostility, and then he looked at the clothes she was carrying. She put them carefully on the chair beneath the window. 'Doctor says you may get dressed today.' Her words were triumphant as if this were the zenith of achievement. 'See, I've brought your uniform.'

He stared at the freshly cleaned and pressed outfit that had been made ready for him. He remembered wearing it with so much pride but that seemed like years ago, almost in another life. He wanted none of it now. All he wanted was to sit down at the grand piano in the drawing room of what was now a hospital and play, play out his anger and his rage, let the keyboard take all his frustration. But there would be no more of that. He lay there helpless and he was shamed by the tears he could feel on his face as he looked up at the white-clad figure looming over him.

She turned away and he guessed she had seen his grief. 'Sorry, Nurse,' he muttered. 'I'm all right now.' He brushed away the tears with the sleeve of his pyjamas and started to pull awkwardly at the bedclothes with his left hand.

'Right then, Captain Buxton. Up we get.' Her voice was gentler and she drew the sheet carefully back and then put her arm round him and helped him to stand. The room appeared to sway and the floor seemed to come up to meet him. 'Carefully now,' she said, and he was glad of the support of her sturdy arms. He had been allowed to get up and sit in a chair for increasing hours each day but every time he'd felt this weakness at the beginning. He gritted his teeth and determined to conquer it.

Dorothy was extremely nervous. She wondered how Clifford would be. The last time she had seen him she remembered his handsome easy strength, the way his uniform enhanced his good looks, and his smile, the smile that had lived in her mind ever since. Then there were his hands . . . she wrenched her thoughts away from his hands.

The hospital smelt of antiseptic, the pungent clean smell pervaded everything and she shivered as she sat in the great hall waiting to be taken to Clifford's room. The house was very splendid and she stared about her with awe. And then suddenly a nurse commanded her to follow and she was there, outside his door, and finally in the room and he was sitting at the window in a wheelchair.

He looked up at her and smiled. 'Dorothy,' he said, 'thank you for coming.'

'Hello, Clifford,' she whispered. She crossed the room and stood awkwardly, feeling the slightly antagonistic scrutiny of the young nurse.

'I'll get you a chair,' the girl muttered.

When she was seated and they were alone, she felt tears welling up inside her but she gulped and forced herself to smile. She had been to some of the other hospitals in Bristol to visit the injured, but always in an organised group of women. They were charged to keep cheerful all the time, not to stare at unsightly wounds and never, never to weep. And of course the men were strangers. This was quite different.

'How are you?' she asked. Her voice was nervous and strained. She had rehearsed this moment so many times, but now it was here the carefully prepared words refused to come.

'More cheerful now that you're here,' he replied. 'And the war is over for me. My mother at least is very grateful for that.'

'Aren't you glad then?'

He paused and looked away from her, turning to stare out of the window. 'Yes, of course. I must make myself happy about it.'

'You don't want to go back!'

'No. I could never want that.'

'I prayed for you. Every day I prayed and you're safe now.'

'Yes.'

The pain in his eyes as he turned to her again pierced her heart and she wanted to scream at the God who had heard her prayers and answered them, but had taken from the man she loved the thing he prized most dearly. Even a leg would have been better lost than an arm. One could walk with a false leg, but never play the violin or piano with only a left hand. And she had never heard him play. It would be a constant grief now. She knew it was his great passion in life, for in each letter he had written he had talked about music and his joy in it.

'Thank you for your prayers,' Clifford said, and then as if answering her thoughts he added, 'Don't blame God for this.' He moved what was left of his arm painfully. 'It's man's evil that causes wars. And some of my prayers were answered too you know.' He didn't enlighten her any further on that point, but remembering, shivered slightly.

Dorothy wondered what he meant but she just smiled at him and decided that she had better not continue this line of conversation. She thought for a second of his father and then of her own mother and her unwavering faith in a good and loving God. Perhaps Clifford had that kind of faith too. Maybe they were right. What a wonderful comforting thing to possess, she thought and wished, for a fleeting second that she shared it.

'I've brought you two books,' she said, changing the subject. She opened her bag and took out a small volume. It was covered in soft leather and she handed it to him reverently. She had saved for a long time to buy it.

He took it and turned the pages slowly with his one hand. 'It's a wonderful present,' he said at last. 'Thank you, Dorothy. You shouldn't have spent your money on me.'

'Someone gave me a copy like it many years ago,' she said. 'And it's meant a lot to me. There is a bit I especially like, a sort of motto.' She recited the words from memory, 'O, how full of briars is this working-day world!'

'A rather gloomy sentiment isn't it? What made you pick that out of a book of comedies?' Clifford asked.

'I was feeling especially low then. It just matched how I felt. It was my fourteenth birthday and I had to start work in the factory the next day. But my mother reminded me that briars have rather lovely blossoms in summer. I've kept the hope in my mind ever since.'

'A remarkable lady, your mother!'

'Yes, I suppose she is. I've always underestimated her.'

'And have the briars had roses on them yet?'

'Just coming into bud,' Dorothy replied, grinning at him. 'It was my copy of that book that started me off on my writing as a matter of fact. Anyway I thought that Shakespeare's Comedies might cheer you in the way they often cheered me. There are photographs of actors too just like in my copy.' She leaned towards him and together they looked at the illustrations. 'I wish I could see one of those plays in a theatre,' she added a trifle wistfully.

'Perhaps you will one day. They do them here in

327

Bristol at the Theatre Royal in King Street.'

'I shall go,' she said. 'After the war I shall go.'

'I'll take you.' The words were out before Clifford could stop them.

'That would be wonderful,' she whispered. Then she pulled another book from her bag. 'This is a novel,' she said apologetically. '*Wuthering Heights*. It's one I've just read and enjoyed very much. I hope you won't consider it a woman's book. Perhaps you've read it?'

'Emily Brontë. No I haven't. Laura used to talk about it a lot. I'll have time to read now.' He took it from her awkwardly, first placing the Shakespeare down on the table beside him. He leafed through it and then put it down too. 'Thank you. I have nothing to give to you.'

'I don't want anything. Just for you to get better.'

'I shall never get better!'

The bitter words shocked her. 'What do you mean, Clifford? Of course you'll get better.'

'Arms don't grow again do they? That's what I mean. To be better is to be whole. I shall never be that.'

She leaned towards him and took his hand. The long sensitive fingers rested in hers and she stroked them gently. Then she looked up into his eyes and saw the pain, and all her brave intentions vanished and she wept.

Immediately their rôles changed. He was concerned for her now. As she looked at him through tear-filled eyes she saw for one unguarded moment his feeling for her showing nakedly in his own. He covered both of her hands with his remaining one and she could feel his returning strength. 'You will be whole,' she whispered. 'Not in the way you mean, but you will be whole. I know it.'

The precious moment was swiftly gone. He regained his composure. 'Yes,' he said. 'I was just being sorry for myself. I'll try not to be. Not while you are here anyway. I apologize, Dorothy.'

She wanted to scream out at him not to be sorry, not to try to be anything that he didn't want to be. She wanted him as he was with all the hurts and miseries and wounds. She wanted to be able to cradle him in her arms, to comfort and console and to bring him healing. Instead she released her hands from his grip and clasped them primly on her lap. 'Is Amy coming to see you?' she asked. It was something that haunted her. She needed to know.

He looked at her and she couldn't read the meaning in his eyes. 'She writes frequently,' he said. 'She was working in a field hospital at the Front as you know. I was taken there actually. I have a very vague memory of her leaning over me and I still feel it was a dream. The face seemed to be yours at first, but they assured me later that it was Amy and that she sat with me for a long time after the operation.'

'Why doesn't she come home?' There was criticism in her tone.

'I believe she's on her way now actually. My father wrote to her and told her to come. They're very busy over there with so many wounded and it's not easy to get leave.'

Dorothy's heart sank and she found it difficult to reply. They sat for a long time after that and talked only about unimportant things until eventually she felt it was time to leave.

'I shall have to go,' she said. 'I won't come again if Amy will soon be here. I don't think she would like it somehow.'

There was immediate alarm in his voice. 'I need to see you, Dorothy. Please come.' Then he smiled. 'I shall want to tell you how I've enjoyed the books!'

She rose and stood looking down at him. She took his hand and pressed it gently. 'All right then,' she said. 'Just once more.'

Then she bent and kissed him full on the lips, a sudden impetuous action that immediately caused her to turn and rush out of the room without waiting for another word or glance. Outside she paused for a moment before rushing through the hall and out into the autumn sunshine. She had seldom felt so shocked with herself. How could she ever face him again, she wondered, furious with herself. But perhaps Amy would soon be here. Perhaps there would be no question of keeping her thoughtless promise to return. With leaden footsteps she walked back into the city.

'Have you heard the news, Dorry?' Rose asked as soon as she was inside the front door.

'No. What news?' Dorothy's heart seemed to fail for a second. News these days was usually bad.

'Good news this time.' Rose's usually placid voice was quite excited. 'It's Arthur. He've got the Military Cross. His mother is that proud. Oh, Dorry, who would have ever guessed it! Arthur Price getting to be so important. He've got home leave for a few days, then he's staying in England as a flighting instructor, whatever that means, and his ma told me that he's now a flight-commander.' Her words tumbled out one after the other and she promptly stuck her sewing needle right into her finger in her excitement. She thrust the injured finger into her mouth and sucked it noisily. 'He just been round to see if you were in. He looked so grand I was quite struck dumb.'

In spite of all the emotions that crowded Dorothy's thoughts, she couldn't help laughing a little at her mother's elation. 'Well, that's marvellous,' she said. 'I'm glad for him.'

'Glad, is that all you can say? Just glad?' Rose sounded suddenly deflated.

'I've just been to see Clifford Buxton, Ma. Had you forgotten? He's lost an arm. He'll never play the piano or violin again. He's been terribly ill.'

Rose looked contrite. 'Yes. What with thinking of Arthur I'd put poor Mr Buxton right out of my head. How is he?'

It was a difficult question to answer. Dorothy really had no idea how he was, not beneath the surface anyway. 'Getting stronger,' was all she could say.

Amy arrived in Bristol on one of the hospital trains and as it steamed into Temple Meads and shuddered to a halt, she grabbed her bag and stumbled out on to the platform. She vaguely noted the lines of waiting stretchers and the tea ladies behind their tables. She felt filthy and so tired that she just stood quite still and stared in a bemused fashion at the waiting helpers and nurses who surged forward eager to offer assistance. They flowed around her all intent on their carefully rehearsed jobs and for a few seconds she felt totally detached and unable to comprehend where she was or what she must do. The sea crossing had been rough and during most of it, and on the train from the port, she had ministered to countless soldiers and now that the ordeal was at an end her mind and her body refused to function normally any longer.

'Amy!' She heard her name called and turned thankfully to see Felicity running along the platform towards her. Then she was gathered up into strong capable arms.

'My dear, dear child! Whatever have they done to you?'

'Oh, Aunt. I'm just so tired!' After that she could remember nothing until she awoke in the back of the Rover. For a second she wondered where she was and then she felt the leather seat and the heaped up blankets around her and she became aware of Felicity at the wheel. She struggled to sit up. 'What happened?' she murmured.

331

Felicity continued to drive steadily through the dark streets. 'You fainted,' she said calmly. 'Just overtired I think. Now lie there until we get home and then it's a bath and some food and bed.'

Amy pulled the wraps more tightly round herself and suddenly remembered sitting right here in the same seat with Clifford weeks ago, months ago, years ago? It seemed as though a whole lifetime had passed since that time. 'How's Clifford?' she asked.

'He'll be all the better for seeing you,' Felicity stated firmly. 'He gets depressed from time to time. Now don't talk any more. Just rest until we get home.'

Amy was glad to obey. Waves of nausea swept over her and she longed desperately for the end of this interminable journey. When they reached the house she was dimly aware of being helped up the front steps and of Myrtle's frightened face staring at her. Then there was the luxury of a fragrant bath and a warm soft feather bed. She sank into its welcoming depths and slept, slept until some of the infinite weariness of the past months had receded a little. And when she awoke next morning Myrtle was ready with hot milk and with an encouraging smile.

It was a full five days before they would let her go downstairs and during that time she was pampered and spoilt.

'You've been more ill than you realized,' Felicity told her. 'You had quite a fever. Influenza the doctor said. There's a lot of it about. You've been working much too hard of course and we're all very proud of you, but you must make up for it now, and you aren't to go back until you're quite well. Geoffrey has written.'

'Thank you for all you've done, Aunt,' Amy murmured. She felt quite unable to protest. 'How would I have managed without you?'

Felicity ignored this remark. 'Your clothes are still

here,' she said. 'I'll ask Myrtle to come up and sort something out for you. She's been looking after all your things. I think you need something a little more fashionable though. We'll have to see what can be done about it.'

Amy sat on the edge of the bed and smiled weakly at the thought of having to order new clothes. She had not given a moment's consideration to what she wore for a long time. 'I'm sure there's something there that'll do while I'm home, Aunt. The latest fashions can wait.'

'I expect your dresses are too long, dear. Skirts have gone up you know.'

'That won't bother me just now,' she said. 'The most important thing is going to see Clifford. Do you think I'm well enough and not infectious any more?'

'I've told him that you'd probably be able to go tomorrow,' Felicity replied. 'I shall drive you in the afternoon and if the weather is warm you can both walk in the garden for a short time.'

'How is he, Aunt? You haven't answered any of my questions about him. Really how is he?'

Felicity was silent. She stood for a moment and fingered the beads that hung down over the bodice of her blue dress. 'It's difficult to say. Sometimes he talks a lot and during other visits he is very quiet and withdrawn. Of course his music was more important than most other things in his life.'

Amy remembered the Dvořák she had struggled through in order to accompany him when he played his violin all those years ago. The music seemed suddenly to come alive in her head and she hastily brushed her tears away. Then she got up unsteadily and walked over to Felicity and threw her arms around her and together the two women wept.

Clifford was sitting before a great log fire waiting for his visitors. He wondered what he was going to say to

Amy, how he would feel when he first saw her. Dorothy had been twice more since that first visit and on each occasion she had betrayed her feelings for him. Not directly of course, apart from that one and only kiss. He had been deeply moved by that, but had put it down at first to her emotional response to his lost arm. The following visits had made him doubt whether that was the only reason. He couldn't understand the easy relationship that had developed between them. With Amy he had always felt protective, even sometimes slightly ill-at-ease, and he had never been able to share his deepest thoughts with her. Dorothy, however, seemed to know what he was thinking before he spoke. Sometimes it was almost disconcerting. He recalled some of the words in one of the books she had given him. The heroine, Catherine, said of Heathcliff that he was a necessity for her, that he was always in her mind. He was, she said, her own being, her very self. He was beginning to feel like that about Dorothy.

He looked into the fire and watched the flames curling around a fresh log that had just been added and he wondered if an intense relationship like that would do for marriage. In the book, the love of Catherine and Heathcliff had only brought suffering. Then he jerked his thoughts back to reality. He was engaged to Amy. He would have to come to terms with that. She was a sweet gentle girl and he could not walk out on her now. He could never hurt her. She had received enough blows in her life recently without another being added. He loved her. He told himself firmly that he was sure he loved her and he cared very much about her happiness and her well-being. She needed him. He could never marry Dorothy.

When Amy came into the room his heart plummeted with fear for her and with compassion. She was so thin, a sort of pale ghost of Dorothy who was all good health and bouncing enthusiasm.

'Hello, Amy,' he said. 'You've been ill they tell me.' He held out his hand to her and she came to him shyly and took it, but only for a moment. 'It was nothing,' she whispered. 'But how are you?'

'Progressing I suppose.' His voice was suddenly bitter. He was infinitely tired of answering that question.

Felicity was still standing in the doorway. 'I shall leave you for a time,' she said. 'Sister has said it's too cold after all for you to go in the garden, but I need some exercise. I shall go and admire the shrubs.'

She withdrew closing the door gently behind her and they were alone. Clifford reached for Amy's hand again and pulled her down on the chair which had been placed beside his. 'I believe you sat with me for hours when I was delirious after the operation,' he said. 'Thank you. I'm sorry I wasn't really aware of your presence. Those days only exist for me in some sort of fevered dream.'

Amy found it difficult to reply. He obviously didn't know about the name he had repeatedly called during that terrible time. She felt tears threatening as they always did when she thought about it. Then angry with herself for giving way to her private grief, she forced them back and tried to smile. 'I'm glad I was able to be there,' she whispered. 'I was praying for you and willing you to get well.'

'And I did.' He smiled at her. 'You're a dear girl, Amy.'

They looked at each other and both were embarrassed, lost as to what to say next.

'How much longer will you be here?' Amy managed at last. 'Aunt Felicity said you are going to a convalescent centre for officers.'

'Yes, a place in the country, and not far from here apparently. I'm looking forward to it.' He laughed a little grimly. 'Then I suppose I shall be demobbed one day and I shall be dragged into Father's factory at last. There's nothing in the way now of course.' Once again the words were bitter and his eyes strayed automatically to the empty sleeve that was fixed to his jacket.

Amy sat quite still beside him, her hand remaining motionless in his. 'I'm sorry, Clifford,' she said simply. 'So sorry.'

Suddenly the door was thrown open and Dorothy stood there staring at them. Clifford closed his eyes against the hostility in her face as she took in the scene before her. Amy pulled her hand quickly away from him and sat stiffly in her chair.

'Sorry to disturb you,' Dorothy said. 'The man at the door told me you were alone, must have made a mistake.' She walked over to the table beneath the window and placed a small bag upon it. 'Ma sent these,' she explained. 'They're her best little yeast cakes. She made them especially for you.' Then she turned to Amy. 'Well hello,' she said addressing her directly. 'Funny we should meet here.'

The two girls looked at each other and there was immediate tension between them.

Clifford glanced from one to the other feeling the antagonism. He looked at Amy's ashen face as she stared at her sister, and then at Dorothy with her bright eyes challenging them both, her cheeks glowing with good health from her walk in the cold air.

'Hello, Dorothy,' he managed. 'Thank you. For the cakes, I mean.' He moved restlessly, his arm suddenly painful. 'Forgive me for not getting up.' Then he spoke to them both. 'You'll have to get to know each other,' he said.

Amy was the first to reply. 'Yes, we shall. We are twins after all.'

'Special kinds of sisters,' Dorothy said. 'That's what Chrissy calls us.' She laughed, a little grim sort of laugh, and she turned to Clifford. 'How are you today?'

she asked. 'Ma wants a full report.'

'I'm all right,' he replied automatically. There was nothing more to say and the silence in the room was heavy, almost tangible.

At last Amy smiled, that generous sweet smile of hers that Clifford used to love. To his disgust – with himself, not her – he now found it irritating. She addressed her sister. 'I'm glad to see you, Dorothy,' she said. 'But we mustn't tire Clifford, must we. I shall walk in the garden for a while and leave you to entertain him. I need some fresh air.'

She rose and went to the door. As she was about to open it, she looked back pointedly. 'My aunt has the car. Perhaps you would like to ride with us when we leave?'

'Thank you,' Dorothy said. 'That's very kind.'

Clifford watched Amy go and knew that he should call her back, insist that he was quite well enough to manage two visitors, but he was silent.

Dorothy watched her too and also said nothing more until the door closed and they were alone. Then she turned to him, 'I'm sorry I chose just now to come. I won't stay long.' She sounded unsure of herself, her usual confidence gone.

'Don't be sorry. I'm glad to see you.'

Dorothy sat down but not on the chair so recently vacated by Amy. She pulled up a small footstool and arranged herself at his feet. She managed a bright forced smile. 'Then I'm happy too, but I won't come again for a while. I mustn't take time away from you and Amy.'

'I don't know how to answer that,' Clifford said. He suddenly felt overwhelmed. His arm ached alarmingly now and his head began to swim. He breathed deeply and made an immense effort. 'I need you, Dorothy,' he whispered. 'You always give me a sense of optimism and challenge. Those are things I need.'

'I think you need peace and quiet just now,' she replied. 'Two of us are no good for you, and you belong to Amy.'

She took his hand and held it between hers and they were silent for a long time, neither finding any words necessary. Then she got up resolutely and going to the table, brought the bag of cakes over to him. 'Have one,' she ordered. 'Ma is a very good cook!'

They both laughed and she took one herself and ate it with healthy enjoyment. As he watched her, with the crumbs falling on to her lap, his tension began to disappear. He ate first one and then another and they laughed again and the world suddenly seemed a happier place.

'I shall not wait until Amy comes back,' Dorothy said eventually. 'I like your mother but I wouldn't want to face the two of them.'

'You won't accept their offer of a ride back?'

'Most certainly not. Can you imagine it? What on earth would we talk about?'

'I can see your point,' Clifford said. 'But my mother is very wise and kind. She would know how to keep the conversation going. She wouldn't be at all accusing. Anyone who cheers me up as you have done is welcome as far as she's concerned.'

Dorothy shook her head. 'I'm not sure of that and I shall definitely not wait to find out. Thank your mother for her offer please.' Dorothy pulled on her coat and gloves and picked up her bag. 'I need the walk anyway. After eating all those cakes I shall grow fat.'

'When will I see you again?'

She felt a painful tug at her heart but smiled bravely. 'I don't think we should see each other for a time,' she said. 'You have your fiancée now and you don't need me.' She was standing at the door and she didn't go back to where he was sitting or wait for a reply. She knew that she mustn't take his hand in hers again. Quickly she opened the door and blew him a kiss and then rushed out, along the corridor and through the hall hoping that she would not be seen. She forced herself to walk decorously down the long drive and out on to the country road, her mind reeling with the knowledge that she was about to lose the man she loved. She had always known of course that he was not hers to lose, but while her sister was so far away she had been able to blind herself to the unwelcome facts. As she walked back towards the town where there was no one to see, she allowed her tears to flow at last.

By the time she reached the tram-stop her anguish was spent and she wiped her face angrily with her handkerchief. Was she really to lose him or should she fight her sister as she had fought her circumstances all her life? As the noisy vehicle carried her homewards she eventually made her decision. She would give Amy a chance. She wouldn't visit Clifford again while her sister was at home. It would be hard, but it was the right thing to do and she would keep true to her resolve however difficult.

She told her old friend Winifred Gale about it later. It was usually to Vera that Dorothy turned when she wanted companionship, but she felt that this was something she couldn't talk about to Arthur Price's sister. She had spent some time with Arthur during his last leave, and now that he was stationed in England for a time he wrote to her regularly. She knew that he still hoped to persuade her to fall in love with him.

'It's the hardest thing I've ever done,' she told Winifred. 'To stand back and let Amy have Clifford Buxton. It's taken more determination than all my efforts to learn things, to type and write and all that. But I could never be happy if I thought that I'd done wrong. I have to be true to myself as well as to

Clifford.' For a second she thought of her mother's God whom she been brought up to worship and honour. If He was good and required justice as she had been taught, then He too must be brought into her decision. To try and steal Clifford away from her sister was definitely wrong, and would probably bring disaster of some sort, she reasoned.

'But what does Captain Buxton want?' Winifred's voice was doubtful.

'He'll have to decide that won't he?'

'I don't think I could do it. Give up a chap I was in love with, without a fight!'

'I didn't say I was giving up completely,' said Dorothy. 'Only until she goes back. Just to give her a chance. If she'm stupid enough to go back to France without fixing a wedding date, then I'll know that she doesn't really love him, won't I, and that'll be different. I shan't feel guilty then. I couldn't do it if I was feeling guilty all the while. I'd never have a moment's peace, and all the time I'd be expecting something bad to happen.'

'A sort of punishment do you mean?'

Dorothy wasn't sure quite what she meant. It was just a feeling she had, a certainty that she must do the right thing. It was important for happiness all round.

'Maybe,' she said. 'I don't really think we get punished for our sins, not down here in this life anyway. But I'm not going to risk it, Winifred.'

'I suppose you'm right,' her friend said. 'Yes, all in all I suppose you'm right!'

CHAPTER FIFTEEN

The journey back to France was not as unpleasant for Amy as the homeward one some weeks before, although it was much more fraught with doubts and misgivings. Physically she was perfectly well now and quite capable of managing the long railway journey and the sea crossing: when at last she heard the sound of distant guns she almost welcomed it for she knew that she was desperately needed here. It was a good feeling. At home, although she had been cossetted and spoilt by Felicity, she had sometimes felt out of place and even superfluous. Perhaps this was where she really belonged, here amongst the wounded and the dying.

She looked out of the window of the train at the battle-scarred countryside and thought about Clifford. In many ways it had been difficult to leave him, but the relationship between them had sometimes been strained and difficult and she had begun to feel that she wanted more time to sort out her emotions, to prepare for her marriage.

'Shall we marry in the summer then?' he had said on that last visit. 'Would you like that, Amy?'

He had been holding her hand in his and she remembered the look in his eyes. She could not wholly decipher it, but she was sure that it contained affection and concern, anxiety too. But was there love, the kind of love she had read about, the magical thing that was supposed to set your blood on fire and your veins tingling? She was ashamed now that her own first thoughts when he broached the subject of their wedding date had been of the war. Would it be over by then? Would she be free?

'If the war should not be ended, Clifford, it would be difficult for me to leave,' she had replied.

Sitting now in the noisy train, she winced. She knew that it was an excuse. She would certainly be able to obtain a release in order to marry and care for an injured service-man. Why had she prevaricated? And why was it that he was always more precious to her when they were apart? It had been exactly the same during the last leave before he was wounded. There was a restraint between them when they were together. In spite of her feelings for him it had always been so. Amy felt that if he were right here beside her now, she would fling her arms around him and say she wanted to marry him as soon as possible. Yet she knew perfectly well that she wouldn't do any such thing, because how she wanted to be, and how she actually behaved in his presence were two totally different things.

He had been kind and affectionate this last time, almost dispelling all her doubts about Dorothy. She thought about his last kisses with pleasure, and resolved to write as soon as she could. She wished to make amends for any perceived coldness on her part. Perhaps she would agree that they should marry in the summer as he had suggested. She was sorry now that she had refused to name a definite date and had even given him the impression that she wanted to wait until the war ended.

An ambulance met the train. It was to take her and a few more returning VADs back to the hospital and as she climbed into it a feeling of expectation and purpose gradually began to take the place of the doubts and insecurities she had been experiencing ever since Felicity waved her off at Temple Meads Station.

'Good time?' one of the girls asked.

'Yes, fairly good,' Amy replied. 'And you?'

'Getting married as soon as I can be released,' her companion told her. 'My fiancé was blinded at Passchendaele. He needs me. I think they'll let me go pretty soon under the circumstances.'

Amy sat in the swaying bumping vehicle and looked at the girl with respect. She wished that she could honestly say that Clifford needed her, sure that if he had told her so – seemed vulnerable – then she would have behaved very differently. In her presence he always put up a front of strength and independence even when she sensed that he was far from feeling those things. She could never seem to get through to the man underneath. She sighed. In those days of his semi-consciousness when he had lain in the hospital, helpless before her, she had loved him deeply, ministered to him with affection – and been terribly hurt by the name of her sister she'd heard so often on his lips. All those things had been hard to forget when she saw him again.

The girl sitting opposite her would have to face a life of much grief and self-sacrifice, Amy reflected as she looked at her, yet in many ways she envied her. To be needed was perhaps the most important thing.

The ambulance made so much noise on the rough tracks that conversation was difficult and the girls sat without speaking for most of the remaining journey. At last the vehicle turned in at the barbed-wire gates of the hospital. The journey had been cold and long, and they all clambered thankfully down and gathered up their kit bags. Amy was rather ashamed of her large suitcase. Felicity had been shocked by her appearance when she came home and had insisted on packing the most unsuitable things for her return. The case was heavy and cumbersome and she stumbled along the path to her billet hoping that Iris would be there. It was almost like coming home!

'Lovely to see you again,' her friend greeted her, kissing her fondly. 'I've missed you and I worried about you when I heard how ill you were.' Then Iris looked at her critically. 'You seem all right now though. I thought you'd be all wan and weary!'

Amy dumped her case on the bed and looked around at the familiar little hut with its spartan furnishings. Where on earth was she to put the new dresses and the coat?

'I'm fully recovered now, but how about you? You've been ill too.'

'Just a touch of fever. Nothing bad enough to get me sent back. I had four whole days in this place though, confined to bed. Not pleasant!' Iris had been sitting on her bed writing a letter. She replaced her pen and paper on the shelf and screwed the top safely back on the bottle of ink. 'I really didn't expect you to come back. I thought you'd manage to get a discharge somehow. It can sometimes be done, I'm told, if you're getting married.'

'Getting married? Who said anything about getting married?'

'Well you're engaged aren't you and he's been badly wounded? Surely that's enough reason.'

Amy slumped down on her own bed beside the unopened suitcase. 'I've been rather stupid again, Iris. He wanted to settle on a date for the summer, but I said that I needed more time. I even suggested that I'd like to wait until the war ends, and now I regret it. I started to have doubts as soon as the train pulled out of Temple Meads, I think.' She shook her head in despair. 'Yes I know it's silly, but I've always been like this. When I'm with him I get scared about the idea of a permanent relationship, and then when we're apart I just long to see him again!' She pulled off her fine kid gloves and twisted the large diamond ring on her finger. 'I always worshipped him when I was a child,' she admitted thoughtfully. 'That's not quite the same thing as being in love is it, though?'

'You sound as if you don't know.'

Amy took a deep breath. 'Well don't all couples have doubts?' she said. 'Sometimes anyway?'

'Perhaps some do,' Iris replied. 'I've never really been in love so I can't tell. I hope I'll know one day, but' – she shrugged her shoulders unhappily – 'with so many men being killed I'm sometimes tempted to give up hope.'

'Fiddlesticks!' Amy said. 'You mustn't do that, Iris. Don't ever do that.'

'Perhaps there might be someone around sometime,' Iris said. 'Anyway we're talking about you. How about everything else? Your . . . your other mother? Did you go to see her?'

'No I did not!' Amy's voice was suddenly determined and cold. 'In spite of the fact that I suppose I am really Amy Miller and not Amy Harding, I didn't go to see her! I don't really know who I am do I? Perhaps that's what's at the bottom of my refusal to give Clifford a definite date for our wedding. How can you get married if you're a non-person?'

Iris stared at her friend a little coldly and then put her hands on her shoulders as though she wanted to shake her. 'Don't be so stupid and don't make silly excuses,' she said. 'Of course you are still Amy Harding. Stop all the self-pity. Your parents gave you their name and that's the one you must keep.'

'My parents? Who are they? A sewing woman and a factory worker, and their name is Miller.' Amy shook off her friend's hands. 'And there's Christabel too. My mother . . .' she paused on the last word. 'I just couldn't face her or the child after hearing what Arthur Price told me.'

'I think you're being hard and cruel, Amy,' Iris said.

'And that's not like you at all. Where has all your compassion gone? You know nothing about Mrs Miller. Just because you don't know who your little sister's father is you're behaving in a very unkind way. I can't understand you.'

Amy felt considerably chastened by her friend's unexpected criticism, enough to be jolted out of her self-righteousness. She had thought much about her mother during the weeks at home and had frequently wondered whether to tell Felicity and Geoffrey what she knew about her small half-sister, but something had prevented her. It was as if this were a stain on herself, something which she wished to push from her mind. If Felicity wondered why she had not gone to visit Mrs Miller she had said nothing, and Amy had not volunteered any thoughts on the matter. It had not been discussed between them.

She had even kept her secret when Laura came home from Cambridge for just two days to see her.

'If you were me you would understand,' Amy told Iris. 'You can't possibly know how it feels one minute to be a person with wonderful parents, and the next to have to accept that they aren't yours at all. And just when you are coming to accept that, to be told that your mother . . . I think it's all this that has made me find it difficult to relate to Clifford properly.'

'Why don't you tell your Aunt Felicity about Christabel? From what you've told me I think she sounds just the person to confide in.'

'I shall have to one day, but I can't yet, Iris. I just can't, and of course I should have to tell Clifford before we marry. That thought was on my mind too. What would he say? He's accepted that I'm not who I was, but perhaps he wouldn't be so keen if he knew that my mother is a whore!'

'You mustn't say that!' Iris shouted at her. 'You must not call her that awful word.'

Suddenly it was all too much and Amy desperately wanted to feel carefree again. Her problems whirled around in her head and made her want to scream at them all to go away and leave her in peace, or at least as much peace as anyone could have here on a battlefield. But there were two kinds of peace she thought, and peace of mind was also desirable, whatever the outward circumstances. Perhaps she was worrying too much about everything. She looked at her friend and grinned at her. 'You're right to be cross with me,' she said. 'I won't say it again, I promise, and yes all right, I'll try to be more sensible. I'll write to my . . . my mother as soon as I can, and I shall write to Clifford this very night.'

'That's good then,' Iris said 'And don't take yourself too seriously. You're just fine really. Maybe a little too full of high ideals sometimes. Anyway let's see what you've got in that great suitcase you've lumped all the way here. I can't imagine what goodies you've brought.'

'No food,' Amy told her. 'Most things are in short supply at home.' She pulled the case towards her and started to undo the buckles of the strong leather straps that had been securely fastened by Geoffrey. Then she flung open the lid and pulled out the dress which lay on top. The sight of its flippancy, so out of place here made her laugh, made her spirits rise a little. 'Let's not quarrel, Iris,' she said. 'Look at this. Aunt Felicity insisted that I had some new clothes and I've brought a few things back. I don't mind if you borrow them sometimes. We're the same size.'

Iris gasped as Amy held up the dress. 'Where are you going to hang it, and when are you going to wear it? It's beautiful but not very suitable for a place like this is it!'

'I'll keep all of them in the case under the bed. There's nowhere else.' She took out each garment in

347

turn and held them up for inspection. 'It will soon be Christmas. There might be some sort of occasion when we want to dress up!'

Iris laughed. 'Well we can hope, but I can't see much possibility. The shelling doesn't stop for Christmas!'

There were three dresses each one a different colour, all simple, with little ornament, the beauty lying in the material and the cut. There was a three-quarter length jacket, too, that matched all three, and long strings of bright beads.

'And hats too,' Iris exclaimed taking one from the case. It was small and round and she perched it on her head and peered at herself in the mirror. 'You've actually brought hats. You'll cut a dash in those, but I can't think when. There's hardly any time to eat and sleep lately, let alone change out of our uniforms.'

'I know. It was stupid to bring any of these things, but Aunt Felicity went to such a lot of trouble to get them and I don't think people at home have any idea how things are over here. I just couldn't tell her. Uncle Geoffrey is my guardian and he might have refused his permission for me to come back if he had known just how bad it is. I hope the dresses don't get any lice on them,' she added. 'Do you know that there were some in my clothes when I arrived home? Myrtle told me that she had the fright of her life when she was taking them down to be washed.'

'Who's Myrtle?'

Amy was just about to say, 'my maid' but stopped herself in time. 'She works for my aunt,' she said instead. 'I don't think she'd ever seen a louse or a flea before. I told her not to tell Aunt Felicity!'

'She's the aunt who was force-fed isn't she?'

'Yes. I don't suppose she'd have been too shocked really. She's pretty down-to-earth, but I wanted to be sure that I would be allowed to return here. I certainly didn't want anyone to know that we catch lice!'

They both laughed.

'But you're almost twenty-one aren't you? Your uncle won't have any control over you after your birthday, will he?' Iris said.

'I shall be twenty-one on New Year's Day and I don't know what say he'll have over me after that. None probably, but until then he could have stopped me returning and I hadn't the energy to argue with him. It was easier if there were no problems. That was why I went along with Aunt Felicity about bringing all these clothes back. It set her mind at rest.' She picked up one of the dresses and held it in front of Iris. 'This one suits your hair-colour,' she said. 'We might get another day off. You never know, we could meet up with Arthur Price and his friends again.'

'You've only just come back and you're talking about leave,' Iris teased. 'It's pretty though, this dress.' A dreamy look came into her eyes. 'I liked Arthur Price and his friends.'

'You shall wear whichever one you like best,' Amy told her. A sudden sparkle returned to her eyes and she laughed. 'Come on, Iris. I'm starving. Let's get over to the canteen and see if there's any food. I've quite missed the stodge.' She folded the clothes carefully and forced the suitcase lid down, then pushed it unceremoniously under the iron bedstead. 'It's going to be weeks before we get any leave anyway. We shall have to forget all about the finery for a long time I expect.' She put on her uniform, fastened her apron and nurses's hat. 'I must report back and get on the duty rota again.'

'Happy Birthday, Dorry,' Rose said. 'And a Happy New Year too. Let's hope this old war comes to an end soon. Just fancy, here we are in 1918 and it's still going on.'

Dorothy kissed her mother briefly. 'Yes. We all want

that. A Happy New Year to you anyway, Ma.'

'I've got a present for you.' Rose took a parcel from the cupboard and handed it to her with obvious pride. 'It's just the usual,' she added. 'But not made-up. I reckon you'd prefer it this way now you've got your own ideas.'

As Dorothy unwrapped the brown paper she gasped with pleasure. Inside was a length of material and a set of pictures of the latest fashions, no frills anywhere to be seen, just smart tailored clothes.

'I thought that I'd make it up for you in the way you want. No more fancy things like I used to sew. You must choose. There's enough for a dress and a loose coat to match if that's what you'd like.'

They both laughed, remembering many previous birthday outfits, then Dorothy spread the soft flame-coloured wool out on the table and its brilliant colour filled the small room so as to lend it a sudden joyousness. 'Thank you, Ma. Thank you for choosing such a wonderful colour,' she said. 'It's so beautiful. Do you think you could get it done for the weekend?' She looked at the illustrations and immediately chose one of a simple dress with a three-quarter length coat. 'That's the one I should like. Material like this needs no decoration.'

'That only gives me four days,' Rose said doubtfully. I'll try though. Why the weekend? What are you doing that's so important?'

Dorothy stared at her mother a trifle defiantly, knowing the criticism that would follow the announcement of her plans. 'I'm going to see Clifford,' she said.

'Oh Dorry, you promised me that you wouldn't.'

'Yes, I know I did. And I've kept my promise. I didn't say that I'd never go again did I? I just said that I wouldn't go for a few weeks. Now I've decided not to be brave and good any longer. I'm going to do just what I should have done a long time ago.'

Rose slumped into the chair. 'And what about Amy?' she said.

'Well what about Amy?' Dorothy repeated. 'That's what you always say to me whenever Clifford's name is mentioned. Amy's gone back to France just as though he didn't exist, back to that precious hospital of hers. I made a promise to myself that I would give her a chance, and if they fixed a date for their wedding and everything was settled, then I'd put him right out of my mind. But there's something wrong between them, Ma. I just know it. I've kept my promise anyway. If I was engaged to him the last thing I'd do would be to rush off and leave him. I'd be at his side all the time helping him through his convalescence. She's asking for all she'll get!' Dorothy didn't want to spoil her birthday or the gift by feeling angry and hurt, but resentment against Amy surged over her again as it so often did. 'She didn't come to see you either, did she, Ma?' she added. 'She was home in England for a good long time and she completely ignored us.'

'That's as maybe, and I dare say she had her reasons.' Rose had been hurt by the non-appearance of Amy as well as worried about her illness, but she had no intention of letting Dorothy share her pain. She would have liked to have made her some new clothes, too. She sighed and wondered for a moment what Amy thought about Christabel. If she suspected that the child was born out of wedlock would she be too shocked to want to come here again? And what if she told Mrs Buxton? These thoughts always sent shivers up and down Rose's spine, but when that happened she turned her eyes heavenward and prayed to her Maker to sort things out. After all He'd want to protect His own wouldn't he, and Mr Buxton was a good Christian gentleman and one of the best preachers she'd ever heard. Surely the Good Lord would look after him and protect his good name even if he had sinned, she reasoned.

With her peace thus secured, she returned to the subject of her erring daughter. 'I think you're doing wrong. Mr Clifford is engaged to your sister and what they do is their own affair and nothing to do with you. You shouldn't go to see him no more, not after what you told me about how you feel for him.'

'But Ma, I truly do love him, and we enjoy being together. If they don't love each other isn't it even more wrong for them to marry just because it was all arranged a long time ago?'

'No it isn't wrong. I told you, Dorry, love grows after marriage. You ought to marry that poor Arthur. He's a good boy and always hankered after you.'

Dorothy gave an exasperated sigh. 'He's certainly not "that poor Arthur" as you call him, and I won't marry anyone I don't love. He's an officer now as you know and probably has lots of girls queuing up to go out with him. But I'm not going to be one of them and that's that! I like him very much and we're good friends. That's all, Ma.'

Rose looked doubtfully at the material that she had bought with such pleasure. She had no wish now to rush to make it up. Not if it was for a weekend visit of which she wholeheartedly disapproved.

Dorothy followed her glance and interpreted it correctly. 'I don't suppose you'll do it for me in time then?'

Rose was silent, a mass of conflicting emotions circling round and round in her head. She loved this daughter, wanted the best for her, but did that include hurting Amy who had suffered so many losses lately? She couldn't find the answer. Perhaps it was better just to let things go along without interfering. All three of her daughters had strong wills of their own anyway and there was little she could really do to influence them.

Even Chrissy, just turned five, was difficult sometimes. At last she spoke. 'Yes I'll do it, Dorry. You shall have it for Saturday.'

The house, now a convalescent home for officers, stood on a small rise with trees behind and a great circular drive at the front. Dorothy paused and looked with awe at the old weathered stone. She had never seen such a beautiful building. Clifford had described it to her in one of his letters but she hadn't been able to imagine anything so lovely. It was an old manor house dating back to the time of Queen Elizabeth he had said.

She walked nervously along the drive, her new shiny black shoes scrunching uncomfortably on the gravel. She eventually reached the door. It had a forbidding air, and she wondered what to do next. There was a great iron knocker and a bell with a pull-rope. She was still undecided when the door was flung open and a smiling nurse greeted her. She was infinitely glad of the girl's friendly smile.

'I saw you coming up the drive,' the nurse explained. 'I believe you've come to see Captain Buxton. He's been waiting for you all the morning.'

Dorothy followed her into the hall and vaguely noticed a great polished table and high walls displaying shields and armour right up to the soaring roof. It was not a bit like the hospital. There was no antiseptic smell, and no wheelchairs to be seen. She shivered a little with apprehension, for it was intimidating. She couldn't imagine living in such a place.

But the drawing room into which she was shown was smaller with flowers in a bowl on the sideboard and she immediately felt more comfortable. The wintery sun was streaming through long windows and Clifford was sitting reading. Her heart thudded with happiness as she saw him. He rose from his chair easily as the door opened and he strode towards her, his one arm outstretched in greeting.

'Lovely to see you at last, Dorothy,' he said. 'I've been counting the hours.'

She took his hand in hers for a moment and then released it. There was so much she had prepared to say in these precious opening moments, but the words deserted her. 'You look so well. I'm thrilled to see you so much better.' It sounded trite but it was all she could manage. She felt the colour flaming to her face, matching her bright new clothes, and she was acutely aware of the interest of the other two occupants of the room.

'Aren't you going to introduce us?' one of the men asked. 'You can't keep such a charming visitor to yourself, Cliff old chap.'

'Just watch me,' Clifford replied with a grin. 'One brief handshake is all you're getting. Dorothy, meet Captains Brook and Davis.'

Dorothy smiled at each of them and shook hands, noticing with a twist of agony that both had two arms, two capable hands. There were no obvious signs of wounds.

They talked of unimportant things for a time, superficial conversation to fill in the difficult minutes and Dorothy found herself silently willing them to leave. Eventually they fulfilled her wish and as the door closed behind them she looked at Clifford. Really looked. She was aware of the tall handsome form, the easy grace, but there was a nervous quickness to every action that had never been there before, and he was smoking, fast, one after the other.

'I hope you don't mind this,' he said indicating the cigarette. 'It helps, you know.'

'Of course not. It just seems strange. You've never smoked before have you?'

'Everyone does here. I enjoy it now.'

They walked over to the window seat and sat down, keeping a respectable distance between them. Dorothy noticed a grand piano standing against the wall, covered with an immense brown cloth. She turned away quickly but not soon enough. Clifford saw her glance in its direction and when she looked at him again she was aware of a sudden bitterness that swept over him like a shutter, taking all light from his eyes.

'I want to throw the cover off that thing every time I come in here. I sometimes wonder how I can sit in the same room with it.'

His words were cold and she wanted to weep for him.

Again she was completely lost for the right thing to say and she silently wished that he knew how much she cared, and how much his grief wounded her too. She turned to the window for escape from her thoughts. Outside the sky was blue and a winter-flowering shrub blazed in full glory at the side of the lawn.

'Are you allowed in the garden?' she asked on impulse. 'Look, the sun is shining.'

She watched him and saw his eyes clear a little. She could almost feel the immense effort that he was making to tune in to the world of ordinary happy things.

Then at last he turned to her and smiled. 'Yes of course I am,' he said. 'I'll show you the lake. It's quite beautiful.'

As soon as they were out of sight of the house, they walked hand in hand along the narrow path that led between old beech trees down to the water's edge. Underfoot the fallen leaves of autumn still made a soft dry carpet and Dorothy was grateful, for her new shoes were uncomfortable. When they reached the end of the small wood they stood together and stared at the wide expanse of shimmering water, and at the swans and ducks which came hopefully towards them.

'We feed them sometimes,' Clifford said. 'No one shoots the ducks any more and they've become tame.'

'I hate the thought of shooting,' Dorothy said. 'It's sad even to end a bird's life just for pleasure. They're so lovely.' As soon as she had spoken the words she realized how they must sound and was appalled at her own lack of thought.

But Clifford laughed at her! 'Yes,' he said. 'I think I hate the thought of shooting too.'

She turned to him. 'I'm sorry,' she whispered. 'I didn't think. I say such stupid things.'

'Nothing stupid about that,' he replied. 'If anyone back from France wanted to shoot for fun, even birds, then I should imagine he would be quite crazy. But come on, let's stop talking about death. We've got some living to do.'

She looked up at him. The distressing mood had been set aside. He seemed almost cheerful. He took her hand and they walked close together and she even managed to ignore the discomfort of her feet in the joy of his nearness.

'Why has it been so long since you last came?' he enquired suddenly. 'I've missed you Dorothy. I didn't know you could be so unkind!'

'Isn't it obvious why I couldn't come,' she replied. 'You are engaged to Amy. You are going to marry my twin sister!'

He was silent for a time and then at last he spoke slowly and thoughtfully. 'My relationship with you is quite different,' he said. 'Amy needs me, always has I suppose, but you are more an equal, a friend. The other half of me.'

She gasped at his words and wanted to shout out at him that he would have to choose, that he couldn't have both, but she was silent and they walked on without saying any more until the path led them round a bend in the lakeside. A small building stood there made solidly of stone, the roof covered with decaying thatch. It fronted directly on to the water.

'What's that?' she asked.

'It might have been a cottage years ago, but it's a boathouse now and there's a room in the roof. We can go in and have a look if you like. It's not locked. Some of the fellows keep some fishing tackle there.'

Clifford pushed open a small door that was set in a larger one and they stooped to enter. It was gloomy inside for there was only one tiny window but Dorothy could just see that there were two small boats pulled up on to the concrete floor and she could smell the unpleasant odour of stale fish. An old spiral staircase led, presumably, to the room above. She wrinkled her nose and shivered.

'It's rather creepy isn't it?' she said. 'And the floor feels slimy and horrid. I'm a bit scared about what I'm walking on.'

Clifford laughed. 'Only bits of old bait I should think,' he replied, 'But wait till you've seen upstairs. I'll go first.' He led the way to the staircase. It was wooden and bare and as he went up each tread creaked alarmingly, but she followed slowly, holding on to the wobbling banister rail. Then suddenly they were up into the sunlight and she gasped in surprise.

'Yes it's lovely isn't it. We think it might have been used at some time as a studio.' Clifford went over to the window. 'This was obviously let into the wall a long time after the place was originally built; must have been some job with the thickness of the walls. It faces south and gets any sunshine that's around.'

The room was square, the exact size and shape of the building, and the walls were plastered and painted white, giving it a bright airy appearance. There were paintings of birds, original watercolours, not

357

particularly good, but attractive in that setting, and a large settee stood opposite the staircase. It was covered with a woven rug and scattered with cushions. A solid oak table stood under the window with a vase of dead flowers set upon it.

'And it has a fireplace too,' Dorothy remarked in amazement. 'Why should a tiny place like this have such a huge fireplace?'

'That's another mystery about it,' Clifford replied. 'You probably didn't notice the one downstairs. The chimney runs right up that side of the building and serves the two. But it's useful. We light a fire here every now and then just to keep the place habitable and to get away from Matron. The gardener lays in supplies of logs.'

Suddenly Dorothy was overcome with confusion as the probable use of this pleasant room became obvious to her. 'Well there's no fire now and I'm getting cold,' she said. 'Hadn't we better go back.'

Then without warning he pulled her roughly towards him and with his one arm he held her tightly and pressed his mouth down on to hers. For a moment she gasped and then, as she felt all the power and the passion in him, she gave herself to his embrace and her arms went round him. They sank on to the settee and she didn't care about the coldness of the cushions. He was on top of her and she wanted to give herself to him totally, holding nothing back. Her hands fumbled with her clothing and she was hardly conscious of the precious new coat and the dress, they were simply garments that were now merely in the way. Then suddenly he was pushing her gently away. He stood up slowly and looked down at her.

'Dorothy, I'm sorry. I shouldn't have done that.'

She sat up hurt and afraid. 'Why Clifford? Why are you sorry?'

'Because I am not free. As you so firmly told me

just now, I am already attached.' There was anger in his voice and he turned away from her.

She jumped up and took two determined strides over to him. She put her hands on his shoulders and spun him round to face her and was shocked by the ravaged expression on his face. But she carried on, regardless. 'Ever since I knew that Amy was my twin sister I've been jealous of all her good fortune,' she shouted. 'Her money, her clothes, her education – and now she's got you too.' Her voice was shrill and passionate. 'And I don't mean to let her have you, do you hear me, Clifford? She can't have you as well!'

A great force of savage energy swept over her and she put her arms round him and kissed him full on the mouth as he had done to her moments before, but with even more passion and more determination. She backed to the settee pulling angrily at her clothes with one hand and holding him with the other. And he responded. She knew immediately and with a great sense of triumph that she had won. Amy Harding could keep her money and her fancy voice. She would never have Clifford!

She moaned with joy and pain, and then with ecstasy as he took her brutally and with all the force of his anger and his youth. It was not how she had imagined it would be but she was filled with elation and satisfaction. When it was over she lay quite still on the soft feather cushions waiting for him to speak. He pulled himself gently away at last and knelt on the floor beside her since there was no room for them to lie side by side. They stayed like that for a long time, without speaking, and then he got up and she watched him struggle with his clothes. She was filled with love and compassion when she saw him grit his teeth as he tried to get his still-bandaged stump back into the sleeve of his jacket.

As suddenly as it had come, the determination and

strength drained from her, replaced with a sober knowledge of what she had done. She looked at Clifford anxiously and a great surge of relief spread over her as she saw him smile. He picked up her dress and coat and put them on a chair and then he came over to her again and sat on the edge of the settee. With the fingers of his left hand he gently traced the outline of her lips and then her neck and breasts.

'My precious Dorry,' he whispered. 'The first time for both of us, and so wonderful. Thank you.'

They didn't talk very much after that, just walked together right round the lake and then back to the house, each hoping that what had happened was not written on their faces for all to see.

'Tea and cakes in the Great Hall,' the gushing young nurse announced as soon as they were inside, and Dorothy was glad of the noise and bustle to distract her. Then it was time to go. A lift had been arranged for her in the motor car of another visitor going back to the city. There was no time or privacy for tender farewells.

'I'll write,' Clifford told her as she settled herself in the back of the large tourer. 'I hope you don't mind my awful writing. It's still difficult with this stupid left hand.'

She shook her head. She wanted to tell him that his large and scrawly words penned unevenly over the page always made her cry, and that those pages were the most precious things she possessed. But all she managed to say was a quiet and formal, 'I'll look forward to a letter.'

Their eyes held for a moment and then he turned away from her.

'A splendid car,' he said making conversation with the elderly chauffeur who was busy cranking the engine.

'A Sunbeam, Sir,' the man said. 'You drive, do you?'

'I did. Can you drive with one arm?' The words were bitter.

The man straightened up and stared at him. 'Don't see why not,' he said. 'Surprising what you can do when you've a mind to.'

Listening, Dorothy was suddenly cheered and she smiled. 'If you can teach yourself to write with your left hand you'll manage to drive somehow,' she said.

'And the first thing I'll do is come to see you.' He was looking at her again and she tried to read his dark eyes. She hoped that there was love as well as deep affection and caring. Her heart beat faster and she could feel colour flaming to her face once more.

Then as the motor carried her further away from him, she turned and waved until they passed through the gates and there was only the darkening sky and the powerful lights of the vehicle piercing a way along the narrow lane.

'Where would you like me to take you, Miss Miller?' her fellow traveller asked.

'The nearest tram-stop please,' Dorothy replied.

'Are you sure, my dear? I am quite willing to take you right home.' The accent was aristocratic and the woman's clothes of the finest quality.

'It is very kind of you, but the centre will be fine. There are some things I want to do before I go home.' Dorothy's words were proud. She could not admit to someone like this that she lived in St Paul's.

Rose was waiting for her when she eventually arrived.

'Well then, what happened?'

'What do you mean?' She blushed at her mother's words.

'What did he say? How is he?'

'He's much better in himself, but depressed still about his arm, about his music and everything.'

Rose was busy with the evening meal and she returned to the scullery. 'And are you seeing him again then?' she called through the open door.

'Oh, Ma. I don't know. I don't know anything. Don't ask me about him.' Suddenly it was all too much and she ran out of the room and up to her own bedroom. They had come to no understanding. She had staked everything on that one desperate bid to take him from Amy, given him her very self. At the moment of her triumph she had been completely confident but now, in the cold little room, the doubts began to surface. She was even unsure of his love in spite of all their shared closeness before this day, in spite of the long letters and deep friendship that had grown between them. Would his sense of duty to Amy still predominate? She removed her new clothes remembering vividly the time only hours before when she had pulled them from her body with such speed. She put the coat and then the dress on large padded hangers and smoothed out the creases. Then she placed them in the big wardrobe. She pulled on her serviceable grey dress, took the pins out of her hair and brushed the long golden waves again and again.

She did everything automatically, her mind on Clifford. How was she going to wait, to survive if she had to watch him marry her sister? A shudder convulsed her slender body and it was followed by a surge of fresh determination. What was she thinking about? This was a contest that Amy must not be allowed to win! Dorothy thought of all her own hard-won accomplishments as she always did when any doubts or misgivings crept into her mind. She had a vast number of published stories to her credit now, her first novel was on submission with a publisher and had received a favourable first reading. At Buxtons she was respected and her job secure, and she had been able to hold her own against anyone on the tennis courts last summer. That was important too. She thought of all those things with pride as she plaited her hair. She coiled each long braid round and round, pinning first one and then the other into neat earphones over each ear. It was a style that she had seldom used lately, but it gave her an added maturity and that was what she needed just now. She lifted her head proudly as she surveyed her handiwork in the mirror.

Suddenly Chrissy bounced into the room and stared at her with Clifford's eyes.

'Hello, Dorry,' she said. 'Have you had a nice day with Uncle Clifford?'

'Who told you to call him that?' Dorothy enquired sharply.

'No one. I just did. What else should I call him? I suppose if he's going to marry Amy though he'll be my brother-in-law. Well I don't know what that means but that's what Mam said.'

Dorothy looked at the little girl and her own contrived composure suddenly vanished. 'Don't you ever say that again,' she said fiercely. 'He's not going to marry Amy, do you hear me!'

The dark eyes looked at her in pain and astonishment. 'Yes I hear you. There's no need to be so cross.' Chrissy removed herself to the doorway. 'Then he'd better marry you I suppose. I liked him that time he came but he's too big for me.'

Realizing what she had done Dorothy was seized with remorse, her moods chasing each other in rapid succession. She grabbed her bag from the bed where she had thrown it and pulled out a large shiny penny. 'I'm sorry, Chrissy,' she said. 'I'm a bit tired that's all. Here have this and go and get yourself some sweets. Forgive me?'

Chrissy's expression changed as she saw the money. She was not often given so much to spend. 'Yes I forgive you,' she said. 'It must be awful being grown up.' She came over hesitantly and took the coin. 'Thank you, Dorry. I'll go and ask Mam if I can go now,' But before she ran out of the room she put her small arms round her sister and Dorothy was suddenly comforted.

'I hope he marries you,' Chrissy said as she left. 'I know Amy's my sister too and I'm supposed to love her, but you're the best, Dorry. I think I love you best!'

Then she ran down the stairs and Dorothy heard her excited chatter in the scullery and finally the back door bang as she ran out to the shop on the street corner.

Dorothy looked at herself in the mirror again before she too went downstairs to lay the table for their evening meal. What a mess all their relationships were in, she thought. How complicated their family tree would be. And when would Clifford be told he shared a sister with herself and Amy? She shivered at the thought and knew that it was a problem that would have to be faced one day.

CHAPTER SIXTEEN

One evening the following week Dorothy flung into the house after work and called angrily to her mother. 'Ma,' she shouted, 'What do you think Geoffrey Buxton has done now?'

Rose winced. She still thought of Mr Buxton with affection and not a little awe, and every time she looked at her precious Chrissy she had to admit that she was glad and even perhaps proud, God forgive her, about what had happened so long ago. She knew it was a sin, but she'd been pardoned by the Almighty and that was that. No good crying over spilt milk, she told herself frequently.

'What's he done then?' she asked. She was used to Dorry's frequent moans about her employer.

Dorothy threw her coat, hat and gloves down on the chair and glared at her. 'He's told me that I mustn't go and see Clifford, that's what!'

Rose took a deep breath. Her first reaction was relief. She had suspected that there would be trouble soon if Dorry went on trying to get the better of poor Amy. But when she looked at her daughter's face she recognized immediately the pain, saw in a flash that this was trouble with no easy solution. And Mr Clifford was a grown man after all. He ought to be able to have what visitors he wanted, surely. 'Why's that then? What did he say to you, deary?' she asked.

'He thinks I'm getting too friendly, that the stress of my visits will upset Clifford. Yes, Ma. He actually called it *stress*! Of course he's trying to protect precious little Amy. That's what it's all about. I haven't been to see Clifford for ages anyway.'

'Well,' Rose said. 'I been telling you all along that you shouldn't go at all.'

'But, Ma, it's wicked interference, that's what it is. He as good as said that I might lose my job if I go on seeing him. Lose my job!' Her voice became shrill. 'I love it there, and I'm good at it.' Suddenly all her anger seemed to collapse, her bright spirit disappear. She sat down at the table and put her head in her hands. Then after a while she looked up at her mother again. 'And that's not all. He's taken that awful Miss Jenkins back into the office, the one who hated me so much. She's been at Wills Factory and she didn't like it. She came to see him and it was just the right time, right for her I mean. He did it to spite me, Ma.'

Rose was quite at a loss. She could find no words of advice or comfort and she hated to hear such bad things said of Mr Buxton.

'What am I to do?' Dorothy went on. 'How can I fight a man like that? He can do anything, even ruin Clifford's life if he wants to. He's evil. Quite evil and ruthless! No one should have that much power over other folks. I can't give Clifford up, Ma. I just can't. I love him. You know that don't you? I love him!'

Rose stared at her daughter and felt her pain as if it were her own. She bent to the fire and lifted the kettle on to the glowing coals, and as she straightened herself her eyes lingered on the latest photograph of her husband. He had sent the likeness in his last letter and she had only that afternoon put it in the battered silver frame on the mantelpiece. She thought momentarily of her own marriage, and desperately hoped for better things for her twins. But nothing seemed to be going right for either of them.

Dorothy followed the direction of her mother's

glance and looked at her father's photograph too. She had never known him really and had little or no affection for him, but seeing that permanent black-and-white smile she couldn't help wondering if there had been an earlier photograph in the same frame when . . . She turned to her mother.

'How on earth, Ma . . . however could you have . . . The thought of you and Geoffrey Buxton together haunts me.'

Rose blushed. She knew that her face was an uncomfortable red all over and she could feel her neck getting hot right down inside the neckline of her dress. 'You mustn't judge,' she rebuked. 'Mr Buxton's a good man. He'm just doing what he considers right for his own, and he's come to think of Amy as his own, too, since he's her guardian and she with nobody now!'

Dorothy snorted her disgust. 'Well that's as maybe,' she said. 'But my happiness is just as important as hers. We're equal, Amy and me, twins, or had you forgotten?'

'I'll never forget that, Dorry. I just wants what's best for both of you.'

'And he's to be the judge of it, is he?' Dorothy could take no more and she stormed up to her bedroom and stood staring out of the window at the flickering lights of the dreary houses, row upon row of them. At least now, after dark, it was only the lights you could see. The ugliness was hidden, but there was little light in her heart.

She had been to see Clifford only once since that wonderful day in January, and the visit had not been a spectacular success. There were other visitors around the whole time and it had rained. They had not talked of anything more interesting than the weather and the progress of the war, and other unimportant things which she had mostly forgotten. She wondered how she was going to manage to see him at all now after his father's decree. There was little she could do about it. The initiative would have to come from Clifford.

A few days later there was a letter waiting for her on the table when she arrived home from work. She picked it up and felt her heart beat a little faster as she saw the unformed writing, but as she read she became more and more dismayed. His arm had become infected again, he said. It had failed to heal completely and he was being moved to a military hospital some distance away where he could get the treatment he needed, a place that specialized in his sort of wound. He told her that he was disappointed that they would not be able to meet while he was away because it was too far for visiting without a motorcar. He hoped, however, to be home by the end of March, or April at the latest.

She was immediately filled with suspicion. Was this part of Geoffrey Buxton's plan? Was there something that she didn't know about? He said he would eventually be sent home. Home! How would they manage to meet in that great posh house with his parents always around? Servants too, to spy and report? She knew, with a frightening certainty that Clifford would have to have made up his mind by then. She couldn't go on keeping her love for him a secret for ever. Yet she was still unsure of him, still feared that his sense of duty would force him into a marriage with Amy, the girl who wore his ring! She looked at her own bare fingers and wanted to weep!

Now that he was ill again she longed to go to him, to be at his side and to be able to show her love and concern for him openly. She thought with anger and jealousy of her sister, Amy, who could quite properly have been there beside him. Why was she not giving comfort to the man she was supposed to love instead of bestowing it on a lot of strangers? She was amazed at this behaviour, felt it was inexcusable. Yet she gloated over it too. She had to admit that she was selfishly very glad that Amy was busy so far away. Yet she was failing to take advantage of the situation. It was all so frustrating.

She read the letter many times, trying to find something that would give her hope, but Clifford had always found it difficult to write with his left hand, and the two pages were filled with large spidery writing that said very little. She felt tears fill her eyes when she thought of the many beautiful pages he had penned to her from France, when he was still whole and confident and they had been so close in spite of the miles that separated them.

He sent her his love at the end, and a row of shaky kisses, but nothing was mentioned of that golden time in the boathouse. She folded the sheets of paper and carried them upstairs to put safely away with all the others. She couldn't look at those earlier ones now. It was almost like seeing something that was past and finished, something precious that would never happen again.

The end of March he had said, perhaps even April! It was now only February and April seemed a whole eternity away!

She went to bed that night still thinking about it and slept badly, only to wake in the morning to find her whole body swept with nausea. Groggily, she sat up in bed. She was never ill. The feeling was totally alien to her. She grabbed for the chamber pot that was kept under the bed, but which she never used, and vomited into it and immediately felt better.

Rose was suspicious. Every morning lately Dorry had been getting up early, getting up and rushing out to the back yard before she dressed. When it had happened three mornings together, she knew that what she most feared must have come to pass. For a time she kept her counsel and said nothing. It would be better if the girl told her herself, but she was filled with guilt. Like mother like daughter! She kept repeating the words over and over in her mind and eventually she could bear it no longer.

It was a Sunday morning and as Dorothy sat at the table staring at the bowl of porridge that Rose had prepared, her face was a deathly shade of grey. Chrissy was still upstairs reading. It was a new craze, and a blessing. She had recently taken to staying in bed on Sundays for an hour, lining all her dolls up beneath the bedclothes and reading to them. Now was the chance that Rose had been waiting for.

'You been sick again?' she remarked innocently.

Dorothy looked up at her with wide red-rimmed eyes. 'Yes, Ma. I've been sick again.'

'Why's that then?'

There was a long silence between them and Dorothy looked down into the bowl, stirring the porridge round and round until Rose felt she wanted to scream at her to put the spoon down and say something.

'I'm going to have Clifford Buxton's baby, Ma,' she said at last. 'I went to the doctor. It's quite definite. It was only the once; like you, Ma, only once, and I've been punished too.'

Although Rose had already guessed, it was still a shock, and visions of Clifford's father flashed before her eyes, compounding her sense of responsibility. She tried to keep calm. She couldn't accuse or blame, for hadn't the Good Lord said that only those without sin should cast a stone?

She looked at her daughter and seemed to see all of the girl's bright hopes and dreams collapse. Dorry had been working so long and so hard to improve herself. And was it all just for this? To have a babe out of wedlock, to struggle and strive for the rest of her life just for a living as Rose herself had done?

'What will you do then, love?' she asked, and her face and voice were both full of compassion.

Dorothy turned pained eyes towards her mother. 'Aren't you shocked? Aren't you going to shout at me and tell me how stupid I've been, Ma? For I have been. I should have known better shouldn't I. Why are you so calm and nice?'

'You don't need to ask that, Dorry,' Rose said. 'And I guessed anyway. It wasn't no surprise. I been wondering what you were going to do. I'll help you all I can, lovey.'

'I haven't made up my mind,' Dorothy said bleakly. 'I'm not going to one of those awful women anyway, if that's what you're thinking. I'd never do that.'

'That was what I was feared about,' Rose said. 'I didn't want that for you. It kept me awake thinking about it.' She remembered that Clifford's father had made some such suggestion to her all those years ago. 'They'm terrible and they do awful things to you.' It wasn't quite what she meant to say, but the danger for Dorry had been on her mind ever since she'd first begun to suspect the truth.

'I shall have the baby,' Dorothy said. 'I'm sure about that, but how we'll manage I don't know yet.'

'Are you going to tell Mr Clifford then?'

Dorothy was looking down at the lumpy porridge again, seeing nothing, her eyes blank. 'I haven't decided yet, Ma. I've got to think.'

'He ought to know as it's his baby. He'd marry you, Dorry, and a child needs a name.' Rose felt that her loyalties were being split right down the middle. She had always loved Amy almost as much as she loved Dorry, and now Amy was the one who might have her rightful man stolen away from her, yet Dorry was the one in need. And after all, she thought grimly, it took two to make a baby. He shouldn't leave Dorry all alone

371

with the pain and the trouble. But men usually did, she reflected.

'I was prepared to fight and fight to get him, Ma. I didn't care what happened to Amy. She's got all that money and everything. But now I'm feeling different about a few things.'

Rose looked at her suspiciously. 'Be you telling me that you don't love him now, and after all the trouble you been and caused?'

'No. I don't mean that at all. I'm nearly dying for love of him! Oh, Ma, you can't know how much I love him.' Dorothy got up from the table leaving the porridge untouched and went over to the window. She stared out at the brick wall that divided their back yard from next door. 'It's just that I want him to come to me of his own free will. I couldn't force him. He'd feel trapped if I told him about the baby, wouldn't he? No one who's trapped into something is ever happy. I'm frightened about telling him and frightened about not telling him too. What do you think that I should do, Ma?' I couldn't bear to lose him.'

Rose considered her daughter's plight and felt quite out of her depth. 'I don't honestly know, Dorry,' she said. 'He'll have to choose between you two, won't he? Between you and Amy I means.'

As soon as she had spoken she realized that it was definitely not the right thing to have said. Dorothy looked at her with angry eyes.

'Don't get me wrong, Ma,' she said. 'I don't care at all what happens to Amy. It's the baby and myself that I care about, and Clifford too. I want the best for all three of us. If I keep the baby a secret for a bit it's only because I want him to come to me freely, like I said.'

'And he might, love,' Rose said. Privately she doubted it. Without being forced to make an honest woman of Dorry he'd probably choose the easy way, wouldn't he? Amy was a lovely girl and already promised to him. Rose was silent for a time, thinking about it all. There was Arthur as well of course. She remembered him coming here on that last leave. He'd looked so grand that she'd almost wanted to faint from shock and she knew that he was really and truly in love with Dorry. Perhaps if he'd take the child as well, she might agree to marry him. Now that would be the answer to all their troubles, she decided.

But there were more immediate problems. Ever since she'd become suspicious she'd started to plan just in case. She knew that as soon as Dorothy began to get big there'd be awful gossip round about. It might be better if her daughter went away for a bit.

'How about you going to stay with that cousin of mine, Elsie Franklin, down in Teignmouth. She got plenty of room I think and she takes in boarders and got a little tea shop or something. She writes to me now and then and she'm always wanting girls to help out.'

Dorothy turned to her mother in surprise and then closed her eyes with the horror of it. After all her efforts to improve herself she was to end up serving in a shop and waiting on other people! Yet as she considered the idea it gradually began to have possibilities. All she wanted at the moment was somewhere to run, some refuge from the jeers and censure that she knew would come when her trouble became known. Most of all she needed to be able to escape from having to tell Clifford as soon as he came home in April. If no one knew about the baby she could be the first one to break it to him, and it would be in her own time. That was important to the rather vague plans that were beginning to form in her mind. She would give him her address in Teignmouth only when she decided that the time was right.

'I owe your Aunt Elsie a letter,' Rose went on. 'Shall I mention it?'

'All right. Ask her. I haven't decided anything yet mind, but it might be a good idea.'

'Teignmouth's nice,' Rose said. 'I only seen pictures, but it's got a pier and sandy beaches with no mud like Weston, and it's got the sea and cliffs.'

Dorothy felt a little happier. She crossed the room and kissed her mother. 'Thanks, Ma,' she said. 'I know it'll all come right in the end.'

She kept visualizing the next meeting with Clifford all the next day. It would be beside the sea in some idyllic place and he would ask her to marry him before he knew about the baby. At about four months she surely wouldn't show too much if she wore the right clothes. She didn't want to compel him into marriage because of this baby. She couldn't bear the thought of seeing the love in his eyes disappear within the bondage of a marriage into which he had been forced. He must come to her because he loved her and for that reason only. At least by going away she'd find out how he really felt.

Rose lost no time in writing the letter and a few days later a reply arrived. She opened it with excitement and hope. 'Yes,' she said. 'She'm willing to have you, Dorry. Very pleased in fact, and she'm a nice lady. You'll like it there. You'll have to wear a wedding ring, she says and she'll say you'm a war widow.' Rose went on reading and didn't notice that Dorothy, too, was engrossed in a letter of her own that had arrived for her on the same post.

'Ma,' she suddenly shouted. 'Listen, just listen to this. Proute & Sons want to publish my book, my whole book, Ma, and they're offering me more than I could earn in weeks at Buxtons. They want another similar one, too, as soon as I can get it written.' She jumped up and did a pirouette around the breakfast table waving the letter in the air, and then she kissed her mother and sat down again. 'You know what that means. I can support myself. Well, not just at first perhaps, but I'll soon be able to.'

Rose became excited too. For days Dorry had been far too quiet and pale. It was wonderful to see a bit of colour in the girl's face again. 'That's marvellous,' she said. 'Oh, Dorry, I'm that glad for you. You been working so hard all these years.'

'I think I'd like to go to Teignmouth, Ma. It seems just the place to write. Can I go? Have you heard yet?'

'You haven't been listening to a word I been saying, have you,' Rose said. 'Yes, you can go. You'll have to help out to pay for your keep and you'll be able to write in your time off. Your Aunt Elsie'll understand. She'm educated like you.' At last everything seemed to be looking up, Rose thought. She poured another cup of tea for herself and drank it thoughtfully. 'So you'll not tell about the baby then, not tell anyone here.'

Dorothy put down the publisher's letter and looked at her mother. 'There are some people that I want to tell, Ma, ones that I know'll keep my secret.'

'Who's that then?'

'Vera Price and Arthur. We've been friends for years and years. I can't just go off and disappear without telling them.'

'Arthur Price? You'm mad.'

'No I'm not, Ma. Me and Arthur have been close for as long as I can remember, and he's asked me to marry him lots of times. He's still got hopes, I know, from the last letter he wrote to me. I've got to tell him, and then he'll be free of me and he'll marry some other nice girl. I want him to be happy. And I couldn't let him find out about the baby just any old way either.'

Rose was doubtful. 'How'll you do it then?'

'I shall write to him and give the letter to Vera to keep for the right time. She'll give it to him when he comes home. I don't want him hearing about it while he's in France flying one of those flimsy aeroplanes that he's so proud of. When he's next on leave will be time enough. I shall swear both of them to secrecy. *I* must be the one to tell Clifford, and only when it's right.'

'You've got it all planned out haven't you?' Rose commented. 'Just like one of them stories of yours! When'll you tell Mr Clifford then?'

'I don't know that yet. I'm not sure about it. I shall wait until he's quite well of course, and until I'm settled in Teignmouth. If he realizes that I'm successful and independent then that might be the right time. He wouldn't feel under any compulsion then would he, Ma?'

It was not really a question that needed any answer and Rose stared with amazement at this daughter of hers. She had always known that she was stubborn as well as clever. Now she realized how determined she was too. 'I'm proud of you, Dorry,' was all she said.

Dorothy was excited and proud too, yet later that day, alone in her room she experienced some of the fears and doubts that she would never show to anyone else. When she went to bed she unlocked the wooden box and took out Clifford's latest letter, hugging it to herself. 'Oh, Clifford,' she moaned quietly, 'If only you were here with me to share my success as well as my troubles. I do need you. I do love you so much!'

Arthur Price watched the plane spiralling to the ground. It circled slowly, smoke pouring from its fuselage and then flames suddenly added to the horror. It was his forty-third victim, forty-three pilots whom he had sent to their deaths, and for the first time he shuddered. The elation he usually felt was totally absent. 'Must be getting soft,' he muttered. 'Huns are Huns after all, not worth a second thought.' He tried to collect his wits, concentrate on getting himself and his aeroplane back to base but he felt numb with dread, not for his own safety, but for the German. He'd actually been able to see the pilot at first, to watch him struggling inside the terrible ball of fire and then mercifully no more details had been visible, only the blazing, falling inferno. Suddenly he was aware of four more scouts on his tail and he came to his senses. He turned and climbed swiftly, blessing the advantages and swiftness of his own machine, and managed eventually to get behind the leader and fire a burst at very close range. The plane went down at once, vertically this time, with pieces falling off the fuselage. It struck the ground swiftly, cleanly, not like the other with its terrifying spiral.

The moment of conscience had passed as quickly as it had come and Arthur's blood was filled again with a fierce desire to down more and more of the enemy. He fired swiftly at another Hun aircraft but it spun away out of reach, then he managed a burst into a third but the plane limped away and suddenly both his guns were silent. He looked round and found that one had finished its ammunition and the belt on the other had broken. But the plight he was in only seemed to increase the passion and fury in his veins and he chased the remaining two enemy planes even though he had no fire power. Then, regaining common sense, he broke away and headed for home.

Once safely landed, Arthur recorded the two Huns accounted for and went to the mess. He sank into a chair and was overcome with unusual fatigue. Later that night his earlier misgivings returned and even in sleep he seemed to see the burning enemy plane, the struggling pilot. Then his dreams turned to Dorothy and he woke himself up shouting her name.

'Give us a bit of peace,' his fellow officer shouted. 'You've been jumping around like a demented frog all night.'

Arthur sat up in bed and rubbed his eyes. 'Sorry, old chap. Didn't know I was doing it. Downed two Huns today and one of them really had it bad. Burning all the way down.' He groped for a match and lit the candle beside his bed. 'God it was awful. I'm going to keep a gun handy to finish myself off if that happens to me.'

In the dim flickering light he could see his friend staring across at him.

'I've never noticed you having qualms before,' James Grantley said. 'What's got into you?'

'Don't know. Wish I did. Perhaps I need some leave.'

The following morning Arthur awoke with his head feeling light and strange and he was shivering, every limb shaking and quivering first with cold and then intense heat.

'Can't be trench-fever, old chap,' Grantley told him cheerfully, 'seeing we're never in the trenches. Just the old influenza probably. You'd better stay there and I'll send someone.'

'You'll not keep me in bed,' Arthur said angrily and he pushed his bare feet out on to the cold floor and immediately swayed dizzily and fell back on the blankets.

His friend looked at him dubiously and then piled some more bedding on top of him. 'No damn good up in the machine like that,' he exclaimed. 'You'd soon come crashing down, and without any Huns to give you a push either. Just stay put for a bit.'

'Seems I can't do much else,' Arthur said weakly.

Influenza it certainly was and a particularly virulent strain, the army doctor told him. He mustn't leave his bed until told, and his friend would be moved out of the room. 'We don't want the whole Flying Corps on its back, do we?' he commented dryly.

Arthur glared at him but the weakness that filled every bone in his body made it impossible to argue. He lay there day after day, his batman ministering to him, and he fumed with frustration when he heard the drone of planes overhead.

Having a batman had been a considerable embarrassment to him at first. 'I'm not officer class,' he confided to his friends when he was awarded his commission. 'More used to serving others than being served as a matter of fact!' But as the days and weeks passed he became more used to it, to the privileges that were accorded to his officer status, and he began to wonder how he would fit back into the overcrowded little house in St Paul's when it was all over. He knew of course that he wouldn't go back there to live, ever. He thought of Dorothy and her ambitions, and when he considered the future she usually figured prominently in it – Dorothy with the learning that she had struggled so hard to achieve.

But after that last leave he was not so sure. She had refused to give him an answer when he told her that he loved her, that he wanted her to marry him. He had asked her more than once. How many times now he couldn't be sure. He had lost count! And now he had been promoted to Captain and a bar added to his Military Cross yet he doubted if those things made any difference in her eyes.

With his body inactive, endless thoughts went round his head and he became more and more depressed about Dorothy. After the third day of fever and intense boredom, he decided that she was not in love with him. It was a hard fact to come to terms with and the usual pace of his life had not allowed him to face it truthfully before. He lay in the hard narrow bed day after day thinking about her and pondering all the improbable things that had happened to him because of the war.

His mind eventually strayed to Amy, to that twin sister of hers, so like her in appearance and so unlike in behaviour. What a shock it must have been to have been brought up in that posh house and then to find out that you came from a poor family, that your parents weren't your parents at all. He shuddered as he thought of it, and then he laughed a little to himself, remembering her horror when he told her about the kid, Christabel. That her ma should have gone a-whoring was a terrible blow to her. His thoughts turned to Rose Miller: it was incredible that she should have found herself a fancy man. Who was it? He wondered if his mother or his sister knew. Vera was a bit of a terror and kept her ear firmly to the ground. He resolved to ask her if he got home soon.

Home . . . surely they would send him to Blighty to recover. Suddenly he wanted to go, to be away from the eternal sound of the guns and away from the need to appear brave, to be the great hero. This influenza must have affected him more than he knew, made him into a real jelly-baby!

On the first day he got up he was greeted by the welcome words, 'It's Blighty for you, Captain Price.' He had struggled into his uniform and walked weakly over to the hut where the doctor held his surgeries for the walking wounded. 'Lucky fellow!' the doctor went on. 'You'll have your womenfolk to wait on you instead of that batman of yours. Should be a pleasant change. Three weeks should do it. Report back then.'

When Arthur Price arrived home in April, he was at first full of a sense of jubilation. This was what most men, both soldiers and airmen wanted, a spot of home leave. He was still feeling weak from his bout of influenza and the thought of a few lazy days with nothing to do seemed infinitely desirable.

Yet after only a short time, the tiny house in St Paul's appeared to be smaller than it had ever been and his many brothers and sisters almost noisier than it was possible to bear. He thought of his friend, James Grantley, and the photographs of the beautiful country house where he lived, and Arthur wondered what it would be like to go home to a place like that. Vera and his mother, perhaps understanding a little, tried to make his convalescence bearable. They gave him a room of his own, for which he was infinitely grateful, and he was very touched by their pride in him and the sacrifices they were making.

He was looking forward to seeing Dorothy again although he feared that he must give up all hope of ever being anything to her other than a friend. He lay on his bed in the small room and thought dully of all those times he had asked her to marry him. Each time the reply had been similar. 'I like you more than I can say, but I can't make myself fall in love, Arthur. I want to, but I just can't.' The words had not always been quite so definite but he knew that the meaning was the same. She wanted him for a good friend and that was all. Well, perhaps he could learn to be content with that for now. He decided to wait another day or so before he called on her. Perhaps then he would feel stronger, more himself.

He still had nightmares about the flames, about dying that way. He was desperately ashamed, for he had never previously known a moment's fear. The horror of it all had suddenly been personalized for him, the game had become reality. He never again wanted to watch a fellow pilot, Hun or not, go down in flames.

The following day was a Saturday and he was sitting in the kitchen wondering what he should do. Tomorrow would be the right day to call on Dorothy. They had often enjoyed Sundays together in the past when they were still at school. He remembered those afternoons in St Andrew's Park and smiled to himself.

Suddenly his sister broke into his pleasant reverie. 'Will you take me out?' she suggested. 'I got things to tell you. No good talking here though. Too many little ears around.' There was a worried look on her face and Arthur hoped that she didn't intend to unburden herself of any of her problems just yet. Vera was a good girl and he had always liked her best of all his parents' brood, but he still didn't feel strong enough to cope with anyone else's troubles.

'Where shall we go then?' he said without enthusiasm.

'On the Downs. We can get a tram. The weather's nice.'

He glanced out of the window and saw that indeed it was a nice day. The sun was shining, a rather weak April sun but warm enough to be reasonably pleasant.

'Right then,' he agreed. 'The Downs.'

When they climbed from the tram at the last stop before the Suspension Bridge, Vera linked her arm proudly through her brother's and he smiled at her. They hadn't talked much during the journey which was surprising for Vera.

'Well, what have you got to tell me?' he asked. 'You've been as close as a clam at home. Not a word about Dorothy even though I asked you a few times. I thought she was your best friend. What are all these things that you couldn't talk about in the house then?'

Vera stalled for time. She didn't know how best to impart her news. 'It wasn't only to talk,' she said slowly. 'I want to be seen with you. You look so posh in that uniform. Makes me feel like a lady walking along arm in arm with a real officer.'

Arthur laughed and realized with a sudden pang of

382

guilt what a great gulf there now was between himself and his family. 'Thanks, Sis,' he said. 'It's nice to be here with you too.'

Vera looked up at him again. She couldn't help looking at him constantly. Fancy having a brother as grand as this! How could that silly friend of hers possibly turn down him down?

'You are still Dorothy's friend I suppose?' Arthur enquired suddenly anxious.

'Yes. We're still friends, but she'm a bit above me now with her being an author and all. She've just got a book taken to be published, a whole book, a love story or something she said. She'm going to get money for it. She've really got brains, have our Dorothy. Well, she have for some things,' she added darkly. 'And then there's that fancy way of talking that she've learned herself.' Vera paused and took a deep breath. 'It be about Dorry that I've got to talk, Arthur. I don't know how you're going to take this. It's something I got to tell you and don't want to. She made me promise to tell you. I ain't letting on about something that I shouldn't!'

Suddenly Vera vividly remembered that day in the playground years ago when she had told Dorothy about Amy Harding. She had been given half a dripping sandwich as a reward for the telling! This time it was different. This time it was her own brother who was going to be hurt.

She looked at him and her heart leapt for love and pride, and anger too. How could Dorry have been so stupid! She shivered, but she had her instructions and she must go through with them however hurtful it might be. She had given Dorothy her promise. It was better out anyway. No good came of hiding things. Although why it was Arthur that the silly girl wanted to tell about her trouble and not Clifford Buxton, Vera couldn't imagine.

'You must tell me now, Vera. We've come up here especially, haven't we?'

She started to tremble at the import of her news and then she blurted it out, closing her eyes for a second as she did so. 'She's going to have a baby!'

She didn't know what reaction she had expected, but it was certainly nothing as violent as that which followed.

Arthur stared at her without comprehension at first and then when the words began to make sense she saw a frightening anger sweep over his face.

'What did you say?' he shouted. 'You little slut. I don't believe you.'

Tears sprang to her eyes. She pulled her arm from his and stood quite still, staring at the complete stranger he had become, her face full of shock. 'How dare you call me that, Arthur. How dare you! It ain't me what's having it. Her, I said. Dorothy Miller, the girl you set your heart on. Well she's gone and done it with that Clifford Buxton, and she's having a baby come the autumn.'

Arthur could feel the blood rush from his face and he swayed on his feet. He was weaker than he thought and he thought he was about to fall. Then he caught his sister's hands in his and his grip was painful. 'Are you really sure? Don't lie to me, Vera.'

She was still angry and now she was overcome with indignation too. 'Would I lie to you about something like that?' she said, trying to regain some shreds of composure. 'She told me herself and she said to pass it on to you, that's why I'm telling you her secret. She said she wanted you told and no one else. She told me to command you not to tell anyone.'

'Command? Was that the word she used?'

I can't rightly remember. Something like that. Perhaps it was another swanky word. Beseeched I think it might have been. Anyway she's wrote you a letter and she bid me give it to you after I'd told you.' Vera searched in her bag and pulled out a cream-coloured envelope and handed it to Arthur.

He took it from her and put it into his pocket. 'I want to sit down,' he said quietly. 'And I'm sorry, Vera, for what I called you.'

'I should think so too,' she said coldly. All the pleasure she had felt in being with him had disappeared, yet she realized that he'd been ill and a certain concern had replaced the earlier pride and anger. 'There's a seat over there.' She pointed across the green and they walked over to the wooden bench without speaking. He slumped upon it and Vera seated herself so that there was as much space as possible between them.

He took out the letter and began slowly to read.

My dear Arthur,

You asked me to marry you more than once and I don't think that I ever fully appreciated the honour you did me. I wish that I could have loved you, for we were always kindred spirits and we could have been very happy.

However Vera will by now have told you, as I asked her to do, that my heart was given to another. I can only thank you for your love and friendship over the years and ask you to forgive me.

I wanted you to know about what has happened to me partly because of our long friendship and also because I wish you to know before you find out from someone else.

There is one thing that I ask of you and that is your secrecy. Vera has promised not to tell anyone else and I beseech the same of you. One day the facts will all come out, but until then please do as I ask. It is important to me that Clifford does not know that I carry his child until the time is right. You won't understand this but please trust my reasons.

Try not to think too hardly of me.

Your friend,
Dorothy

Arthur read it over twice more and then screwed the paper into a tight ball and squashed it fiercely in his hands. 'Where is she?' he demanded. 'I want to see her.'

'She've gone away to the country somewhere. No one but her ma knows. She won't tell for fear of Mr Clifford finding her.'

'Why doesn't she want to tell him, for goodness sake?' Arthur had never felt so shocked and devastated in his life. Until this past minute he had still retained some faint hope that Dorothy might at last change her mind, come to love him and marry him. Now his dreams were totally shattered. She carried another man's brat. He couldn't believe it. And that letter! Trusting him not to tell! He wanted to go up to Clifford Buxton and knock his head off!

Vera read his thoughts. 'Clifford has been wounded, badly. Lost an arm and been very ill. His right arm too and he can't play the violin or piano any more.'

'I don't care about his bloody arm,' Arthur shouted. 'Pity he didn't lose something else.'

Vera looked at him in horror. This wasn't like her quiet, gentle brother. For the first time in her life she was frightened of him, and of the white-hot fury in his face. He pushed the ball of screwed-up paper into his pocket and sat there with his fists clenched and his eyes full of hatred. He seemed to be completely unaware of her presence and she didn't move, desperately hoping for the mood to pass.

He stared across the road, seeing nothing. So even revenge was not to be permitted him. He could never face an injured man with this terrible rage. He thought about Clifford and then closed his eyes and covered his face with his hands. For a second the vision of the stricken German pilot flashed into his memory again. He couldn't erase it from his mind and in moments of stress as well as in his dreams he was frequently revisited by the sight of that terrible downward spiral, the engulfing flames. He didn't know how long he sat there and eventually he began to shiver, his whole body shaking.

Then another astonishing thought came to him. He voiced it aloud. 'That letter,' he said. 'Do you think it might be . . . might be an appeal for help, Vera. Could she want me to marry her, look after her, bring up the child?'

His sister shook her head. 'No, Arthur. I'm sure she don't mean that. Do you want to? Would you?'

For a few paralysing moments Arthur thought about it but he felt too shattered for the facts to make much sense. He bent his head and covered his face with his hands. 'I don't know,' he said at last. 'If she loved me, perhaps, but she doesn't. She never will.'

Vera was filled again with anger at her friend and love for her brother. She gently took his arm. 'Come on,' she said. 'We'm going over there to get a cup of tea. You'm still not well enough to sit here in the cold.'

He allowed her to lead him across the road and into the pastry shop. They found a small table in a corner at the back and she ordered a pot of tea and some cream cakes. He ate automatically and at last began to feel the warmth seeping into his bones again and the anger dissipating into grief for Dorothy.

'How will she manage?' he asked at last. 'Do you know what she's going to do?'

Vera was relieved. He seemed calmer. 'She told me

that she'm going to live with some relation and do her writing. She've bought a typewriter and she'm going to write as hard as she can she says. This relation got a tea shop or something and she'll help out for her keep.'

'Devon,' Arthur said. 'She once told me that she had an aunt in Devon. I forget where though. Not that I want to know,' he added hastily. His impulse to rush off and find her had diminished.

'Her mother's helping her a bit with money too,' Vera said. 'Till she gets on her feet. Well she can't do nothing else, what with her being the same way a few years ago, can she?'

'How can she help? They haven't much, have they?'

'They're not doing so badly. She makes a fair bit with the sewing and its my opinion that they get some from elsewhere too! In fact I know they do.'

Her voice was mysterious and Arthur looked at her, wondering what she meant. 'They get some dollars from the father in Canada now and then I believe,' he said. 'Dorothy told me once.'

'Yes and there's some more comes regular.' Vera put another piece of cream cake into her mouth and was glad to have something else to talk about. Perhaps the further piece of information she had discovered about the family would distract her brother a little.

'You mean from . . . ?' Arthur had always known that Vera would unravel the mystery about Mrs Miller sooner or later. Now that she was probably about to do so, he had sudden qualms about knowing.

'Yes. From Christabel's Pa. I've found out who he is! It was something I overheard Dorothy say to her mother one day. No one knows that I know.'

He looked at her and wondered if he could cope with any more shocks right now. But then he couldn't bear not to be told either.

'Oh, Vera,' he said miserably. 'Why must you keep

finding out about things that don't concern you?' He wanted to shake her for being such a busy-body. 'It's nothing to do with us is it? And how can you be sure?'

'Oh it's true all right. You needn't be feared of that. And I found out by accident, didn't I? I couldn't help it. I wasn't standing with my ear to the keyhole if that's what you'm suggesting!' She was defensive and inclined to be angry again. 'It's a terrible burden to keep all to myself, Arthur. I haven't told no one since I found out and that were months ago. I want to tell you. Will you promise to keep it a secret?' she added anxiously.

'How can I until you tell me?'

Her face went grey. 'I can't say if you don't promise.'

He looked at her and an unexpected surge of affection for this sister of his took the place of the previous irritation. She had so little compared to himself, compared to Amy and even Dorothy for that matter. He glanced at her thin figure and her crimped waves and tried to force himself to smile. 'All right then. You have my promise. It probably isn't important anyway, but I won't breathe a word to a soul unless there's a very good reason to do so.'

She had to be content with that, although what he meant by it she couldn't be sure. 'It's Mr Buxton,' she whispered. 'Mr Geoffrey Buxton. That's who Christabel has for a father!'

For a second Arthur was silent, frozen into immobility. Then, as all the implications of the incredible piece of news he had just heard entered fully into his mind, he started to laugh. He laughed so loudly and for so long that two women at the next table stopped eating and stared at him and he continued to laugh, completely unaware of the spectacle he was making. It was a nervous, almost uncontrollable reaction. At last he ceased and mopped his eyes and then took another gulp of the cold tea in his cup. 'Geoffrey Buxton,' he said. 'Geoffrey Buxton!' His voice was like steel.

'Thank you, Vera. Thanks a lot.'

Suddenly Arthur's desire for revenge overcame all other considerations. Clifford Buxton had taken the girl he loved, made her pregnant, ruined her life. Now he would confront him with the results of his filthy lust, prevent him from marrying the sister. He thought of Amy for a moment, of her innocence and her bravery. She had been wronged too. Then there was Geoffrey Buxton's adultery, the bigoted self-righteous Geoffrey Buxton was heading for a fall as surely as his son. A glow of satisfaction swept over Arthur as he thought of the years when he had served these two, chauffeured them about, called them 'Sir'. They had made a mess of their lives thinking of no one but themselves and he was going to be the one to tell them so. Things would be evened up at last. He now had the power to destroy them both.

Vera stared at him. She felt almost paralysed with apprehension, sure there was something terrible behind that awful laughter. 'But you promised not to tell,' she pleaded.

'Oh no, not really. I said that I wouldn't do anything with your priceless bit of knowledge unless there was a very good reason to do so, and there is a reason, Vera. Believe me there is.'

She looked at the expression on his face and knew that he must be ill – in a way she didn't understand. She had seen soldiers with shell-shock. Perhaps this was something like it that fliers got? She was filled with regret at her own stupidity. What awful string of actions were her words going to set in motion?

She stood up and took the bill the waitress had left beneath his plate. 'Come on,' she whispered, aware of the interested stares of all the other customers. 'Pay the bill, Arthur. I haven't any money. We must get home.'

He took the scrap of paper and, beckoning to the

girl, left a large tip. But once outside he started to laugh again and Vera tried to lead him to the tram-stop. 'Oh no, sister dear,' he said. 'I'm not coming home. Here's some money for you.' He pushed a sovereign into her hand. 'You go on. I have business to attend to.'

She was frantic. 'You must come home,' she said. 'You're not well. Please come.'

She pulled at his sleeve, but he shook her off. 'I'm just going to call on my former boss,' he told her. 'I'll see you later. Tell Ma I'll probably be late. And I've never felt better in my life!'

She knew it wasn't true. Something very strange had happened to him but there was nothing more she could do. Hopelessly she watched him walk swiftly away from her along the broad tree-lined street, knowing that this time she was going to be the cause of something dreadful. She stumbled away in the opposite direction. Perhaps she should throw herself off the Suspension Bridge as others had done! As she walked towards it, she felt that she could never face anyone again.

CHAPTER SEVENTEEN

Arthur strode through the familiar streets of Clifton and turned into the drive of the Buxton home. He felt distraught and slightly hysterical, and he began to think that perhaps Vera was right when she said that he was nowhere near well yet. He wasn't sure now just how he was to achieve his aims. The strange trembling had returned to plague him, the weakness that had started only a month or so ago, just before he went down with influenza. He'd felt it when he'd had to face the Hun, when he'd seen that plane on fire. And he felt it now, for his anger against Clifford had not diminished. There was no mercy in his heart and the demand from Dorothy for secrecy failed to register. It made no sense to him at all. Yet the man for whom he felt such hostility had been wounded, was still suffering Vera had said, and had only been home a few days. He tried to come to terms with these facts, tried without success to curtail his fury.

He went to the front door and pulled the bell-rope. It was not long before a maid whom he vaguely recognized opened it. Her face lit up when she saw him.

'Captain Price isn't it? You want to see the master? He's out but Mr Clifford is in. Would you like to speak to him?'

'Yes, he'll do very well.' He watched the smile fade from the girl's face as she heard his angry tones.

'Will you wait a minute, please,' she said, giving him a strange look. She went into the house, leaving him standing on the doorstep. But she came back eventually and showed him into a small study that opened off the hall. 'I've told Captain Buxton that you're here,' she said.

Arthur stood awkwardly, staring at the many shelves of books. He had never been in this room before. It was on the north side of the house and was cold and cheerless, which did nothing to stop his shivering. He heard the girl's footsteps in the hall and then others, a man's, but the room began to revolve around him and he was only vaguely aware of Clifford Buxton smiling at him, left hand outstretched in greeting, before the nervous thudding of his heart reached unbearable proportions. He looked for some support and then fell heavily to the floor, his head hitting a small stepladder used for reaching books on the top shelves.

When he regained consciousness he was lying on a sofa and a woman was sitting beside him whom he recognized through mists of pain and confusion as Felicity Buxton. He had no idea why she was there or how he came to be in this place and his head throbbed alarmingly.

'Where am I?' he asked, struggling to sit up but failing.

'You fainted,' Felicity said putting a restraining hand on his arm. 'You've been ill I believe.'

'Yes.' He could see Clifford standing near the window and he experienced an unexplained shiver of antipathy for the man. Yet he had no idea why. He felt a stab of fear as he realized that something strange had happened to him, something of which he had no remembrance. There was a darkness in his mind, nothing more.

He turned to Felicity. 'I can't remember anything of the last hour,' he said. 'I know that I was with my sister before I came here.

'It must have been the bad fall you took,' Felicity

said and her voice was gentle and calming. 'Unfortunately you hit your head as you fell. It's only concussion I think, but it does sometimes take one's memory away for a short time. 'We've sent for the doctor and he will be here soon. Just try to rest.'

Arthur turned to Clifford and stared at him. He saw the empty sleeve pinned to his jacket and was immediately saddened by it, but also there was the nagging antagonism that he couldn't understand. He and Clifford had liked each other well enough previously. What had happened that he was unable to recall? He closed his eyes and desperately searched for some clue.

'I'm sorry to cause you all this trouble,' he said to Felicity. 'And I really think that I should go.' He struggled again to get up and this time felt some returning strength, and his head was not spinning quite so much.

There was a knock at the room door as he spoke and Myrtle came in. I'm sorry, Madam,' she said. 'Doctor's out and won't be back until this evening. I left a message though.'

By this time Arthur had struggled to his feet. 'I insist on leaving,' he said. He was feeling more and more uncomfortable in Clifford Buxton's presence. 'You have been very kind but I'm truly better now. I promise that I shall see the doctor who has been attending me and I shall tell him about this relapse.'

Felicity looked at him doubtfully. He certainly seemed to be a little recovered but not well enough to walk out of here alone. 'Then I shall drive you right to your door,' she said. 'Fortunately we have two motors at the moment. Amy asked us if we would look after her father's until she had decided what is to be done with it.'

Arthur desperately wanted to get away on his own but the thought of walking or even waiting for a tram was too daunting. 'Thank you,' he said. 'I should be very grateful.'

His memory of the events of the afternoon returned to him slowly during the journey. He sat beside Felicity and felt his heart thumping furiously as his emotions took over again. He tried to give polite answers to the various questions she asked but all the time he was longing for the journey to end. When at last they reached his home, he climbed down from the vehicle and was ashamed of his thunderous thoughts as she smiled at him.

'Now don't forget, Captain Price,' she directed. 'Please get your doctor to have another look at you. You aren't well yet, you know.'

'I promise,' he replied. 'And thank you for all your trouble.'

Vera opened the front door as Felicity drove away. She had regained a little of her composure but her face was still grey and drawn. 'Thank goodness you've come,' she said. 'I've been that worried about you. You'd better tell me what you've gone and done. I never thought to see you driven home by Mrs Buxton. Did you tell 'em about Dorothy?'

'No I didn't, so you needn't fear.' He staggered slightly as he spoke and he pushed past her and climbed the narrow stairs to his room. 'I fainted when I got there,' he called back to her. 'Hit my head and couldn't remember a thing until now. Concussion they said it was.' He laughed grimly. 'So your secret is still safe. I'm going to lie down for a bit.'

He closed the door and took off his uniform, flinging it on to a chair. Then he got quickly into bed and lay there thinking about the extraordinary events of the day. He acknowledged that the strange fainting episode and the short memory-block that followed it had saved him from making a complete fool of himself, and from betraying Dorothy and his sister too.

'Cup of tea?' Vera said half an hour later. She put her head round the door and seeing that he was awake she placed the cup and saucer on the small table beside the bed. 'What happened, then?' she asked.

'I told you. I couldn't remember anything. Lucky for you I couldn't!'

Vera looked at him with a worried expression on her face. 'I shall tell Ma and she'll get the doctor again,' she said. 'You'm important now Arthur. We can afford the doctor for you!'

It was not until the middle of the night that he suddenly remembered the letter that he had screwed up and pushed into his pocket. He got out of bed unsteadily and opened the door of the big wardrobe where Vera had put his clothes. He felt in his jacket. He pushed his hand into each pocket and as one after the other yielded nothing, he started to panic. His heart began to race and he could feel the colour draining from his face. He went through each pocket again more and more feverishly but still there was nothing.

Arthur went back to his bed and sat upon it like a man in a trance, trying to remember. Then gradually he managed to recall the details. At the Buxton front door he had taken the crumpled piece of paper and held it fiercely in his hand like some explosive weapon. His unreasoning fury had taken over both his normal common sense and his loyalty to Dorothy. All he had wanted to see at that moment had been his enemy's face when he read the words.

He clenched his hands together in an agony of shame at his remembered behaviour. Now that the rage had passed he knew that more than anything in the world he wanted to keep the secret as he had been asked to do. He had loved Dorothy for a long time and he didn't want to let her down now. The thought that had occurred to him when he'd first read her letter came to disturb him again. Did she want his help? Could he accept her now, Clifford's cast-off? Vera had said quite firmly that this was not why she had written. She was probably right, and he realized that he was, in any case, in no state to ponder anything so disconcerting. All he wanted to do was sleep, sleep and forget.

Overcome by weariness, by the after-effects of his influenza, and by the nervous exhaustion that the endless months of war had induced, he crawled back into bed and, pulling the blankets tightly around his shivering body, wept. He was shamed both by what he had nearly done and by his weeping and when at last he fell into a restless sleep, his dreams once again were of an aeroplane circling to earth in a mass of terrifying flames, but the face that he could see in the cock-pit was Dorothy's.

Geoffrey Buxton was late home that night. He drove the motor carefully into the old coach house and closed the heavy wooden doors, locking them securely. He thought of Arthur Price as he often did at this time of day. It had been good to have a chauffeur to attend to all these tiresome chores. He walked wearily to the front door and bent to retrieve a piece of litter that was lying there. The lack of good staff really made life difficult. Even the gardener only came twice a week. There would have been no rubbish lying about in the old days, he reflected. He let himself in and looked around for somewhere to drop the offending scrap and then he stared at it. It seemed to be a letter. Perhaps he should glance at it before throwing it away. It might be something important that one of the family had dropped by mistake. He needed his reading glasses which were at the bottom of his briefcase and with a short grunt of annoyance he pushed the paper into his pocket and went upstairs to his bedroom to wash and change before dinner.

His suit was always left for Myrtle to put away while they were dining. She came into the bedroom later and put the jacket on to a big shaped hanger and then she took the heavy wooden press and prepared to put the trousers in it. Something in one of the pockets was making an unsightly bulge and she removed it and placed it on the chest of drawers before making sure that the creases were in the right places and the press securely fastened. She glanced at the thick cream paper and wondered why Mr Buxton should have it in his pocket. He was usually most particular about the line of his trousers. It had been screwed up tightly but the outer edges had become unrolled. Her curiosity overcame her and as she glanced at it she could see the words, 'My dear Arthur'. She stood undecided for a moment knowing that she shouldn't read any more. Then she couldn't stop. She came to the end and quickly she crushed it again in her hand and dropped it on the carpet as though it were alive. Then she bent and picked it up and placed it back on the chest of drawers. He must have read it or it wouldn't be screwed up. If he hadn't then she could save a lot of unhappiness by destroying it, but if she did that and he asked her . . . She simply couldn't believe what she had just read. And why did Mr Buxton have a letter from Dorothy Miller to Arthur Price in his pocket?

The more she thought, the more worried she became and the more miserable for Miss Amy. Eventually she decided to put the letter in the corner of the armchair, pushed down so that perhaps Mr Buxton might not see it. Then if he forgot about it she could rescue it the next day and put it safely in the fire. If he asked about it, she could say that it must have fallen down there.

It was Felicity who found the letter. She picked it up idly the following afternoon and smoothed the crumpled page. The more she read the more horrified she grew. Like Myrtle she held it in her hand as though it had a terrifying life of its own. She carried it to the window and read it again and then folded it carefully and put it in her pocket. She couldn't begin to imagine how it had come to be half-hidden in the back of the chair in her husband's room and she was sure that he knew nothing of its contents. Had he read those words he would not have breakfasted so normally this morning. Clifford would have been summoned before him. He would probably have been turned out of the house by now!

She walked downstairs like a woman in a trance and went into her small study. She sat there for a full half an hour and every possible course of action was examined in her mind. It was tempting to burn the letter. She looked with longing at the flames leaping cheerfully in the grate. But they wouldn't dispose of the awful news the letter contained. And of course Arthur Price knew! Suddenly she realized why he had come yesterday and why his behaviour had been so strange. He was in love with Dorothy Miller and Clifford had taken her from him, and in this terrible way too! But why had Dorothy written to Arthur and not Clifford? There seemed no sense in it.

The more Felicity pondered the situation the more complicated it appeared to be. And the longer she strove to find some way out of the predicament, the more furious she became with both Dorothy and her son.

At last she got up and walked across the hall towards the library. Clifford spent a lot of time there nowadays. She knew he couldn't bear to sit anywhere near the piano for long and the thought made her guilty about her anger. Nevertheless she entered the room, and closed the door behind her. She stood unsmiling and Clifford looked up, his greeting freezing on his lips as he saw her face.

'What is it, Mother?' he asked. 'Is there bad news?

You look as if you've seen a ghost.'

For reply she walked slowly across the carpet and held the letter out to him. Then she sank into the other large leather armchair beside the fire and covered her face with her hands so that she could not see his expression as he read.

There was a long silence and finally she looked at him. 'Can it be true?' she asked, hoping for his passionate denial. All her anger had drained away. It had always been difficult to be cross with Clifford. Geoffrey had been quite harsh with him during all his growing-up years and she had tried to make up for it.

But now he stood there pale-faced, staring at the letter incredulously and she knew that he was hardly aware of her presence.

'Why to Arthur?' he said. 'Why did she write to him and not to me? It's my baby!' He turned the paper over and then back and read it again and again. 'Where did you get it?' he demanded. 'Where did you find it and who else has seen it?'

Felicity's heart was thumping with fear. So it was true then. She had hoped it might have been some strange trick of that girl's. But her son obviously acknowledged its truth. 'I found it pushed into the side of the chair in your father's room,' she said.

'Then he . . .'

'No. He couldn't possibly have read it. He wouldn't have been as pleasant as he was at breakfast this morning if he had any idea of the contents of that letter.' Felicity knew her husband very well and she was completely sure about that.

'How did it get there then?'

'I have absolutely no idea except that Arthur Price must have had it yesterday. That probably accounts for his strange behaviour. So it's true then, what she says?' Felicity still wanted him to deny it, wanted to grasp at any small possibility of reprieve.

'Yes, if she says so, it's true.'

'What are you going to do?'

Clifford stared at his mother with a remote look in his eyes, as though he wasn't really seeing her at all. 'Find her of course,' he said in a flat empty voice. 'I must find her and . . . and see why she has hidden herself away from me. I shall ask her to marry me.'

'Your father will never allow it!'

'He has no power over me now. I'm an adult.'

'He can cut you off, refuse to take you into the firm.'

'I shall have an army pension of some sort I think. We can live on that.'

'Have you forgotten that you are engaged to Amy?' Felicity demanded.

'No, Mother. I have not forgotten that. I have loved Amy for a long time.'

'And she is right for you. You cannot hurt her so badly, Clifford.'

'Don't you think that I have already done that?'

Felicity closed her eyes by way of reaction. 'You will have to write to her,' she said. 'You will have to beg her forgiveness and understanding, and knowing Amy as I do, I am sure it will be forthcoming. We can settle money on Dorothy Miller for the upkeep and education of the child.'

Clifford was angry and his arm throbbed so much that he almost cried out with the pain of it. All he wanted to do was get out of the room, out of the house, and find Dorothy, tell her that he loved her and wanted to be with her for ever. Yet his mother seemed to think that money would solve the problem, solve everything. Surely she couldn't be so naïve!

Then suddenly into his mind came a little worm of doubt. Dorothy could not possibly love him or she wouldn't have behaved as she had. There were so many unanswered questions. He had thought it strange when she had told him in a letter that she was going away, that she had given up her job and she didn't want anyone to know where she was. She had said it was because she needed peace to write her next book. Now he understood the real reason, but why had she not come straight to him instead of writing to Arthur Price? He remembered Price's stormy face yesterday, before he'd passed out. He'd always liked him, a decent chap. He reminded himself uncomfortably that he was not Price the chauffeur now, but Captain Price of the Royal Flying Corps and with a Military Cross too. He began to feel a searing jealousy. Why should he be the first one to know about this child?

Felicity was watching him and she saw the conflicting emotions flash across his sensitive face. Clifford was a grown man now, yet this latest infection in the pathetic stump of his arm had set him back a great deal. He was flushed and she knew that he should not have to cope with a problem of this magnitude. It seemed that for Arthur Price too the strain had proved too much. The war had left a terrible legacy, she thought, when it did such things to strong young men.

She went to her son and longed to wrap her arms around him as she had when he was little, longed to hold him and send the problems away. Instead she just stood there and hoped he could feel her love. She put out her hand, touching him gently, wanting to drive away the resentment she could feel in him. 'Tell me how I can help you,' she said. 'Don't leave me out, Clifford.'

Her words and the familiar gesture brought an element of comfort to him and he was suddenly aware of her support, wondered why he had doubted it. It had always been there ever since he could remember. 'Thank you,' he said quietly. 'Forgive me. That's what I need from you, Mother. Forgiveness, for I have been very foolish. And if Dorothy should marry me, could

I ask you to accept her as you would have accepted her sister?'

He suddenly realized that this would be the hardest thing he had ever asked of his mother. Knowing of her protective love for Amy, how could he expect her to take Dorothy into her heart?

'What about Amy?' she said, and there was a flat hopelessness in her voice. 'She wears your ring, Clifford. She loves you.'

'Does she, Mother? Are you sure of it? Or did we all just imagine it to be so, Amy as well? Why did she go back to France if she loved me so much?'

'She felt it was her duty.' Felicity collapsed into the chair again and pushed back the hair from her forehead with a nervous gesture, her usual calm efficiency deserting her. 'In some ways I hope that she does not love you too much. Then she will not be so badly hurt.'

Clifford felt a wave of shame spreading over him when he thought of his treatment of Amy. He remembered her clinging affection for him in the early days. But she had been so different on that last leave, much more independent and even slightly cold.

'She changed so much,' he said. 'When she heard about her true birth she seemed to become a different person.'

'It was her experience of the battlefield that changed her,' Felicity said. 'And are you sure you're not merely making excuses for your behaviour, Clifford?'

'Perhaps I am,' he said, yet as he spoke he remembered clearly those last visits in the convalescent home. Amy had been ill-at-ease with him, almost glad when it was time to go. He was still holding the letter and he glanced down at it, at Dorothy's handwriting that he knew so well, and he felt again a deep hurt that it was not penned to him. Perhaps he was going to lose both Amy and Dorothy? Instead of having to choose between them, would they both reject him? He longed now, more than ever, to find Dorothy and confront her.

He looked at the letter's date. Some time had elapsed since it had been written. How long had Price had it? How long had he known about the baby? He felt jealousy suffuse him again and he began to sweat, though who he was really angry with he was not entirely sure.

'So Arthur must have dropped it and somehow, by some strange mischance it got into my father's room and remained unseen by him!' he said 'It sounds pretty improbable.'

Felicity sighed. 'We shall never know what happened, but I think you should burn it before it causes any more havoc.'

'Havoc?' Clifford repeated the word. 'Is that what you think about it then, Mother?' But he went to the fire nevertheless and held the sheet of paper above the flames. Then he dropped it and watched, fascinated as Dorothy's momentous words curled and burned, brightly at first, and then more slowly until there were only charred bits of black and grey soot left to be carried up the chimney in a whirl of smoke. With their going he felt a great sense of loss and he continued to stare into the fire as if expecting some sort of inspiration, but none came.

The letter was gone, but the problem with all its doubts and fears remained. Then he suddenly realized that there was joy too. He had to admit that unexpectedly, in the depths of his heart, a sudden happiness had arisen. He was surprised by it, tried to hide it from his mother.

Felicity, watching him, tried to understand and accept but she couldn't help feeling anger for the girl who had brought such shame to them all. She shivered with apprehension, too, when she thought of her husband's reaction! But she said nothing. Her son was a grown man. He would have to make his own decisions.

Then Clifford turned to her. 'I'm sorry, Mother,' he whispered. 'Sorry to bring you such worry.' He kissed her gently on the cheek. 'I have to be alone for a bit to think things out. Do you mind?' He walked as calmly as he could over to the door and up to the privacy of his room. He noticed Myrtle staring at him as he climbed the stairs and as he registered the expression on her face, he guessed that she too had read the letter. How long then would the secret be his? He knew with a deadening fear that he would have to tell his father soon. He had faced barrages of enemy fire time and time again in appalling raids over the top from the trenches. He had marched for miles through mud and filth and achieved the rank of captain, yet suddenly the thought of facing his father with the news that Dorothy Miller was expecting his child seemed more daunting than any of those other things. If only his father had more understanding of human love and desire, he thought. If only there were some small flaw in the stern and authoritarian figure, the blameless preacher. Then perhaps . . .? But there was nothing. Geoffrey Buxton appeared to think himself above reproach.

The following day Rose Miller was stitching a new frock for Christabel, for Geoffrey's child, and there was another length of material cut out and ready to sew for Dorothy. She would need some bigger dresses soon. Geoffrey Buxton's money had paid for both. She thought about the situation as she worked. Well, she couldn't criticize Dorry, however stupid she had been, but she couldn't understand the girl's reluctance to say anything to Clifford Buxton. He ought to know. It was his right. And she'd gone off to Devon in a bit of a hurry too, before she needed to really. Rose hoped that everything was going well down there in Teignmouth. It was a nice place by all accounts, but she missed Dorry, and Chrissy had been grumpy and bad-tempered ever since she'd left.

There was a sudden and unexpected knock at the door and she stopped her machine to heave herself from the chair. So much sitting made you stiff, she thought, as she pushed her hair from her forehead and went out through the narrow passage to the front.

Clifford Buxton was standing outside. After the first shock she welcomed him and ushered him through the door, hoping the neighbours hadn't noticed. From the look on his face perhaps he knew after all! Well it would be a relief if he did, whatever Dorry said, but if he didn't then it was going to be difficult. She hoped that she wouldn't give anything away.

'I'm glad to see you, Captain Buxton,' she said. Her eyes strayed to his empty sleeve and she was flustered. 'I was sorry to hear about your arm. Our Dorry told me that you'd had a bit of a setback with it.' She looked at his pale face and thought sadly that no young man should look like that.

He smiled and tried to ignore her obvious discomfort at his presence. He felt considerably uncomfortable himself. So much depended on this visit. He had to find out where Dorothy was, and if possible discover why she had behaved so strangely. Rose Miller possibly held the clue to both mysteries.

Yet he couldn't go blurting out his questions immediately. How would he know whether Dorothy had told her mother about the baby? Might she possibly have kept it a secret, merely saying that she was going away to write? He thought it was extremely unlikely but it wouldn't do to risk giving anything away until he was sure. He would have to phrase everything he said with great care.

She was still staring at his empty sleeve and it made him nervous. He glanced down resentfully. 'Yes, it was a bit of a shock when I had to go for more treatment, but I think all's well now,' he said, trying to dismiss it casually as though the missing bit of himself were merely a piece of unwanted flotsam. He was stalling for time, watching her, trying to fathom the expression on her face. 'I hope you don't mind my calling on you like this, but I should really like to contact Dorothy,' he said, changing the subject and trying to sound matter-of-fact. That much at least was safe. He had given nothing away.

He saw the blush redden her cheeks. 'She don't want no one to know where she is, not for a bit anyway,' Rose said. 'She made me promise.'

He shook his head in amazement and consternation. 'Why though, Mrs Miller? Why doesn't she want to see me?'

'If you give me a letter for her I'll post it on.'

He was beginning to feel angry. 'It's ludicrous,' he declared. 'Like something out of a storybook.'

Rose twisted her hands together anxiously. 'She has her reasons, Captain Buxton. She'm not just being difficult, and I knows that she wants to see you later on.'

'Then why are you withholding her whereabouts, for goodness sake? Why can't I go to her now?'

Rose's agitation was increasing and Clifford was aware that he too was becoming flustered. The pain in his stump began to trouble him and he winced. It was time to stop playing games. She must surely know all the facts. She was Dorothy's mother after all. The more he watched her the more sure he became. From the colour of her face and the worried set of her mouth it was quite clear that she knew he was the father of the baby her daughter carried, the cause of all the trouble! He felt guilty and ashamed. They were emotions he was becoming used to lately! He decided to prevaricate no longer.

'Mrs Miller,' he said. 'I have found out about Dorothy's . . . Dorothy's predicament. I love her. I want to go to her. Please don't stop me.'

Rose gasped and sat down heavily at the table. 'I don't rightly know what to do then,' she said. 'She gave me my instructions, and she was quite firm about it all. How did you come to find out, Captain Buxton?'

'It's a strange story and I hardly know myself how it all happened. Did you know that Dorothy wrote to Arthur Price and told him about it? I read the letter.'

Rose was dismayed. Dorry had particularly said that no one but Vera and Arthur should know. Her secret must be kept from Clifford until it was the right time to tell. 'I told her not to write to Arthur,' she said. 'But she wouldn't listen. She wanted him to know.'

The worm of doubt returned. 'Why? Why did she write to him and not to me?' He almost shouted the words and was immediately contrite. 'I'm sorry, Mrs Miller,' he added. 'I don't want to be rude to you, but to tell you the truth I was very dismayed about that, about her writing to Price.'

Rose looked at him with sudden understanding. 'Oh, you got nothing to worry about there, Captain Buxton. She and Arthur have been friends for years and years, just friends mind you as far as my Dorry was concerned. He wanted to marry her, see. He kept on asking her lots of times, but she fell in love with you didn't she?' Rose paused for breath and shrugged her shoulders. 'When she found she was going to have your baby, well then, she knew that Arthur must give up hope and find somebody else. She wanted him to be free of thinking about her, of thinking he might still hope that she'd change her mind. I know it sounds daft and I told her that it was, but she's stubborn is our Dorry and she would have it her way. She'm a good girl though and she didn't want him hurt more than was necessary.'

Clifford felt relief sweep over him. It sounded plausible, just the kind of thing Dorothy would do. He felt that his whole life was suddenly resurrected. He had no need to be jealous of Arthur Price any longer! It was more likely to be the other way round. He remembered with some discomfort the traumatic episode of the previous afternoon.

'But why didn't she tell me as well?' he asked. It was the most important question, the one to which, as yet, he had no answer. 'And why does she not want to see me?' He stared at Rose. 'Why was I not supposed to know? It is, after all, my baby!'

Rose blushed again. She was not used to mentioning certain embarrassing conditions to young men, to any man for that matter. But she could try to explain Dorry's reasons for rushing off in that silly way.

'It's just that she didn't want to trap you into marrying her,' she told him. 'Because of the baby, she meant. She've always wanted to be independent. She says that she can manage, and that if you married her just because you thought you ought to, then neither of you'd be happy. Now she'm an author she'm really proud, and says that she got no need of anyone's charity.'

'Charity!' Clifford snorted in disgust. 'Charity! I'm not offering her charity, Mrs Miller. I love her and I want to marry her. Baby or no baby I want to marry her. I wanted that long before I knew about the baby!'

Rose felt tears spring to her eyes. So it was going to be all right after all. This rather splendid young man sitting opposite her was really going to marry Dorry! She could hardly believe it. 'Then I think I'll be able to give you her address,' she said. 'As long as I'm sure, Mr Clifford.'

'Sure?'

'Sure that you . . .' Rose was embarrassed again. 'Sure that you love her and all that. Really love her I mean. She was worried that you'd just pretend you did

410

out of a sense of duty, for the sake of her good name and all!'

Clifford laughed in relief. Then he leaned across the table and took Rose's hand in his and gripped it tightly. 'Thank you, Mrs Miller,' he said. 'Thank you. And yes I do really love her!'

Then suddenly Rose thought of her other daughter and all her happiness collapsed like a pack of cards. 'What about Amy?' she said faintly. 'You'm engaged to marry Amy!'

Clifford felt the pain in his arm again and he closed his eyes for a moment before replying. 'I think my relationship with Amy has been rather like Dorothy's with Arthur Price,' he said at last. 'We grew up together, drifted into our engagement because it was expected of us. During her last leave she made it fairly clear to me that she thought we had made a mistake. Nothing was actually said . . .' He paused, realizing that it all sounded like excuses. 'Then she went back to France,' he finished lamely. 'I shall write to her immediately of course.'

'Amy's my girl too,' Rose said. 'I feels for her. She sends me letters you know, quite regular. She's changed.'

'What do you mean, *changed*?' Clifford was intrigued that Mrs Miller should apply the same word that he himself had used when he spoke to his mother about Amy yesterday.'

'Well she's not the frightened little Amy that I knew years ago when I used to make dresses for her. She'm a young lady with a mind of her own now. She seems to be independent somehow. It comes out in her letters.' Suddenly Rose knew, without any doubt whatsoever, which one of her twin daughters was the more vulnerable, and the knowledge surprised her. It was Dorry with all her bright breezy ways who needed reassurance now, and someone to love her, although she would deny it of course. She was the one who was all soft and crumbly underneath her bold front. 'Amy'll be all right,' she declared. 'You mark my words, Mr Clifford. Amy'll be all right.'

'I hope my father shares your optimism,' Clifford said, and in those few words shattered all Rose's new serenity.

'Do he know?' she asked, horrified at the thought. 'I can't think that he'll be very pleased!'

Clifford laughed bitterly. 'My mother knows but not my father. He'll probably turn me out, cut me out of everything and refuse to have me in the house or business again.'

Rose stared at him in horror. 'He'd never do nothing like that, Mr Clifford,' she said. 'He's a good man, your father.'

'You don't know him, Mrs Miller. He may sound good from the pulpit, and of course he is in many ways. He's upright and fair and all that, but he's too good. I mean, he has no ordinary human failings. He can't understand things like . . .' He broke off and wondered why he was telling this woman so much, unburdening his thoughts and fears to her.

Rose, looking at the worried young man before her, suddenly recalled that day so long ago now when the father he was speaking of had made love to her. She thought of his hands on her body, the masculine feel of him. He was the last man she had known. Then it became clear to her that if Geoffrey Buxton did indeed react as his son predicted, then she would have to tell. For the sake of Dorothy's future she would have to tell her long-kept secret and force him to acknowledge that all human beings were ordinary mortals with ordinary failings that had to be forgiven and forgotten. For Dorothy's sake she would do it. It was probably better out in the open too. She had a feeling that somehow that interfering Mrs Price had found out, or guessed. Then there was Chrissy to think of. For her sake too it might be better told. The only one to suffer would be poor Mrs Buxton.

She sighed and for a time Clifford sat there watching her and wondering why she had reacted so strongly over his remarks about his father.

'So you think your pa is too good,' she said at last. 'That's a strange thing to say. If he's that good, then he won't turn you out.'

'You don't know him. That's obvious. He'll be absolutely furious.' Clifford shivered at the thought of his father's wrath.

Rose sat down at the table and was quiet for a moment. Then she looked at him and smiled grimly. 'If he is furious, like you say, Captain Buxton, and if he turns you out, just you come straight back here to me. I've something to tell you that might make things different.'

'Whatever do you mean?'

'Never mind for now. Just do as I say. And don't be scared of him. There's no one what's perfect, and him least of all. And I know that if you plucks up your courage and faces up to him, it'll make a great difference to my Dorry. She'll be sure that you really love her then, won't she? Otherwise you might have to persuade her a bit of that. She'll never marry you unless she'm quite, quite sure. That was what she said!'

She wouldn't be drawn any further and Clifford was consumed with curiosity over what she meant about his father.

Eventually Rose got up and went to the fireplace and took a card from behind the clock on the mantelpiece. 'Here it is, her address. Perhaps you could copy it down.'

With some difficulty Clifford took a silver pencil from his pocket. His trembling fingers didn't help. He found a notebook and opened it out on the table, and then he laboriously scrawled the address, hoping that he could read his writing afterwards. 'Teignmouth,' he said in dismay. 'Devon, I believe.'

Rose watched his efforts with a sudden rush of pity and wished that she had been more thoughtful and given him the card, copying the words out for herself. 'Yes, she'm staying with her Aunt Elsie, my cousin,' she explained. 'She keeps a tea and cake shop down there. She'm writing in all her spare time and helping out in the shop. You know about her book of course.'

'Yes, she wrote and told me. She said that was why she'd gone away!'

'That were a half-truth,' Rose said. Then on a note of pride, 'But she got paid good money and she bought one of them typewriters. A great big black thing, and heavy too to take all that way, but she reckoned it was the most important thing in her trunk!'

Clifford laughed. 'I'm glad for her,' he said.

Then Rose changed the subject again: Geoffrey Buxton was very much on her mind. 'Now just promise me that you won't worry about that father of yours,' she directed firmly. 'He've got no right to stand in judgement over anyone.'

Her voice was mysterious but oddly confident, and all the way home Clifford couldn't get the words out of his head. He decided not to tell his mother of his visit, but something in Rose Miller's bearing as she said goodbye to him had given him hope, and it was with a new strength that he entered his father's study the following morning.

CHAPTER EIGHTEEN

Clifford stood in the study facing the man who had dominated him for so many years. It was a bright Sunday morning, but the sunshine outside did nothing to dispel his agitation. He had spent some sleepless hours the previous night wondering just what he was going to say, and also pondering Rose Miller's strange words. He could not possibly imagine how she might be able to affect his father's attitude to him or to anyone else for that matter and he had decided eventually to ignore her remarks. She was obviously exaggerating the importance of whatever it was she knew and he had enough to worry about without getting involved with any other concern.

'You are coming to Chapel with me this morning, Clifford?' His father's words were almost a command rather than a question.

'Probably not, Father. There's something I have to tell you though.' Clifford glanced nervously at the bookshelves that lined the walls, and then out of the window at the clear sky and the sunshine that never shone into this gloomy room.

Geoffrey was sitting at the large desk making some final notes for a sermon he was to preach later that day. He put his pen down on the ink stand and looked at his son. 'Yes. What is it? You sound particularly dismal for such a lovely day.'

Clifford tried to summon all his reserves of self-confidence. He was angry with himself for his fear, remembering all the nightmare situations he'd lived through in France without feeling the sort of trepidation he felt now. He took a deep breath. 'I intend to break off my engagement with Amy,' he said. 'I wanted you to know before I write to her.'

For a second there was chilling silence and then Geoffrey spoke slowly, his words calm and cold. 'I trust that I am not hearing correctly,' he said. 'If I am, then please explain yourself.'

'It's quite simple really,' Clifford said, trying vainly to believe that it was. 'I do not think that Amy feels for me as she once did. She made it clear during her last leave and although we didn't talk about it I believe that we both knew that things were not as they used to be between us.' He took a deep breath and marvelled at how callous his words seemed. For an agonizing second he could see himself as his father must be seeing him, and the picture was not a pleasant one. He suddenly felt ashamed and a concern, almost a kind of love for Amy, as in the past.

His father was looking at him coldly. 'And does Amy agree with your conclusions?' he asked. 'I presume that you have given some thought to the effect such a course would have upon the girl who has promised to marry you.'

'I have thought of little else, Sir. As I said, no words were spoken between us about the possibility of breaking off our engagement, but I feel sure that it was in her mind. Why would she have left me to go back to France if things had been otherwise?'

'She deemed it her duty. Amy is a highly principled young lady.'

There was a silence during which both men assumed postures of extreme antagonism. Standing in front of his father's desk, Clifford felt at a distinct disadvantage. At last Geoffrey spoke again and his tone was almost menacing. 'Is there anyone else you have set your mind upon? I have heard rumours and until now I have chosen not to believe them.'

Clifford could feel his heart beat a tattoo in his chest, each beat echoed by a stab of pain in his arm. 'I intend to marry Dorothy Miller, Sir.' He spoke quickly and then pulled himself up to his full height and tried not to think about the throbbing pain.

'Just as I feared, as I have feared for a long time in fact.' Geoffrey said. 'And to think that I had a hand in that girl's rise from the factory.' He got up from his desk and walked to the window and stared through it. The silence in the room was threatening. Eventually he turned and Clifford could not understand the inscrutable look on his father's face. He spoke eventually and his voice was completely firm, brooking no argument. 'But it cannot be,' he said in level assured tones. 'I absolutely forbid it. You cannot possibly marry a girl like Dorothy Miller, and you certainly cannot break off an engagement as easily as you obviously think. You will stop seeing the Miller girl and you will write to Amy today and tell her to come home and marry you immediately. There is nothing more to be said.'

Clifford felt anger rise in him like a tide, dispelling all his fear and his doubts too. 'I am a grown man, Father and I will not obey you as I once did. What you say is impossible. Dorothy Miller carries my child.'

Geoffrey took a step towards him, his face now contorted with fury and he raised his hand a fraction and then lowered it. 'Then you will remove yourself from my home by the end of this week. You will take your whore and leave Bristol. I do not wish you to work in my factory and I shall cut you out of my will completely. Now get out.' The voice was quiet and low again, brooking no argument.

Clifford turned and walked from the room. His rage at his father was absolute. He had expected disappointment and anger but this cold and unreasoning assumption that he, Geoffrey Buxton, was to be obeyed without question was not be borne. He went up the stairs to his own room and sat down at his desk, remaining there motionless for a long time. Then he pulled some writing paper towards him and cursed aloud at the loss of his right hand. Awkwardly he dipped the pen into the glass inkwell and started to write to Amy. The letters were ill-formed, like those of a small child. They strayed across the paper in a way that dismayed him. He had spent long hours learning to write again with a left hand that frequently refused to do his bidding. This letter was important and he wanted to get it right, wanted Amy to accept what had happened with the least hurt. He knew that there was blame, that he had behaved badly in many ways. And he still had a large place in his heart for the girl who had once loved him, perhaps still did, the girl he had loved too but more as an extension of Laura, another sister.

An hour later, and after many attempts, he had finished and he wrote Amy's name on the envelope. His mother would have to write the address. He hoped that his news wouldn't bring Amy the grief it might have done a year ago. He couldn't help feeling anxious for her. Would she ever come to look upon him in friendship again as she had years ago? Like a brother?

No one had come to his room during the hour and he wondered what had happened downstairs, what his father had done and said. He was glad that he had prepared his mother for the trauma. She would have been expecting an explosion of anger and he was sure she would be able to deal with it, although this made no difference to the regret he felt for causing her such pain.

Then his thoughts turned to Dorothy as they constantly did, and he knew that he must go to her as soon as possible. There was still a terrifying niggle of doubt in his heart, that perhaps she might refuse him. He had been thrilled to hear of her latest success with her book, but feared her new-found independence might cause her to question whether or not she wanted to marry him. And after all he was rather a liability now. He had no job, little money and no prospects, and he was only half a man into the bargain! He glanced angrily at his empty sleeve and thought of the career he had wanted. He could have earned a good living for both of them with his music. He got up and slowly went down the stairs. There was no sound. His parents would be in Chapel by now. He longed to talk to his mother but he knew that she would not be alone until tomorrow. But, despite his doubts, he was amazed at the detachment he felt, at his ability to decide what he must do. There was money to be drawn from his bank on Monday, and then he would go to Teignmouth.

He knew that he could not stay here in this house today, not with his father coming home from Chapel full of holiness and righteous anger. There was only one place in Bristol now where he might be welcome, one person who would listen to his plans. He walked down through the quiet Sabbath streets to St Paul's and knocked on Rose Miller's door once more.

'Sit down and have a cup of tea, Captain Buxton,' Rose said. 'If you'd honour us, me and Chrissy, perhaps you'd like to have a bit of dinner with us too. It's lonely without Dorry and I managed to get some meat yesterday so we're having a proper stew.'

'Thank you very much,' Clifford said. There was an appetizing smell coming from the little scullery, and he was grateful for the invitation. He hadn't realized how hungry he was.

Rose bustled about laying the table, finding the best

419

cutlery, making suet dumplings and sorting out some cakes for afters.

She had been in a state of intense agitation ever since Clifford's visit yesterday, but she was quite determined that if Geoffrey Buxton behaved badly over the affair, then she would definitely tell.

She could hear Chrissy playing next door, her bossy voice coming clearly over the wall that divided the two back yards. Chrissy was always the leader in any game, always the one to give the orders. Rose laughed a little grimly to herself as she thought of Geoffrey Buxton and the dominant personality that he had so obviously passed on to his daughter.

'So you've gone and told your father have you, Captain Buxton?' she asked breathlessly.

'Yes. I told him this morning.'

'And how did he take it?'

'Just as my mother predicted. He said I was to get out of the house and out of his life if I married Dorothy.'

Rose felt a great surge of maternal anger. After all, she reasoned, Dorry was more hers than Amy really. Amy had been brought up by someone else. And what was so wrong with Dorry anyway?

'He's got no reason to think himself so much better than you or anyone else,' she said indignantly. 'You just listen to what I have to say, and then you might be able to get him to change his mind.'

Clifford wondered what she could possibly mean. 'I've no intention of going begging to him after what he said to me this morning, Mrs Miller,' he said. 'Whatever you have to tell me will make no difference to that.'

'Well, that's as maybe,' Rose said stiffly. You must make up your mind, but just you wait while I tell you. It's about Chrissy so I must say it now before she comes back.'

420

Clifford looked at her in some surprise and impatience. He couldn't think that the thin, plain little girl had anything to do with all the problems that occupied his mind, but he said nothing.

Rose was holding a large wooden spoon and rich gravy dripped from it. She went out to replace it in the stew-pan and then she wiped the table and finally sat down. 'I've kept this secret for over six years,' she said at last. 'And now the time has come when I must tell. If he'd been understanding and kind like I always thought he was, then perhaps I never would have told. Not that he haven't been good to me,' she added hastily. 'But that don't come into it.' She paused and twisted her hands anxiously together. 'You seen my Chrissy haven't you? Well, she's your half-sister. Your pa is hers too!'

The words were so staggering, the pictures they conveyed to his mind so outrageous that Clifford wanted to jump up and walk from the room. He was amazed at his own reaction, at the overwhelming desire he immediately felt to protect his father from the implications of what this woman before him was saying. Geoffrey Buxton might have been a tyrant of sorts during all his boyhood years and just now acted as a despot, but there had always been, in the family, a certain reverence for his integrity, almost as though they were all proud of it in a complex way. He gulped on the tea she had given him and pushed the cup away across the table.

'It's not true. You're not telling me the truth are you, Mrs Miller? I mean, my father . . .' Suddenly he thought of his mother whom he loved so much and he covered his face with his hands when he realized what this would mean to her. If it were true of course. Eventually he looked up at Rose.

She was sitting very still and he saw tears in her eyes. 'Would I have said such a thing if it weren't the honest

421

truth? I'm a Christian woman, Captain Buxton. Apart from that one fall from grace, I've always kept to the Good Lord's ways as best I know how. Your pa sends me money regular for Chrissy's upkeep. He knows that she's his.'

Clifford felt that in all his twenty-three years he had never been so shocked. His whole world seemed to spin about him in pieces. The future became filled with horrifying uncertainties. How could his father behave like that and then go on preaching hell and damnation to sinners every Sunday?

Rose seemed to read his thoughts. 'We all fall sometimes you know, Captain Buxton,' she said. 'There's not one soul on this earth that's perfect.'

'I certainly know that,' Clifford replied, thinking of himself. 'But I've always felt that my father thinks that he is pretty much beyond reproach.' The words were bitter and spoken with sarcasm.

'Well now you know different, don't you.' Rose's voice was quiet and measured. 'But I think you'm wrong when you say that he thinks he'm near perfect,' she added. 'He knows that he did wrong as well as anyone. He believes that he'm forgiven and that's the end of it. That's what he believes!'

Clifford tried to digest this piece of information and he had to agree that his father's reasoning probably went along those lines. But the theology still made little sense to him. 'There are others from whom he needs forgiveness as well as from God,' he said, thinking bitterly of his mother. All the implications began to churn about in his mind. 'Does Dorothy know?' he asked suddenly.

'Yes. Of course she knows. In fact I hope she'm the only one what do know, apart from him of course.'

Clifford tried to take a grip on himself. 'I don't know what you want me to do about it,' he said. 'But for the sake of my mother I think that I must keep silent.'

'That's up to you, Captain Buxton. I told you because I want the best for my Dorry. You can tell your pa that you know or not, just as you want. You and Dorry can talk it over when you go to see her. I don't mean you to blackmail him to take you back or anything like that. I'd never 'ave told you if I thought you'd do that. And I shall go on keeping silent. But I sometimes thinks that perhaps it ought to be told one day soon. I've felt bad about deceiving your poor ma all these years. I'd not want her hurt, but knowing the truth and coming to terms with it sometimes be the best way of going on.' She paused and looked at him wistfully. 'I know it might sound a bit selfish, but I'd like to have her forgiveness. I've wanted that for a long time, to tell her how sorry I am.'

It was a long speech for Rose, and Clifford listened, desperate to get out of the house and walk in the clear April sunshine, always his panacea when things were difficult. All his desire for food had disappeared, but just as he was wondering how he would achieve an escape Chrissy came into the room.

She stared at him. 'Hello, Captain Buxton,' she said. 'I'm glad you've come. Are you going to marry our Dorry?'

Clifford looked at the child – his half-sister – and he saw immediately a look of Laura, a look of his father. Rose was certainly telling the truth. He had seen it before but it had meant nothing then.

'Yes I am. If she'll have me,' he replied.

'That's good then, and are you going to have dinner with me and Ma? It's stew today.'

The two questions seemed to have equal importance and Clifford wasn't sure whether he wanted to laugh, cry or scream. 'Yes,' he said again. 'Yes please. Your mama has asked me to stay and have some.'

Chrissy turned to Rose. 'Did you hear, Ma? He

called you my mama? Can I say that instead of Ma or Mam? It sounds nice.'

'Yes, dear. I think I should like that,' Rose said. 'Mama! It's posh, but that's all right.'

Clifford ate the food that was set before him without too much difficulty in spite of his state of mind. It was delicious and he found that he was enjoying it.

'My Dorry can cook like this,' Rose informed him proudly and he smiled, thinking that it would probably be necessary for her to do so. He had to remind himself that he only had his army pension to live on now.

As soon as he decently could, he excused himself. 'I shall go down to Devon tomorrow,' he said. 'Is there anything you would like me to take to Dorothy?'

'Just a frock,' Rose said. 'She'll be needing bigger ones soon and I've got one finished already and another almost done. I'll give you the one that's finished.' She went to a drawer, took out a parcel and handed it to him, and he felt the colour rush to his face. A mixture of both pride and shame overcame him. That their one short time of loving should have been the cause of this was both horrifying and wonderful.

Rose followed him to the door and suddenly was overcome with happiness. As she looked at the personable young officer standing there, all her mother's love surfaced once more. She wanted this man for Dorry more than anything in the world, perhaps even more than she had wanted her to marry Arthur. If it was what Dorry wanted of course, and she was pretty sure of that! After all, she reasoned to herself, Amy had her money. She was a rich young woman, and money could get you anything you wanted, well almost anything. 'Give her my love won't you, Clifford,' she said, using his first name. 'You'm a good man. I trust you to do what's right about what I told you, and to look after my precious Dorry too.'

For reply he bent and kissed her gently on the cheek

and then he strode out of the house and quickly away through the narrow streets and up the Ashley Hill towards the country, where he could breath deeply and think what next to do.

Amy received three letters all at once. She glanced at them and set them aside to read later when she had a little spare time. One was from Clifford. His funny writing was on the envelope, just her name, and underneath it the address written neatly by Felicity. Then there was another from her solicitor. And a third with a Gloucestershire postmark.

A few hours later she sat on a wooden bench in the spring sunshine and read Clifford's letter. She sat there for a long time with the pages in her hand, staring through a blur of tears at the daffodils blooming in their hundreds, planted three years ago in happier times; she sat so still that a small bird hopped very close, almost on to her boots. So it was all over. This was the final closing of her old life. For a few moments there was an emptiness in her heart and a grief for all that might have been but as she sat there the mists began slowly to clear and the sense of loss diminish. She had known for a long time that her love for Clifford did not match up to all the things she expected of the love between a woman and a man. She frequently felt that it was not enough for marriage. There was some missing element that she did not fully understand. Perhaps it was the difference between loving someone and being in love! She had always loved Clifford in a way, and it was to him that she had turned in the difficult times of her life. When she was young she had needed his praise too. She laughed a little as she remembered the Dvořák and her endless struggles to become proficient and earn his approval. She had no need now to prove anything to anyone. She had become confident of her ability to cope with her life. Here, in this little bit of hell she had come to terms with all the disappointments and tragedies that she had suffered and she felt completely whole now. It was a good feeling, and she knew that she was able to face this latest situation without too much trauma or too many tears.

Yet in spite of her brave resolutions she shivered a little when she thought of Dorothy Miller. This girl was her twin sister and Clifford had . . . she didn't want to think of them together like that! She remembered the times when he had called out so frequently in his delirium. Always the same name, always Dorothy.

She folded the letter slowly, and placed it back in its envelope. She knew that she would never have ended their engagement herself. Not after the amputation of his arm. How awful though if they had married each other out of a sense of duty, with no true romantic love between them. She shuddered and gradually relief took the place of loss. When the war ended she would be free to do what she liked. For the first time in her life she was totally alone and totally free. It was a strange and not altogether an unpleasant feeling.

The second letter, from her solicitor, was a large affair and she had difficulty in opening it. She scanned the page quickly and her heart filled with relief again. So all the legal problems were overcome. Her father's will had been accepted. The case had been won and she was the sole legatee. Everything was hers as he had wished. She was rich as well as free. The news was too much to take in all at once and she turned to the third letter.

It was from Arthur and she read it eagerly. He had been sent to England to recover from influenza and had succumbed to some other illness as well, a sort of minor nervous breakdown he said. But he was well now and would be returning to France in May or June to rejoin his squadron. He said that perhaps they might meet again one day. The letter was beautifully written and she read it twice over and then folded it and placed it, like the others, in its envelope and back into the large pocket in her apron. Then she walked slowly to her room and locked all three into the small box that she kept for her special things.

Before she went back to the wards again she untied the ribbon that hung round her neck and took Clifford's ring from it. She looked at it for a moment, holding it in the palm of her hand and watching the sun glinting in a myriad of colours on the diamonds. Then she unlocked the box again and placed the ring carefully inside Clifford's letter. She tied the ribbon firmly round the envelope and placed it right at the bottom of the box with the others that he had sent.

She looked in the mirror and breathed a deep sigh of sudden contentment. 'As soon as the war is over,' she told her reflection, 'I shall travel. I can do just whatever I please. I shall go round the world. Perhaps I might go to Canada to find my real father. I shall start a new life.'

Clifford sat in the train that every minute was carrying him closer to Dorothy. He hugged the amazing knowledge of his father's infidelity to himself and wondered what he should do. His mother, the one to whom in the past he had often taken his problems, had to be considered first. What would she want? Would she wish to know? Would she ever be able to forgive? And Rose said she needed forgiveness from Felicity. Was that too much to ask of any woman? Then there was the little scrap of a sister, Christabel. What would be the best for her? But also filling his mind was Dorothy. For her sake should he confront his father?

He was no nearer a solution when suddenly the train was right at the sea's edge. He gasped at the beauty of it and watched the waves, grey and threatening, rolling towards the shore as though they would encompass the whole train. He knew that he would soon be in Teignmouth and Dorothy would be in his arms. Arms! He always thought of them in the plural until he angrily remembered.

He had written to say that he was coming, and he hoped that she would meet him, but there had been no time for a reply. During the whole journey he had been anxious about his reception. He knew that he had staked his future on this meeting. If she didn't want him . . . he could not bear to think what he would do if she told him to go home again.

He leaned anxiously out of the window as the train steamed into the station and saw her waiting for him on the small platform. He pulled his bag from the rack, impatiently fumbled with the awkward door and then he was out and they were running towards each other. He dropped his bag and held her with all the strength he could muster.

But after that first hungry embrace his words were almost condemning. 'Why did you not tell me? Why Dorothy?'

She put her finger on his lips. 'Later, my darling. Later we'll talk. Just let's be together now.'

He had to release her in order to pick up his bag, but she put her hand over his and they walked out of the station saying no more, but in perfect accord.

The three-storeyed house was narrow and painted white with frilled net curtains looped back from the bay windows at either side of the front door, and there was a sign at the gate that said, 'Teas, Home-made cakes, soups and sandwiches.'

Aunt Elsie was a large handsome woman and she welcomed him with a firm handshake and a broad smile. 'Glad to see you, Captain Buxton,' she boomed. 'Heard nothing else but how good-looking and brave you are and all that. Glad to see it's all true!'

Clifford blushed somewhat. 'Thank you Mrs Franklin,' he replied. 'I'm very grateful to you for looking after Dorothy.'

'Don't mention it my dear boy. It's nothing. In fact I'm glad of her help. Very good at cake-making is your Dorothy and we need lots of cakes and and scones each day in the shop. Now let me show you to your room so you can unpack. It's right up at the top of the house.'

They left him alone to sort out his things and he was grateful. He still didn't like to be watched as he struggled with his one hand to accomplish all the ordinary everyday tasks that he used to take for granted.

The room was small but spotlessly clean and he looked around with pleasure and a sense of peace, a feeling of having reached a safe haven at last. When his suitcase was empty he heaved it awkwardly on to the top of the wardrobe and looked out of the tiny window. He could just see the sea between the houses across the road. He stood there for a long time and knew that this was where he wanted to be. After all the trauma of the past months, this was home. And perhaps it was here in this peaceful little town that he would start a new life with Dorothy. Filled with optimism and an unusual enthusiasm for the future he went down the stairs.

'Will you marry me, Dorothy?' he said just an hour later. They were walking along the stone jetty above the beach and he stopped and caught her hand tightly in his.

'You really want me then, Clifford,' she said. 'Not just because of the baby.'

'I really want you,' he whispered. 'You have no need to ask something like that. I thought you knew. I wondered if you wanted me!'

'But do you truly love me?' she persisted, ignoring his last remark.

'I truly love you,' he said.

'Then, yes. I will marry you.'

There was no need to say any more. All his doubts vanished as if they had never been. They stood together, aware of no one but themselves. A train steamed past them on the line that ran close to the sea and they cared nothing for the interested passengers who only saw a glimpse of an officer and a girl. For Dorothy and Clifford all the complications of their lives could be sorted out tomorrow. Only today counted and the certainty of their love.

For Dorothy the relief was enormous. The man she loved had come to her freely and without coercion. She pulled away from him for a moment and looked at the waves that were breaking lazily on the sandy shingle beneath the path. A gull called eerily in the grey sky and a sense of peace filled her. 'I'm so happy, Clifford,' she whispered. 'I don't think I've ever been so content in my entire life. Always, always I've been fighting and striving for something. Now I don't have to any more.'

He held her closer and smiled. 'You'll never stop striving,' he said. 'But now we'll do it together.'

'I promise that you will have to listen to every word I write. You can be my severest critic.'

'No good at all,' he said. 'I shall approve of everything.'

They both laughed and swung hand in hand along the promenade.

CHAPTER NINETEEN

Arthur had mixed feelings when in May he was declared fit enough to return to duty. A full report of his illness had been written. He had suffered a severe attack of influenza they said, followed by a time of nervous exhaustion due to an irrational fear of fire.

'Irrational?' he said to one of his fellow officers when he returned to France. 'Watching a man spinning down in flames nearly every day of your life would make anyone afraid of fire! Stupid bloody doctor!'

'Well the Red Baron's no more,' his friend said. 'So perhaps we've a bit more chance of getting back alive. I expect you read about it in the papers.'

'Manfred von Richthofen,' Arthur remarked to himself, thinking with respect and fear of the legendary German pilot. 'Yes, I heard. How many of ours did they say he accounted for?'

'Eighty, I think. Pretty deadly. There were celebrations here when we heard the news.'

Arthur shuddered. The newspaper had reported jubilantly that von Richthofen had come down in a fireball. For anyone it was a terrible fate. He wondered if he would ever overcome his fear of a death like that. He was supposed to be cured, but he knew in himself that every time he went up into the sky he would experience that fear again. Constantly he would fall asleep only to dream of his own burning descent. He had not been plagued by these phobias when he'd first started flying and he heartily wished to be free of them now.

The fact that he had been given command of a squadron made his terror more significant. He knew that any weakness he betrayed in front of his men might well cause the death of one of them during combat. It was an awesome reflection. They were all afraid sometimes, of course, and it was his job to give them courage and leadership. He squared his shoulders and determined to do this, however much the panic raged inside.

His life quickly resumed the old pattern of flight after flight, combined with the training of those under his command, and as he struggled to keep his fears in check, the problems of home gradually receded from his mind.

But he sometimes thought of Dorothy and more often now of Amy. He had written to Amy while he was in England and recently he had to admit to a feeling of empathy with her, for she too was working in pretty awful circumstances. He could imagine what a field hospital must be like and sometimes he shuddered at the nightmare quality of his thoughts. That a girl with Amy's sheltered upbringing should be exposed to such experiences seemed just too improbable. Whenever he thought about her it was with immense respect.

He often recalled the afternoon they had met at Le Montaine and he hoped that the pleasure could be repeated. It had been a wonderful interlude in a life that was surrounded by constant gunfire, battle and death. She had replied to his letter briefly but there had been no definite promise of another meeting. She had said that she would write again.

Vera seldom corresponded and he was surprised one morning to receive an untidy envelope that could only be from his sister. He opened it and looked at her misspelt words and faulty English with a measure of impatience and yet also with affection. But in spite of the doubtful writing, the news she had to tell held his attention. Dorothy was in Teignmouth, in Devon, she said. She and Clifford had married there quietly. They were settling down and working in a little tea shop. Dorothy was writing her second novel and Clifford was doing some teaching. She couldn't tell him if they intended to return to Bristol but she thought that there was a rift between Clifford and his parents.

Arthur put the letter down and stared out of the window at the skudding clouds and he felt a sense of loss as though part of his life were now closed. He had known it was so ever since he'd heard about the baby, but this was the end, like the firm and final shutting of a door on his youth. He allowed his mind to stray to England, to an imagined scene of peaceful fields and sleepy Devon towns where the smell and noise of war was unknown. Then he slumped on to his bed, put his head in his hands and wept for all that he had lost: for the war, for his dead comrades and for the future that he frequently felt would never be his.

That afternoon he headed a patrol over enemy lines. He placed his men in positions where they could achieve some success if attacked and when he was sure that he had done all in his power for their safety, he charged off on his own. The wind tore at his fragile craft and he was filled with a great sense of power. The whole sky was his and what did Dorothy matter now, or anything down there on the ground far below! He saw some enemy planes in the distance and with a feeling of complete detachment he headed for them until he was at point-blank range. Then all the frustration and anger he felt was aimed at the Hun and he watched with both elation and horror as he sent yet another two of them spiralling to the ground in flames.

Arthur's elation was only temporary, however. During the actual times that he was in the air, and particularly when he was in combat, he felt free and full of power and strength; but as soon as he reached the comparative safety of his room, or the mess, his turbulence returned.

A few days later he received a letter and he immediately felt cheered as he recognized Amy's writing on the envelope. She had two days' leave which she intended to take at Le Montaine, she said. It had become her favourite seaside resort, and could he meet her there? She had lots to tell him.

She was sitting at a table outside the small café, a tall glass in her hand, and the wind blowing her fair curls round her face. Arthur roared up the street on a motor bicycle that he had borrowed for the day.

He smiled at her, parked the bike carefully and then came quickly up to her and took her outstretched hand in his. 'Lovely to see you, Miss Harding,' he said, and his heart lurched for a moment as he saw Dorothy's face in the fair features.

'Captain Price. You're better now?'

'I think so. But tell me about yourself, and about home. And what's all this news that you mentioned? I've been consumed with curiosity.' He called for coffee and then sat down opposite her.

For a moment she felt shy, wondering if she had been terribly forward in writing and suggesting this meeting. Then she remembered her new freedom and laughed a little to herself.

'Well,' she said without preamble. 'My engagement to Clifford is a thing of the past, but you must have known that of course, as Dorothy and he are married!'

'Yes . . .'

'And Clifford's father has thrown him out of the house, out of the factory and out of his will!'

Arthur grinned, but hastily tried to hide his amusement. Well it served him right he thought privately,

434

but he endeavoured to keep his thoughts to himself. Aloud he said, 'My sister wasn't sure when she wrote to me but she believed that there was a rift between him and his parents. A pretty awful state of affairs I suppose.'

'I feel sorry for them,' Amy replied. 'I've written to Mr Buxton and asked him to do nothing on my account. I said that I was not in love with Clifford and that I certainly did not intend to do anything about breach of promise as he advised me. I also told him that I hoped that he would forgive Clifford and reinstate him.'

Her words amazed Arthur. He drank his coffee slowly, thinking about what she had said, comparing it with his own reaction, his own anger. He beckoned the waiter to order more coffee, and when he spoke to her again his words seemed unconnected. 'Tea would be better, wouldn't it,' he remarked absently. 'I wish they could make decent tea in France!' Then, full of humility and admiration for this quiet slim girl in front of him, he smiled. 'That was a very generous thing to do,' he said.

Amy stared at him and blushed at the look of surprise and sudden affection in his eyes.

'Well I could do nothing else. After all I feel sad for them.'

'For Clifford and Dorothy you mean?'

'Yes. I know you may think that I have cause to be bitter, but honestly I don't feel that. In fact, now that the initial shock is over I'm happy about it.'

'You said you were not . . . not in love with Captain Buxton. Is that really true? You were engaged to marry him.'

'I always loved him in a way. He was necessary to me. That's really what it was I suppose. When my mother died I turned to him, and at other times of crisis too. Then I came over here and learned to be independent.' She paused and a far-away expression passed over her face. She stared out to sea and then back to her companion. 'Do you know how I first knew about his feelings for Dorothy?' she said.

'Tell me.'

'I was nursing him. He was delirious and he kept calling out her name every time he opened his eyes and saw me. 'Dorothy,' he said over and over again. He spoke my name only a couple of times, but hers repeatedly, and with such longing! I knew then, and from that time I began to have doubts about my own feelings, too. It was as if the two things went together.'

Arthur suddenly wanted to take both of her hands tightly in his, wanted to comfort and protect her from further hurt. The anger that he had felt towards Clifford Buxton on that never-to-be-forgotten day in Clifton came back to him in full measure. It took a moment for him to realize that his outrage this time was not because of Dorothy!

She was suddenly aware of the effect her words were having on him and she smiled. 'Don't be cross at Clifford. No one can help falling in love. It's something that just happens. And he was terribly ill. He didn't know what he was saying.'

Arthur, watching her, marvelled again. 'You amaze me,' he said. 'How can you be so forgiving?'

She laughed at him. 'It's not a case of being forgiving. It just doesn't hurt me any more. No one should live with grudges. They're too damaging and the person they damage is the one who has them.'

'True,' Arthur said. 'You'd better teach me a bit of your philosophy then.'

'Are you still upset?'

He paused and thought about her question. Was he? Was he still jealous? After a moment's consideration he decided that the hurt was definitely passing. If Amy could forgive and forget then certainly he could. 'I'm

436

beginning to live again,' he replied.

'Did you love her?'

'Yes, I suppose I did. I definitely did.'

'Do you still?'

'You ask a lot of personal questions, Miss Harding.' He laughed as he spoke and wondered what to reply. Dorothy was often in his thoughts, but he had to acknowledge that Amy took up quite a share of his dreaming time too. 'I'm learning to forget her,' he said ambiguously. 'In fact I am quite sure from this minute that I'm learning very fast.'

She blushed as his meaning conveyed itself to her and changed the subject hastily. 'Can you think of anything that might bring Mr Buxton to change his mind?' she asked. 'About throwing Clifford and Dorothy out I mean. I've just had a letter from his sister, you remember, Laura Buxton? She tells me that there's a great gloom over the house and Aunt Felicity is quite devastated. Of course Clifford still has his army pay and he'll have a pension Laura says, but they'll be pretty poor unless Dorothy makes a lot of money as a writer. And he hasn't got his music now to compensate.'

'I still can't imagine why you are so concerned. Can't we talk about something else?'

Amy looked contrite. 'I'm so sorry. I'm being very boring, but Laura and Clifford have been like brother and sister to me ever since I could remember and I'm very fond of Aunt Felicity. They're almost like my own family. And I try to have some affection for Dorothy. She is my twin sister after all, and twins are supposed to be special.'

Arthur stared at her and suddenly into his mind came the piece of information Vera had imparted to him that day on the Downs. He remembered her words clearly. Geoffrey Buxton and Rose Miller! Christabel was a Buxton! He spoke quickly without considering.

'I think I may have a weapon that could be used!'

'A weapon? What do you mean?' There was a startled expression on Amy's face.

He was almost sorry that he had spoken and then he remembered that he had already told her about Mrs Miller and Christabel, but he hadn't known who the father was then. It had been quite a shock to Amy to discover that her small sister was illegitimate. How would she take this further disturbing piece of news? But he had started the telling. There was no going back.

'Please Arthur, do tell me what you mean,' she asked again.

He knew that she had sensed his sudden reluctance and he hesitated, played with the cup and saucer on the table before him. 'It's going to be a blow, Amy,' he said gently.

She stared at him with large wondering eyes. 'If it's unpleasant I would rather hear it directly from you. Tell me,' she said. 'So much has happened to me that there surely can't be many more bad things left!'

He pushed the cup away and looked straight at her without flinching. 'Mr Buxton is Christabel's father,' he stated simply. 'I didn't know before.'

Colour flooded her face and she clasped her hands together tightly in horror. 'You can't mean that my . . . that Mrs Miller and . . . him? It's too unthinkable. Arthur, are you sure?'

'Quite sure. He pays towards Christabel's upbringing, and he insists that no one should know.'

'Then how did you find out?' There was slight hostility in her voice.

'I have a sister called Vera whose whole purpose in living seems to be discovering bits of information about other people and then passing on the secrets where necessary.' He felt disloyal as he spoke. 'Well actually she isn't as bad as she sounds, and she can keep a secret very adequately. I don't know what would happen if she couldn't.'

Then suddenly Amy's mouth began to twitch a little and Arthur looked at her in alarm, wondering if she were about to burst into tears. But it was her laughter that completely discomfited him. He had quite forgotten that he had experienced the same reaction.

'Don't you see?' she said at last. 'Don't you see how funny it is?' My saintly Uncle Geoffrey falling for Rose Miller! It's the funniest thing I've heard for a long time.' Then she was off again in peals of hilarity. Arthur stared at her, dismayed, not knowing what to do.

At last she found her handkerchief and mopped her eyes. 'That was terrible of me, wasn't it?' she said, suddenly calm again. 'I can't think what came over me. But it's such a shock. And of course I should be thinking of what this will do to my poor Aunt Felicity and Laura too.' She looked across at the sea lapping lazily at the harbour wall and Arthur felt a sudden tug at his heart-strings as he watched her and thought of all the traumas she had coped with during the past few years.

'I'm sorry that I had to tell you,' he said. 'But it's probably better you know now rather than find out later.'

She turned to him and when she spoke her voice was measured and slow. 'I still can hardly believe it, but I'm truly grateful to you for telling me.'

'Do you want to do anything about it?' he asked.

'Face him with it, you mean or face her, my mother? I couldn't. Just imagine!'

Arthur tried to imagine and totally failed. 'Vera said that Dorothy knows, so I presume that Clifford does too,' he said.

'Then why doesn't he confront his father?' Amy queried. 'If anyone should do so then I think it must be Clifford.'

'Of course,' Arthur agreed. 'Presumably he'll benefit when the sorry tale comes into the open.'

'His father will have to take him back then, you mean!'

'Yes, of course. He couldn't have double standards could he?'

'So there's a way for Clifford to be reinstated.' The relief in Amy's voice was obvious. 'Then I shall not think about it any more,' she added. 'It's up to him.'

'I expect he's thinking of what it would do to his mother,' he said. 'That's probably why he's remained quiet so far.'

'Of course.' Amy looked quite stricken. 'Poor Aunt Felicity. What will she do?'

'I've no idea. Walk out on him I should think.'

'She'll never do that. They love each other, you know. I've lived there with them. He's quite different with her, and she always has her own way!'

'I've lived there too, remember. Not in the house of course!'

Amy was immediately contrite, remembering the difference in the way they had each been reared. He was an officer now, well-spoken, self-educated. She thought again of the young chauffeur whom she had called Price and regarded as just a servant, and she was embarrassed. She wanted to share her other news with him, but this latest turn in the conversation made it more difficult. She was conscious suddenly of the great gap that still existed between them, a gap not caused now by birth, for in that they were fairly equal.

But she was wealthy. She had no need to find a husband now if she didn't wish to, no need to work at all for the rest of her life. For a moment the prospect seemed almost obscene, then she laughed to herself and determined that she wouldn't let anything detract from her new-found sense of freedom and happiness.

She was silent for a time, feeling a great admiration

for Arthur Price and for all the things he had accomplished, not least his wonderful war record. Then she smiled at him and gently touched his arm, pulling her hand away quickly in case he should misunderstand. 'You are always the one with important things to tell me,' she said. 'Now I have something to tell you.'

He looked at her and felt alarmed for a moment but the smile on her face allayed his fears.

'My solicitor has written at last,' she said. 'He says that everything has been settled in my favour. My father's will remains as he intended it.'

There was a pause and his eyes held hers for a long moment. 'So you get the house after all?' he said.

'Yes, and everything else. I'm quite rich, Arthur. It's rather an awesome responsibility. I can't go back yet, of course,' she continued. 'Aunt Felicity is looking after things for me, but do you know what I have decided to do when the war is over?'

Arthur tried to be happy for her. 'No,' he replied. 'I can't guess.'

'I shall sell the house as soon as I can. I am quite determined on that. I always hated living in St Paul's. I shall buy myself another little one, somewhere nice, by the sea perhaps, and then I shall travel. Papa always said he would take me to Venice and Rome and Florence, places like that. And then I might go to Canada and find my . . . my real father. I've seen his photograph, but I have a sort of fear about knowing what he's like, a ghost that I want to lay. Then I shall come home and settle down to be an old maid!'

He laughed at her, but her words frightened him a little. There was a brittleness about them that he didn't like and he experienced a surge of fear for her. In spite of her air of independence she was so vulnerable, and this unknown man, her natural father, could so easily be yet another disappointment. If the little he had heard of him from Dorothy were true he certainly would be. Then there would surely be the fortune-hunters. Even Frank Miller might try to get his hands on some of her money. Arthur shivered at his thoughts and tried to tell himself that it was not his concern. He could do nothing for her now. He could offer her nothing. Her considerable wealth would always be a barrier between them. He looked at her and wondered how it felt to be able to say, 'I'm quite rich.' He tried to change the subject. 'What about your mother?' he asked. 'Do you still feel bad about Mrs Miller?'

'Because of Chrissy you mean?' Amy considered for a time. 'Well, of course this latest amazing piece of information puts a slightly different perspective on it. Uncle Geoffrey! I'd never have thought it possible in a thousand years. Yes, perhaps I might be able to feel differently now although I'm not sure exactly why!'

The coffee was finished and Arthur paid the bill and they walked along the beach together in the warm afternoon sun. The guns were still booming with terrible menace in the distance.

'The war's changed,' Arthur said. 'It shouldn't be long now before the end.'

'Are you just being optimistic?'

'No. We're striking the Boche infantry from the air, and that helps the poor old tommies down below. You know of course that the Royal Flying Corps and the Royal Naval Air Service have merged now, don't you? We are the Royal Air Force.' There was great pride in Arthur's voice. 'We'll probably be called the RAF.'

'We've a lot more tanks as well, haven't we,' Amy commented. 'And the Americans are helping us, too, and the Canadians and Australians. Oh, Arthur, I do hope you're right about it ending soon. There are so many wounded and killed coming back from the Front every day, thousands and thousands, some of them victims of that awful mustard gas. These have been awful years. I'm longing to start my new life, but when I think about it I almost feel guilty for having survived.'

She looked up at him and smiled and his heart thudded uncomfortably as he took her hand for a moment and pressed it gently. He suddenly believed himself to be a little in love with her. He wanted to throw his arms round her right there on the warm sand, but then common sense intervened. Perhaps it was only because she was so like Dorothy that he felt this overwhelming desire to protect and cherish her. But the war wasn't over yet anyway was it! There were still hordes of Boche planes to be gunned down. He gritted his teeth and tried to control himself as the nightmare pictures returned to haunt him yet again.

When they parted later that day Amy noticed that the strained look on his face had returned. It had not been there earlier. And when she held his hands in hers and he bent to kiss her gently on the cheek, she wondered at the trembling in him. She was sure it was not on her account, and she worried. 'Please keep yourself safe, Arthur,' she whispered to him. 'I shall need a friend when we get back to Bristol!'

'We'll celebrate the end of the war together perhaps,' he said.

'I shall look forward to that very much.'

'Before you go off on your travels?'

'Before I go on my travels!' she repeated and she smiled and waved until the motor bike was out of sight round the corner of the village street.

CHAPTER TWENTY

Geoffrey was feeling decidedly anxious. Bristol was full of Americans, soldiers about to go to the Front and therefore, he judged, with doubtful morals and nothing to lose. In view of this he regarded the girls in his factory with a stern fatherly concern: weak females whom he must strive to protect. One balmy day in June he gathered them together and stood in front of them on an improvised platform, looking around at the assembled company severely.

Vera Price, listening to what he had to say marvelled at his hypocrisy. He lectured them for more than half an hour on the evils of fraternizing and she knew perfectly well what he meant by that even if some of her friends were not so sure.

'What's he mean?' the girl next to her whispered.

'Going with the Yankees,' she whispered back, and was immediately glared at by the supervisor.

'They have a special day,' Geoffrey boomed out at them. 'As some of you may know it is called Independence Day and it takes place soon, on July the fourth. This year they will celebrate it here in Bristol. They have been invited to march through our streets to the Drill Hall in Old Market where they will be entertained to lunch. In the evening there will be other celebrations. I have to warn you that any girls from this factory being seen with any Americans on that night, or any other, will be called to my office the following morning and sacked.'

His words were received in silence, but during the dinner hour there was a buzz of anger as the girls discussed his ultimatum. Vera was the most militant.

'If I want to go out with one of they Yankees, I shall bloody well go out with one,' she said. 'And nothing that Mr High and Mighty can say'll stop me, so there.'

'You'll lose your job!' Her friend was looking at her with awe.

'Huh. I won't for sure.' Vera had kept her secret for a long time but frequently, now, she was sorely tempted to tell. 'I know something about him that'll stop him sacking me or any of us for that matter. You wait and see!'

'Go on, Vera. I don't believe you. You'm just saying that. You can't know anything about Mr Buxton.'

'Oh yes I can, and it'll be the biggest shock in his life when I tells 'en what I knows. So don't listen to a thing he do say. Do just what you wants.' She grinned at those who were crowding round her. 'Only don't get caught out and land in the family way,' she added, 'like some I could name!'

She wouldn't be drawn any further and the girls drifted slowly away finding a place outside to sit in the sun, eat their sandwiches and talk about Mr Buxton's pronouncement and Vera's tantalizing remarks.

Laura Buxton, down from Cambridge for the summer, was rummaging through her wardrobe. She sighed in exasperation and turned to her mother who had just come into the room. 'I need some new things, Mama. Where's the best place to go?'

'You can buy ready-made now, but I think a dressmaker is still the most likely to give you just what you want,' Felicity replied. 'I've been wondering lately about going to Mrs Miller. Patricia always employed her, and her work was excellent. You remember Amy's dresses when she was little?'

'Yes of course, all frills and furbelows. But I was sometimes envious!' Laura laughed. 'Do you think she could manage the latest styles, much plainer and well cut?'

'I'm sure she could. Why don't we go and ask her? I have to go down and check over Amy's house some time soon. We could call then. It's only a few streets away.'

Laura hesitated for a moment and then looked at her mother with a suddenly dubious expression on her face. 'We're forgetting something aren't we?'

'Yes,' Felicity said. 'She's Amy's mother. It always seems so improbable to me that I constantly put it right out of my mind. My memories of Patricia are still fresh and clear and I can see only her when I think of Amy.'

'Yet you and Papa knew about Amy's birth long ago didn't you? Before the rest of us?'

'In my head I knew, but in my heart I refused to accept the knowledge.'

'So do you think we ought to go?'

'I really don't see why not. I should like to get to know her a little. She's rather sweet. I've met her a couple of times.'

Laura went to the window and stood for a minute looking out at the summer garden with its row of standard rose trees and well-kept lawns. 'You know of course that Amy didn't go to see Mrs Miller when she was last home.'

'Yes. I felt she was wrong, but I couldn't persuade her to change her mind.'

'It's strange isn't it, about Christabel I mean? I can't imagine a woman like that having . . .' Laura tailed off her sentence. Although she believed herself to be fully emancipated, sex was one of the few taboo subjects that she could not discuss with her mother.

'I don't think that she has any permanent relationship with anyone now,' Felicity said. 'Not with her being such a regular worshipper at the Chapel. One of the elders would find out and accuse her if she had. She's still married of course. Her husband is in Canada, has been for years.'

'It's strange isn't it! Being married and living apart for so long. But who could have been the child's father then, Mama? Have you any idea?'

'None at all, and it's no concern of ours really, is it? We'll call on her tomorrow morning and ask about some dresses.'

'We can watch the American Independence Day parade on the way,' Laura commented. 'The soldiers are marching through the town apparently. Papa told me.'

The visit to Rose was brief for she was surrounded by flowing lengths of sparkling silk that had to be made swiftly into a ballgown for an important client.

'Fancy wearing that just now,' Laura commented as she stared at its exuberant colours.

'Some folk don't like to think too much about our lads in the trenches,' Rose commented. 'Having things like this takes their mind off it.'

Felicity was turning the pages of some pattern books and she drew Laura's attention to the latest fashions, simple dresses and quite short. 'I wish I'd been able to wear things like this when I was your age,' she said. 'When I think of all the layers of petticoats and those awful tight waists I suffered!'

'They was pretty though,' Rose said. 'I liked making them.'

'You made lovely things for Amy,' Laura replied. 'I used to envy her when I was little.'

Rose looked down. 'I always liked sewing for Miss Amy,' she murmured. Then she took her tape measure. 'I'll just measure you, Miss Buxton and you can bring the material and make the final choice of patterns

448

next week, if that's all right for you.'

Laura stood before the fireplace and held her arms up so that Rose could measure her. She glanced at the mantelpiece and suddenly her attention was riveted on an envelope propped up by the clock. It was unmistakably one of her father's. He always used the same kind, large and made of thick creamy paper with a mottled watermark. But it was the writing that stood out so clearly. She would recognize his elaborate copperplate anywhere. She stood transfixed and then speedily recollected herself and looked away, but not before she realized that Rose had noticed. For a moment their eyes met and she watched fascinated as Rose crushed the tape measure in her hand and a blush crept up from her neck until her whole face seemed to be on fire.

Nothing was said between them. Felicity, quite unaware, was talking about inconsequential things and as Rose gradually regained her composure Laura began to wonder why she had blushed so furiously. If it wasn't for that, she would simply have assumed her father was writing about matters to do with the Chapel, for wasn't Rose Miller concerned with the running of it? Laura seemed to remember something being said about cleaning the meeting room. Perhaps that was her job? But if so, why the guilty reaction?

When Laura returned on her own with the material the following week, Rose was pale and worried. There was considerable discussion about the style of the two dresses that were to be made, but she was obviously very preoccupied about some other matter.

At last when everything was settled she turned to the subject that was concerning her. 'Have you heard about the trouble in your father's factory, Miss Buxton?' she enquired. 'I'm feared that there's more to come.'

'No,' Laura said. 'I've heard nothing.'

'Then perhaps I shouldn't say.'

'Well, you'll have to now or I shall think that it's something truly awful.'

'It's about my friend's girl, Vera Price and a couple of others too. They been silly enough to be seen out with Yankees down Old Market. Twice it were. They been reported and Mr Buxton, well . . .' Rose wiped her forehead and her eyes were infinitely troubled. 'Well, pardon me Miss, but your father told them all that if they were caught with Yankees they'd be getting their cards. Fancy losing your job just for going out with a lad.'

Laura was appalled. 'Are you sure of this, Mrs Miller? I can't think that my father would be so severe.'

Rose looked at the clock and Laura, following her glance, remembered the letter that had been there on her last visit. She had come to no conclusion about that. But today there were other things to think about.

'This afternoon she got to go and see him in his office. Her ma told me. Four o'clock he's going to see all three of them.'

Laura shivered at yet another example of her father's harsh judgements. 'I wish I'd known before,' she said. 'I'd have talked to him about it, but he said nothing to us.'

'I'm feared there's going to be trouble over it,' Rose declared. 'I know that Vera Price. She got some of her brother's spirit and go, even though she's a girl. She'll not take it lying down.'

Laura privately wondered what being a girl had to do with it, and then she suddenly realized who this Vera was, that Rose was talking about. She must be the sister of Arthur Price, their ex-chauffeur. She had heard about his rise in the Royal Flying Corps, about his illness and his dramatic visit to their home when she was away in Cambridge. So the Price family would have yet another grievance against the Buxtons!

She tried not to let her misgivings show. 'I'll ask my father about it and see if I can persuade him to change his mind,' she said. 'He never used to listen to me, but now I'm at Cambridge he treats my opinion with just a little more respect.'

'It might be too late,' Rose said, her voice full of gloom.

Laura decided that she must try to cheer things up a little. 'There's nothing done that can't be undone,' she stated. 'I promise to speak to him after dinner tonight. He'll be in a good mood then, and more likely to listen favourably.' She stood up and started to put on her jacket.

'You'll have a cup of tea before you leave, won't you Miss Buxton?' Rose asked anxiously. 'I've got some fresh seedy cake made. That'll make us both feel a bit happier!'

Laura laughed and sat down again. She had heard that there was very little that a cup of tea and a slice of Rose's home-made cake couldn't put right.

Vera and her two friends stood outside Geoffrey Buxton's office door trying to keep up their brave defiance. At last the 'Come in' was heard and one by one they shuffled into the room. He was sitting behind his large desk, with Miss Jenkins full of vindictive triumph beside him. Vera looked at her scraped-back greying hair and grim old-fashioned frock with disdain. If I ever get to look like that, she thought, I'd go and drown myself! With her confidence reinforced, she turned her attention to Mr Buxton. The pictures that formed in her mind made her want to laugh in spite of her nerves. Him and Mrs Miller! Just to think of it was too funny!

He looked at them, and his brown eyes seemed to bore into them.

'So you have seen fit to disobey my instructions,' he stated without preamble. 'You were all observed with American soldiers last week, not once but twice.'

Vera wanted to ask who had seen them, who had been detailed to do the spying, but she forebore, keeping her bombshell for later.

'Have you anything to say for yourselves?' he questioned. 'Are there any excuses you wish to make?'

Suddenly, goaded beyond endurance, Vera spoke. 'I don't rightly think we need excuses, Sir. Our free time is our own!'

'Of course, you are correct,' he replied icily. 'Yes, your free time is your own, but I have my freedoms too, and one is to choose those whom I wish to employ in my factory.' He turned to the woman beside him. 'You have their cards, Miss Jenkins?'

With a grim smile of satisfaction she indicated the file on the desk. 'They are all in there, Sir. All stamped and made up to the end of the week.'

For a moment Vera remembered Dorothy. Keeping these cards had been her job. She'd loved it and had been sad to leave. And now she was married to this man's son. To think of it made Vera shiver.

'So you will all take a week's notice,' Geoffrey said. 'And I hope that a lesson will have been learned.'

Then Vera took a deep breath. She was annoyed at the trembling that shook her thin body. It was the same as her brother felt when he saw those burning planes. She remembered his description of the nervous shaking that was almost impossible to control. Well, he flew his aeroplane in spite of it and she wouldn't flinch either, wouldn't be intimidated by anything, least of all by Geoffrey Buxton sitting there in front of her like God. Only God was probably kinder, she thought!

'Before you hand them cards over, Sir,' she said, 'There's some things that I'd like to say.' She moved a step forward and gripped the desk to stop the

452

trembling. Her hands felt clammy and ice-cold and she noticed the marks they made on the immaculate polished surface. 'Don't you think you should give a thought to Christabel before you do anything rash, Sir? For I know all about her and her ma.' She paused for effect and to catch her breath. Then she added triumphantly, 'And them what lives in glass houses shouldn't throw stones.'

There was a terrible silence. She could feel herself swaying and the room appeared to be going round in alarming circles. Then she looked at Geoffrey Buxton and her own weakness disappeared as she savoured her victory, for she could clearly see that that was what she had achieved. He was white, like a ghost, staring at her blankly. She had expected a terrible anger, yet there was none. He reminded her of a balloon with its air leaking out slowly, until there was nothing left but a shrivelled shell of rubber.

She was suddenly aware that the others in the room were regarding her with horror-filled eyes.

Then Geoffrey spoke. 'Would you all leave us please except you, Miss Price.'

Without another word the girls filed out.

'You too please, Miss Jenkins,' he said.

The older woman stiffened and then, reluctantly, she too swept out of the room.

When they had all gone Vera backed to the wall and stood at the closed door, her fear returning now that she was alone with him.

'So?' he questioned. 'Explain yourself please.'

Vera gulped. How was she to say the things that needed saying to this man? 'Well,' she eventually began. 'It's just that I know that Christabel Miller is your daughter and if you can do that, why then, you got no right to make rules for the likes of us.'

There was a long silence.

'How many people know about this?' he said at last.

'My ma, but she won't tell. Then there's your Mr Clifford and Dorothy and my brother Arthur, and maybe Miss Amy Harding. She been seeing Arthur in France and I reckon he might 'ave told 'er.'

Geoffrey Buxton stood up and appeared to sway in front of Vera's eyes. Then he gripped the table as she had done earlier. 'I want you to go now, Miss Price. Can I have your word that you will not spread this any further until I have decided what to do?'

She glanced pointedly at the folder of insurance cards that was still lying on the desk.

He followed her glance. 'Don't worry about those,' he said, and he opened a small drawer at the side of the desk and placed them carefully in it. 'I think that I can promise you your job, and those of your two friends as well, if you keep faith with me.'

Suddenly she was sorry for him. It must be hard to have your whole life crumple about you, for that was how she saw it. She felt sorry for that nice Mrs Buxton too. A sense of doubt filled Vera. Had she done the right thing? Was she just being selfish? What would Ma say, and Mrs Miller?

'I've kept your secret for a good long time now,' she whispered. 'I'll keep it a bit longer. My friends don't know what I meant when I said what I did. I ain't told 'em any more'n what you heard. And there are plenty of Christabels around. They don't know who I meant.'

She was conscious of his relief and then he stood up and spoke slowly, all the confidence gone from his voice and his bearing.

'Then go please,' he said. 'Leave me. I shall call for you to come to my office tomorrow.'

Geoffrey walked out of the building and through the dusty streets. He walked for miles, alone and in turmoil. He saw nothing of the Park Street shops or the view from Brandon Hill where his feet unconsciously

454

led him. He walked from there into Queen's Road and through Whiteladies Road up to the Downs. He strode across the expanse of open space seeing nothing of the beauty, the great trees and the dumps where he used to play as a boy. The Suspension Bridge came into view and he stopped at last and stared down at the soft mud far below. It seemed infinitely desirable. But he resolutely turned away and headed back towards the city. He couldn't go home yet. It wouldn't do to arrive home earlier than usual and without his motor car.

His legs were not used to so much walking and his whole body began to ache, matching the agony of his mind. He was unused to the mechanics of public transport, but he waited nevertheless at the next tram-stop and climbed wearily on board when the lumbering vehicle appeared. It carried him much of the way to St Paul's and within half an hour he was knocking at Rose Miller's door.

She opened it, took one look at his face and ushered him inside. 'Dear me, Sir. You look that ill. Come and sit down and I'll make a pot of tea. The kettle's nearly boiling.' She asked no questions, just accepted his need.

He slumped in the large chair, his arms trailing limply over the thick padded arm rests. 'I can only stay a minute or two, Mrs Miller,' he said. 'But yes, I will have a cup of tea.'

She said nothing, but busied herself with the making of it. When it was finally ready, she took a cup and saucer from the set of best china ones in the cabinet and poured carefully, then handed it to him. She poured one for herself in her old chipped cup and perched gingerly on the edge of a small chair that was set some distance away in the bay window.

'I shall come straight to the point,' he said. 'Vera Price has, in a way, threatened me. I was about to sack her when she told me that she knew . . . knew about

Christabel, and I gathered that she would tell all and sundry if I did not withdraw her notice.'

Rose nodded her head. She was not at all surprised at his news. 'I always thought them Prices had found out somehow. Vera's a good girl, but a busy-body. What are you going to do then, Sir?'

Geoffrey was silent for a moment, not knowing at first how to answer. His meditations during his long walk had not been pleasant. He had learnt many things about himself during the past hour and a half, most of them far from pleasing, and he now had great misgivings about his behaviour that afternoon in the factory.

He put the cup down on the hearth and picked nervously at the threadbare chair-arm. 'The thing is,' he replied at last, 'how do you, yourself, feel about people finding out about . . . ? If our brief . . . liaison were to become common knowledge how would it affect you? Would it be very terrible?'

She avoided his eyes. 'No, not terrible. Most of my friends know that Chrissy haven't got a father anyway.'

He flinched at the unconscious implication, but Rose went on as if unaware of what she had said.

'They'll be surprised of course if they ever find that she'm yours.' She paused and took a sip of tea. 'It's you what'll suffer most,' she said. 'You and your poor wife.'

Geoffrey's heart raced as he thought of Felicity. He had been rehearsing what he would say to her and he was terrified. For the first time in their marriage he felt totally inadequate. He closed his eyes as if to blot out the confession that he must make. Then his thoughts turned to his children. Laura and Clifford? How would they react? According to the Price girl, Clifford knew already! 'Oh dear God,' he whispered aloud, and Rose looked at him in amazement. He ignored her. His treatment of his son suddenly horrified him. In the light of his own behaviour how could he possibly have been so unfair?

Rose couldn't believe that he had taken the Lord's name in vain. She stared at him sitting there with his head in his hands. Perhaps he was praying? Well maybe he had need to, she reflected. She was beginning to feel a little more assertive. It was time she spoke up for Dorothy!

'My Dorry kept our secret for years and years,' she said. 'She've known for a long time!'

Geoffrey raised his head and stared at her. Of course, Dorothy Miller who had plagued him at work for so long. He realized now why she'd had that slightly supercilious look on her face from time to time. He had tried to think it was just because she had brains and abilities far above most of the other girls. Now he knew better. He was horrified at the idea of her knowing about his . . . his adultery all along.

'She could have told any time,' Rose persisted. 'But she'm a good girl and she knowed the damage it would do to your poor wife, Mr Buxton and to . . . well to everyone.'

So Felicity was 'his poor wife'. He flinched at the words. The confession he would have to make this evening seemed even more terrible. Felicity had never been 'poor' in her entire life, either in material goods or in spirit; yet perhaps he, in his selfishness and stupidity, had caused her to seem so to a person like Rose Miller.

'Yes, well,' he said. 'It seems that I am in debt to your daughter for upholding my good name in my factory.'

Rose was encouraged by his apparent humility. 'Could you see it in your heart to pardon her then?' she said. 'Her and Mr Clifford?' She was amazed by her own daring.

'Pardon them?' Geoffrey was surprised by her use

of the word. He thought that in her eyes they would not be in need of pardoning. Suddenly he began to see his own behaviour more clearly. He had always hated the word hypocrite, yet this was just what he was. He knew that, however painful, he had to make amends to all the people he had wronged and misjudged. 'Yes,' he said quietly. 'I shall pardon them as you say, although I think it is I who need the pardoning!'

Rose felt fit to burst with happiness, but she had not finished yet. 'There's Chrissy,' she said. 'I've worried a lot about her. She'm a bright little thing and already she've asked now and then about her pa. What'll I tell her? She mustn't find out from someone else. Too much of a shock that'll be.'

Geoffrey tried to muster his reserves of composure. The child was important, his own daughter after all, and must be considered before anything else, he told himself sternly.

'I think that we must both tell her,' he managed to say at last. 'I want to be here when you do, Rose.'

'How about now then? She'm just upstairs in her bedroom. Would you like to tell her now?'

Geoffrey felt a tremor shake his whole body. In spite of his noble sentiments he had not thought to have such an important encounter right at this moment. It was the last thing he felt he could cope with when all his thoughts were with his wife. But before he could make any excuse he heard the child's footsteps on the stairs.

Chrissy had heard the door bell when he'd first rung and she had been listening on the landing ever since, her head pushed through the wide space in the banister rail. She didn't understand much of what they were talking about, but when she heard her name she came slowly down and stood shyly in the doorway. She stared at Geoffrey.

Rose lost no time in making the introductions. 'This

is Mr Buxton, Chrissy,' she said. 'You always told me that you wanted a pa. Well now, you got your wish.'

Christabel walked uncertainly across the room and stood beside his chair. 'Are you really my pa?' she asked.

Geoffrey knew that this was a day he would remember for the whole of his life. Never had so many conflicting emotions crowded in upon him all at once. The child before him was flesh of his flesh. He could see it plainly in her face and he felt a sudden protective urge for the little girl.

'You can call me that if you like, but it's a secret for now,' he said. He noticed the straight hair hanging loose about her shoulders and the great satin bow tied on the top of her head. Somehow, in spite of all the worries that filled his mind, she tugged at his heartstrings. She reminded him so much of Laura as she used to be.

'Can I call you Papa like Miss Laura?' she asked.

Speechless, Geoffrey heaved himself out of the chair. 'Yes, you may,' he said and he took her hand in his and stared at it as though he had no idea what to do with it. Then, embarrassed, he stooped and kissed the top of her head, and turned hurriedly to Rose. 'I shall not call again, of course,' he declared. 'But, if my wife agrees, I would like to see the child sometimes, and I shall arrange for her to go to a boarding school when she is older.' He walked as quickly as he decently could through the door and into the passage. Before he went into the street he looked back at Christabel. 'Look after her for me,' he whispered to Rose, and then he strode away, back to his factory, his motor car, and back to Felicity.

For the whole evening Rose pondered on what might be taking place in the Buxton home. But had she been able to see the two main participants in the drama that was taking place, her amazement would have been greater than she could ever have imagined.

The confession had been made, the forgiveness asked for and granted, and Geoffrey was kneeling on the floor with his head bowed in his wife's lap. On Felicity's face there was a smile and she stroked his meagre hair gently. There was a silence between them. There had been no scene, no accusations. All the response he had received had been a gentle, 'I guessed that there had been someone, my dear. I've known for a very long time, but I knew too that you were not constantly unfaithful. I couldn't have borne that. So it was Rose Miller. I should have known. Christabel is so like Laura.'

Then he had given an account of the visit today, and his assurance that he felt nothing at all for Rose apart from a responsibility for the child.

'You must see Christabel frequently,' Felicity told him. 'We must arrange for her education. After all she is your daughter, half-sister to Laura and Clifford, and to Amy and Dorothy as well.'

The irony of the situation was not lost on either of them, but Geoffrey could not see the smile that Felicity continued to wear. It was not callous or triumphant but one of calm and unexpected happiness. She was relieved that at last she knew the truth, and with her husband's confession and new humility came the confident assurance that only good would follow. For so many years she had longed for him to be a true partner to her. Now perhaps at last her prayers were about to be answered.

It was while they were still seated in that position that Laura breezed in upon them intent upon taking her father to task for his ultimatum about the American soldiers.

She stood at the door and gaped. Geoffrey looked up and she saw the tear stains on his face and felt that this must be some bizarre dream that she had chanced upon. He struggled to his feet and turned away.

'Tell her,' he directed and Felicity held out her hand indicating that she should sit down. She listened with increasing bewilderment and when it was all told, it was her mother's serene smile that most amazed her. She ran from the room eventually but she was unable to cry, unable to think, and it was not until Felicity came to her later that she managed to come to terms with what she had heard.

'Don't be too distressed, darling,' Felicity said. 'I'm glad, truly glad. Don't you see what it means? Now, at last, you have a father who has frailties and faults like the rest of us. Oh, of course he always had them, but until today he wouldn't admit to them. That is what has always made him so difficult to live up to.'

'And Clifford?' Laura said. Her quick mind had already grasped the implications of this new state of affairs.

'Yes, Clifford and Dorothy will be forgiven and invited back,' Felicity told her. 'We have already discussed it.'

'And I have a little half-sister,' Laura said. 'Chrissy, the child named after Miss Pankhurst. I liked her. She looks a lot like me.'

EPILOGUE
November 1918

'So the war's over at last!' Arthur sat once more at a table in the small seaside café at Le Montaine and smiled at the girl opposite him. 'We'll all be going home,' he said. There was a radiance on Amy's face that he had never seen before.

'What are your plans, Arthur?' she asked. 'Isn't it wonderful to be able to think about next year, to know that we have a future and a hope!'

He laughed. 'I haven't any ideas at the moment. Some of my pals are thinking of going into test-flying. There'll be a lot of advance in aeroplane design soon. Not for me though. Not yet anyway.'

The November sky was grey and dismal, and the sea wild, but there was little that could dampen their spirits.

'I'm going to travel for a bit, as I told you last time we met, and I shall go to Canada next year,' Amy said. 'Just for a few weeks. I need to make sure of my roots, find Mr Miller.'

'It could be rather a shock. Do you think that you should go alone?' There was great concern in his voice.

'Laura is coming with me. It'll be a holiday for both of us. I don't think I'll be upset really because I've thought about it a lot, tried to prepare myself, and I'm not expecting too much. I'm not searching for a new father. No one could ever replace Papa.'

Arthur was relieved. She seemed to have everything well under control and if Laura Buxton was to be her companion then not much harm could come to her. He remembered the tomboyish, capable Laura with slight amusement. She had never been at ease with him in those days when he had been her father's chauffeur.

'I'm glad that Miss Buxton is going with you,' he said. 'Young ladies shouldn't travel alone!' He realized that he must sound extremely patronizing and he laughed at himself a little.

Amy stared at him and then laughed too. 'It's different now, Arthur,' she said, and she tossed her smartly bobbed hair. It had been cut by a young French hairdresser in the very latest style and gave her a new sense of freedom and assurance. 'We're the bright young people of the future now, you know, not your poor supressed females any longer.'

'I'm not sure that we men are going to find all these changes to our liking,' Arthur replied. 'Some of us rather preferred the self-effacing fluffy little things that used to be.'

'You're teasing of course!' Amy grinned at him.

'Yes, I suppose I am.' Then he became more serious. 'Tell me all the news from Bristol. My family don't write much and I'm rather out of touch.'

Amy took a deep breath. 'There's a lot to tell,' she said. 'And most of it is good. All of it in fact. Where do I begin. With Dorothy?' She looked at him carefully, wondering what effect her words would have. Was he still regretting Dorothy? There was no response, no flicker of extra interest in his eyes. Perhaps he had recovered, just as she had.

'I heard all about the baby of course,' he said. 'A girl, and born in Bristol. Vera managed to tell me that much.'

'And fully accepted by Felicity and Geoffrey. Even my mother is to be at the christening, and they've asked me to be godmother. Just imagine that?' She paused and took another sip of coffee. 'Clifford is working in the factory and making the best of it. That piece of news came from Laura. She says that she has persuaded him to play duets with her sometimes so he hasn't given up his music entirely. And he's happy. He and Dorothy have a house in Redland.'

'And how do you feel about Mrs Miller now?'

Amy sighed. 'Yes. My mother. She's very sweet really and I think that I shall grow to like her very much, perhaps even love her eventually. I hope to buy her a little house of her own if she'll accept it from me. She mentioned once that she always wanted to live by the sea so it could be at Clevedon or Portishead, or even Weston. I shall suggest it when I feel the time is right. I want to buy a motor car and drive her around a bit when I go home so that we can get to know each other.'

Arthur's face suddenly became hard. Amy's words stressed the difference between them. Her vast wealth made an almost impenetrable barrier. 'You're not going to live with her then?'

'I don't think I could. I must have my independence now. Christabel is going to boarding school, by the way,' she added. 'Geoffrey is seeing to that.'

Their meal finished they left the café a little regretfully, knowing that they would probably never meet again at this place which had become precious to both of them. They walked along the beach, the harsh sand scrunching beneath their feet and gulls wheeling and soaring in the angry sky.

Then Amy was suddenly aware of her companion's mood. 'What is it, Arthur?' she asked, turning to him, her voice full of concern. She knew of his struggle with his nervous fears of burning planes, but it couldn't be that now surely. 'You must be glad that the war's over?' she questioned.

'Of course I am,' he said. Then he suddenly took her hand in his. 'I shall miss you, Amy. We've shared a lot of sorrows together, haven't we?'

'You don't have to miss me. We both live in Bristol, or had you forgotten?'

'No. I hadn't forgotten. It's just that . . .' he paused, groping for words and finding none.

Suddenly she understood. 'My money,' she said. 'That's it, isn't it! You're jealous, Arthur Price! And you a major too.'

She knew that his latest promotion to the rank of major, given to him during the last month of the war, had been a wonderful achievement bringing him immense satisfaction. But when it came to his relationship with her, she realized even that apparently didn't compensate for his lack of inherited wealth.

She looked at his woeful face and suddenly laughed merrily, feeling that to cheer him out of his mood was the only thing she could do.

He tried to release his hand from hers but she held it tightly putting her other one over it.

'Not jealous,' he said. 'Not at all. I'm glad for you, but St Paul's isn't Clifton, is it? That's what I mean.'

'You're talking a load of rubbish,' she told him, amused at his comparison. 'I'm St Paul's born and bred, and please remember it.' She thought of Rose Miller and smiled to herself. 'And it was your grandma wot brought me into the world and give me away, Arthur Price, and you'm not to forget it, see.'

He winced, hearing her imitate the language of his childhood, the accent that he had struggled for so long to leave behind. Then his sense of humour prevailed and he, too, laughed. 'Well, Amy Harding-Miller,' he replied. 'I've nothing to offer you at all, so if you want me as much as I want you, it's you that'll have to do the asking.'

She dropped his hand and clasped her own together in mock supplication. 'Then as a new, free, and totally emancipated woman I'll do it,' she said. 'Arthur Price, will you walk out with me now and then?'

'Pleased to, Madam,' he replied matching his tone to hers. And he swept her into his arms and kissed her.